MW01199481

CLAW

KATIE BERRY

For Frances Amelia, who always believed.

Acknowledgements:

Special thanks to Paulina, Thomas, Terry, Jen, Tara, Michael, Marcie, Erin and Shana. Your support and enthusiasm have been a constant comfort to me as I have brought this story through to completion. I am forever grateful to each and every one of you.

-Katie Berry

Preface

This book is the culmination of several years of work and hundreds of hours of research. I have taken liberties here and there with how certain jobs are done in a small town. In addition, I hope the Conservation Officer Service of British Columbia will allow me my flights of fancy regarding how their officers actually operate. But most things you will read are based upon factual information. There are certain elements, of course, that are more of a fantastic nature, but that's why you're here, to read something where the everyday meets the not so everyday. I hope you enjoy reading this book as much as I enjoyed writing it.

Katie Berry
November 28th, 2019

CHAPTER ONE

The towering bonfire crackled in the centre of the large clearing, the fresh-cut firewood drying out as it burned. Huge plumes of smoke billowed into the cold night air, blending with the thick fog that surrounded the camp, adding to the limited visibility. Every once in a while, a new pocket of resin in the unseasoned wood would explode, shooting out yet another red-hot ember seemingly in search of the first flammable thing it could find.

Jerry Benson noted with frustration that he still seemed to be one of those flammable things and scooted his camp chair back from the blazing fire another metre. He cursed under his breath and brushed the remains of the latest smouldering, red fleck from his neon-blue parka, not wanting it to burn through the fabric and ruin his new winter-wear.

"Hey, Jer! You look low! Incoming!" Tyler said, lobbing another beer. Jerry snapped out of fire suppression mode and deftly caught the canned beer in one hand. He placed it in the snow beside his chair, next to the other beer he'd barely touched.

"Gotta keep up, bro! This booze isn't going to drink itself!" Tyler took a large gulp from the huge bottle of bourbon he held. He placed it into the snow next to his chair and picked up a fresh can of beer that had been chilling in the snow. Cracking it open, he washed the burning remnants of whiskey down his throat in a long, thirsty swallow. After a belch loud enough to shake the snow from the overburdened trees around them, Tyler smiled contentedly, closed his eyes for a moment, then took another small sip of beer, savouring his barley beverage.

Jerry shook his head slightly in disbelief, saying, "Thanks, Ty, but I think I'm okay for now. I'm not in the mood tonight."

Tyler's eyes popped back open, and he leaned drunkenly toward Jerry, almost falling out of his chair in the process. A look of incredulity crossed his face, and he said, "Not in the mood? We're out here in the great Canadian outdoors, bombing around on our sleds, enjoying nature and getting drunk! How in the hell can you NOT be in the mood?"

Jerry yawned. "Just tired, I guess. It was a long drive."

Tyler belched loudly at this news, then settled back into his chair once more.

When Jerry had learned that his college brothers were heading out on a snowmobiling expedition into the Kootenay region of BC for their yearly vacation, he'd been all over it and jumped at the chance to join them. But his excitement this year wasn't because he still enjoyed coming along on these annual booze-fests with the boys. No, it was for a different reason this year. After a decade and a half, he was tired of coming home from a week of drunken debauchery and feeling like Ray Milland from The Lost Weekend for several days afterward. This year was supposed to have been the year he told the guys he was done with the party animal thing.

But it seemed as if fate were egging him along on this particular frat-brother vacation in spite of his reservations. The real reason he'd been excited this year was the fact that their destination just happened to be near the site of a recent seismic event in the interior. And this event was in a region with a rich history of gold strikes, making it an opportunity too good for him to pass up.

As a Professor of Geology at The University of British Columbia, Jerry Benson had been studying the Cascade Mountain Range for over a decade. The amount of gold mined from the area in the late nineteenth century and into the early twentieth had been phenomenal. As a geologist, Jerry also knew there was still much more just waiting to be discovered in the region. Thanks to a significant earth tremor that occurred in the Cascadia subduction zone just after the new year, he hoped that it might have exposed some potential new sites in which to hunt for the valuable yellow metal.

***

Earlier that afternoon, with camp set up, GPS unit in hand and a few other tools of the trade thrown into his backpack, Jerry had set out looking for the fault line at the epicentre of the recent earthquake on his rented snowmobile. The machine was equipped with an eye-poppingly bright paint job that seared the eyeballs on contact. He'd dubbed it the 'Waspmobile' as soon as he'd laid eyes upon it, thanks to its neon-yellow and black colour scheme along with its high-pitched, droning engine. Just looking at the damned thing made his temples throb.

Departing much later than he'd wanted, Jerry knew he was operating under a time constraint — the hours of daylight left to explore were precious few. But he praised serendipity once more, when only five and a half kilometres along, at the base of the Kootenay Glacier, he discovered the opening to a promising cavern in the cliffside. According to his GPS, it was centred almost directly over the new, quake-causing fault line.

Gold Ridge was usually spared much of the fog and low cloud that had been socking-in the city of Lawless and the valley below for the last few weeks. Up until now, Jerry had enjoyed a beautifully clear afternoon as he'd searched for the source of the fault. But his delightful day came with a bit of a caveat: despite being located high above the valley cloud, quite often in late winter, just as the sun set behind the local mountains, rapidly dropping temperatures created a freezing ice fog. It crept down off the Kootenay Glacier, a pellucid presence that coated everything it touched in a slippery crystalline crust — any attempts at travel were a very difficult and dangerous time. The last thing Jerry wanted, was to be caught off-guard by the freezing frost. He knew he needed to leave enough time to get back safely to camp to avoid this hazard.

Tumbling out of the cavern's entrance was what appeared to be a geothermal aquifer. Jerry knew there were already several hot springs located around Lawless, making it a popular destination for people looking to soak away their aches and pains. This new hot spring would add to the Province of BC's already impressive total, which boasted eighteen out of the twenty-one confirmed to be in Canada.

Kneeling, Jerry measured the aquifer's temperature. At just a hair under one-hundred degrees Celsius, it was an excellent example of the province's true volcanic nature. It was far too hot for human use, and anyone unfortunate enough, or stupid enough, to try using this hot spring for skinny dipping would find their skin sloughing off like a blanched tomato before canning — definitely a 'look but don't touch' situation.

He took one last, quick look into the aquifer before entering the cavern and froze in his tracks. Glinting enticingly in the middle of the boiling stream was several of the largest looking gold nuggets he'd ever seen, some of them easily the size of golf balls. He grabbed a broken branch from the base of a nearby tree and fished a few of the nuggets out, examining them once they'd cooled enough.

As a geologist, without even having to break the ore open, Jerry Benson knew that what he held in his hands wasn't pyrite, but real gold. The rounded edges and corners of the nuggets in his hands were the telltale sign of authenticity as they had none of pyrite's harder, more angular surfaces.

Jerry was now officially more than a little bit intrigued as to what lay inside this cavern. Standing, he added the nuggets to a plastic sample bag, then placed them almost reverentially into his backpack. He adjusted the shoulder straps of the pack and prepared to enter the steaming black underworld in the rock face before him.

Suddenly, Jerry's mind registered what his eyes picked up only moments before — the trees in the surrounding forest were casting lengthening shadows. Time had gotten away from him while he'd been examining this golden aquifer and the sun was now almost kissing the rim of the glacier — the remaining daylight was growing short. Above, the first probing tendrils of ice fog began cascading off the ancient ice toward him. "Looks like I've overstayed my welcome." He turned to face the cavern's entrance, saying, "You'll have to wait until tomorrow to get your turn."

Several small rocks tumbled off the rock wall near the opening, as if to show it was paying attention to Jerry's promise. They bounced along the narrow ledge leading up to the cavern's entrance for a moment before tumbling with a splash into the sizzling stream below.

In spite of his precautions, he'd been caught off guard by the rapid movement of the fog, and soon found himself enveloped in a swirling grey cloud. Carefully turning the snowmobile around, he sat in the icy mist a moment longer and pulled out his GPS unit. With a couple of quick button presses, he tagged the precise location of the cavern in the device's memory. He smiled, knowing he could relax this evening with the boys, his GPS receiver assuring him he would have an easy trip back in the morning to explore the inside of this potentially valuable new find.

***

Jerry yawned again and smiled sadly as he looked over toward Tyler. The man was now slumped sideways in his chair, temporarily unconscious due to too many trips to the watering trough over the last few hours. A small drift of aluminum beer cans was piled high next to Ty's chair, a silent testament to his powerful thirst so far this evening. Over the years, Tyler had fancied himself as the de facto leader of the group, and when they were out on one of their yearly 'Four Bros' adventures, it seemed inevitable that he would make sure there was plenty of alcohol available. He constantly monitored everyone around him, making sure they were as well-lubricated as he was, and if they weren't, he'd keep pestering them and pushing the booze on them until they were.

This year, Jerry's other college brother, Nick, had decided to buy a Texas Mickey-sized, three-litre bottle of Jack Daniels. It was the kind that came with a handle to help you steady the big jug on your shoulder, just like Granny did on the Beverly Hillbillies, while you sloshed some of Tennessee's Finest, Old No.7 down your parched throat. Usually, Jerry knew Nick only brought along a forty pounder, but this year he'd decided to super-size it for some reason, most likely at Tyler's behest.

Jerry closed his eyes for a moment, but every time he did, visions of dollar signs danced behind his eyelids as he envisioned the golden nuggets he'd found. That was the other reason he wasn't drinking tonight; he didn't want to get smashed and then have to get up early tomorrow morning with a throbbing head and try to navigate the treacherous, ice-slicked path back to the cavern on his high-pitched, droning Wasp-mobile. Just the thought of spelunking around a cavern half-tanked was scary enough, but when you threw in the fact that it could easily have dormant lava tubes scattered throughout, some of them possibly dropping thousands of metres into the darkness below, it was just insane.

No, stumbling drunkenly into one of those black holes was not an appealing idea. He knew he'd have to add the concept to the ever-growing list that comprised the bulk of his pet project, a book he planned on self-publishing later in the year called, "Darwin's Herd Thinners" (working title only) — falling into a seemingly bottomless pit while inebriated would have to be at least death number two hundred and thirty-five according to his calculations. He'd have to check his notes to verify it when he finally got back near a cell tower and was able to access the cloud-saved data on his cell phone once more.

Jerry loathed taking notes on his iPhone when his four-thousand-dollar laptop was just sitting at home, keeping warm and dry. But he wasn't about to expose his MacBook Pro to the foggy, icy air he'd seen floating around Lawless recently, so home is where it was going to stay, and he knew he'd just have to suck it up. The last thing he needed was Tyler trying to play World of Warcraft on his laptop in the middle of sub-zero temperatures and have him bork his computer because of some condensation issue shorting-out the motherboard.

The smoke and fog parted momentarily, and Jerry saw Nick sitting across the roaring fire, looking a little green around the gills. Nick wobbled back and forth in his chair for a moment, then looked down in disgust at something in his lap, wiping his mouth with the back of his hand.

Jerry worried that when he wasn't paying attention to Nick at some point, perhaps during a moment of limited visibility due to the smoke and fog, his friend might choose that time to ooze off of his camp chair and roll into the blazing bonfire like a large, drunken log. If something so unfortunate came to pass, he figured it would be death number two hundred and thirty-six for his new book. Nick had been doing his wobbling routine next to the flames for the last half hour now. So far, every time he'd wobbled, he'd wake up just enough to stabilise himself, then take another gulp of beer from the can jammed between his thick legs, and also maybe a chug of bourbon if the bottle of Jack were nearby. After a few minutes, his buddy would begin to doze off again, wavering back and forth in his seat near the fire as he swam in and out of consciousness, threatening to immolate himself accidentally once more.

Mostly with Tyler's help and a half dozen or so of the aforementioned beers, Nick had downed almost a third of the bottle of whiskey over the last couple of hours. Now, when he wasn't perched precariously on the precipice of passing out, he was constantly getting up and staggering through the shortcut that lead to the forest behind his chair. Each time he disappeared, he'd invariably hollered out that he was, "Unrenting some more beer!" When Nick was coherent and sober, he usually said, almost sagely, "You can never truly buy beer, you can only rent it."

Looking across the fire at Nick, it appeared to Jerry that some of the beer and whiskey might have come back out the wrong end of Nick and found their way onto his lap. He shouted over the colossal blaze to Nick, "You doing okay, buddy? It looks like you're having some issues!"

Nick's head snapped up. He looked through the smoke and haze for a moment at Jerry with bleary eyes, as if considering an answer, then leaned forward and puked into the campfire. It hissed and sputtered as the vomit vaporised in its searing heat as if Nick's stomach spew was an affront to its blazing dignity.

From his vantage point at the head of the fire, Tyler saw this latest occurrence and hooted with delight, tossing another can of beer toward Nick, saying, "Glad to see you made more room brother, here's another!"

With red-rimmed eyes, Nick watched the beer roll through the brown-coloured slush. It came to rest against the side of the air mattress of Jerry's other college brother, Matt. Already sound asleep, Matt was stretched out on top of his air mattress near the campfire, basking in its warmth. He'd taken several hits off of Nick's bottle of JD, in addition to a couple of the 'special' medicinal cigarettes he'd also brought along. Jerry glanced at his watch and saw that it had been at least fifteen minutes since his friend had last been vertically oriented. With his purple toque pulled down over his eyes, Matt was using his backpack as a pillow. His long, dark, dreadlocked hair spilled out over the pack's sides like a dead octopus on a rock.

To aid in their camping experience, when the Bro-Squad (Tyler's idea) had first arrived at the clearing that afternoon, they'd driven the snowmobiles back and forth across the clearing several times. Ty's plan was to flatten down the snow so that they would have a relatively level spot in which to camp and not have to slog back and forth as they traversed the site. When they were done, Ty told them to make sure they all backed their sleds in, so that they were all facing skis-out and ready to go for the next day's activities. That way they'd be able to blast out into the snow in the morning without wasting any of their valuable time jockeying them around.

Jerry yawned and glanced over his shoulder with longing toward the tent where his sleeping bag lay but couldn't see it through the heavy fog. They'd erected the six-man structure at the backside of the clearing, safely away from the bonfire's shooting embers, next to where they'd parked the snowmobiles. At Tyler's back, the trail the four sleds made on their way into camp that afternoon disappeared and reappeared like a mirage, occasionally obscured by the smoke and fog that rose in serpentine coils into the night air. Wide and spacious, the trail was almost like a road in the snow, easily marking their progress into the centre of the clearing. Off to Jerry's right, through the undulating mist, he caught the occasional glimpse of his own, single snowmobile trail, coming in from the direction of the forest that backed onto the campfire.

Trying to get comfortable, Jerry felt something lumpy digging into his side. He reached into the large, outer pocket of his jacket and probed around for a moment, then pulled out his GPS receiver. Surprised to see that he'd left it on, he checked the battery level indicator and was relieved to see its charge still appeared to be almost full. He turned the unit over in his hands, marvelling at the technology. Though he had GPS on his cell phone, it wasn't the same as this device. His cell phone used Assisted GPS, not true GPS like the unit he was holding. At any given time, this GPS receiver linked directly to a minimum of four Global Positioning Satellites circling the planet. His cell phone, on the other hand, relied on cellular repeater towers to assist its location-tracking capabilities with no direct link to any satellites. Out here, without a single cell tower in sight, the phone now acted as nothing more than a glorified camera, alarm clock and flashlight combination. If something happened to one of them while they were out here, in the middle of nowhere, they were on their own.

Jerry jumped as another bubble of sap in the green wood exploded with a pop, sending more embers churning high into the shifting fog. He was happy to see that he was now far enough away to no longer be a target of flying cinders, but still close enough to feel the warmth of the fire. He turned off the GPS unit to conserve its battery and placed it back in his jacket pocket.

Leaning over, Jerry reached down and grabbed the beer in the snow next to his chair. He took a small sip and watched the wandering fog rolling in waves out of the darkness toward him. It washed over him and merged with the billowing smoke from the green wood burning on the fire, making him cough. Looking around the camp with somewhat watery eyes, he saw that apart from the circular oasis of light and warmth that the bonfire provided, the rest of the camp now lay encrusted under a glistening white frost of ice.

Jerry placed the almost full beer back into its snowy cup holder. Thanks to his current lack of interest in pounding back the booze like the rest of the Bros, when he'd informed them of his new, healthier lifestyle, they had enthusiastically nominated him as the designated driver for the trip before they'd even left Vancouver. Jerry had no problem with that.

***

On the drive up from the coast, they'd encountered a little bit of thick, patchy, low cloud on a couple of the mountain passes as well as some compact snow and slushy roads. It was nothing too concerning as Tyler's massive Dodge Ram 3500 pickup was a four-wheel drive. Still, Jerry was glad the roads had been good. He wasn't a huge fan of driving through inclement weather in a monster truck loaded with loud, sloppy drunks, so that had been a relief.

But it had been a long trip. The drinking and rowdiness had started almost as soon as they'd left. Tyler had brought along a flask to share with Nick and Matt, getting them pre-lubed for the party like he was. When they stopped that afternoon at the Osoyoos Holiday Inn, Jerry had felt relieved to be out of the pickup truck and the eye-watering whiskey fumes that filled the cab. Almost before the truck stopped, Tyler and the boys were stumbling out the door and heading to the hotel bar for a few dozen more drinks and an evening of partying. Of course, trying to get everyone awake and moving before five o'clock the next morning had been quite a challenge. But thanks to the three large double-doubles from the local Tim Hortons, he'd managed to pour the boys back into Tyler's Dodge and had them underway again before sun-up.

After several hours of following scenic Provincial Highway #3, Jerry turned off onto Highway #3C and headed north toward the Kootenay Glacier and Lawless. Just after nine o'clock, they crested the apex of the Golden Mile pass. Taking a break, Jerry pulled off of the highway onto an adjacent viewpoint overlooking the valley.

The view was breathtaking. Snow-covered mountain peaks jutted like broken teeth through the dense fog that filled the valley bottom — a blanket of grey that smothered the city of Lawless below. Sitting majestically in the distance at the back of the valley, the Kootenay Glacier poked its head through the clouds, its ancient ice shining a brilliant white as it bathed in the morning sunshine.

Continuing their journey, they descended into the grey twilight toward Lawless, heading for the sporting goods outlet where they'd reserved their snowmobiles. After a few wrong turns in the fog, they arrived at an ageing aluminum Quonset hut on the outskirts of town.

As they finished up the rental paperwork, the tall, bald-headed proprietor behind the counter asked Tyler, "Did you boys come prepared?"

With amusement, Jerry watched Tyler, who had been at the cash register preparing to pay. Ty greeted the man's question with a blank expression as if he were wondering whether the guy behind the till was also trying to sell him a pack of prophylactics or something.

But then the shopkeeper had continued and clarified things by saying, "Despite the many standout geographical features of Lawless and the lovely Kootenay Glacier area, using any of them to navigate in the middle of winter around here is about as helpful as a driver's licence to a blind man, thanks to all this goddamned fog!"

Tyler continued to stare at the man.

"So I'd recommend you carry, at the minimum, at least one other GPS unit for redundancies sake, in case something happens to your friend's there," the proprietor finished, looking over at Jerry, who had been fiddling around with his own GPS unit while he waited.

Caught off-guard, Jerry took a second and then agreed, explaining to Ty that his cell phone-based GPS was crap out in the backcountry and that he'd better listen to the man.

Tyler stared at the shopkeeper and then Jerry with the same blank expression for several more seconds as if deciding whether they were bullshitting him or not — or perhaps thankful that he hadn't said the first thing that had popped into his head about the pack of condoms. He sighed as if relieved, saying, "All right, add one on to the bill."

The smiling shopkeeper said, "A wise decision, my friend." He turned and looked at the small inventory of shrink-wrapped GPS receivers hanging on the wall behind him and grabbed the top unit, which, from what Jerry could see, was also the most expensive one. Ringing up the total on the till, the proprietor said, "These things sell like hotcakes every winter when the fog hits. You're really lucky you came when you did since I just got more of these units back in stock last week!"

Looking rather unimpressed with his good fortune, Tyler briefly glanced out the foggy window toward the last stop they would be making before heading up into the mountains for their vacation. Barely visible across the street, a tall blue lotto sign revolved atop a black and white marquee advertising a small, squat cinder block convenience store next to it. The flickering letters proclaimed The Gas 'n Gulp to be the proud purveyor of 'Liquor, Lotto and Groceries'. Tyler was no doubt already checking off items on his mental shopping list once they got across the road to the convenience store. Jerry looked through the window himself, thinking without a shadow of a doubt that when Tyler checked out at the convenience store, there would be plenty of the first two advertised items in his basket and very little of the third.

Tyler turned his attention back to the shopkeeper and said, "Gee, thanks. Seeing as I'm that lucky, maybe I'd better pick up a couple of 6-49 tickets across the street."

The shopkeeper said nothing, and only grinned, ringing up an impressively high total on the cash register's LCD screen.

***

Smiling lightly as he recalled their morning at the rental shop, Jerry reached down and grabbed his beer in the snow once more, taking another small sip. He grimaced from the Lucky Lager's slight aftertaste and placed the can back on the ground. A twinge in his lower back reminded him how stiff he currently was from the long drive over the last couple of days, and he was paying for it now. Thinking of the day ahead of him tomorrow, he started making mental notes of things to check the next day. His eyeball-searingly yellow snowmobile was at the top of the list. If there were any mechanical problems with the machine, he didn't want to be in a situation where he'd be snowshoeing it back to camp. Number one, he didn't have any snowshoes, and number two, the snow was quite deep, easily up to his waist and over his head in some places. GPS unit or not, he'd be slogging through kilometres of this clammy crap if something happened, and that was definitely not on his list of fun things to do on vacation.

Looking to his left, Jerry saw that Tyler was nodding in and out of consciousness as well now. Sprawled in his camp chair, Ty's legs stuck out, his head nodding forward onto his chest. Every few seconds, his head would snap up, and his eyes would fly open. After a brief, myopic glance around the camp, he would gradually close them once more as his chin slowly sank back down onto his chest.

Though he'd moved farther back from the bonfire that the boys had built, thanks to the comforting warmth of the blaze, Jerry felt like he, too, might just fall asleep if he weren't careful. He stifled a yawn. This wasn't where he wanted to sleep tonight; no, he'd rather be in the warm, cosy confines of his sleeping bag, which just recently began calling to him with its siren song of sleep.

Jerry's eyelids began to droop, on the edge of nodding off himself, when he heard what sounded like someone struggling, quickly followed by the rustling of dry brush. His eyes snapped back open, and he looked across to where Nick had been doing his wobbling act moments before. A brief gap opened in the swirling smoke over the fire. Nick's camp chair was laying on its side in the snow, with Nick nowhere in sight. "Nick!" Jerry called, thinking that his friend may have finally succumbed to alcohol and gravity and tumbled into the campfire.

"Shit!" Jerry jumped up from his canvas chair and stood to see if Nick's smouldering body lay in the muddy slush next to the fire, but the fog and smoke had stopped cooperating — he couldn't see anything through the haze.

Moving quickly, Jerry rounded the fire, calling out, "Nick! Where are you, brother? Are you okay?" Next to Nick's overturned camp chair, the bottle of JD lay on its side in a small pool of its golden contents, most of which had already disappeared into the slushy mud. Only a few drops of the tan fluid from Tennessee remained in the jug now.

Jerry righted the bottle, saying "That's going to put a damper on the party!" Standing, he called out to the forest, "Nick! What's going on, big fella? Did the Jack catch up with you finally?"

The thick brush behind the campfire remained mute to his enquiry. Sighing, Jerry decided to give Nick a few more seconds, just in case he was puking, or maybe back there playing with his bait and tackle in the dark. In the meantime, he would walk over to Tyler, give him a good swift kick and tell him it was time to pack it in for the night. As he turned, another rustling noise came from the bushes at his back, followed by what sounded like muffled screams of pain.

Jerry moved toward the gap in the brush that lead to the forest beyond. The grey mist seemed to thicken as he approached as if trying to foil his investigation. "Nick, what in the hell are you doing, man? Are you trying to scare me? Cause it's not work..." His voice faltered as he moved beyond the fire's light, the frigid fog enveloping him as he edged forward into blackness.

The light from the campfire had given Jerry temporary night blindness, and his eyes were having a hard time readjusting. He thought briefly of using his phone's flash as a light source in the fog but knew from experience it would only illuminate everything around him as a diffuse grey mess, making it even more difficult to see.

Reaching out with his hands in the hope of touching something bush or tree-like, he paused for a moment when he felt twigs scraping along the back of his right hand. He continued moving forward using that as his guide and edged into the thickening mist. After seconds that seemed like minutes, Jerry's eyes gradually started adjusting to the lack of light, and he was able to discern the vague shapes of trees and brush in the swirling fog ahead.

"Nick! Stop screwing around, bro!"

After taking several more slippery, stumbling steps, the churning mists parted for Jerry, seeming to draw back like the curtain at a carnival sideshow. It was as if an invisible barker were showing him an amazing new attraction, saying, "Hey! Come check this out, my friend! You won't be disappointed!"

Jerry stopped, his mouth dropping open as he rubbed his eyes in disbelief. "What in God's name?"

It looked like something had fallen on Nick. Jerry moved a bit closer and could see his friend's snow boots sticking out from under the edge of this humongous, grey rock, his legs spasming in pain. "Jesus, Nick…" He inched forward, hesitant, knowing that what he was seeing was impossible. How could this slab of stone have fallen on top of his friend out here in the middle of this forested plateau, with no rocky overhangs anywhere in sight? There was no way this could be happening! It just Did-Not-Compute. He moved forward to aid his friend.

A sudden spasm of movement shuddered through the slab of stone and Jerry stopped dead in his tracks, his breath catching in his throat. He finally saw the thing for what it was. The rough, stone-like texture of this 'boulder' was actually grey, matted fur. The thing on top of Nick had a rough, angular head the size of a Mercedes-Benz smart car. Broad, sinewy muscles contracted beneath the creature's tangled, filthy pelt.

Gore-stained fangs nearly twice the length of the World War One bayonets that Jerry collected at home tore into Nick with a savage fury. Jerry knew he should be running, but he stood transfixed and rooted to the spot.

The beast slowly rose from the ground, revealing legs the diameter of thick tree trunks. Nick's torso hung from the corner of its mouth, a river of bloody drool washing over it and spattering onto the frozen ground below. In one practised motion, the creature flicked its mouth open, jerking its head up and back at the same time, drawing Nick's body deeper into its nightmarish maw. Now, only a single, blood-soaked leg hung from one dripping corner of the creature's mouth. Finishing its current bite with a brief, snapping crack of its jaws, dozens of razor-like teeth amputated Nick's protruding leg as surgically as any scalpel. The severed limb, still encased in Gortex, dropped to the frozen ground with a soft thump as dark, venal blood flowed out of it onto the red-smeared snow.

As Jerry struggled with his rising gorge, he began paying attention to a small voice inside his head. The little voice was very quiet at first, but it gradually became louder and louder, growing ever more insistent that he listen to it. Jerry's brain finally provided him with a bingo and he realised that this little internal voice was trying to tell him to get his ever-loving ass out of this place, while the getting was good and the monster was still ignoring him, preoccupied as it currently was eating Nick (no offence, bro — RIP).

Spinning on one boot heel, Jerry tried to speak a single word of warning aloud, but his fear-tightened vocal cords refused to cooperate, and the word remained dammed-up inside. But fear demanded that he keep trying, and after several more desperate seconds, he found his voice, and the word gushed from his mouth, "Monster!"

With his verbal dam ruptured, Jerry was finally able to access the rest of his fear-flooded vocabulary, and a string of colourful metaphors poured out, growing louder and louder the closer he got to camp.

"Holy shit! Jesus Christ! Sweet Mother Mary! It's a goddamned monster!" Scrambling and slipping in the ice-covered snow, he could barely see his hand in front of his face. He ran for his life toward the sanctuary of light and safety that the glow of the campfire promised.

"Tyler! Matt! Wake up! Something just ate Nick!" Jerry crashed through the brush, stumbling to a stop near the bonfire between the two men. He wasn't particularly surprised that his verbal early warning system had had little effect, seeing how drunk everyone currently was.

On Jerry's right, Tyler was now completely slumped over sideways in his chair, snoring loudly. To his left, Matt was still out cold on top of his air mattress, drool coming from one corner of his mouth.

Panic made Jerry decide to upgrade his attempts to rouse his friends from verbal warnings to feats of actual physical violence, at no extra charge to either of them. He grabbed Tyler, pulling him upright in his chair at the same time. "Ty! Wake up! There's some kind of monster here, and it's eaten Nick!" He gave Tyler several hard shakes. The man stirred for a moment and grumbled something to the effect of Jerry going away and leaving him the fuck alone; then his head dropped forward onto his chest once more.

"Shit!"

Jerry sprinted around the edge of the fire to check on Matt, squelching through the mud, almost slipping and falling into the fire himself. He jammed his muck-covered boot into his sleeping friend's thigh several times with increasing vigour. "Matt! Wake up, dude! We have to go! Nick's dead!" Matt continued to rock his impression of a dead octopus at the beach, snoring softly.

"Son of a bitch!" Jerry said, looking back over to Tyler. He saw that the man was slumped sideways in his chair once more, showing no signs of consciousness. Giving Matt one last, good kick, he ran around the fire and grabbed Tyler, this time by the collar of his parka. Pulling the man upright with his left hand, Jerry began slapping his friend repeatedly with the open palm of his right.

Sputtering and swearing, Tyler came back around, grabbing at Jerry's hands. "Shit! What in the goddamned hell do you think you're doing, bro?"

"There's a huge goddamned monster over there, bro, and it's eaten Nick!" Jerry shrieked at his friend.

"What? What kind of gag do you think…" Tyler said, feeling pissed at Jerry's goofing around after everyone had already started chilling for the night.

"Ty, it's not a fucking gag!" Jerry said in exasperation. He turned around and saw Matt still sound asleep. "Goddammit!" Jerry raced back and proceeded to kick his comatose comrade once more, this time with a renewed fervour, alternating between shouting, then kicking, "Wake!" — Kick — "The!" — Kick — "Fuck!" — Kick — "Up!" — Kick.

No response.

Jerry shouted over his shoulder to Tyler, "Do something to help me! We've got to get the hell out of here!" Bending down, he grabbed Matt's legs and tried to drag his friend off of the air mattress, but he was too heavy. Jerry knew if he tried to roll Matt off the mattress, he'd end up rolling the unconscious man directly into the fire, much like he'd been worried about Nick doing to himself about a half a lifetime ago, or so it seemed.

Looking back, he saw Tyler now sitting upright in his chair, elbows on his knees, grinding the palms of his hands into his eyes as he simultaneously tried to wake up and sober up. Jerry stumbled back around the fire and yanked Tyler's hands away from his eyes. Kneeling in the snow, he placed his face directly in front of his friend's and tried to speak in as calm a voice as he could manage, but it still came out all at once, in one quick breath like some sort of scream-speak. "There is a gigantic monster over there, and it's eaten Nick! And you and me and Matt are going to be next unless we get our collective asses out of this frozen hell!"

From behind Jerry and Tyler, on the other side of the campfire, a dry, thirsty voice said, "What have you been doing, bro? My side here is as sore as shit! And I think you might have busted one of my freaking ribs!"

Jerry turned, a smile rising on his face when he saw Matt finally awake and communicative. His friend was propped up on one elbow, glaring across the fire at him. But Jerry's half-baked smile quickly deflated as a massive, gore-covered paw shot out from the tall brush over Matt's head.

Four sabre-like claws gleamed in the firelight, each one easily a half-metre in length. Matt looked up at this claw-tipped paw, still half-stoned. "Man, that must have been some potent shit!"

At the sound of Matt's voice, the taloned appendage paused, hovering over him, as if unsure what to make of these strange noises coming from its prey. It suddenly slammed down onto Matt's prone body with an ear-ringing pop that ruptured both the man on top and the air mattress beneath. Jerry winced as Matt's arms and legs shot out to both sides as he was crushed, a final, breathless, "Gak!" escaping from beneath the grotesque, bloody paw. With frightening speed, the gargantuan limb yanked back into the bushes, clawing its prizes of Matt's body and the now claret-soaked air mattress along with it.

"Holy shit!" Tyler yelled in disbelief. He jumped up, pushing away from Jerry's grasping hands and ran toward the tent, stumbling and sliding in the ice-slicked snow, then slipped inside.

Stunned, Jerry said, "Tyler! Where are you going? What are you doing?" He was left standing alone near the crackling fire, the fog and smoke swirling like phantoms around him.

"Just hang on a sec!" Tyler hollered from inside the tent. Moments later he came tearing back out and stumbled to a halt next to Jerry in the ice-covered snow. "Bring it on, motherfucker!" Tyler shouted defiantly. Clenched in his right hand was one of the biggest handguns Jerry had ever seen.

Using his left hand, Tyler firmly pushed Jerry back behind him by a couple of feet while he pointed the pistol into the fog, saying, "Stand aside, brother!"

Jerry backed up a bit more, a hysterical giggle building in his throat as he wondered if Tyler was going to inform the monster that he was holding one of the most powerful handguns in the world and that it was capable of blowing its head clean off? Perhaps also asking if it was feeling lucky? No, he doubted that very much.

Tyler aimed at the brush where Matt had been dragged and started shooting, emptying the entire clip from the .44 Auto Mag into the thicket.

The sound of the gun was enormous. Jerry felt like he'd lost the hearing in both ears from the concussive blasts of Tyler's hand-cannon. He watched the bullets shred the fog as they travelled to their mark, slamming into the thick brush, a shrapnel of twigs and small branches flying in every direction.

"Son of a bitch!" Tyler whooped, still pulling the trigger on the now-empty magnum. He looked over at Jerry, "Do you think I got it?"

"I think you can volunteer to go and take a look for yourself since you're the one holding the howitzer there," Jerry said, looking at Tyler's handgun.

"Yeah, I guess you're right." Tyler reached into his pocket and pulled out another magazine of ammunition. He ejected the spent one and slammed the fresh clip home in a single, fluid motion. "You can back me up." Tyler moved toward the bushes once more.

"Whaa...? With what? Harsh language?" Jerry asked incredulously as he fished around in his jacket pockets for something to use as a weapon. He pulled out the only thing he could find, his GPS unit. He turned the screen on, pointed the device toward the bushes and said in a quavery voice, "You want me to tag its location for you or something? It's right the hell over there!"

Holding his left hand up toward Jerry asking for silence, Tyler edged toward the thick brush, hunched slightly forward, the knuckles of his right hand growing white from the death-grip he held on the pistol. Tyler now cupped the bottom of the gun with his left hand and angled his right foot slightly back and to the side across from the other. Jerry thought it was called the 'Weaver Stance'. He didn't know why that particular bit of information would pop into his head right now, but he was pretty sure Tyler didn't need him riddling him with shooting stance questions at the moment.

Tyler moved slowly forward. A metre from where Matt had been dragged off, he stopped, froze and shouted, "Whatever the fuck you are, if you're not dead yet, you're going to be soon!" He stepped through the break in the brush and disappeared into the swirling smoke-filled mist.

"Tyler! Where are you going? Don't go in there!"

"I'm fine," Tyler called back. "I think I got it or maybe scared it off!"

"That would be great," Jerry said, relief flooding his voice.

"Shit, I don't see Nick or Matt's body," Tyler said, then added after a pause, "Holy Christ! What the fuck did that thing do to them? Oh my God! The blood! There's so much goddamned blood!" Tyler retched hard, sounding repulsed by the signs of the slaughter.

Jerry started to move toward the bushes when Tyler suddenly popped out of a gap directly in front of him. He leapt backward, saying, "Christ! Don't do that!"

"Sorry, Jer, but I think it's gone," Tyler said, wiping the corner of his mouth with the back of his hand. "I saw what looked like tracks heading the other way in the snow. I must have scared it away, thanks to this baby." He patted the gun lightly as he held it in his hands as if it were a good little guard dog that had done its job.

"Thank God! Then let's just get the hell out of here and call the RCMP or the marines or something. Speaking of which…" Jerry pulled out his iPhone. The signal strength bars were still at zero. "Shit!"

"Well," Tyler said, nodding toward Jerry's phone, "first of all, we're at least fifteen klicks from civilisation in the middle of the fucking nowhere. And second of all, like you pointed out, there aren't any cell repeater towers anywhere nearby for a signal. So, unless you've suddenly found a satellite phone, good luck with that, brother."

"Can't hurt to check," Jerry said with a shrug.

Taking charge once more, Tyler said, "Okay! let's get the fu..." His words were cut off in mid-sentence by the sound of something slicing through the air at his back. His eyes went wide, and he fell to his knees, the magnum dropping onto the slush in front of him. Tyler began shrieking in agony, slumping forward into the snow, his hands spasming in tight knots of anguish.

Jerry gagged when he saw the four ragged furrows that had been carved diagonally across Tyler's wounded back. Each one welled with blood; long strips of mangled white flesh dangled from the wounds like pieces of overcooked lasagne. He had been eviscerated from behind, and most of his skin, clothing and internal organs now lay in a spreading crimson bloom on the frozen ground at his back. As Tyler bled out, he did the only thing he was capable of doing now, and he screamed, and screamed, and screamed.

Jerry held his hands up to his ears to block out the blood-curdling sound of his friend's anguish. "Ty! Oh shit! Oh my God!" He couldn't move and felt his mind begin to slip, losing its traction from the unreality of the situation before him.

With a crack of snapping branches, the beast burst through the fog-shrouded bushes in front of Jerry and dropped down onto Tyler's writhing body. The huge, grey creature tore into the squirming, screaming man, as Jerry staggered back in horror. Right in front of his eyes, his best friend was being devoured by this monster from hell, and he could do nothing to stop it because Tyler had fallen on top of his pistol. As Jerry backed away through the smoke and fog, he caught a glimpse of sword-like claws, crimson-covered fangs and great gouts of steaming blood spraying everywhere into the misty darkness.

"Jesus Christ, holy shit, sweet mother…" Jerry backed up toward where the snowmobiles were parked, never taking his eyes off of the spot in the fog where the beast was ravaging Tyler. Almost falling over the closest machine as he stumbled backward into it, Jerry spun around and jumped on board without looking — Tyler's ride, it turned out, but the keys were missing.

"Son of a bitch!" he muttered. There was no way in hell he was going back now to look for the keys in Tyler's pockets and threw himself toward the next sled only to find the same result, no keys in the ignition.

"Shit! Jerry rasped. Sprinting toward the next sled, he was delighted to see it was his blinding yellow Wasp-mobile, and apparently, he'd left his keys in the ignition. "Yes!" He hopped on board and turned the engine over. The machine roared to life, and Jerry twisted the throttle so hard he thought he might snap it off. Looking back over his shoulder, he regretted it almost at once.

The giant predator ploughed through the bonfire, red-hot embers and burning logs exploding into the darkness like flaming matchsticks as it raged toward him.

Jerry gunned the engine. The snowmobile rocketed into the grey void of fog as he attempted to put as much distance between himself and the beast as he could. He followed the trail that they had forged through the snow on their way into camp that afternoon. There were hazards up ahead, but he knew he couldn't slow down, or he'd risk having the beast catch up to him. Still, he knew he was pushing his luck.

Glancing down at the glowing speedometer, Jerry saw he was ripping along doing almost eighty kilometres an hour in the darkness, surrounded by ice fog on an unfamiliar trail in the middle of nowhere. A sense of self-preservation kicked in, and Jerry made himself back the throttle off just a little bit. He didn't want to miss a turn and have a rollover, or god-forbid hit a tree. If that happened, then he'd be royally screwed.

The fog seemed to coagulate around him. He gradually slowed his speed and felt his sense of panic increase. The farther he got from camp, the thicker the fog became. Soon, he couldn't see his hand in front of his face, let alone the trail from the edge of a precipice. He finally stopped, feeling stymied as to what he should do next. Blue light bathed his face as he turned on his cell phone, checking for a signal once more. "Shit! Still no bars!" he complained.

Perhaps sensing a change in the air pressure around him, Jerry wasn't sure, but he glanced to his right just as something whisked through the mist with the speed of a locomotive toward his head. "Jesus Chr…" Jerry ducked down and leaned forward into the windshield of the snowmobile as some of the longest and sharpest looking claws he wished never to see again sliced through the space his head had been occupying only milliseconds before.

Still hunched down and leaning so far forward he thought he might break his nose on the windshield, Jerry Benson aimed the snowmobile for the centre of the trail and twisted the throttle to the max. He shot blindly forward into the freezing fog, praying that the nightmare was now behind him.

CHAPTER TWO

Wiping his hands on a rag, Austin Murphy stood back, folded his arms, and contemplated the lethal weapon before him. He stroked his salt and pepper beard for a moment, then moved to one side for a better view.

The 105mm howitzer gun gleamed dully in the weak daylight of the foggy January morning that filtered through the workshop windows. It was a couple of minutes before eight o'clock, and Austin had just finished doing the final safety check and lubrication of the olive drab cannon. He'd arrived early at the shop today to make sure the gun was ready for business as soon as the fog departed, whenever that may be. Over the last ten years or so, the build-up of the winter snowpack high in the mountains had been increasingly hard to bring down thanks to fluctuating weather patterns. With the air cannon they'd used for decades now ailing and in need of replacement, the howitzer had been decided upon by the city as a more effective solution for triggering controlled avalanches in the area.

As the head of road and highway maintenance for the city of Lawless, BC, Austin Murphy was also the liaison for the region with the Provincial Highways Department. Making sure the local roads were safe for everyone 365 days a year, 24/7 was his job, and it was one that he took quite seriously. It kept him more than busy each winter and practically every other season as well.

In keeping with the changing climate pattern in the area, this year had been foggy and soggy with minimal new snow. Most of the precipitation so far this winter had fallen as rain, at least down at the valley bottom. Up in the local mountains, however, it had been a different story — just cold enough to allow numerous layers of heavy, wet snow to build up to dangerous levels. Every few weeks, a high-pressure system seemed to come through to break up the monotony of the fog, giving them a few days of clearing but also freezing everything solid in the process. Then, yet another warm front off the Pacific would push over the coastal mountains and dump even more wet snow onto the local hills. It was a pattern that repeated most of the winter, making the entire snowpack very unstable and putting the Golden Mile Pass leading into the valley at risk on a regular basis.

There was only one way to access Lawless, and that was through the pass. If it weren't for the constant vigilance of the Lawless Public Works Department's throughout the winter, the town would be completely cut off from the rest of the world for over four months of the year. Not only would that affect food and supplies coming into the town, but also the tourist trade as well seeing as Lawless was currently home to one of the busiest little casinos in the interior of the province, The Golden Nugget Casino and Resort.

Up until the turn of the millennium, the population of Lawless ballooned every winter, as skiers, snowboarders and snowmobilers made the local mountains their winter playground, and Lawless had been more than happy to welcome them. But thanks to the warming trend over several decades, the winter fogs and mild temperatures had forced the closure of the ski hill. It was a sad day for the town, causing severe revenue loss to many of the businesses and residents in the area who relied on the tourist trade.

With the help of a pair of local entrepreneurs, the resort reopened after a major renovation and now operated as a casino and buffet restaurant, making it a major draw for tourists to the area once more. For the more adventurous, the mountains surrounding the Kootenay Glacier still provided more than adequate conditions for some quality winter recreation. World-class cross-country skiing and snowshoeing were also still possible at the higher alpine elevations, including snowmobiling, or sledding, as the locals liked to call it. Heli-skiing, popular in other areas of the province, was not possible around Lawless due to the almost constant cloud layer that smothered the valley in wintertime.

Last week, the weapon in front of Austin had garnered quite a few stares from passersby when he'd towed into town behind the Lawless Public Works truck. Once verifying everything was operational at the shop, they'd needed to run a couple of tests of the new 'snow-blower-upper' and Austin decided to take it out to the local quarry for that purpose.

'Snow-blower-upper' was the name that Austin's son, Alex, had given the gun the first time he'd seen it. When asked if he'd like to join his father and Trip at the local rock quarry to test fire the gun, the boy had almost passed out from excitement at the thought. The gun worked exceedingly well, punching huge holes into the side of the gravel quarry. It left all three of them literally vibrating, not only from excitement but also from the concussive blasts of the cannon.

Towing the large-wheeled gun behind the Works truck also had a positive impact on people's driving habits, Austin discovered. Due to the height of the Chevy Silverado's trailer hitch, the gun barrel of the howitzer pointed almost directly at eye-level into the windshield of whoever was behind him. Once most drivers realised what they were following, they decided to keep a very long and very safe following distance.

"Tailgaters beware," he said with a smile, still gazing at the gun. He picked up an empty shell casing that he'd placed near the gun and marvelled at it. At ten centimetres in diameter, the howitzer shells were huge. He hefted it in his hands, feeling the weight of the projectile. It was one serious looking piece of hardware that would surely make any snowpack quiver in fear, or so he hoped. Without propellant or explosive charge loaded, the casing still weighed almost ten kilograms, not something he'd want to drop onto his snow-booted foot. He looked forward to using one of them for real in the next few days, if the fog let up a bit.

Austin didn't want a repeat of what happened just after the start of the new year when significant seismic activity had shaken things up in the area. The ground tremors had been large enough to loosen quite a bit of the snowpack along the pass, and several large avalanches of snow and rock came tumbling down as a result. It had kept the seven thousand residents of Lawless and its visiting tourists isolated for several days while Austin and crew dug them out from one side of the pass while provincial work crews cleared the other.

Fortunately, after the quake struck, it had been bitterly cold with minimal new snow, allowing for a quicker cleanup. Just seeing the blue sky around Lawless was a rare treat after the seemingly incessant fog they'd had for such a long stretch. The attitude of everyone in town had improved for the better for a while, no doubt thanks to the added vitamin D they'd been absorbing from the sun after such a long absence from its rays.

That changed just after the middle of January when a warm front, affectionately called a 'pineapple express', blew in from the coast. A fresh load of heavy, wet snow dumped on top of the hard cold-pack still in the mountains. The fog returned for another extended visit soon after, creating more issues for Austin. It severely limited the visibility when he needed to assess the avalanche risk, varying anywhere between slightly crappy to really shitty on a daily basis. So, for the past week, he'd been hoping for some clearing to assess the avalanche risk.

This morning, Trip Williams was coming with him to the valley's fire lookout tower. Trip was his assistant, right-hand man and long-time compadre. They planned to assess the avalanche risk from the tower's lofty heights and hoped to have a clear view of the mountain tops above the thick valley cloud in order to make a determination. If it were a go, they would come back for the howitzer later. But as of right now, things didn't seem too promising, and it looked like a repeat of yesterday — another grey, featureless day in limbo.

Carefully placing the shell casing back into the storage locker and locking it up, Austin flicked off the shop lights and walked through to the offices at the front of the building. First stop in his search for Trip was the lunchroom, since today was doughnut day, or Wednesday to the rest of the world. Knowing his long-time friend's routine, Austin was fairly sure that's where he'd find him.

Clara Carleton, the office manager, brought in a dozen doughnuts and coffee from Tim Hortons on hump day each week. She liked to treat her boys, as she called Austin, Trip and Larry on nightshift, to a weekly treat. So, it was almost a given that Trip would be in the lunchroom right now with his arms wrapped protectively around the box of artery-clogging sweetness, picking out the 'good ones' for himself. The 'good ones' were the honey-glazed crullers. Clara always ordered at least a half-dozen of them just for Trip. She knew he'd be a Mr. Cranky-pants all day long without his morning sugar fix, so she ordered accordingly.

Entering the lunchroom, Austin was pleased to see that his prognosticative abilities were still up to snuff, as there sat Trip, working his way through a honey cruller. "Morning, Trip! Which one are you on now?"

Trip chewed for a moment before responding around a mouthful of doughnut, saying, "Mumber free." A cavalcade of crumbs tumbled from Trip's mouth onto his bushy white beard as he spoke.

Austin gave a thumbs up, saying, "You're doing great today, buddy! Only three left to go! I'll catch up with you at the front door when you're done; I'm just going to check-in with Clara first."

Trip was in the middle of washing down his progress with a huge gulp from his prerequisite, extra-large triple-cream, triple-sugar coffee. He set the cup down with his left hand, giving a big thumbs up in return. In his right hand, a fresh cruller sat poised for imminent consumption, its thick glaze sparkling like ice in the fluorescent lights overhead. Austin thought he might have detected a slight smile as well, but with Trip's thick, white beard, it was sometimes tough to tell. Shaking his head, a grin on his face, he turned and walked through to the front offices to greet Clara.

The City of Lawless did not have the largest municipal maintenance department by any means. Apart from Austin and Trip, there were only two other employees that worked at the public works yard: Clara, who had been sitting behind her desk since time immemorial, and Larry, the snowplow/sander/grader driver. Larry was most likely already heading home for some much-deserved sleep after a long night of keeping the roads plowed, sanded and safe — after grabbing his two chocolate long johns, of course. Although Austin suspected that the only thing Larry had moved around the night before with his plow blade was more of the nebulous, grey mist.

Walking by the kennel, he saw the small, caged room was thankfully empty today. Due to the need to consolidate offices in such a small town, the Public Works Office also just happened to be the office in charge of animal control for the City of Lawless. With a smile, Austin thought someday he might just want to add 'Chief Cook & Bottle-washer' to his business card as well.

"Morning, Clara," Austin said, pushing through the glass door into the inner office.

"Good morning, Austin!" Clara beamed. "How's the newest addition to our little family doing today?"

"Sorry?" He said, puzzlement showing in his hazel eyes.

"I mean your new baby, that olive drab bundle of joy sitting in your shop, of course!"

"Ah, yes," he laughed. "It's looking good! Baby should be ready to go boom-boom as soon as the fog lifts. Speaking of which, any word on that? I haven't checked the weather."

"Well, according to the latest from the weather office, we're in for a few more days of this depressing crap before we get some relief." She shook her head sadly.

"That's just lovely."

"Yes, indeed. And by the way, you've got a cleanup in aisle three." Clara smiled sweetly as she spoke the phrase, using their inter-office nickname for fresh roadkill on the highway.

Austin said with a tired grin, "Okay, I'm game. Which part? Fresh fruit or frozen foods?"

"Frozen foods, just about five klicks before the turn-off to the resort."

"Messy?"

"Ray Chance called it in on his way to the casino this morning. He told me he hit something with his SUV and caved in the whole hood. According to him, he wasn't sure what he'd hit at first, but once he got out and looked at the damage, he said, and I quote, 'It was one of the biggest, butt-ugliest, goddamned raccoons I've ever seen in my life! And now it's all over the goddamned road and my Land Rover!'" Clara smiled lovingly as she recalled the conversation. "I thanked him graciously for the call and told him I'd let you know about it as soon as you came through the door this morning, of course."

"Thank you for your efficiency, as always, Clara. It certainly sounds like that man has seen his fair share of homely raccoons over his lifetime," Austin said with a slight smile.

Clara smiled ruefully in return, cautioning, "You know how he is, Austin, he'll be calling me every hour checking to see if you've done it yet, caterwauling that it'll be scaring the tourists away having a dead raccoon spread across the highway."

"No doubt," Austin said, shaking his head. "We wouldn't want to affect business at the casino!"

"Lord, no! So, could you and Trip be a couple of sweeties and swing by and scrape it off the asphalt on your way to do the avalanche assessment this morning?" Clara smiled broadly, concluding. "When Chance called it in, Larry was already heading home, eating his long-johns."

"I figured as much. That shouldn't be a problem, Clara." Austin wasn't surprised Ray Chance would have a bird over something like that. As the general manager and part-owner of the casino, Chance also sat on the town council and was one of the wealthiest men in the area. Austin knew as well as Clara did, as soon as there was something that might affect the almighty tourist dollar at the Golden Nugget Casino and Resort, Ray Chance would be on the phone to the other half of the resort's ownership, the Mayor of Lawless, Bob Nichols. Chance would complain vociferously, making sure that whatever the problem was, it got looked after. Heaven forbid anybody turned around and left Lawless with a couple of dollars remaining in their pocket.

"What's not a problem?" Trip asked, coming through from the lunchroom. He brushed doughnut crumbs from his beard as he spoke, then looked down at his stomach and frowned. Though successful in removing the crumbs from his beard, he'd only managed to move them to a lower berth and now had to go to work brushing them off of his more than ample belly. Trip's six doughnut breakfasts had caught up with him over the past few years, of that, there was no doubt, Austin noted sadly. When Trip first started working at the public works yard about a dozen years before, he had been a much slimmer man. In fact, he wouldn't be surprised to get a phone call from Alvin down at the fire hall someday in the near future regarding Trip. That would be the call where the fire chief tells him they had to cut Trip free from a piece of City Works equipment with the jaws of life due to his ample mid-section getting him trapped behind the wheel.

Clara chirped brightly to Trip, "We've got a scratch and sniff five klicks out on the valley highway. And it sounds like you might want to bring a shovel and big bucket, big fella."

Trip sighed, "It couldn't have been on Larry's shift, could it? All right, I'll throw them in the back of the truck and see you in the front yard, Boss." He stomped back through into the darkened shop, brushing at crumbs stuck to the front of his light brown Carhartt coveralls.

"Sounds good, Trip." Turning back to his office manager, Austin said, "Okay, you have yourself a fun-filled day m'dear." He zipped up his parka, preparing to leave. He started to push the front door open when Clara said, "Oh, yes! There's one more thing I just remembered!" She seemed very excited about her news.

"What is it, Clara?" This must be very big news indeed — he didn't remember the last time he'd seen her so animated.

"Well, it sounds like Ray Chance called everyone he could think of this morning," she said with a small grin.

"What do you mean?" Austin's brow knitted together.

"During his second call of the morning, Ray told me he also called the new conservation officer to help deal with the mess. And then, the new conservation officer contacted me right after I hung up with Chance!"

"That is good news!" Austin interjected. They'd been without a conservation officer in the valley since Carl's recent disappearance.

"Absolutely! The officer said they should be out at the scene by the time someone from Public Works got there," Clara finished, a twinkle of mischief sparkling in the corners of her eyes.

"Sounds good, what's their name?" Austin noted Clara's playfulness and wondered what she wasn't telling him.

"Chris Moon."

"All right, now I'll have a name to put to the face. Thanks, Clara."

Austin stepped through the door and as the pneumatic closer pulled it slowly shut, Clara called out behind him, "Make sure you don't miss any bits and pieces!"

The green and white Lawless Publics Works Chevy Silverado pulled up to the front of the building, stopping in front of Austin. The bucket and shovel looked primed and ready to go, strapped in between the two snowmobiles on the pickup's steel deck.

Austin climbed into the passenger side, saying, "Take me to the Moon, amigo!"

"Huh?" Trip looked to his friend, with a 'what the hell is he talking about now' expression on his face.

"Never mind, it's time for our roadkill roundup! Let's load 'em up and move 'em out!"

"Rawhide! Yee-haw, you got it, Boss!" Trip enthused with a grin, quite possibly.

CHAPTER THREE

Crouching down, Christine Moon gently probed the animal's remains with the end of her collapsible shovel. The collision with Ray Chance's SUV had scattered the 'raccoon' across both sides of the highway in numerous wet, bloody chunks. She had to stop and turn her head to catch a quick breath of fresh air every few seconds as the carcass was exceedingly pungent.

She stood to get a better look at the accident scene, but the fog wasn't helping things as it swirled past her, continually obscuring her view. From the markings on the more intact parts of the creature, it did indeed look like a raccoon. But from the amount of blood and gore spattered around, it appeared to have been from more than one animal — perhaps it was a family of them? If it were only one raccoon, it must have been the size of a black bear, which was crazy! Most of the raccoons Christine had ever encountered were not much bigger than a medium-sized poodle, and the largest one on record wasn't more than thirty kilograms.

A green and white Chevy Silverado appeared out of the fog across the highway, and she paused her probing for a moment. The pickup turned on its rack of amber emergency lights and pulled a u-turn, parking behind her Dodge Ram.

Christine glanced surreptitiously from beneath the brim of her hat, pretending to be engrossed in examining the roadkill. Two men emerged from the truck. The taller one, sporting a neatly trimmed Van Dyke beard, approached her through the swirling mist. He was rather handsome. His salt and pepper beard cast a striking contrast to his short, slightly greying brown hair which sprouted from beneath his green Lawless City Works baseball cap. The second man was still at the truck, rummaging around in the back.

Glancing into the fog and trying to watch his step amongst the carnage strewn across the road, the tall man's attention wasn't on Christine until he arrived onto her side of the highway. She stood to face him. He stuck out his right hand to introduce himself and looked up for the first time. "Hi there, I'm Austin Murphy from Lawless City Works, and you are… a woman!"

"And I see you are a very observant man!" Christine shot back. She shook his hand, a smile dancing across the corners of her lips.

Still apparently caught off guard, the man said, "Sorry, but when Clara back at the office told me I'd be meeting the new conservation officer for the area today, she didn't mention you were a woman."

"Yes, and I have been for quite some time now. I hope that's okay?" Her smile continued its hypnotic display for a moment longer before diminishing to a more business-like expression.

"Absolutely! It was just a bit of a surprise, that's all. Your predecessor, Carl, was much taller, hairier and a lot crustier than you are."

Still with a trace of smile, Christine said, "Well, thanks for the heads up! I'll try to keep the hairiness and crustiness to a minimum, but I can't do anything about the height!"

"I don't think that'll be a problem." Austin smiled back, thinking she was also a heck of a lot better looking than Carl had ever been. And the only hair he currently saw was long, blonde and spilling out from beneath the back of her ranger hat in a loosely-tied pony-tail.

"I'm Christine Moon, by the way, but you can call me Chris." Her hypnotic smile returned as her ice-blue eyes drilled into his.

"Sorry! Pleased to meet you, Chris." Austin Murphy grinned again, his cheeks glowing slightly, perhaps from embarrassment.

Ambling out of the fog, the other man arrived onto the scene, his attention also on the gristle and gore scattered across the road as he approached. Clasped in his work glove covered hands was a large, metal bucket and a long-handled shovel. He was much shorter than Austin and almost bald except for one hell of a bushy white beard, and his flushed cheeks seemed redder than Okanagan cherries in springtime. Surveying the mess near their feet, he intoned, sombrely, "I think we're gonna need a bigger bucket."

Austin turned to his co-worker, saying, "Trip Williams, I'd like you to meet the newest conservation officer for the area, Chris Moon!"

Placing the bucket on the ground, the man looked up from the gore, extending his hand as he did. His eyes widened for a brief moment when they locked onto Christine's face, and he said in astonishment, "You're a girl!"

"Yes, I am! Thanks!" Christine replied, taking the man's proffered hand.

Appearing to grin slightly, he said, "Caught me off guard, sorry. Pleased to meet you." As he pumped her hand vigorously up and down, she thought he might have possibly grinned again, then blushed even harder but his beard made it hard to tell.

Christine bathed the man in her smile's radiance. "Pleased to meet you, Trip Williams." The shorter man's grip was firm but slightly sticky — with what, she didn't really want to know. "Say, fellas, I was wondering, since you're doing so well with your gender identification today, maybe you could put some of those powers of observation to work and help me figure out what the heck this thing all over the road is?"

"Absolutely," Austin said.

"Yes, ma'am." Trip agreed.

"Awesome! Thanks, guys!" Christine said, clapping her hands and rubbing them together. She pointed several metres away into the fog, toward the road's shoulder where a white chunk of skull gleamed. "Well, first of all, if you look over there at that large cranial fragment, you'll see there isn't another piece like that anywhere around that appears to be from a different animal."

"But it looks to be way too much blood and entrails for it to have been just one single animal." Trip observed, shaking his head.

"Exactly!" Austin agreed. "Ray Chance swore it was only one raccoon he hit, but judging by all the assorted bits and pieces, it has to have been more than one."

Trip concluded, "And if that were the case, that would mean this raccoon had been the size of a black bear, and they never get that big!"

Concurring with Trip's assessment, Christine nodded, saying, "I know, and I was wondering about that!" She looked down at the mess, adding, "I was hoping that once we get everything scraped into garbage bags, perhaps you could help me put it in the back of my pickup truck? Pretty please?" She blinded them with her smile once more, then said, "I have a friend on the coast who's a zoologist, and I want to reconstruct it and send some pictures of this creature to her. Hopefully, she might be able to help us figure out what this thing is!"

"Okay, Trip, you heard the lady! Pluck it, bucket, and bag it!"

"You got it, Boss," Trip responded. He reached into his outer parka pocket and pulled out a spare pair of rubber gloves, handing them to Austin, saying, "I didn't want you to feel left out."

"Thank you, you're a scholar and a gentleman, Trip!"

"De nada," Trip said, beginning to pry a piece of the semi-frozen carcass from the asphalt with his shovel.

Once the trio had finally scraped everything off the road that they could scrape, they stood near the back of Christine's pickup and surveyed the mound of heavy-duty, transparent garbage bags in the truck bed.

"There's definitely no way that's one raccoon." Trip said with finality.

"Well, hopefully, my friend Zelda can help out," Christine said. "But I've got to run. Thanks very much for your help, guys! It was certainly great to meet you both, and I'm sure we'll see more of each other around town, soon." As she spoke, she noted Trip's cheeks blooming a lovely shade of rose and thought he might have possibly smiled as well but was unsure due to the density of his facial follicles.

Austin took off his rubber gloves and extended his right hand to shake hers once more, saying with a grim smile, "Nice to meet you as well, and maybe next time we meet it won't be in as gory a situation."

"We can always hope," Christine said, briefly shaking Austin's hand in return. She climbed into her dark-blue Ram 3500 and flicked the strobing amber light rack into high-intensity mode. Turning the vehicle carefully around, she slowly drove away into the mist.

Austin turned to Trip as they watched Christine depart, saying, "So, what do you think?"

"Well, she's a lot prettier than Carl was."

"I mean, what do you think that thing was on the highway?"

"I don't know. I've never seen anything like it. But what I'd like to know is how fast Ray Chance was going when he hit the damned thing. It looks like it exploded!"

"Trip, you know Ray doesn't worry about things like speed limits or using caution while driving in the fog!"

"Or anywhere else for that matter!"

"Too true! Alrighty then! Let's continue on to the lookout tower to see what we can see."

"I don't think today's gonna be any different than yesterday," Trip intoned.

"Well, with the altitude the lookout is at, I think we might get lucky and be able to see something today." As he spoke, the day grew slightly brighter, as if the sun had heard him and was trying to accommodate him by burning off a bit more of the fog and low cloud. Climbing into the truck, Austin thought that just perhaps, things were starting to look up.

CHAPTER FOUR

Pressing the intercom button with one beefy finger, Ray Chance squawked into the speakerphone on his desk, saying, "Roxanne! Did you call to see if the public works yard has scraped that goddamned raccoon off of the highway yet?"

An unruffled, musical voice emanated from the speaker, "Yes, Mr. Chance, I checked with them an hour ago, and they said they had their best men on it."

Chance jabbed the intercom button with his finger once more and groused, "Best men? Hmmph! If that Trip Williams is one of their 'best men' then we're already in trouble." He was still pissed about running into that damned raccoon this morning. Remaining seated, he rolled his leather chair over to the window and looked down at his SUV, faintly visible in the fog. With a sour expression on his face, he observed the damage.

Now that it was daylight (or as close as they were going to get with this constant frigging fog) he saw the damage to his Land Rover's front end was much more extensive than he'd initially thought — it looked to be easily in the tens of thousands of dollars. Though still drivable, the passenger side front fender had taken the brunt of the impact, with the headlight smashed to shit. And then there was the windshield which was cracked in three different places. He sighed and closed his eyes for a moment, trying to shut out the sight of his damaged Rover, but it was still there in the darkness, seemingly burned into his retinas.

In a brief flash of memory behind closed eyes, Chance recalled the collision. The raccoon came out of nowhere, stepping from out of the fog in front of the Rover. It collided with the SUV's fender, momentarily gaining flight capability for the first and last time in its life. This was just about the same time it exploded, bouncing off the hood as it disintegrated. The Rorschach pattern now sprayed over the pearl-white Rover made his once pristine baby look like an abattoir on wheels. "Bastard," he muttered to himself, his face a mask of disgust as he looked at the bits of fur and gristle still stuck in the front grill of the vehicle. He'd have to have Watkins from maintenance scrub it down later today.

From her small desk in the outer office, Roxanne Rooney buzzed Chance's phone. Spinning around in his chair, he stabbed the intercom button, saying, "Yes, yes? What is it?"

Roxanne looked over her drying fingernails at the man standing across the desk from her. "Mr. Chance, Mr. Watkins from maintenance is here to see you." The man in question had slunk into the reception area with a dour expression on his face just a moment before, asking to see Chance. Roxanne had asked what the agitated-looking man was there to see Mr. Chance about, but he hadn't seemed particularly keen on sharing the reason with her.

"Watkins?" the intercom crackled. "Perfect! Just who I wanted to see! Send him in!"

"You may go in Mr. Watkins," Roxanne said, smiling sweetly and nodding to show he could enter. Watkins gave her a slight nod in return followed by a small scowl that he was trying to pass off for a smile, but with little success.

The maintenance man reaffirmed the death-grip he held on his toque, still bunched together in his hands, and shuffled into Chance's inner sanctum. He nodded briefly, then turned and closed the heavy door with his back to the room, cringing slightly when Ray Chance brayed behind him, "Watkins! Perfect timing! I was going to call you with a quick job, but you beat me to it!"

Turning to face his employer, Watkins said, "Actually, Mr. Chance, I was here to…"

"Sit down, man, sit down!" Chance barked.

"Yes, sir," Watkins said, taking a seat in the leather armchair on the other side of the desk opposite Chance.

"Well, what is it?" Chance asked abruptly. "We haven't got all day, so spill it!" He leaned forward as he spoke, the smell of his breakfast brandy drifting across the desk toward Watkins. Just smelling alcohol so early in the morning made Bill's stomach do a backflip. His eyes began to water from the fumes, and he cleared his throat slightly before continuing. "Well, sir, there's been a problem with the gold up at the cavern and…"

"Keep your voice down!" Chance interrupted. He lowered his voice and continued conspiratorially, "I told you we're keeping this completely under wraps until we know how much is in there!"

"Sorry, sir," Watkins said, softly.

Watkins briefly recalled the day he'd come across the new cavern and the start of his current predicament. He'd found it by accident just after the recent quake that the area had experienced. Out in the company Snowcat on the resort's back acreage, he'd been checking for any damage from land or snow slides that may have impacted the security fences surrounding the now-defunct ski runs. Chance had told him with that part of the resort permanently closed, it was imperative to make sure no one was accessing the untended runs for shits and giggles. The last thing they needed was a lawsuit from the family of some yutz who'd decided to get stupid and try to ski or snowboard down one of the closed runs, no doubt killing themselves in the process on a dry patch of rock or a tree stump. You could never be too careful in regards to human stupidity, as it knew no bounds, Ray Chance always told him.

Near the western edge of the Kootenay Glacier, with the last of the daylight beginning to fade, Bill had stumbled across the cavern. He was running parallel to the property line on top of Gold Ridge when he'd spotted it. At first, thinking it was just another rockfall from the tremor, he dismissed it, but then saw the steam rising into the air.

Despite the fading light, he thought it best to check things out quickly. To his delight, he'd discovered the steam was from a new hot spring. A waterfall gushed from a sizeable wound in the rockface about three metres up. It pooled at the bottom, feeding a boiling stream which ran next to a narrow ledge leading up into the darkened cavern. He tested the temperature in the rushing water with his finger and yanked it back out immediately. It was scalding hot.

Steam made it difficult to see clearly, especially once his glasses had started fogging up. When he stepped into the darkened entrance, he took them off for a moment to wipe the moisture from the lenses. The wire-framed glasses slipped from his fingers as he did, tumbling onto the uneven cavern floor. He cursed aloud, hoping he hadn't cracked them. Bending to pick them up, he spied an enticing blur lying next to his spectacles, and he picked it up as well.

Putting his glasses back on, Bill carefully scrutinised the glittering object in his hand. His eyes widened when he saw it was a nugget with a yellowish tint. It certainly didn't look like pyrite, of which he knew there was already an overabundance in the area. Pocketing the rock, he scanned the ground around his feet and discovered not only a few more of these exciting nuggets but dozens and dozens. He loaded up his pockets and high-tailed it back to the resort as fast as the Snowcat would go, eager to tell Chance of his find.

It was only in hindsight that Bill realised the error of his ways. Chance was very excited and more than willing to have the nuggets tested. A week later, the results came back, and Chance was through the roof — they were pure, solid gold. Bill remembered being glad he'd initially neglected to hand over the other dozen or so large nuggets to Chance that he'd kept hidden in his inner jacket pockets.

Ray told Bill he would need to keep his mouth shut and that no one else must know of the discovery, adding he would be very well rewarded for his silence and would receive his fair share of the riches. Chance said that he wanted the cavern explored to find out how much more potential this gold strike had. If it were as good as it seemed, he said they needed to extract as much of the rich ore from the cavern as they could before the gold fever brigade swarmed into the area. Once word of this particular find got out, there would be a tsunami of business opportunities from people flooding in, looking for their own claims. Chance said he wanted to make sure that he and his business partner were riding the crest of that wave, even though they were already both stinking rich.

Watkins mind snapped back to the present when Chance said, irritably, "So what's happening, man? Spill it!"

"Well, you remember when you said I should get somebody reliable to help us out in exploring around up there and doing a bit of mining, just to see how much gold was in the cavern?"

"Yes."

"Well, you remember I hired my cousin, Willy Wilson, and his son, Willy Junior?"

"Yes, yes, well?" Chance leaned closer, inundating Watkins in another wave of alcoholic vapour.

"Well, I don't know where they are." He shrugged his shoulders as he spoke.

"What?" Chance almost shrieked, then lowered his voice. "Did they quit?"

"I don't know. I think they might have gotten caught in a cave-in, or maybe fallen into one of those damned deep holes in there somewhere."

"What? Are you sure they just didn't take some of the gold and blow town? They're probably sitting on a warm beach somewhere with a cold drink in their hands right now."

"No, sir! When I was up there to see them last week, they were just getting situated, and it was going really well. They told me that there was a major vein of gold running through the cavern right down to the back end and that it branched into a whole mess of other tunnels and caverns they hadn't checked out yet. They were really excited about the find and said that they'd be exploring farther back into those areas soon. When I finally made it out there early this morning, before starting my shift here, I discovered the place was empty."

"What, they've gone missing?"

"No sign of them at all! All of their equipment is still there, though, and there's plenty of ore left. I just can't figure out what happened."

"And you called their house?"

"Yessir. There was no answer, just the machine picking up. I stopped by, too, but no one answered the door."

"How did things look the last time you were up there?"

"Well, they were camping just inside the entrance to the cavern. They had a tent set up and everything. And there were about two dozen or so sacks of ore that they'd mined so far, lined up along one wall. But when I got back up there early this morning, they were missing along with the sacks."

"What!" Chance almost shrieked again, and then quickly dropped his voice back to a more conversational level. "And you didn't think to bring any of those sacks back last week?"

"No sir, I was going to bring the whole load back today, but they were already gone when I got up there."

"Just to clarify things," Chance repeated, "So now the pair of them are gone, along with the nuggets, but their equipment is still there?"

"Yessir, but there was one other thing, Mr. Chance."

"Yes, what is it?"

"Well, I said that I thought they might have fallen down a hole somewhere, or gotten caught in a cave-in, but I think there may be another explanation. I poked through the things they'd left behind. It was a real mess. There was a backpack torn to shit, and the tent was shredded, like an animal had been rummaging through it to get at some food, but that's all I found. I'm wondering if maybe a mountain lion or something else living in the cavern might have gotten ahold of them."

"Was there any blood?"

"Not that I saw, but it's so damned steamy in there, you can't see your hand in front of your face sometimes. The only thing I saw was the torn pack and tent, and all their tools were scattered around the place."

"Then I think you may just be jumping at shadows, Watkins. It's evident with the gold missing that those two bastards took it. They probably loaded everything up as soon as you were gone and damaged a few things to make it look good, then skipped town. They're probably sipping Mai Tais on a beach in Acapulco by now!" Chance fumed.

"I dunno, sir, my cousin is a very reliable and hard-working fella. I find it hard to believe that he and his son would just take off like that."

"Watkins, you've heard of gold fever, haven't you?"

"Yessir, kind of."

"Well, then let me tell you something, Bill.' Chance leaned across his desk once more, sending a fresh wave of brandy fumes washing over Watkins, along with a new wave of nausea.

Chance continued; his words slightly slurred now. "Watkins, believe me when I say I have seen my share of avarice, or greed, especially after running this casino for the past fifteen years. Make no mistake, some men seem to be the most upstanding people, paragons of virtue as it were, but when it comes to gold, they'll stop at almost nothing to get it! Do you understand me?"

"Yessir."

"Good! Even the most strong-willed and disciplined of men can succumb to the seductive call of that precious yellow metal. Never doubt that for a moment."

"But I don't think…"

"I don't pay you to think, Watkins, I pay you to do!" Chance slapped his hand on the surface of the large oak desk to accentuate his point. "We need to get somebody else to take their place right away so that we can continue with our little mining expedition unhindered by the issue of theft. But before we do that, I think we need to bring up our friend from the coast to sort things out."

Oh, no, not him, Watkins thought. He was afraid to ask, but did so anyway, hoping the answer was negative, "You don't mean Oritz, do you?"

"Yes, Oritz! I'm going to call him right away to get his ass up here. I'll arrange a charter to fly him into Castlegar if the friggin' airport there is open. Hopefully, he should be here by tomorrow afternoon. If he makes it, at least I know HE won't screw me over." Chance was pleased to see the mention of Oritz's name was enough to make the other man's eyes widen substantially. Watkins sat there for a moment longer, looking like he wanted to say something else. "Yes, Watkins, was there anything more?"

"Do you want me to get some other people to do more digging for you in the meantime?"

"No, I'll have Oritz handle that once he gets up here. That's everything, for now, so get going!"

His toque still clenched in a right-handed death-grip, Watkins stood, moving toward the door. He placed his left hand was on the doorknob when Chance spoke again.

"One other thing, Watkins." Chance was pleased to see the other man's shoulders tense as he called out his name.

"Yessir?" He turned reluctantly to face his employer once more.

"I'd better not find out you were in any way involved in whatever happened up there," Chance said this in a low, cold, voice, any hint of intoxication now gone.

"What? Of course not! Absolutely not!" Watkins said vociferously, shaking his head rapidly back and forth.

"That's good. Because you'd better think twice about screwing me over, or you'll have to deal with Oritz when he gets here.

"I only have your best interests in mind, sir."

"Keep it that way."

As Watkins turned, Chance said, "And one more thing!"

With a small sigh, Watkin's looked back over his shoulder. "Yes, sir?"

"I also want you to clean all the shit off of my SUV from that goddamned raccoon that I hit before you're done for the day!"

Watkins sighed again and nodded. He turned back to the door and exited the office, pulling the door quietly shut behind himself. As the door clicked closed, he heard Chance pick up his phone and begin dialling — no doubt calling Oritz. Bill breathed deeply once back in the reception area, trying to get the smell of brandy out of his nasal passages only to have it replaced by the sharp scent of fresh nail polish.

Roxanne Rooney looked up from repainting her long, cherry-red fingernails, saying, "Is everything okay, Mr. Watkins?"

Shuffling through the glass outer door into the hallway beyond, his back to her, Watkins muttered, "Yes, ma'am, things are just golden."

CHAPTER FIVE

The green and white Lawless City Works truck pulled to a halt in front of a large mound of snow blocking the road. Lookout Road was not plowed all the way up during winter, and any further progress up the mountainside toward the forest observation tower would be by snowmobile. Trip leaned forward on the steering wheel and looked out the windshield at the shifting grey miasma before them. With a grunt, he said, "Well, Boss, that looks just dandy."

Trying to work up his own enthusiasm, Austin bumped his fist gently into Trip's shoulder, saying, "Another day in paradise, my friend! Let's get this thing done!"

Austin backed the snowmobiles down the angled ramp of the truck's sled deck onto the snow-covered road. Trip topped them off with fuel from the large, red auxiliary tank situated behind the truck's cab. When they were ready to go, Austin took the lead with Trip following, and they began their climb into the thick mist.

The fire lookout was approximately fifteen kilometres from town on the eastern side of the valley, almost directly across from the Kootenay Glacier. Austin noted that the avalanche advisory he'd put into effect in this section of the valley seemed to be working as the narrow, winding road leading up to the lookout appeared to be untouched by any sledders or cross-country skiers.

The pair of Arctic Cats cut through the heavy snow with ease, powering them effortlessly around the numerous switchbacks snaking up the mountainside. If the weather cooperated, Austin hoped to have clear skies at the lookout, rather than thick, grey fog, but he was still concerned they might have another down day and be unable to see anything.

His trepidation was misplaced, he discovered, as they neared the final leg of their ascent. The mist grew thinner and thinner until, finally, beautiful blue skies broke above their heads. Rich morning sunlight washed over them as they neared the apex of the mountain. Austin slowed his snowmobile down for a moment to enjoy the view. Finally, a break! He grinned and gunned the engine. Half a kilometre later, he and Trip pulled up near the base of the lookout tower.

Austin surveyed the relatively fresh layer of fluffy white goodness that lay atop the previous accumulations. It would be treacherous to navigate on foot since the snow was over four metres deep in places. He strapped the snowshoes he'd brought along onto the soles of his boots. Without the webbed-wonders, he would sink into snow well over his head. Before plodding up the slight incline to the base of the tower, he paused for a moment, then turned to his friend and said, "Alrighty then, Trip." Austin's breath plumed in the frigid air. "I'm ready for a little climb to see what we shall see." He tightened the straps of the pack on his shoulders in preparation for his ascent. "Are you sure you don't want to tag along?"

Looking up at the snow-covered, wooden monolith in the distance, Trip said, "I think I should keep an eye on things down here, maybe."

"A little too much verticality for you, Trip?"

"Course not! But I thought you might need me down here to keep an eye on the sleds, just in case."

"Just in case an elk or coyote comes along with thoughts of grand theft snowmobile on their minds?"

"Yeah, sure, something like that," Trip agreed with a slight nod.

Austin sighed and smiled, saying "I suppose I'll be fine on my own. Shouldn't be more than half an hour or so."

"Sounds good, Boss." Trip replied, relief evident in his voice. "I'll keep the engines warm."

Austin flopped his feet up the slope to the tower. When he arrived at the ladder, he brushed the snow from the first exposed rung and sat down, removing his oversized footwear. He placed the snowshoes flat on top of the snow next to the ladder in anticipation of his return journey. Swinging around, he started to cautiously climb the ladder, knocking the accumulated snow off the rungs with his thick-gloved hands as he went. Feeling a bit of a chill in his legs, he suddenly realised he wasn't wearing his ski pants. With the mild weather and lack of snow back in town, it was easy to forget how bitterly cold it was at the top of these mountains.

Using the widely accepted average of about three-and-a-third degrees per thousand metres, Austin figured it was easily ten degrees cooler here at the top of the mountain than it was down in Lawless. As usual, when he froze his ass off, he marvelled at the extremes of temperature measurement between the Celsius and Fahrenheit systems. In Celsius, a separation of fifteen degrees could mean the difference between going somewhere in a light spring jacket or bundling up in a parka and long underwear. Whereas in Fahrenheit, fifteen degrees was only the difference between a balmy daytime high and a pleasant nighttime low. As the wind gusted around his legs, he was thankful that he had at least worn his heaviest work pants as they offered him some protection from the elements.

Several long minutes of climbing later, Austin arrived at the top of the tower. It was the tallest one in the Kootenays, rising over fifty metres with a magnificent view when the weather cooperated. Luckily, today was one of those days. He looked around and surveyed the fluffy, cotton batten-like consistency of the valley cloud below. Lawless was socked in from one side of the valley floor to the other — the temperature inversion was in full effect.

Above the valley cloud was a different story. It was a brilliant, blue day, with visibility that stretched for what seemed like hundreds of kilometres in every direction. Austin just stood there and soaked it in. It had been so long since he'd seen the sun. That was one of the unfortunate things about living in a valley in winter, he reflected, you can only enjoy the scenery about nine months of the year. That was especially true now, with the change in the local climate over the past few decades.

Austin pulled a pair of Sunagor binoculars from his backpack and removed the lens caps. With the extreme magnification the binoculars provided, it was easy to see every detail up close, almost like he was there, even from dozens of kilometres away. He surveyed the mountain peaks, paying particular attention to the ones that loomed over the backcountry near the resort. The seismic event had brought down a lot of the old snow, clearing most of the buildup when it shook the area just after the new year, but there were still a couple of areas that needed to be looked at after the recent snowfalls.

Before the inversion socked them in, two new systems had blown through, creating new trouble spots toward the southern side of the valley, where Highway #3C climbed over the Golden Mile pass into Lawless. They needed to bring down the heavier-looking parts of those peaks before any new snow fell. If those came down in an uncontrolled avalanche, the entire town would be cut off once more until the pass could be cleared. The weather was working in his favour somewhat for the moment at least, as there was no new precipitation forecast for the immediate future.

Pulling a portable handheld laser sensor from his pack, he made some measurements, jotting them in his logbook and on his map. He now had the coordinates of the precise locations he wanted to hit with the howitzer. With everything recorded for future reference, he could hopefully aim the gun from down below and still have some hope of clearing the heavier sections of snowpack, even if the fog were still impeding visibility a bit. The danger wasn't too serious at the moment, but it was something that he and Trip needed to address over the next few days.

Austin gave the valley one final scan with the binoculars, enjoying the view, before packing everything away. He stopped when he got to Gold Ridge above the resort. Something seemed to stand out against the blinding white of the snow, catching his attention. He zoomed the binoculars to their full one-hundred-and-sixty times magnification. "What the hell…" He suddenly wished he had another thirty or forty-times magnification as he squinted through the lenses.

There looked to be a campsite situated near the top of the ridge, close to where the glacier rested. It was just past the point where the valley cloud washed up against the rock-face, like an ocean of cotton-batten lapping against a barren, rocky shore. The cloud kept interfering with Austin's view, blowing past the site and obscuring it, causing him to zoom back out and then try to locate it once more.

His brow knitted in concentration as he peered through the binoculars, trying to dial in their focus a little bit better. There seemed to be something seriously wrong at the camp. He couldn't be entirely sure, but it looked like a large tent was partially collapsed, its fly flapping in the icy breeze. The ground around and under the tent seemed to be packed down by a group of snowmobiles parked there. Austin could clearly see the trail they'd made in the snow to get to the camp. Even more intriguing was the snow around the campsite, especially near the cold campfire. It looked red — very, very red. "Jesus Christ, what the hell happened there?" He quickly noted the coordinates of the camp on his map and returned the binoculars and laser sensor to his pack.

Ten minutes later, Austin was almost back on the ground. He mused how climbing a ladder was almost like going somewhere in the car — it always seemed longer to get there than it did to come back. Despite his concern about the campsite, he moved carefully down the icy rungs. He didn't want to take gravity's express elevator to the bottom. Once back at snow level, he reattached his snowshoes for the short slog back to Trip and the snowmobiles.

Taking one final, lingering bite of the Snickers bar he held in one gloved hand, Trip savoured the milk chocolate, peanuts and nougat. He was stretched out on the seat of his sled, feet resting on the handlebars, enjoying the sunshine like a sea lion basking on a rock.

Austin called over to him as he approached, "Hey there, Nancy Greene! How'd you like to take a trip?"

Crumpling up the candy bar wrapper and stuffing it into his Carhartt's pocket, Trip said, "Sure, where to, Boss?"

"Gold Ridge. It looks like something might have happened to a campful of sledders."

"Do you think we'll have enough daylight left?"

"I'm hoping there should be a couple of hours left by the time we get there to at least check it out. That said, we'd better get going before the ice-fog rolls back in there for the evening."

"Should we call search and rescue?"

"No, don't bother Jake at his day job quite yet. We don't know what's happening up there at the moment. It might be just a group of hunters gutting their kill and making a mess, or it could be something much worse. We'll check things out first and then make a determination." With a grin, Austin concluded, "Remember, you're with a professional helper-outer now!"

"Right," Trip recalled, "I keep forgetting you joined Lawless Search and Rescue last month. I guess that makes us more than qualified then."

"Once again, Trip, you've crystallised my thoughts!" Austin said, revving his Cat. He popped it in gear and hollered, "Wagons ho!"

Happy to be returning to the warmer temperatures at the valley bottom, Trip turned his sled's engine over and followed Austin down the mountain, shouting "Yee-haw! You're the boss, Boss!"

CHAPTER SIX

Mayor Bob Nichols briefly massaged his temples, then ran his fingers through his thinning white mane. He'd just gotten off the phone with Ray Chance informing him what had happened up at the cavern. As usual, whenever he talked to the man, he felt like he was getting another migraine.

And thinking of headaches, he suddenly recalled a similar phone call with Chance about two weeks ago, just after the earthquake. Nichols had been in the middle of surreptitiously expropriating more funds from the town's meagre budget when his private line began to ring incessantly. It had been Chance, full to bursting with excitement about the discovery of the gold.

Today, Chance sounded almost as excited as he had been that day, but in a different way. Chance's excitement today was not about finding gold, but rather because he thought he was missing some. Ray had been livid about the loss of gold up at the cavern, supposedly stolen by Watkin's cousin. Yes, it sounded like everything was going according to plan. Turning his chair back to face the man sitting on the other side of his large desk, he frowned slightly, saying, "All right, Reggie, please bring me up to speed about our little operation on the hill, if you will."

Chief Reggie VanDusen of the Lawless Police Department sat across the large teak desk from the mayor. He shifted uncomfortably, his straight-backed wooden chair creaking in distress under his ponderous weight. The chief grunted before he spoke, trying to find a more forgiving position in the small chair's seat with little success. He sighed in exasperation, then said, "Okay, Olsen and I arrived at the cavern yesterday afternoon. We were going to rough-up and run off the lackeys Chance had hired to do the digging and appropriate whatever they'd mined, just like you wanted. Except when we got up there, nobody was around. But just to make it look good, we tore the tent to shit and threw their camping gear around the entrance like some animal had been through it. But all of the gold that they'd mined was still there at that time."

"Did you check the entire cavern out? Just to make sure they weren't down at the back?"

"We checked pretty thoroughly. Some of their tools were scattered all over the ground farther back, almost like they'd just dropped them where they were standing and beat their feet the hell out of the place for some reason."

"You checked 'pretty thoroughly'? Either you did, or you didn't, Reggie! What about the gold? Do you think they might have blown town with some of it and left what you found to make us believe something had happened to them?"

"We liberated all the sacks of gold we found so that Chance's man, Watkins, would think his cousin and son had bugged out. But I'm not sure if he believed that was what happened, though. According to him, the pair was as honest as the day is long. But you never can put too much stock in what some people say under duress."

"What do you mean, duress?"

"I mean that lately I've been leaning on Watkins pretty heavily for information about the operation up there, and he's kept me right up to date so far. That boy sings like a canary in a coal mine."

"Perfect." Nichols smiled at this news.

VanDusen continued, "It didn't look like his cousin was working too hard, though, that being said. But then again, they didn't have to. The gold in that cavern runs all the way through to the back and into other tunnels and sub-caverns we never even got a chance to explore. So, in answer to your question, Mr. Mayor, no, I don't think they absconded with any gold. Plus, I think the two of them were too goddamned lazy to have worked any harder than they did."

"You know, Reggie, gold can make a man do things they'd never normally consider. Even the laziest of men can get energetic with enough motivation, and it sounds like there's plenty of that up there."

"Well, there was no sign of them anywhere. The back of that cavern turns into a real maze, as I said. And then you've got that bloody aquifer running through it all creating so much frickin' steam that you can't see a goddamned thing! It's a regular deathtrap up there..." he trailed off, shaking his head.

"Sounds like you need to watch your step."

"Oh, hell yeah! If a fella took a wrong step and tumbled into one of the pools fed by the hot spring, it'd be game over, man! You wouldn't be dragging your sorry ass back out cause it's hot enough to flash-cook a damned lobster! And then, if you missed out falling into one of those, you could still kill yourself falling into one of those huge frickin' holes in the goddamned floor! There's big ones and small ones. They're kind of round and look more like tubes really. At least a half dozen of 'em closer to the back. Goddamned tough to spot in all that steam, too! Constable Olsen almost bought it when he stumbled on a rock near the edge of one. If I hadn't been right there and grabbed him by his jacket collar in time, we'd be advertising for a new constable right now!"

"Did you look to see if there were any bodies at the bottom of these 'holes' at that time?"

"Yeah, we looked, but there was nothing. At least no sign of anyone at the bottom from what I could see. They're really, really deep. The flashlight I've got is over two-thousand lumens, and even it couldn't pick out the bottom. I dropped a few rocks down a couple of them but gave up listening for them to hit bottom after a minute or so. I figure they probably go all the way to goddamned China! They're a great place to lose somebody." The chief smirked.

"All right let's back it up a second and see where we stand. You said you think they may have killed themselves by accident or might have been attacked by something and panicked, perhaps falling into a hole or a pool. But you collected all the gold?"

"That's right, once we determined they were MIA, we grabbed all the sacks we could find and took them back to town with us."

"No evidence that you or any of your men were ever there?" Nichols leaned forward in his chair.

"We're not complete amateurs, you know," VanDusen growled.

"That's open to debate," the mayor said, scowling back.

Ignoring the comment, VanDusen said, "No, we made sure. Anybody looking for them would probably think they've bugged out with the gold."

"And speaking of which, how much did you get and what did you do with it?"

"I have it all in a secure location somewhere here in the valley. And we picked up two dozen sacks all together." What VanDusen conveniently neglected to tell the mayor was that the secure location he was using was the root cellar in the basement of his house.

Nichols pulled out a desktop calculator from a drawer and placed it on his expansive desk. "Twenty-four bags of ore, you say?"

The chief nodded in confirmation.

The mayor clicked at the calculator's keys for a moment, then asked, "And how much do you think each one of them weighs?"

"I'd say just a little over twenty kilos each."

Nichols continued rapidly pecking away at the adding machine's number pad for a moment longer, then said, "Good lord!"

"What is it?" VanDusen leaned forward in anticipation.

"At current gold standards that works out to over thirty-two million dollars Canadian!"

VanDusen's eyes widened slightly. "That is a tidy sum, to be sure, Mr. Mayor, but there must be at least ten times that amount still stuck in the walls up there."

Nichols rubbed his hands together and grinned so hard that it looked as if his head was going to split in half. VanDusen thought he could see the mayor literally vibrating in his chair with excitement at the thought of the vast fortune the cavern contained.

Regaining his composure, Nichols said, "Good, I wouldn't want Chance to know that I'm compromising our little partnership. As far as he knows, he and I are fifty-fifty partners. I don't need him to know I'm dipping into his half, and I want it to stay that way. I need you to keep an eye on things up there, Reggie. With Chance sending our friend, Oritz up to the cavern to use as his 'security specialist' it should work out well for us. I'll try and persuade him to come over to the dark side, as it were. However, if it looks like his loyalty only lies with Chance, then I expect you to introduce him to one of those bottomless pits up there, just like you undoubtedly did with Carl. It sounds like they're going to come in handy."

"Wait a minute! That was never part of our agreement! It was supposed to be a one-shot deal with that conservation officer! Now you want me to waste that crazy bastard, Oritz for you?"

Nichols made a concerned face, puckered his lips a bit, then said, "Waste is such a harsh term, Reggie. I prefer something more laid back, like 'have an accident' or help them 'meet their maker'. It so much more friendly!"

"Semantics, Nichols! Either way, it's going to cost you more!"

"How much more?" The mayor shifted forward in his chair, the aged leather creaking as he did.

"I want half of what I'm stealing from the cavern for you."

Nichols's face went white with rage. "You avaricious son of a bitch!" He slammed his open palm down on the ornate teak desk. Leaning slightly out of his seat, he finished, "That's goddamned highway robbery!"

"I'm a highwayman then!" VanDusen smiled thinly, trying to adjust his position once more, his chair groaning in protest. "Anyway, I'll need the extra contingency money. It's not cheap to erase people you know. And besides, you're the one that just upped the ante, Mr. Mayor. Chance won't make any waves — he wouldn't want any bad publicity that would affect the casino, would he? He'll definitely want to keep things on the down-low, so no word gets around about the gold, at least not until most of it's been extracted. And there's also one final thing you're forgetting."

"What's that?" Nichols asked, his rage barely contained.

"The fact that you don't want Chance knowing that you're making premature withdrawals from his half of the fortune as well as your own!"

Nichols sat back in his chair. He rested his elbows on the armrests and tented his fingers under his chin. "That's fine, Reggie. But if you screw me over, you're going to find yourself out of a job, or worse."

The chief hefted his bulk out of the chair. His cowboy boots cracked against the hardwood floor of the study as he sauntered toward the door. Before opening it, he paused and turned back toward the mayor. Hand resting on the doorknob, the chief said, "I'd recommend you be careful of who you threaten, Mr. Mayor, there's still plenty of room in those pits in the cavern floor." He quietly closed the door behind himself. Through the heavy oak, he heard one single word uttered by the mayor, "Bastard!"

Reggie VanDusen smiled.

CHAPTER SEVEN

Christine Moon stood looking at the large, black polyethylene tarp on the floor of the conservation office workshop. About to examine the raccoon, the last thing she needed was blood and guts dribbling out of the garbage bags all over the floor while she pieced it back together. Walking to the large, steel-slat roll-up door that took up most of one wall, she grabbed the chain hanging next to it and pulled down hard, cranking the door wide open. She needed to keep the room cold to avoid defrosting her ring-tailed roadkill. In addition, the fresh, fog-filled air wafting in was an added bonus as the stench from the creature was nauseating.

After arriving back from the accident scene, she'd unloaded fifteen garbage bags from the bed of her truck, leaving them outside the workshop bay door momentarily. Now, she grabbed one bag in each hand and began the task of moving them inside to the tarp. The twenty-five-millimetre thick plastic bags did little to staunch the stench of the creature. Grabbing another quick gulp of fresh air before going back inside, she said, "All right, let's see what you actually look like, my stinky little friend."

It was not unlike putting together a rather disgusting jigsaw puzzle, Christine noted with grim amusement. Carefully examining each gory garbage bag, she began the stomach-churning task of putting the various bits and pieces back together. First arranging them by colour, she next toured around the putrid parts, orienting them as needed. The striped and ringed pattern of the fur on the creature aided her greatly in aligning things. The skull was the easiest, still mostly intact, except for a portion between the left temporal and occipital lobes which had made contact with Ray Chance's Land Rover.

As much as the creature looked like an indigenous raccoon, it didn't fit within the same genus as any of those found locally. The needle-sharp teeth of the animal were particularly interesting, especially the canines - much longer and sharper than anything she'd ever seen in a regular raccoon's mouth. And the size was astonishing. Any of the examples she'd seen in the wild were never anywhere near this large. Most of the time, their scavenging diet didn't allow them to get much bigger than eight to twenty kilograms, but this creature looked to be over a hundred.

Using her cell phone, Christine took a photo of the skull to send off to a classmate from college now living on the coast. The picture of the creature's skull and canines would most certainly pique her friend's curiosity. After many years of study, Zelda Wolowitz was now a professor of zoology at Simon Fraser University and widely respected in her field. Christine hoped to give Zelda something to whet her appetite while she took more detailed, high-resolution photographs of the animal with her Canon Digital Rebel camera. She smiled at the caption of the cell phone photo as she clicked the send button. It read, 'Would you like to know more?'

Ten minutes later, she finished shooting the little stinker and checked her cell phone. A text message from Zelda was waiting for her. She was happy to see her colleague was definitely more than just a little eager to see the new, higher-res images. Zelda's reply to Christine's picture was only one word long, and it was one that she rarely used on others, "Please!"

Satisfied that she'd covered the animal from all angles, Christine took the camera to her office and transferred the pictures to her laptop, uploading them to her cloud storage account at the same time. With cloud access, Zelda wouldn't have to deal with any issues of oversized emails containing the data-hungry photos getting rejected by the servers at her end. And if there were any other pertinent data concerning the creature, Zelda could upload it to the same account and share it with Christine immediately.

With everything done, Christine returned to the garage and stood in the loading bay door, surveying the creature laid out before her on the tarp. She was going to have to bite the bullet and use a government requisition to buy a chest freezer to store the creature temporarily. But it was going to have to stay where it lay for now. She wanted to have the carcass on display in front of her during the teleconference with Zelda later that afternoon.

Though it was now quite cold in the room, at the valley bottom, it wasn't quite cold enough to keep her funky friend frozen solid. Soon enough, it was going to be more pungent inside the shop than a garbage dumpster in the middle of an August heatwave. And she definitely didn't want that scent lingering around the building as no amount of potpourri could hide it; of that, she was quite sure. And as much as she wanted to leave the large door open while she was gone, she didn't want to attract anything else wandering the area. A rotting raccoon was most assuredly a scent that would bring the local scavengers running. Sighing with regret, Christine took one more massive inhalation of fresh, foggy air and rolled the steel door down, securing it with the attached chain once more. She double-checked that the heat was all the way down and turned off the light, firmly closing the weatherproof door that separated the shop from the offices.

The phone suddenly began ringing at the front of the building, and Christine hurried through to her office, arriving just as the answering machine picked up. Her recorded voice echoed through the empty building, "You have reached the Ministry of Conservation for the Kootenay Interior Region. If you have a wildlife concern or complaint, press one now…" Christine picked the handset up, automatically disengaging the recording.

"Good afternoon, Ministry of Conservation. Officer Moon speaking, how may I help you?"

Sounding relieved, an elderly woman at the other end exclaimed, "Finally! I've been trying to get through and speak to someone at your office all morning, dearie!"

Christine looked down at the LED call counter flashing on the top of the answering machine and was surprised to see she had twelve missed calls while out and about. She mentally chided herself for neglecting to switch her call forwarding over to her cell phone when she went into the field earlier that morning. After a glance at the caller ID, she saw all the calls were from the same number, the one to which she was currently connected. This woman was not the type that was content to leave just one message, or so it would seem.

"I'm sorry, ma'am, but I was unavailable out in the field all morning. Is there something I can help you with?"

"Well, you'd better stop standing out in your field, dearie, you've got bigger problems now!"

"Yes ma'am, what seems to be the issue?"

"First of all, cut out that ma'am crap! This is Geraldine Gertzmeyer out on Highway #3C calling! My wild turkeys are all dead!"

Christine thought the poor old dear sounded almost ready to burst into tears. "I'm so sorry to hear that, ma'am, I mean Mrs. Gertzmeyer. What happened to your turkeys?"

"They're all dead! Didn't I just say that? Didn't you listen to my messages?"

"I only got back to the office just now, Mrs. Gertzmeyer. If you…"

The woman cut her off, saying, "It doesn't matter, dearie! What does matter is that some vicious, wild animal has slaughtered all my wild turkeys! I don't know if any escaped since its such a mess out there, but I hope some of them got away!"

"That's very unfortunate. But how can I assist you, Mrs. Gertzmeyer?"

"You can assist me by coming out to see what some bastardly thing did to my sweet, precious little babies! Come and see, and then go out into the forest, find it and kill it!"

"Okay, Mrs. Gertzmeyer, please calm down for a moment. I should be able to pop out to see you this afternoon. Now tell me where you're located, exactly?" Christine jotted down the address the distraught woman gave and assured her she would get to the bottom of the wild gobbler killing spree. Since she didn't have anything else pressing at the moment, she decided to head out to the woman's property after first requisitioning the chest freezer,

Before departing, Christine glanced at the large topographical map on the wall of her office. As the crow flies, Geraldine's acreage was only a few kilometres away from the scene of the raccoon's demise — directly in line with the Gold Mountain Casino and Resort.

Killing the office lights, she looked toward the shop and sniffed the air. Currently, there was no smell emanating through the thick, insulated door, thank goodness. She shuddered briefly, thinking that the darkened room where the foul-smelling creature now rested must be as black as the hole from which it must have recently crawled out. She turned and left the building, locking the door behind her, saying, "Curiouser and curiouser."

CHAPTER EIGHT

Easily visible on a clear day, Gold Ridge was a sight to behold. Its rocky prominence jutted out at the back of the valley and ran for several kilometres before terminating at the base of the Kootenay Glacier. Unfortunately for the occupants of the Lawless City Works truck, today was not one of those days. Thick fog obscured the road ahead, giving Trip little time to react to the numerous twists and turns when they suddenly appeared out of the ether. Compounding things, once they'd ascended high enough to be above the moist inversion layer of fog, it was replaced by a layer of ice fog. This caused the road to quickly change from damp and grippy to white and slippy in a matter of seconds. It made an already slow journey even slower.

Austin sighed and looked away from the blank windshield, glancing down at his cell phone. The screen was off, but he was watching the signal strength bars in the upper right corner of the phone's OLED always-on display. When the bars were at their weakest, they'd be getting close to the end of the winding logging road. And that looked to be right about now, Austin noted with a slight smile. "Looks like we're just about there, amigo."

"Yup, I'm on it, Boss," Trip said, glaring through the windshield.

Looking up from his phone, Austin grinned when he saw Trip's expression. It was so intent, he half expected to see laser beams shoot from the man's eyes at any moment, vaporising the fog ahead and clearing the way for them. When he finally tore himself from Trip's intent gaze, he looked back through the windshield and saw they were just arriving at the end of the plowed portion of the road.

Pulled off to one side of the wide turnaround, a white Dodge Ram 3500 sat parked, a large, empty trailer attached to it — the kind big enough to haul several snowmobiles. Both truck and trailer had a thick layer of ice frost coating them from the night before, just now starting to melt thanks to the sunlight that was beaming through the weakening fog.

"Looks like we've found the source of our vacationing camper's rides up to the ridge," Austin said, pointing to the rental company decals on the side of the trailer that read, 'Phil's Freakin' Fun Machines'.

Looking at the GPS unit affixed to the dashboard of the City Works truck, Trip said, "Well, we're still about ten klicks from where you figure the camp is, though."

"Yeah, I know. Time for some more sledding." Austin took the GPS unit off its mount on the dashboard and climbed out of the truck.

Trip once again topped off the fuel tanks in the snowmobiles as Austin unloaded them. Looking up at the sun now burning through the fog, Austin figured that they might have about four hours of daylight left before a fresh helping of ice fog rolled off the Kootenay Glacier once more with the setting of the sun. "We're going to have to make this quick. By the time we get there, there won't be much daylight left."

Trip nodded in agreement, firing up his sled as he did. Austin followed suit, and together the pair cranked their throttles and shot up the mountainside toward Gold Ridge, following the trail the campers had left behind in the frost-crusted snow. The higher they went, the thinner the fog became. Suddenly, the grey day gave way to brilliant blue skies. Austin blinked in the sudden brightness. Pulling a pair of citron-hued sunglasses from an outer pocket with one hand, he slipped them on, continuing to pilot his sled with the other. He still held hope that all would be well with the campers when they arrived.

Half an hour later, his optimism vanished when they rolled into the campsite — it looked like a slaughterhouse. Scarlet was sprayed everywhere across the snow-covered ground. Several particularly nasty looking swaths of crimson coated the area near the cold campfire.

Shaking his head in disgust, Austin said, "Jesus Christ, what the hell happened here? Were they hunting illegally, then gutting their kill all over the place?"

Trip responded, "I dunno, Boss. If that were the case, we'd see some carcasses around here somewhere, wouldn't we? So far, we've just seen lots and lots of blood. This is bad, real bad." Trip pointed toward the frozen campfire, "There's a lot more blood over there." Red appeared to be the colour of the day in the frozen slush. It looked like something, or someone had been crushed into the snow like a bug and then dragged off, judging by the trail leading into the bushes. A wave of nausea washed over Trip, and a small spark of fear ignited in his belly. Where were the bodies of the animals they'd killed, or for that matter, the bodies of the campers? So much blood but not a limb or a scrap of flesh anywhere in sight was very strange and very, very bad.

Ribbons of fabric from the shredded tent fluttered in the light breeze. Next to it, three snowmobiles sat waiting patiently for riders that might never return. A rope dangled from a nearby tree branch, the food that had hung from it scattered across the frozen ground below. Many of the packages looked torn and eaten.

Moving toward the fire pit, Trip poked through the ashes with his toe and suddenly froze at what he saw. He called out to Austin, "Boss! Come here, quick!"

Hearing the edge in Trip's voice, Austin approached the frozen fire pit with trepidation. Standing next to the ashes, he shook his head, saying, "What the hell?" Firmly set into the frozen mud and blood near the edge of the cold campfire were several large, deep impressions. As the head of the Lawless Public Works Department as well as Animal Control for over a dozen years, Austin had seen his share of tracks and prints from various animals indigenous to the area — but this was something new. The spoor looked like a bear's, but not like any in his experience.

Trip gazed at the prints, thinking similar thoughts to Austin's. "That looks like a bear track, but not from one that I've ever seen! And look at those toe and heel marks, and the length of the claw impressions! The size of it is incredible! I mean, holy shit!" The tracks were at least three times the size of any bear track Trip had ever seen, black, brown or grizzly, and he had seen his fair share of them all. He looked around nervously, wondering if the animal that had left the impression in the muck was anywhere in the vicinity at the moment, and wished he'd brought his rifle. "Do you think it ate everyone?"

"Your guess is as good as mine, buddy. Whatever 'it' is, judging by the amount of blood around here, yeah, there could be a very good possibility of that." Austin glanced about and found another of the enormous prints and followed them to a set of fresh snowmobile tracks leading away from the carnage. "I think whatever happened to the other campers, one of them might have gotten away before becoming something's midnight snack. I wonder if it was the guy with the gun?"

"Gun?" Trip inquired.

"Yeah, there are at least a half dozen spent cartridges just over there." He pointed toward several brass shell casings gleaming in the snow on the other side of the fire. "Looks like they're from a large calibre handgun — a magnum, I think."

Shaking his head, Trip said, "That's some pretty heavy stopping power, but it doesn't look like it was able to stop very much."

Several minutes passed as they searched the camp for survivors. Frowning, his hands on his hips, Austin surveyed things for a moment longer, then said, "I'd say our only option now is to follow that other set of tracks heading away from the campsite." He pointed toward tread marks winding into the trees away from the main trail, leading toward the edge of the ridge. If the snowmobile he and Trip were about to follow kept going in the direction it was going, he knew things weren't going to end well for the driver.

They motored along the outer rim of Gold Ridge for a short while, until Austin's worst fears were realised. They slowed to a stop, and he felt his heart drop. While the ridge itself dog-legged to the right, the snowmobile's tracks they were following didn't, and it appeared to have gone over the side. Killing the Arctic Cat's engine, Austin walked cautiously to the edge of the precipice and looked down into the churning clouds. Underneath the sea of grey, it was six-hundred metres straight down to the valley bottom. Shaking his head, he said, "Poor bastard…" Turning to leave, he glanced one final time into the roiling mists below. They parted briefly, allowing him a better view. His eyes widened as he caught sight of something bright-blue resting on the brink of a narrow ledge jutting out from the cliff-face about five metres down. He shouted, "Trip! Hurry! Get the rope! I think there's a survivor down there!"

Trip struggled through the snow toward the cliff edge, a bundle of rope slung over one shoulder. He looked downward, but the cloud had obscured the view once more. "You sure about this, Boss? It's a long way down if you're wrong."

Austin smiled slightly, saying, "Yeah, but I know what I saw, and I'm sure."

Trip nodded and said nothing more, handing Austin one end of the rope.

Continuing, Austin said, "Here's what's going to happen, my friend. You're going to tie one end of that rope to your snowmobile, and I'll tie the other end to me. Once I get down there and scope things out, if I'm able to help, I'll tie this rope around the two of us and give you a holler. Then you can slowly pull us back up with your Cat," Austin nodded toward Trip's snowmobile, concluding, "Emphasis on the word 'slowly', please, since I don't want us getting torn to shreds on the rock face when we come back up."

"Gotcha. Sounds good, Boss." Trip gave one end of the rope to Austin and slogged back through the snow to his sled. Restarting the motor, he quickly turned it around and tied the other end of the rope onto the back of the machine's seat. He stepped off the sled and gathered the rope's slack, feeding it through his arms in order to act as a conduit for it to pass through while he lowered Austin.

With the rope secured about his waist, Austin backed cautiously toward the edge of the cliff. Trip braced himself, then leaned back and pulled hard. "Go for it, Boss!" he grunted.

The rope now taut, Austin leaned back over the edge, then rappelled down out of sight. Sharp rock threatened to tear at his parka as he descended. He needed to keep his legs moving, gently pushing away from the rock to avoid contact while Trip smoothly lowered him down.

Glancing through the swirling cloud at his feet, the closer Austin got to the person in the neon-blue parka, the greater his concern grew. The victim was unmoving, resting near the lip of the lower ledge. One arm drooped over the side, the survivor's gloved hand stretching out as if trying to idly grab some of the clouds as they floated by.

Austin's boots touched down on the narrow ledge about a metre from the body, and he hollered up, "I'm on the ledge!"

Above his head, Trip's voice floated down. "I'm on it, Boss! I'll lose the slack then retie you to the sled. Don't go falling off while I'm doing that, okay?"

"Thanks for your concern, buddy! I'll try not to!" Austin called back, smiling grimly. He scowled as he glanced toward the sun, which now seemed to be arcing across the sky toward the western side of the valley much more quickly than he would have liked. Untying the rope from his waist and bundling it in his hands, he scuttled along the ledge on hands and knees toward the injured person. He knelt in the snow next to them but could only see the back of their blue-hooded head. They faced away from him as if looking out over the cloud-covered valley, enjoying the view. Austin gently touched the victim's shoulder, saying, "It's okay, my friend. My name is Austin Murphy, and I'm here to help you."

The blue parka jerked suddenly and called out in a man's voice, "D-don't let it eat me! Keep it away!" The man bucked and twisted, trying to roll away from Austin, almost taking them both over the edge in the process. Luckily, Austin had been expecting some sort of reaction, and he grabbed the man's outer arm just in the nick of time, pulling him back before he accidentally finished the journey to the valley bottom that his sled had already taken the night before.

"N-no! S-s-stay away from me," the neon-blue man said, his voice frail and weak, body trembling from exposure and fear.

"It's okay, buddy. I'm Austin Murphy. I'm with the city of Lawless, BC and also part of the local search and rescue. I'm going to help you to the hospital and get you fixed up, okay?"

The man said nothing.

Austin tried again, gently touching the man's shoulder. "What's your name, my friend?" This time, he kept his grip firmly on the man's shoulder in case he tried anything else too aerobic for the limited space of the narrow ledge.

"D-don't let it get me, please don't let it get me…" the man muttered again, delirious.

"I'm not going to let it get you, buddy, but I'm going to have to move you a little bit here to see how you're doing." He spoke calmly, trying to reassure the man. "I'm going to do it nice and slow, just to make sure we don't injure you anymore, okay? So, let's try this again. My name is Austin Murphy. What's yours?"

"J-J-Jerry. Jerry Benson."

"Nice to meet you, Jerry Benson. So, here's what's going to happen. We're going to get you off this ledge and then get you on your way down the mountain to the hospital, okay? So here we go." Austin gently grabbed the man's shoulder and rolled him away from the edge. Touching the man's arm to aid in the roll-over, Austin grimaced as he felt protruding bones — it was obviously broken. Jerry groaned in pain from the movement.

"How's it going, Jerry? Are you holding up, buddy? Let's just see if we can get you sitting up, okay?" Austin firmly hauled the man upright using his armpits, helping him into a seated position against the rock face. This time, Jerry screamed.

"What's happening, Austin?" Trip's baritone voice boomed down from above, filled with concern after hearing Jerry's shriek of pain.

Austin looked upward into the clouds swirling overhead and shouted, "Yeah, we're okay! Thanks, my friend!"

"W-who are you talking to?" Jerry asked, confused, still groggy from pain, exposure and dehydration. "Is it God?" Hope swelled in his voice as if he thought he might be having an epiphany. He stuttered as he finished, asking, "A—a-are you an angel?"

Austin looked Jerry straight in the eyes and said, "Sorry, my friend, far from it. But I'll try to be a bit more gentle the next time, okay?" Jerry nodded slightly in understanding, and Austin continued, "Unfortunately, that time is now. So, here we go, let's see if we can get you standing upright." Austin slowly stood, easing Jerry up by the armpits with him at the same time. Jerry moaned once more, swaying in Austin's arms, but finally made it to a vertical orientation.

Leaning Jerry face-first against the cliff face, Austin tied the rope around the man's chest and underarms, and then did the same to himself, tying his body to Jerry's from behind. He shouted up into the clouds once more, "Okay, Trip! I've got him tied to me! Now pull us up, nice and slow, just like we discussed! It's sharp as shit along this rock face!"

"You got it, Boss!" Trip hollered back.

Trip started his sled's engine, revving it a few times. Austin held the slack rope away from himself and Jerry. He didn't want it tangling around their feet when Trip started to move and have him drag the pair of them up the cliff face upside-down. That would most definitely be an unpleasant experience. As that thought passed through his mind, there was a sudden tug under his armpits, and he and Jerry slowly began to rise into the clouds. Austin continually pushed them away from the cliffside with his feet and hands to make sure they didn't get hung up and flayed alive as they ascended the serrated rock.

Halfway up, Jerry's broken arm bumped against the sharp rock, and Austin winced as the man shrieked in his ear. Jerry went limp, the sudden jolt of pain overloading his internal pain circuitry. Probably for the best, Austin thought. They continued their ascent a few centimetres at a time, Trip crawling the sled ahead, pulling them slowly to safety.

When they were within a metre of the top, Austin hollered, "Trip! Put it in park and get over here!"

Trip killed the engine and hopped off the snowmobile, pushing back through the snow toward the edge of the cliff. Tentatively peeking over the side, he saw Austin and the injured man dangling just below him, an ocean of cloud lapping at their feet. Glancing over his shoulder, Trip saw the sun racing toward the horizon, just starting to settle near the edge of the glacier.

"Better hurry up, Boss, or we're going to get stuck out here," he intoned gravely.

"Thanks for the heads up, buddy!" Austin responded, already well aware of the time constraints under which they were operating. "Now, do you think you could break up some of this snow near the edge over our heads first, and then pull us the rest of the way up?"

"You got it, Boss!" Trip got down on his knees and stretched his arms out as far as he dared. He began to pound away on the thick crust of snow above the heads of Austin and the injured man, shouting, "Incoming!"

Just below, while reluctant to let go of the rope, Austin knew he had to have faith in the knot he'd tied around them. He covered both of their heads with his forearms and gloved hands. Chunks of snow and ice rained down around them from above as Trip cleared a path for the final leg of their ascent.

After several seconds, Trip shouted, "Okay, all clear, Boss!"

"Great, Trip! Now pull us up the rest of the way! Real easy, just like before!"

Trip jogged back to the snowmobile and gently twisted the throttle, moving forward, but looking over his shoulder as he did. After several tense seconds, two heads popped up at the edge of the cliff, like a couple of prairie dogs looking for predators in the noon-day sun. Stopping the sled's engine, he trudged back through the heavy snow, still grasping the rope firmly. He leaned backward and began pulling Austin and the survivor the rest of the way up by hand.

Austin clawed into the snow to find the rocky ledge beneath as Trip continued to heave mightily. When Austin's arm finally shot into the air, Trip reached down and grasped his friend's hand, bringing both men first to their knees, and eventually, their feet. Jerry groaned, unsteady on his legs after many hours of inactivity lying on the ledge.

"Okay, let's get him onto your machine," Trip said. They supported Jerry on either side. Part of the time, they walked, but at other times they dragged the semiconscious man through the snow toward Austin's snowmobile. They placed Jerry behind the sled's controls, and Austin sat down behind. He held the man upright while Trip secured the rope around the two of them. Austin now found himself looking over the injured man's shoulder in order to pilot his machine down the mountain.

"Okay, Trip, now tie that rope around us once more, and put it around his uninjured arm as well, in case he wakes up excited. I wouldn't want to lose Jerry here on a bump going down the mountainside or have him clock me one with a panicked hand. Not to mention the fact that the last thing I'd need would be to have his hands flying up in front of my face if he regains consciousness, especially while cornering one of those drop-offs on the way back."

"You got it, Boss." Trip checked that they were well-secured together and that the rope would still be easy to untie once the time came to transfer the survivor to the waiting truck below. With confidence, he said, "He's not going anywhere now!"

"Awesome job! Now, if you could follow along behind us just in case I need a hand along the way." Austin started his sled and turned it around.

"I'm on it, Boss." Trip mounted his snowmobile and glanced toward the glacier as the brilliant, blue sky began fading toward the violet of twilight. The first waves of ice vapour began to curl off the top of the monolithic chunk of ice as he watched. Lawless was in for another grey, impenetrable evening once that settled on top of the inversion. He shook his head.

Austin revved his engine a couple of times. "All right! Let's get moving before we have to spend the night out here ourselves!"

Trip heard relief heavy in his friend's voice, and agreed, saying, "You got my vote, Boss!" He cranked his throttle, and a plume of snow kicked out from the sled's track as he fell in line behind Austin and Jerry. His mind was awhirl with questions. What had attacked this man and his friends? What was lurking out there in the local forests? What sort of creature was able to wreak such havoc on a group of armed men? And how did it get to be so huge? He suddenly realised he was dawdling and falling behind and twisted his throttle hard to catch up to Austin and Jerry.

There was one thing that he knew for certain. When he arrived home to his little bungalow on the outskirts of town this evening, the Winchester Carbine he kept propped in his hall closet was going to get a thorough cleaning and then loaded up from a fresh box of hollow-point shells. Of that, he had no doubt.

CHAPTER NINE

Highway #3C curved its scenic way through most of the valley bottom. It ran parallel to the chunk of Kootenay goodness that Geraldine Gertzmeyer called home for several kilometres. Christine Moon drove cautiously through the fog, spying numerous faded signs dotting the tops of decaying fence posts along the side of the road. The signs appeared every kilometre or so, popping out of the fog as she passed. 'Private Property!', 'Keep Out!' and 'No Trespassing!' were just a few of the many colourful greetings sitting atop some of them. But it was the last one that had to be Christine's favourite. A hand-painted sign with large red lettering cut right to the chase, reading, 'No Hunting, No Fishing, No Nothing, Go Home!' Obviously, Geraldine was a woman who liked to make sure her animals were safe and who enjoyed her privacy. Smiling to herself, Christine turned onto the property and followed a narrow lane leading up to the house.

The turkeys on Geraldine's acreage weren't indigenous to the region. They had been introduced to the area by BC Fisheries and Wildlife many decades before. The population had thrived, despite living in a harsher climate. They were now a regular part of the spring and fall hunting season — except around Geraldine's property, apparently. On a final bend in the tree-lined lane just before the main house, a yellow caution sign proclaimed that section of the laneway to be a turkey crossing. Seeing no turkeys currently lined up to cross the road, Christine proceeded cautiously up the lane.

Pulling her truck around the circular entrance at the front of the house, Christine found Geraldine Gertzmeyer sitting on her veranda in an Adirondack chair, waiting patiently. The elderly woman was bundled up in an oversized green parka and Sorel boots to keep warm, a thick quilt across her lap. Protecting her from the elements, a covered porch ran the entire length of the front of the house, wrapping around both sides. The petite, white-haired woman watched Christine emerge from her truck, and a surprised expression crossed her weathered face. "You're not Carl!" she exclaimed as Christine approached. "He was a lot hairier!"

Christine smiled and nodded at the comment. "Yes, ma'am, I get that a lot."

"I'm sorry, dearie, but when I talked to you on the phone, I thought you perhaps were a new secretary Carl had hired. Where is he, anyway? Couldn't he make it?"

"Actually, I'm the new conservation officer for the region. Carl Kuehn is no longer with the service." Slinging her work backpack over her left shoulder, Christine walked up three low steps and extended her hand to Geraldine, saying, "My name is Christine Moon."

The woman shook it lightly, saying, "Well, that's too bad! I liked Carl!" After a beat, she added, "But I'm sure you'll do just fine at the job, dearie! It's nice to meet you!"

Christine noted that, although the senior's hands were not gloved, they were very warm to the touch, which she found surprising for someone of Geraldine's obviously advanced years — the woman couldn't possibly be a day under ninety-five.

"Thank you! Nice to meet you as well. And I'll try my best," Christine said, still smiling.

The woman's face became serious. "I hope Carl filled you in on my situation before he left?"

"Actually, no, he left rather abruptly. Perhaps you can fill in the blanks for me?"

"Sit down, dearie!" The woman gestured toward another chair that matched hers, separated by a small, square table. Christine nodded and sat down, putting her pack on the floor beside the chair.

Before speaking, the woman wrapped her arthritic hands around a large, vat-sized mug. She took a delicate sip of the steaming beverage. The paper tag hanging off the side of her mug proudly proclaimed it to be a hot cup of Earl Grey tea. With her whistle whetted, Geraldine told Christine of how she and her late husband, Norbert, had raised unwanted and abandoned animals from all over the Kootenays during their life together. They especially loved the ones that had come from an abusive environment or could no longer be cared for by their owners for whatever reason. When they came to her acreage, she explained, they were well tended to the end of their days. That was, up until Norbert's passing several years ago. Feeding and tending the animals on her own had been too much of a challenge for Geraldine after that. Though reluctant to do so, she'd been forced to give most of them away to good homes where she knew the owners weren't going to abuse or harm them in any way.

Taking another sip of tea, Geraldine continued, "The only thing I couldn't give away was the gosh-darned wild turkeys! They just keep coming back, year after year, God bless 'em! That's probably because I keep feedin' 'em!" She cackled at her joke, then said with a wistful look in her eyes, "I adore their small, wrinkled, bald heads — they so remind me of Norbert! I just love seeing 'em clucking and gobbling about the place. Makes me feel a little less lonely. Most years around here, I get a dozen or so of the little cuties. But last year was a real bumper crop of 'em!"

"More than twelve?" Christine politely inquired.

"That's right, dearie! One fine spring day, mama and papa turkey showed up with eighteen of the little gobblers wandering along behind 'em! Can you believe it? Eighteen! Gotta be a record!" She beamed with obvious pride.

"Yes, ma'am, that might be one for Mr. Guinness," Christine said, smiling encouragingly.

"They'd been all over this property up until yesterday. In fact, they usually nested in the pine trees just in back of the house."

Christine nodded in agreement, knowing that the wild birds were likely to do so at night for safety reasons. The average citizen of Lawless would be quite surprised to learn of the large birds' nocturnal predilection. Most people operated under the impression that because the turkeys were usually seen going about their daily business in a more pedestrian mode, narrowly avoiding collisions with local cars and trucks as they gobbled their way about town, then they must be earthbound creatures and incapable of flight. But that was actually quite far from the truth. The reality was that they were more than capable of flight over short distances compared to their domesticated brethren, sometimes up to distances as far as half a kilometre.

Christine recalled hearing about an incident a few years back near Fruitvale, an area of the Kootenays blessed with an overabundance of the tall, gawky creatures. This particular wild turkey decided to stretch its wings across a busy roadway, directly in front of a speeding pickup truck. The fifteen-kilogram bird caved in the truck's windshield, breaking the driver's nose and so startling him that his turkey-tainted truck careened off the road into a mud-filled ditch. It severely damaged both the vehicle and the driver's reputation, who also happened to be a very well-respected local outdoorsman. For many years after that, when hunting season came around, the man was forced to endure the nickname bestowed upon him by some of the more flippant locals in the area, 'The Turkinator'.

Geraldine continued, "The little ones were just about old enough to be leavin' their parents, but now they're all gone!" The woman's eyes welled with moisture as she recalled the loss of her babies. Lifting a corner of her glasses, she swiped at the tears with one bony knuckle. "Here, let me show you what that horrible thing did to them." The elderly woman pulled herself upright from the chair and grabbed a walker sitting next to it. She began slowly rolling along the porch toward the rear corner of the house, Christine at her side.

"Are you sure they just didn't leave on their own," Christine asked as they toddled merrily along.

"No, dearie, I'm pretty sure some bastardly thing ate 'em!"

"All eighteen of them?"

"That's right, all eighteen of my little Norberts as far as I know! Something horrible came through here last night and had a wild turkey dinner and gobbled 'em all down!" She looked prepared to spit on the porch floorboards as she spoke, but apparently, decorum got the better of her at the last minute, and she cleared her throat instead.

Rounding the side of the house, the back of the acreage came into view. "Just see for yourself!" Geraldine said, taking her hands off the walker. She lifted her arms in a grand gesture, encompassing the scene of the massacre, just in case Christine missed something. Blood and feathers were smeared across various spots on the ground. The elderly woman finished, saying, "All of my babies, dead and gone! Eaten by some horrible creature!"

Christine looked about the yard. There were bones, blood and guts scattered everywhere, the remains of several birds to be sure, but not quite the eighteen that Geraldine espoused. Perhaps the ones that didn't get eaten may have literally flown the coop in their panicked attempts to flee the predator attacking them and had fled the area permanently as a result.

"What do you mean, ma'am, when you say 'creature'? How do you know it wasn't coyotes or perhaps a badger?" Christine asked.

"Look at the prints that the thing left behind on the ground!" Geraldine pointed to impressions in the earth amongst the blood and feathers. "There ain't no way that's a coyote or a badger!"

Christine walked down a small flight of steps to the back yard for a closer look, leaving Geraldine on the veranda. The impressions in the ground were larger than a coyote's, that was certain. Bending down and looking closely at them, she thought they were large enough to be a match for her dismembered guest lying on the concrete floor back at her shop. Removing her gloves, she took her Canon out of her pack and snapped numerous digital photos of the scene, especially from close-up. She wanted to have detailed shots of the spoor for Zelda down at SFU. But a picture, despite being worth a thousand words, was not quite as verbose as a cast impression, she thought to herself with a smile.

Removing her backpack, Christine knelt next to a particularly good, deep impression where the bloody slush was still frozen around the print. No blood or feathers were contaminating its clarity, and it looked to be a prime candidate. First returning her camera to the pack, she removed a one-litre, stainless steel water bottle along with a plastic bag labelled 'dental stone'. As she placed them on the ground near her feet, she recalled her first day in training using dental stone to make an impression at the academy. Along with the rest of her class, she was surprised to learn that it was the same product that dentists and denturists used to create positive replicas from the alginate moulds they made of patient's teeth. Crouching down, she smiled, thinking that day was now many hundreds of impressions ago.

Shaking her head at the memory, Christine took a small amount of the white powder in her hand and proceeded to scatter it about the depression left by the beast, lightly coating the entire surface of the print. Only a dusting of powder was needed at first to establish a 'crust' inside the impression. Unlike casting a mould of a print in the dirt, she couldn't just pour the mixed dental stone into the frozen impression all at once. The stone warmed slightly as it cured and it would have melted the snow, ruining the casting. Taking her bottle, she poured some of the water into the remaining stone in the bag and proceeded to knead it like it was dough until it reached the proper consistency. She then slowly poured the pancake batter-thick mixture into the powder-lined impression.

With just about a half an hour to kill while the casting firmed up, Christine had time to explore. She stood, turned around and saw Geraldine sitting patiently on the fold-down seat of her walker. Christine asked, "Do you mind if I poke around the property a little bit more while this casting dries?"

"You go right ahead, dearie! But be careful of that thing, whatever it is. I'm sure it likes to eat lovely young ladies like yourself, just as much as it likes wild turkeys!"

"Don't worry, ma'am. I'll make sure I'm very cautious."

"All right, then. And when you're done, you need to come in for a nice cup of tea to warm up. And stop calling me ma'am, my name is Geraldine!"

"That sounds nice, thank you, ma'am. I'm sorry, I mean Geraldine!"

"That's better, dearie!" Geraldine said over her shoulder as she wobbled and rolled unsteadily toward her kitchen to make tea for her guest.

The back yard of the house really was a mess. Christine checked out the immediate scene of the carnage a bit further, then moved into the fog. A wide path resolved out the grey before her, and she followed it for about a kilometre, then stopped. A choice now stood before her as she tried to figure out from which direction the animal might have travelled.

The path branched in two. The wider of the two trails moved slightly downhill, leading toward an acreage and perhaps a barn, if she had to guess, but couldn't see anything for sure due to the limited visibility. The other path wound up the mountainside, disappearing into the fog. She nodded to herself, that looked like a more promising candidate.

Several sections of brush appeared partially trampled by something moving through it, most likely her predator. Noting the direction of travel the creature took through the flora with her GPS unit, she thought about following it a bit farther but felt a tickle of anxiety along the back of her neck. Already aware that the fog was making her feel anxious and claustrophobic, she felt there was something else feeding her sense of disquiet.

With a flash of clarity, she realised the cause of her unease, and it was from two different sources. Firstly, she was unsure if the creature that had killed the turkeys might have perhaps had a mate. There was no evidence to say that it did, but what if there was another? She looked around in the gloom and listened hard, straining to hear any sound that might be a threat. Hearing nothing, she remained on edge, nonetheless.

The other cause of her disquiet was that she realised she was naked and that she'd traipsed into this shifting labyrinth of fog-shrouded trees unarmed. Her .30-06 was resting comfortably in the gun rack in the back window of her pickup truck at Geraldine's house. How could she have been so stupid and forgotten it! She shook her head in disbelief, mentally chiding herself for forgetting something so important, especially in her current situation. That was a rookie mistake if ever there was, and one that could cost her her life.

Knowing she'd gotten lucky so far, Christine decided to hit the pause button on her little search operation and literally stick a pin in things for now. Activating her GPS, she grabbed a colourful, yellow, digital pin on the touch screen and dropped it onto her map for future reference. Though she was unable to see where she was thanks to the mist, if need be, she could at least find this spot again at a later date.

Fifteen tense minutes of navigating later, using only her GPS receiver as a guide, Christine was finally back at her truck. She opened the driver's door and was relieved to see her Remington, waiting faithfully for her in the gun rack. After a few seconds of mentally flogging herself one more time for forgetting the damned thing, she remembered there was one more task she wanted to complete at her truck before going inside for tea with Geraldine.

Pulling out her GPS unit once more, she quickly extrapolated the creature's trajectory based on its current incident locations. She made sure to include the attack at the house as well as the site of the creature's ultimate demise on the highway. The animal appeared to have come from the direction of Gold Ridge, and there was only one other property directly in line with Gold Ridge. It was situated on an acreage directly adjacent to Geraldine's: The Golden Nugget Casino and Resort.

Shaking her head in wonder, she said, "First, giant exploding raccoons, now a wild turkey smorgasbord, and all within the vicinity of the resort. What next? Coyotes dealing Texas Hold'em, while the deer and antelope play slots in the lounge?" She grinned slightly at her own joke, gazing into the fog. Her sense of disquiet returned. She uneasily turned her back to the forest and climbed the porch steps to see Geraldine and the cup of hot tea awaiting her inside.

CHAPTER TEN

"You asshole!" Manny Oritz shook his fist at the shithead in the red Toyota Prius that just cut in front of his Hummer H1. Unconcerned about his speed or the law, he flew along the High Occupancy Vehicle lane, sometimes weaving back into the non-HOV lane to pass slow-assed drivers in his way. Though he was likely breaking most provincial and many federal transportation laws at the moment, he was okay with that. The only other occupant of the vehicle, Oritz's constant travelling companion, required no seatbelt by law and remained mute, saying nothing of his driving. The sleek, black Glock 17 sat cocked and ready to fire on the passenger seat beside him.

Manny Oritz was many things to many people, but a nice guy was not one of them, and he didn't have a problem with that either — in fact, he owned it. Then again, most people who hired Manny never hired him for his manners and sparkling personality; they hired him for his persuasive abilities and dedication to the highest bidder.

Over the last decade, he had worked in varying capacities for Ray Chance and Bob Nichols as the pair had sought to get the Golden Nugget Casino up and running. Officially, he'd worked for them as an on-again, off-again 'Security Consultant Specialist'. At least, that's what it said on the T4 he gave to the Canada Revenue Agency each year. When he thought about it, he really was more of a Manny-of-all-trades. There'd been several bumps along the way that he'd smoothed over for his employers. Sometimes the bumps were small, such as greasing somebody's palm to look the other way. Other times, they were quite large, almost man-sized, in fact, requiring a pick, a shovel, and a nice deep hole somewhere.

Chance had called him the previous day saying he'd wanted him up at some new cavern they'd found ASAP. He'd babbled on, saying he wanted Manny to check things out up there and keep an eye on the place for a little while, but wouldn't say why. At first, it sounded more like a glorified security guard position, and he almost declined the job. But after Chance offered him an ungodly amount of money and told him he'd already chartered a plane to the interior of the province for him, Manny had changed his mind. He was now on his way to YVR to catch it, and he was running late.

"Cocksucker!" Manny stomped on the Humvee's accelerator and roared up behind the small, red Japanese import. He started flashing his lights and honking his horn aggressively as he wove back and forth behind the car like a cobra ready to strike.

A gap appeared in the traffic to his right, and he took it. He cranked the wheel hard and shot into the next lane, cutting off a Honda Fit that was approaching rapidly in his review mirror. Manny flipped his finger at the Honda driver and shot forward past the red Prius. With another crank of the wheel to the left, he cut in front of the hybrid and then stomped his foot on the brake pedal. As his brake lights flared red in the other driver's face, he shouted, "That'll learn ya, ya piece of shit!"

The red Prius behind him reacted to the H1's brake lights and swerved to avoid Manny's suddenly slowing vehicle. It was too much, too fast, and the other driver, an elderly woman, over-corrected and lost control of her car. She slammed into the concrete barrier that separated the highway from opposing traffic and spun around several times.

Oritz gloated as he glanced in his rear-view mirror and saw the small car come to a smoking halt. Throwing his middle finger up in salute once more, he accelerated rapidly in a cloud of diesel exhaust and took the turnoff to the airport, unable to stop grinning from ear to ear as he did.

Arriving at the outermost long-term lot of YVR, he skidded the massive SUV to a halt. He collected his bag and the Glock from the passenger seat beside him and opened the driver's door. Before he exited, he separated the coloured wires hanging down from the broken ignition lock and killed the engine. He smiled, thinking how great Vancouver was to live in, thanks to so many accommodating people leaving easy-to-steal vehicles all over the place.

After a brisk walk to the main terminal, Manny Oritz swaggered into the Vancouver International Airport and scoped the rubes. The place was surprisingly busy. As he thrust through the throng, he overheard a group of young women discussing their vacation plans at a resort in Mexico. Across the lobby from them, a cluster of young men had started partying before boarding their plane, sipping discretely from cans of beer inside brown paper bags as they waited for flights to warmer and no doubt more girl-filled destinations.

His pocket vibrated, and he pulled out his phone. The charter company had just texted him he was going to be departing an hour later than planned due to circumstances beyond their control. "Son of a BITCH!" Manny hollered as he read the message, startling a group of white-haired seniors in loud Hawaiian shirts and muumuus as he stormed along.

The VIP lounge was a very sedate and muted affair in comparison to the main part of the airport, just how Manny liked it. The decor, though bland, had no doubt been designed to calm nervous travellers. The well-stocked bar had almost every variety of booze a person could imagine, and then some. Not that he wanted a drink at this time of the day, God no! He stepped up to the bar and the attendant approached him, asking what his poison was. Frowning at the man, he ordered a ginger ale.

Manny paid without tipping and sat down at the end of the bar. With a moment to reflect, he suddenly shuddered as he thought of where he was going. It wasn't from fear, though, it was from disgust. Inhaling deeply of the filtered, bland air in the lounge, he tried to clear his nasal passages, but it seemed he could already smell the cloud of brandy fumes that would be emanating from Ray Chance when he saw the man this afternoon. There was no time of the day that wasn't a good time for a drink for that boy. Oritz scowled and shook his head as he thought of the booze the man poisoned himself with — he seemed to have absolutely no respect for his own body.

Speaking of bodies, with an hour to wait, Manny was bored. He decided it was now time to indulge in one of his favourite hobbies, fucking people over. After a quick glance around, he was rewarded with a likely-looking prospect. At a small table near his end of the bar sat a rather sloppy-looking business traveller. The short, balding man's gaze was fixed on a small tumbler of amber fluid before him. Manny sniffed the air deeply once more, and now knew the reason for his olfactory flash-forward to later in the day, the man he was about to fuck with was currently drinking the same crappy French brandy that Ray Chance did.

Oritz grinned as he thought of the fun he was about to have. Reaching into his jacket pocket, he extracted a black leather wallet that contained a very believable reproduction of a CSIS ID. He flipped it open briefly, admiring the craftsmanship of his friendly neighbourhood forger back home, Bobby Dubois. In the picture, Manny was glowering at the camera. He took a moment to adjust his current expression to match the photo, losing the slightly insane grin that was presently residing there. Now in character, he pulled a pair of black Ray-Bans from an interior pocket and perched them on his aquiline nose, then slicked back his dark, wavy hair with both hands.

As if to admire the arriving and departing planes, he stood and sauntered toward a massive, plate-glass window, glancing at the small man's carry-on luggage tag as he passed. Oritz paused at the window for a moment, then approached the man from behind. Placing his left hand on the traveller's shoulder, Manny spun the man's swivel stool around to face him. With his most stone-faced expression, he addressed the wide-eyed businessman. "Excuse me, Mr. Anderson, I need to ask you some questions regarding your destination today." The man's face went white, and his wide-open eyelids flew even farther apart when he saw the CSIS ID in Oritz's right hand. Apparently, he now had this man's attention.

"I-I-I'm sorry?" the man stuttered nervously; no doubt flustered that this officer of the law that stood before him had called him by name.

Manny watched the man's reaction and mentally clapped his hands together in glee. It was time to rattle some bones in this man's closet. Still looking very serious on the outside, despite his excitement on the inside, Oritz said, "I'm agent Tom Davis with CSIS."

After flashing the ID for a moment, Manny pocketed it and looked down at the man. He stared for a moment, not speaking, allowing the guy to stew in his own juices. When he'd wandered past moments before, he'd noted Anderson's name on a plastic, laminated tag on his carry-on luggage. According to that tag, Oritz was now fucking with a Mr. Robert Anderson.

Manny pushed forward with his spiel, saying, "We've had you under surveillance for the last little while now, Mr. Anderson, and we are aware of your connections in Detroit." Oritz had also noted the man's destination tag attached to his carry-on luggage, DTW — short for the Detroit Metro Airport.

"My connections?" the man squeaked from fear-tightened vocal cords.

Oritz smiled inwardly, loving how Bob Anderson was now the living embodiment of the expression 'sweating bullets'. Rivulets of sweat poured off the pudgy man's consternation-knitted brow.

"Yes, Mr. Anderson, we've been monitoring your email and voicemail for the past several months and are aware of your activity south of the border." Manny kept his voice low, calm and slightly threatening.

"But I'm just a software developer." The man's face was white now.

"We know you're much more than that, Mr. Anderson." He moved closer to the man, towering over him.

"Really! I just make apps for iPhones!"

"You need to come with me, Mr. Anderson."

The man blanched as Oritz spoke those words. "B-b-but I haven't done anything!"

Oritz pulled out the handcuffs he kept in his pocket for special occasions like this and slapped them onto Anderson's wrists. "Dead or alive, you're coming with me." He pulled the man to a standing position with one beefy hand, then grabbed the man's carry-on bag with the other. Anderson had changed colours from 'white with fear' to a lovely shade of 'beet-red from embarrassment'. Oritz almost laughed aloud, thinking the guy must be part chameleon. He pushed the dishevelled man along in front of him, herding him toward a small, unlocked utility closet in a quiet corner that he'd reconned earlier on his way into the airport.

"W-where are you taking me?"

"I need to ask you some questions in the interrogation room, Mr. Anderson. If you answer them correctly, I'll let you go. If I suspect you're lying, I'll be taking you in. Then, you'll be spending a very long time in a very small cell after I charge you with espionage."

"What? Espionage? I'm no spy, really!"

"That's what they all say, Mr. Anderson." Manny smiled behind the man's back as he shoved him into the utility closet. Glancing at his wristwatch, he noted the time for him to have fun was growing short. He stepped inside, shut the door and locked it. Spinning Anderson around once more, Oritz growled, "Now, it's time to ask you some questions."

This was the part Manny loved the best. Though he usually never harmed anyone too much when he pulled this routine on unsuspecting strangers, there were always exceptions. Sometimes, someone would get panicked and tried to flee from his 'police' presence. But he usually found a good whack upside the head with his Glock brought them back around to their senses.

He was just a simple man at heart who loved to intimidate people and make them sweat, and a majority of people were quite cooperative in that regard. Quite often, they'd sing like a little tweety bird, spilling all sorts of dirty little secrets to him. This naturally segued quite nicely into Manny's other favourite hobby, blackmail. Several months later, once his victims had almost put the traumatic experience out of their mind, he'd contact them. All of the embarrassing things they'd unwillingly shared with him while under duress during their initial 'consultation' were then used to extort more money from them. Though Anderson was dumpy looking, the gold Rolex on wrist belied his true wealth, and Oritz was always looking to further his own retirement efforts.

Ten minutes, and several thousand dollars in donated jewellery and cash later, Oritz slipped back out of the supply closest. Grinning from ear to ear once more, he realised his sour mood was now gone. He ruffled through a thick wad of bills in his hand and found he almost looked forward to his flight to the interior of the province now — almost but not quite.

Since Lawless was basically a no-fly zone in wintertime these days, Manny's flight was into Castlegar's regional airport instead. He sincerely hoped that his upcoming flight to that mountain town wouldn't end with it living up to the nickname given it by the locals, Cancelgar. That small city suffered some of the same meteorological woes as Lawless, thanks to winter valley cloud affecting inbound and outbound flights to the region. Though not as pathetic as Lawless weather could be, Castlegar was still problematic and came in a close second. He shook his head dolefully as he thought about it. The last thing he needed was for his flight to get rerouted due to bad weather and end up in some even more God-forsaken place, like Trail, or heaven forbid, Cranbrook.

Oritz discreetly riffed through the thick wad of bills in his hand once more before stuffing them into his jacket pocket. He was already mentally calculating how much money Ray Chance was going to pay him as he thrust through the doors into the charter waiting area. A grin of avarice threatened to tear his face in half as he passed a group of blue hairs. Several of the old biddies looked at him uneasily, noting the slightest hint of insanity behind his smile. They quickly glanced away in fear when he turned his gaze toward them. Crazy as a shit-house rat, one ex-associate had once called his lunatic leer. And he was more than okay with that — in fact, he owned it.

CHAPTER ELEVEN

The Lawless and District Health Centre, known in a previous life as 'The Hospital', was built in 1897 at the height of the town's wealth. The city founders determined that a larger medical facility with more doctors was needed since the single, local physician at the time was kept extremely busy. Doc Brown sometimes put in twenty-hour days patching up residents and rogues alike who found themselves at the wrong end of a knife or gun. It was one of the oldest buildings in Lawless and also served as the regional medical centre for many smaller communities nearby, including Driftwood and Silvervale. Four gargoyles decorated the corners of the main building's parapets. The winged demons, along with the rest of the intricately cut stonework had been hand-hewn from a local quarry — it had been built to last. Despite the now quaint appearance of the building on the outside, it was updated and modern inside with two new wings added onto either side over the last two decades.

Sadly, Austin reflected, something not as updated and modern were the cellular repeaters around Lawless. The mountainous terrain and lack of towers wreaked havoc with local cell phone reception. He'd been trying to call the medical centre to put them on alert regarding their impending delivery of Jerry, but the lack of reception had foiled his attempts to do so. With Trip at the wheel and their emergency lights on, they were making good time through the fog, and ten minutes away from the hospital, Austin was finally able to get through. He told the emergency room what their ETA should be, and the attendant on duty replied they would be standing by for their arrival.

Amber lights flashing, Trip pulled the Works pickup truck under the covered emergency entrance. "Okay, Jerry, here we are!" Austin said, looking over at the man. He'd been fading in and out of consciousness and muttering to himself since they'd gotten him into the truck. Austin wasn't surprised to see that he was currently unconscious.

The hospital had been as good as its word — waiting outside the emergency entrance were two orderlies with a stretcher. The disparity in size between the two men couldn't have been more pronounced. One was extremely tall, almost seven feet if the height marker on the doorframe behind him were anything to go by, while the other attendant couldn't have been more than five feet in height. Mutt and Jeff, Austin thought, that's what his dad would have called them.

"Hey, guys! Here's your patient," Austin said, jumping down out of the truck. He stepped aside so the orderlies could extract Jerry and put him onto the gurney.

"What happened to him?" Mutt asked.

"Fell about five metres onto some snow-covered rocks. He has a fracture in his right forearm, plus exposure for an undetermined amount of time. We believe he may have been attacked by an animal of some sort as well, so I would check him for bite marks, too, with rabies and all, you know."

"We'll check all his nooks and crannies," Jeff said, tucking Jerry into place on the gurney while Mutt strapped him down for transport.

The orderlies wheeled the stretcher through the airlock into the emergency room. Austin tagged along, wanting to speak to the ER Doc on duty to fill them in about Jerry's condition.

After moving the truck out of the way, several quiet minutes passed for Trip, and he was just beginning to doze off when Austin climbed into the truck once more.

"Hey, Sleeping Beauty, we need to go to the cop-shop now so that I can report this."

Giving his head a slight shake to clear the fog from his napping brain, Trip blinked and said, "You got it, Boss."

Located just around the corner, the police station appeared out of the fog as they pulled into the lot. Almost as old as the hospital, and just as solid, it appeared bland and unimpressive, lacking flair. More sombre and industrial-looking of a structure, it was designed to instil a sense of fear and respect, rather than health and wellbeing like the hospital.

The Lawless Works truck pulled up to the marble column-framed entrance. Austin released his seatbelt and opened the passenger door of the truck, saying, "Okay, I'll run in and file a quick report with Fred inside…" He paused before climbing out, feeling his phone vibrating in his pocket. Pulling it out, he found a new voicemail waiting. "Hang on a second, Trip." He autodialled the number to retrieve the message, putting it on speakerphone so Trip could hear.

"Hi, Austin!" Clara's voice chimed. "That nice, young conservation officer called and would like you to stop by to see her this evening at about six o'clock at her office if you could make it. She said she has some very interesting news regarding that scratch and sniff out on Highway #3C this morning."

Austin deleted the message and hung up. "Looks like we've got one more stop when we're done here, Trip, if you're up for it."

"No problemo, Boss. I'll just chill here while you give the 5-0 the lowdown, same as the hospital."

"You're awe and some, my friend! Back in a few minutes."

"De nada, Boss." Trip pulled out a Snicker's bar and began to unravel the wrapper with an almost comical look of anticipation on his face.

Austin smiled and checked his watch. It was 5:30 P.M. He should have just enough time to fill the local constabulary in on the mess up at Gold Ridge and still make it over to the conservation office for six o'clock.

As he pushed through the large, revolving, brass-framed entrance door, Austin marvelled as he always did when he saw the police station's interior. Apparently, it had last been renovated about 1975, and it showed. The chairs in the waiting area were day-glow orange plastic — the kind of colour that makes your eyes start to ache after looking at it for more than a few seconds. The walls of the lobby were almost as nauseating with a yellow and orange-striped paint job that made you want to ask the desk sergeant on duty if you could have fries and a Coke to go with your misdemeanour.

The LPD's seven-member force included an elderly German Shepherd named K-12. The ageing dog was so named by its owner because he got along great with the children whenever he toured the schools, from kindergarten right up to grade twelve. He lay on the floor next to the front desk, gentle snores coming from his greying muzzle. The senior sniffer kicked its legs in the air, occasionally grazing the leg of his equally grey-haired handler. Desk Sergeant Fred Paulson was currently scribbling away, filling out a report and ignoring the dog's naptime knocks against his socks.

"Looks like he's running down some perps there, Fred." Austin nodded his head toward the dozing dog.

Looking up from his paperwork, Fred said, "Hey Austin! Yup, he's always on the job, that dog! What can we do for you this afternoon?"

"Well, I've got something that'll perk you both right up."

"You don't say! What's that?"

"Might have some missing persons and a possible bear attack."

"Hmm… Now that is interesting. I'd say you've got our attention!"

At the mention of the word 'bear' the elderly canine raised its head from the floor for a moment, then dropped it back down with a thud and a resigned sigh. It was as if the dog's advancing years had affected not only its ability to get up off the floor but also its ability to get excited about pretty much anything at all anymore, even bears.

After Austin filled Fred and K-12 in on the events at Gold Ridge, the desk sergeant told him he'd make sure get to some of the boys out there by first light to investigate things. Austin thanked him, scratching the sleeping dog's head as he did. Pulling a one-eighty, he pushed back through the revolving door. Walking down the steps to the street, he blasted off a quick text to his son, Alex, asking him to start dinner without him this evening since he and Trip were running late.

"You look less than impressed," Austin said, pulling open the passenger door of the Works Silverado.

Trip looked up from his phone's screen, a scowl on his face. He turned his phone around, and Austin squinted at the screen while Trip held it less than a foot from his eyes. The current NHL league standings were scrolling across the screen, and Austin now understood the reason behind his friend's glower. He and Trip were both in a hockey pool with several city workers from other departments, including fire and police.

Trip had been doing quite well in his picks, at least up until right about now, judging by his newly frown-knitted brow. Austin winced when he read the standings and shook his head in commiseration, saying "Ouch! That's gonna hurt your average. Okay, my friend, one more stop today and then we're calling it quits. I know with scores like that, you'd probably like a beer out at Fred's right about now."

Trip stuffed his phone back in his pocket with a sigh. "You read my mind, Boss, but I'm up for one more stop." He started the engine. "Where to?"

"To the Moon."

"You already used that one, Boss."

"I know, but it never gets old."

With a grin threatening to sprout through his beard, Trip said, "Yeah, it does." He put the truck into gear and drove forward into the swirling mist.

CHAPTER TWELVE

Christine Moon stood looking at the carnage. Bag after bloody garbage bag of dismembered body parts surrounded her. Thankfully, each bag now had a number on it. She'd decided that some form of labelling would be good to have on the bags for whenever she needed to put stinky back out on display for further examination. Though she'd only placed the trash bags into the newly delivered chest freezer a couple of hours earlier, the squishy bits and pieces inside had firmed up quite nicely within its icy confines. Hopefully, that would keep the smell to a minimum for the next hour or so while she gave the boys a rundown on the raccoon when they arrived.

Carefully lifting the dental stone reproduction out of the container near her feet, Christine held it next to the pad of one of the raccoon's still intact paws. A quick comparison of the two verified her suspicion — the predator preying on the wild turkeys at Geraldine Gertzmeyer's and the furry stink-wad surrounding her on the floor of the shop looked to be one and the same.

"Well, well, my smelly little friend, it looks like we've identified the turkey gobbler," she said, smiling at her own pun.

She placed the casting back in its container, standing up in the process. The buzzer at the front door suddenly activated as someone entered the front office. "I'm in the back!" she called out.

The heavy, insulated door to the shop opened, and Austin Murphy walked through, closely followed by a rather morose-looking Trip Williams.

"Hi, Chris," Austin said with a slight grin, "Good to see you again."

"Thanks, Austin, you too!" Christine said, smiling softly. She looked past Austin to Trip, saying, "Hey Trip, how're you doing? Did you see those NHL standings on TSN? Crazy stuff, huh?"

Trip brightened, surprised by Christine mentioning one of his favourite sports. "It made me feel like I was living in an alternate universe for a moment!" he enthused, a grin trying to flourish from beneath his thick, white whiskers.

Christine smiled once more. She'd remembered seeing Trip looking at hockey scores earlier that morning while she'd briefly talked with Austin after they finished picking up the scraps of the disassembled scavenger. He'd seemed so quiet when she'd first met him. Throwing the hockey reference out there, she hoped it would help bring him out of his shell by sharing a common interest — and it seemed to have worked. His cheeks now flushed beet red, making him look like a short, bald Santa Claus, only dressed in tan and orange for safety, instead of red and white for Christmas.

"So, what's the word on our putrid little friend here?" Austin asked, poking the nearest body part with the toe of his boot. He wrinkled his nose from the smell of the rotting carcass. Its stench was almost palpable despite the fact it was still frozen and surrounded by thick plastic bags.

"Yes, Rocky Racoon here is getting a bit ripe, isn't he?" Christine concurred.

"I think you could use an Airwick or two in here, Chris, or maybe a case of them," Trip said, his eyes narrowing to a 'stink-eye' expression as he sniffed the air. He looked like a person who'd just walked into a stall in a public washroom, only to discover the patron before them had just suffered a bout of explosive diarrhea and forgotten to flush. "Did you figure out what it is, yet?" He nodded toward the creature, still squinting from the aroma.

Deciding she'd kept the pair hanging long enough, Christine said, "Yes, we think we may have identified this creature. Although in doing so, it looks like we may have opened up more questions than we answered."

"What do you mean?" Austin asked. He removed his ball cap and ruffled his short silver-brown hair.

"Well, as you can see, it looks like a raccoon, but not like any that I've ever seen." She walked around the tarp as she spoke, circling the larger parts while stepping fluidly over the smaller ones.

"Me either." Trip added.

"Exactly. But when I showed the digital pictures of this animal and the picture of the casting to my colleague, Zelda, she almost fell out of her chair!"

"Really? Why?" Austin cocked his head.

"Because this creature doesn't exist, at least not anymore."

"Not anymore? What do you mean?" Trip asked.

"That's the part that floored Zelda, and me," Christine added, moving toward a laptop computer on a nearby workbench.

"Well, don't keep us in suspense! What did your colleague have to say?" Austin asked, eyeing the laptop's screen.

"Let me show you." Christine tapped the spacebar of the laptop, and a full-colour artist's rendering of what the animal may have looked like in life blinked onto the screen. For comparison, next to the animal in question stood the silhouette of an adult human, with a Volkswagen Beetle in the background for contrast. The creature was easily the size of a black bear, looking to be almost two metres tall if it were to stand erect. Trip and Austin looked at the picture on the screen, dumbfounded. Christine let them soak in the image for a moment before continuing.

"That is one mother-loving huge raccoon!" Trip said, eyes wide and unblinking.

Christine nodded, saying, "Gentlemen, I'd like you to meet 'Chapalmalania Altaefrontis', or more commonly known as a giant raccoon."

"Where would something like that come from?" Austin questioned.

"More to the point, WHEN did something like that come from?" Christine countered.

Trip added, "I know when I've gone hunting, I would have remembered it if I'd seen one of those things skulking around out in the forests!"

"Well, that's not surprising. Apparently, our friend here lived during the late Pleistocene era and has been extinct for over fifty thousand years, give or take a millennium or two."

"What? That's impossible!" Austin said, his mouth agape from surprise.

"You read my mind once again, Austin," Christine said, playfully. "Those were my exact words!"

"Does it only eat meat?" Trip asked.

"Actually, it was an omnivore and would eat just about anything. Fully grown, these creatures weighed between one-hundred and one-hundred and sixty kilograms, and they were much more aggressive than their modern-day, garbage-picking cousins. And it turns out our putrid friend here had recently partaken of a wild turkey dinner sometime late last night, before shuffling off this mortal coil earlier this morning."

"Turkey dinner?" Austin wondered.

"Yes, Geraldine Gertzmeyer had most of the wild turkeys living around her property killed and eaten by something last night. And I believe this may have been our culprit."

"Geraldine's turkeys?" Trip said. "That's just wrong; she loved those birds!"

"I know, she showed me some of her photo albums over tea this morning when I was out there," Christine said, smiling in recollection.

"Then that would certainly explain the abundance of guts and entrails all over the road when Ray Chance hit this thing — it must have been still digesting those birds. And it must have been damned full, too! No wonder it exploded like it did from the impact!" Trip said.

"You're right, Trip," Austin agreed. "But I'm also wondering if this might somehow maybe be related to the shitstorm we found up on the Ridge this afternoon?"

"What did you find?" Christine asked, her own interest now piqued.

"One very cold and very scared man, and a LOT of blood," Austin replied.

"What? Up on Gold Ridge?"

"Yeah, it looks like an attack occurred at a campsite up there. Must have happened sometime in the last twenty-four hours; otherwise, the survivor we found wouldn't have made it due to exposure," Trip added.

"A survivor?"

Austin said, "Only one, but it appears that several people may have been attacked at the site, though."

Christine inhaled sharply, "Omigod! Was anyone killed?"

"We don't know for sure," Trip said. "But there wouldn't have been even one survivor if he hadn't gotten lucky when his sled went over the edge of Gold Ridge."

"What? He survived the drop?"

Leaning against a stainless-steel countertop near the laptop, Austin said, "Well, fortunately, we were able to extract him from the ledge he landed on, then we brought him into the hospital ourselves."

"How's he doing? Is he conscious?"

"Not yet. He's in the ER at the moment. The Doc there thought he seemed kind of delirious and said she was going to keep him sedated until she could stabilise his vitals. But, hopefully, we should know a bit more later tonight or tomorrow when he wakes up," Austin said.

"Then I need to talk to him as soon as he's lucid to find out what happened," Christine said, her mood brightening a bit. "There's a good chance it could have been this creature that attacked him."

"I don't know about that," Trip interjected.

"What? Why's that?"

"The tracks we saw in the snow out there were way too big to have belonged to this animal," Trip concluded.

"Too big? Really? Did you take pictures?"

"No, sorry, we were otherwise occupied," Austin said.

"How big was this print, anyway? Any idea what it was?"

"Slow down a second. The tracks we saw in the snow looked to be at least three times the size of any bear I've ever seen," Trip said.

"Three times the size? Did I miss the signpost up ahead and we've already stepped into the Twilight Zone here?" Christine asked.

"Well, they looked like they hadn't been affected by any melting and they were huge — and Trip and I have both seen our fair share of bears and their tracks," Austin concluded.

"Then we need to get out to that camp at first light tomorrow to check it out!" Christine said excitedly.

Austin responded, "That's what I thought you were going to say. Let's call it a night then, and queue it up for tomorrow morning. We'll swing by here for you at oh-six-hundred."

"I'll be here with bells on."

"Actually, something a little bit warmer than just those might be in order," Austin said with a grin.

"Bells and thermal underwear, then," Christine said, walking the men into the front office to see them to the door.

"G'night, Chris," Trip said, blushing once more.

"Goodnight, gentlemen. I'll see you both in the morning." Christine smiled lightly as she locked the door behind them, watching the men walk to their pickup. A moment later, the truck's headlights flared alive, and with a peep of the horn, they drove off into the foggy night.

She turned and leaned against the door for a moment. The cold glass caressed her slender neck, sending a chill down her spine to match the one already created by her racing thoughts.

What the men had described at the campsite seemed beyond belief! But was it somehow possible that what they said was true? In addition to the giant raccoon, was there something else now prowling the local forests with an appetite for fresh meat? Something hungry for more than just a turkey dinner? Something that made the raccoon on her shop floor look like small fry in comparison?

Christine Moon shuddered and flipped off the office lights. "Time to put someone back on ice," she said, wrinkling her nose as she walked back toward the closed shop door.

CHAPTER THIRTEEN

Manny Oritz was perturbed. His charter flight had made him late. He'd been rerouted through Kelowna due to fog shutting down Castlegar's airport just like he'd feared might happen. He'd finally blown into Lawless in the late afternoon driving a Jeep Grand Cherokee that he'd liberated from the Kelowna airport's long-term parking lot.

After a brief meeting with Chance at the resort, the tipsy turd had given him a GPS receiver with the coordinates of the cavern already punched in for him. But no matter how hard he pressed, the tubby little tit wouldn't tell him what was actually in the cavern and kept acting all cloak and dagger-like about the whole thing. The more Manny thought about it, the more curious he was to get up to the place and check things out.

Despite his misgivings, at least the snowmobile Chance had lent him seemed to be top of the line. The Polaris 800 moved with assured traction and control as he worked his way up the mountainside. After several monotonous kilometres of following the GPS almost blindly through the fog, billions of pinpricks of white starlight suddenly painted themselves across the inky-black canvas of the cloudless night sky. It was definitely not a sight he was used to seeing after living down on the coast. Down there, light pollution made it difficult to see anything in the sky at night, other than the moon on occasion. Manny grinned, pleased to finally be able to see where the hell he was going. Several kilometres later, he could go no further and cut the engine on the sled.

A field of scree lay before him. Beyond it, the mountainside rose up almost vertically. At its top, the Kootenay Glacier hulked starkly over the valley. Freezing white mist poured off the lip of the glacier, flowing rapidly down to settle atop the moist cloud layer in the valley below. Oritz had been to Lawless several times before in the winter and knew of the weather they received at this time of year. When Chance told him on the phone that they were having another inversion and that the fog was thick as shit, it came as no big surprise. Oritz knew how depressing this area could be in the wintertime and wasn't pleased to be back in it. Sitting for a moment longer in the crisp, clear air, he watched the lights of Lawless twinkle beneath its incessant, fluffy blanket. Yeah, tonight seemed like any other winter's night in this dismal part of the world. Shaking his head, he removed a flashlight from a side pouch on his backpack. He turned it on, then slung the pack over his shoulders, securing the straps.

Ray Chance said he was suspicious about what was happening up here. Two workers had disappeared under mysterious circumstances, and he didn't know how far he could trust his business partner, Mayor Bob Nichols. Plus, he was less than impressed with the calibre of people his handyman, Watkins, had been providing up to this point. As he'd handed the GPS receiver to Manny, he'd said he wanted someone that he could rely on to keep an eye on things.

Oritz knew Chance's trust in him was not misplaced — he was a real stand-up guy, especially if the money was right. In keeping with that spirit, as soon as he'd gotten off the phone with Chance the day before, he'd contacted Bob Nichols. He was curious to see if he knew what Chance was up to. The Mayor obfuscated for a moment regarding the cavern, then proceeded to double what Chance was paying him. Nichols also asked Manny to keep him apprised of the situation 'up the hill', as he put it. Not a problem, he'd said at the time, telling the mayor he couldn't buy someone more reliable than Manny Oritz — unless there was a better offer somewhere else. Of course, he didn't mention that last part to Nichols. He smiled crookedly for a moment in recollection. Yeah, it looked like things were certainly going to be more than all right after all, especially if you worked both sides of the street at the same time as he did.

Oritz stood at the bottom of a narrow path that sloped upward into the moisture-laden entrance. A waterfall gushed next to the opening, water spraying into a steaming pool below. He shone his six-cell Maglite toward the veil of vapour obscuring the cavern's opening but could see nothing of the interior. His light's beam reflected off a thin layer of ice on the rock that sparkled like a million diamonds. The mist from the small waterfall was starting to coat the ledge's narrow path, freezing to the rock as it cooled in the crisp evening. It was getting more than a little slick. He'd have to be careful later since he didn't want to slip and fall into the hot water below.

As soon as he stepped inside, Manny realised the reason behind Chance's reticence to talk about what treasures the cavern contained. Through the swirling vapour, he spied a thick band of gold ore running along the wall off to his left, disappearing into the dark, steamy depths. Next to this wall was a small campsite. He made a cursory examination of the area, noting the damage to the tent. It looked like claw marks, but it was hard to say. On the ground near the cold campfire, an LED camping light lay on its side glowing dimly.

"Must be running on those bunny batteries," he said with a grin, kicking the light with the toe of his boot and watching it roll back toward the entrance. He explored deeper into the cavern to see what else this amazing looking hole in the wall contained — perhaps the missing men, or even more gold? That's what he was here to find out. He moved deeper into the black recesses of the cavern.

Chance told him he suspected he might be getting screwed over by his business partner, Bob Nichols. He'd said in retrospect how much he lamented being naïve enough to bring the man in on the project in the first place. He'd told Oritz if he found any evidence of subterfuge on the Mayor's part, he wanted to know right away. Manny completely understood Chance's point of view, due to his previous encounters with the mayor. Bob Nichols was one greedy son-of-a-bitch, and Manny wouldn't put it past him to grab all of the gold for himself. Yes, he was truly was a man after his own heart. Oh well, as long as Manny got the rest of the money deposited into his offshore account after he finished, he didn't give a flying fuck one way or another who ripped off who — or was it whom? He shook his head for a moment to dispel the errant thought of grammatical correctness from his avaricious brain.

With thick vapour coiling near his feet on the cavern floor, Manny's vision was severely limited, and he moved slowly, watching his step. Nearing the back, he found it quite challenging to traverse the uneven ground without falling into one of the numerous boiling pools of water that fed the cavern's interior streams. He knelt next to one, deciding to dip a finger in to test the temperature, only to pull it back out immediately, cursing under his breath. The water was searingly hot.

"Not many people gonna soak in there for too long," he muttered, sucking his overheated fingertip.

There were additional hazards farther back, including gaping black holes in the cavern floor. Manny shone his light into several of them to gauge their depth. Though the beam of the light was extremely powerful and usually able to penetrate hundreds of metres into the darkness, it did nothing here and was quickly devoured by the hole's depths. There was nothing, just endless inky blackness that ran all the way to the bottom, wherever that was. He had thrown rocks into several of the black voids as he passed by but hadn't heard any of them hit bottom. "I may never need to dig another hole," he said, smirking to himself.

Shining the light along the cavern walls proved to be very illuminating as well, as the beam reflected back more of the warm yellow glow from the thick veins of gold running through them. He shook his head as he marvelled at the fortune this cavern contained. It wasn't surprising that Chance suspected Bob Nichols was up to some shenanigans, now that Manny knew how much wealth was up here.

At the back of the cavern, there were numerous rounded tunnels in the ore-laden walls. These entrances ranged in height from over three metres for the largest, down to less than one metre for the smallest. Probing with his light, the opening in the middle was more of a small nook, and he saw nothing of interest. The tunnel on the right wound off through the steam at a slight angle, descending into the bowels of the earth. But the leftmost entrance, which was also the largest one in this section, looked very promising. He spied another thick stripe of the precious yellow metal twisting off along the tunnel's walls into its depths and whistled out loud. This vein seemed even more substantial than the ones near the entrance. It went quite a ways inside from what he could see, but he first needed to get by some sort of blockage. A rockfall obstructed the tunnel. It was squarely in the middle, so it looked like a no-go in that direction, but he was still curious.

Oritz stepped forward and cast his flashlight's beam into the depths of this new tunnel. He stopped for a moment and sniffed the air, squinting his eyes at what he smelled. There was a rancid, rotten odour of spoiled meat coming from it.

Just as he was about to turn back, something caught the corner of his eye.

The rockfall juddered ever-so-slightly in his light's circle of brightness. He blinked several times, thinking it must be a small bit of trickery caused by the sharp relief the shadows cast against the tunnel walls as he flashed the high-intensity beam around. Or perhaps it could be he was just so goddamned tired after his flight in, coupled with the drive and snowmobiling afterwards that he was seeing things. It had been a long day, and he figured his mind must have been playing tricks on him just now.

Sighing loudly, he turned to explore elsewhere when the mass of rock quivered again. This time, he leaned forward, straining to see through the steam. His eyes widened, and he began slowly backing up once he saw what was actually blocking his way. It was neither a deceit of the light nor his mind throwing his eyes a few capers and japes, just for yuks.

"Madre de Dios!" His voice was strained and ragged. He stumbled backward, his flashlight dropping from his hand in a panicked spasm.

The grey mass in the tunnel stretched itself out, then turned toward him. This was no rockfall; this was something much, much worse. His mind went into survival mode and he quickly back-pedalled, dodging into the smaller tunnel to his right. He had to duck to enter and hoped against hope that the abomination that had been emerging from the darkness of the other tunnel couldn't follow.

The monstrosity roared and tried to thrust its head into his small sanctuary, gnashing teeth like razors less than a metre from his face. Its enormous girth blocked it from entering the small nook into which he'd squeezed. Jaws snapping and cracking, the beast spewed thick cords of saliva into Manny's sweat-slicked face. Wave after wave of fetid breath washed over him, making his eyes water from the stench.

With little success bulldozing its way in, the beast changed tactics and reached in with one of its log-like paws trying to hook Manny with its scimitar claws and drag him out like some two-legged, man-sized salmon. But the massive size of the predator's muscular shoulder made it impossible for it to stretch its paw in as far as it would like, thwarting its attempts at snagging its prey. The beast's hunger seemed to feed its rage and frustration, and it redoubled its efforts to reach him. Roars and shrieks ripped through the cavern as the thing probed the opening with sickle-sharp claws.

Oritz pushed as far back as he could into the hole in the wall he was currently occupying. He strained with all his might, pressing himself back into the uneven cavern wall, the sharp rock jabbing into his spine. It seemed as if his subconscious mind were trying to embed his physical body into the rock face at a molecular level to get away from the thing trying to eat him.

The beast eventually recognized things weren't going its way, and it backed out of the nook, perhaps to look for prey elsewhere that was more easily accessible.

Drenched in sweat, Manny wheezed in relief, his breath coming in short, panting gasps. He felt as if he might collapse from the overdose of adrenaline that was currently coursing through his body, his heart racing like a hummingbird's. After several more minutes — or maybe it was hours, he wasn't sure anymore, he decided it was make or break time. "It's now or never, hermano," he said quietly to himself.

He poked his head out of the small sub cavern, peering into the darkness. With no sign of the beast in the immediate vicinity, he ventured into the swirling vapour. Up ahead, glowing brightly, his flashlight lay where he'd dropped it earlier, its heavy-duty batteries keeping it energized.

"Yes!" he hissed with excitement. Picking up the torch, he briefly shone it about, then clicked it off immediately. The light was so goddamned bright! He realised as he picked the torch up that he'd basically just broadcast his whereabouts to the predator if it was still nearby. He stuffed it back into his pack and shook his head — his stupidity had undoubtedly made life much easier for whatever the fuck was lurking around trying to eat him in this grey, steamy hell.

Despite his reservations about light, he knew he had no choice and pulled out his cell phone and turned on the screen to use it as a torch, turning the brightness level down low. He couldn't walk blindly forward because of the gaping pits in the ground, not to mention the pools of boiling water. With the toes of his boots, he slowly felt his way along the rough terrain, the dim glow from the phone doing little to illuminate the hazardous way ahead.

Pausing for a moment, he tried to get his bearings in the steam. It looked like he was about halfway through the labyrinth of pools now, just a little past the series of black holes in the cavern floor, if his memory served correctly. Ever so slowly, he edged closer to the front of the cavern, a few centimetres at a time. He listened desperately for any sound from the predator, but the only thing he could hear was his blood roaring in his ears.

His foot suddenly brushed into a small pile of rocks near the edge of one of the pools. The rocks clattered and bounced along the lip for a moment before falling into the scalding water with several wet plops.

"Shit!" he swore under his breath. Manny froze in place, listening intently and praying the beast hadn't heard his life-endangering clumsiness. Apart from the trickle of water from the streams and pools nearby, there was no other sound except the rapid staccato of his heartbeat. He remained frozen to the spot, cell phone screen off, not moving for several minutes as he imitated a stalagmite, not daring to make a sound. Keeping the phone shielded, with its screen still as low as the brightness level would allow, he carried cautiously forward, still feeling amped by the recent adrenaline rush caused by the beast's attack.

Embers of hope grew into burning flames of salvation inside his chest when he saw the faint glow of the camping lantern. It was still near the entrance next to the small tent where he'd kicked it. It seemed with the beast no longer anywhere in sight that escape might now be a possibility. Maybe it had gone on the prowl into the forest, looking for a meal that was easier to get at. If that were the case then, and he made it out of here alive, he'd be on a plane back to Barcelona faster than he could say, 'Adios maple syrup!'

Oritz began walking faster, a half-smile forming on his face, and he became heedless of the uneven stones scattered across the floor, not caring if he kicked them about by accident. He hurried through the steam, the small LED camp lantern's glow providing a tantalising hint of escape, just up ahead. "Yes, yes, yes!" he hissed. Inside his chest, the flames of salvation became a conflagration, consuming all rational thought.

The entrance beckoned enticingly, the starlit darkness outside not as deep as that of the steamy blackness inside. Fear propelled his leg muscles forward, their fibres burning as they re-awoke to the concept of flight instead of fight as a possibility for survival for the first time ever in Oritz's life.

There was a sudden eclipse of the faint lantern light as something moved across the entrance, blotting out all hope of escape.

Manny whipped the Maglite from one pocket, and the Glock 17 from the other. He turned the light on, and his mind turned off, unable to accept what it saw standing before him. "Mierda!"

The predator had been lying in wait just outside of the illumination of the lamplight as if it knew Manny would be using the light as a beacon to aid in his escape. It reared up and roared, towering above him, its grotesque, grey head scraping the stalactites, five metres up.

"Puta Madre!" Oritz screamed, unloading the Glock in the direction of the beast. He lunged to the right, then changed directions at the last moment as the creature came down onto its forepaws and charged toward him. He had effectively faked the creature out and was now running past it. A renewed sense of hope flowed through his burning leg muscles as he sprinted toward the entrance.

But urgency had distracted him from his prognosticative abilities; he now discovered they had been spot-on as he bolted into the freezing night air, his footwear only making tentative contact with the ice-slicked rock surface outside. The vapour from the waterfall had worked its magic on the sloping ledge, making his route of escape into something far more dangerous than anything he could have ever anticipated.

"Shit!" He tried to keep his balance, hoping to slide along the icy surface like a child finding their first frozen puddle of winter. But his boot-clad feet wouldn't cooperate and slid out from beneath him as their aggressive tread lost traction on the fresh coating of satin-like ice. His haste had made him blind to the hazard, and he cursed his stupidity as he fell.

"Son of a bitch!" he shrieked, landing hard on his back, and knocking the air out of himself. His momentum carried him down the slippery slope at an alarming rate. The bottom of the ledge dog-legged to the right lining him up perfectly for a fall into the superheated stream below. He knew he had to do something, and he had to do it now.

Seemingly with wild abandon, he began casting his hands and feet about, trying to snag onto something. But the ice thwarted his attempts at deceleration, its surface being far too slick for him to gain any purchase, and his complimentary ride on the cavern's latest attraction, 'The Afterlife Express' continued.

In a last-ditch effort for salvation, his hand hooked onto a small outcrop of rock not covered by ice, a reflexive grasping motion that stopped his rapid descent with a sudden, arm-wrenching tug. Panting in relief much like a small dog on a hot day, Manny dangled over the deadly drop. He prepared a list of options in his mind to help him deal with the current situation. After only a brief moment, he realised he was fucked six ways from Sunday, no matter which way he sliced this avocado.

Behind his head came the sound of the creature moving down the sloping ledge toward him. His mind suddenly cleared, and he felt a renewed surge of adrenaline defogging his brain. He pulled upward with all his strength, trying to climb back up onto the ledge. But because of his angle, with his feet hanging the way they were, he was unable to leverage himself back to safety, and his thick rubberised soles only weakly scraped at the moisture-slicked rock face.

The beast, however, had no problem negotiating the sheer ice of the ledge. With its stiletto-like claws acting as crampons, it gained easy purchase on the thick layer of frozen water that coated the rock. Manny craned his neck around and saw the beast slowly plodding down the slope toward him, saliva flooding from its jaws.

"Jesus, Mother Mary," he whispered, still unable to catch his breath. He was stuck between a rock and a hot place. Any which way he ran it in his head, he was screwed. If he let go, he'd plummet three metres into a deep stream of boiling water that must easily clock-in at one-hundred degrees Celsius. And if he didn't let go, he was a meal for this motherfucking monster. With a silent prayer, he made his choice and let go of the rock.

A huge taloned paw speared through his chest and shoulders, impaling him and dragging him upward. He screamed with pain he'd never known as he was pulled up toward the beast's dripping gorge.

Manny Oritz had been many things to many people, but a nice guy had not been one of them. As a result, he knew that someday, somewhere, he'd be taken out by someone, somehow. But he'd never seen himself going out like a sushi dinner for some abomination from hell. "You piece of sh…" he shrieked in rage and pain, as the creature's jaws closed around his skull.

133

Natural sutures between his brain plates separated, folding in on themselves and pancaking his brain as the animal clamped its jaws shut. The predator's eyes closed as it began to chew as if savouring the first taste of this elusive new prey.

Searing pain consumed Manny Oritz's last thoughts as the beast devoured his brain and then his body.

After a short while, its meal finished, the carnivore lumbered into the foggy night. Pausing for a moment, it sniffed the moist night air, its tongue licking crimson covered lips. It moved into the forest, searching for more fresh meat to staunch its insatiable hunger.

CHAPTER FOURTEEN

Austin rose early, being careful not to wake Alex. Usually, he wouldn't be up this early, unless it was a hockey practice morning. But today they needed all the light they could get at the campsite to see if they could figure out what had happened on the ridge. His goal was to be mobile, and on the road as soon as daylight broke. Stopping by Tim Hortons was a given on his way to meet with Trip and Chris, so he'd grab a bagel and coffee then.

Alex had turned fifteen last month, and Austin was more than okay with leaving the boy home alone to look after himself on the days he had to leave for work early. His son could be relied upon to get himself up, dressed, fed and out the door to school in the morning without any problems. Though the expression was as hackneyed as the day is long, Austin knew in his heart that Alex really was 'a good kid'.

Smiling as he thought of his son, Austin pressed a button on the remote control attached to the sun-visor over his head. The chain-drive clacked and whirred as the wooden framed door rolled up on well-oiled hinges. Austin started the Honda Pilot's engine; its brake lights flared alive, gleaming in the darkened garage like a set of hungry, predatory eyes. Pausing for a moment before he backed out, he grimaced when he glanced into the Honda's rear-view mirror to see what weather the new day had brought. He'd hoped to be able to see the end of his laneway this morning, but it didn't look like that was in the cards today. Squinting harder into the grey ghostland, he commented to himself, "Yep, if anything, this crap looks even thicker today. How is that possible?"

But he knew it could be worse. The fog could have been the freezing variety that sometimes hit at this time of year when the temperature inversion cleared temporarily. Though the damp, grey nothingness behind his Honda limited his visibility to an extreme degree, it didn't pose the same navigational hazards as the freezing mist. He knew all too well that when the treacherous freezing fog finally did creep down into the valley bottom, all hell usually broke loose on local roads just like it was the first day of winter instead of halfway through.

Few things in life are inevitable, except for death and taxes, and maybe one other thing, Austin reflected. At the beginning of each winter season when slippery roads were now going to be the norm, it seemed many people spontaneously forgot how they managed to navigate those same roads the previous year. In his experience, owners of four-wheel drives were usually the first ones in the ditch after a fresh snowfall or ice fog — their overblown confidence in the words 'four-wheel' and 'drive' printed on the sides of their vehicles blinding them to the hazards of the winter roads ahead.

Austin scowled once more at the sombre, grey, featureless morning. Today was a prime example of the reason the ski hill in Lawless was now closed — the incessant winter valley fog. Thanks to milder temperatures that came with global warming, regular low cloud and thick mists that limited visibility had been the final nail in the coffin, ending downhill skiing in the area. Back in 1982, when he was still in high school, the fog hadn't started settling in for weeks on end as it did now, and the resort was a thriving concern providing access to world-class skiing with breath-taking vistas. Year after year, the resort experienced a tremendously busy ski season thanks to record snowfalls.

But fog hadn't been the sole reason for the ski resort's demise, although it had been a major contributor. The other compounding factor was when the Sinclair Development Corporation, then owner of the resort, had been judged liable in a lawsuit concerning another of its properties up the coast from Vancouver. The resultant settlement cost the corporation over one-hundred million dollars in 1982, which was closer to a quarter of a billion dollars today. The money had been awarded to the relatives of the victims of the incident to provide some closure. Each one received nearly one million dollars in cold, hard cash. It was a tidy sum to be sure, but hardly worth the life of a loved one as many of the bereaved had lamented at the time. When all was said and done, it came to be known as 'The Sinclair Incident' and made international news. Many observers compared it to other events such as the Mary Celeste and the Roanoke Colony.

At the stroke of midnight, New Year's Eve, 1981, ninety-eight beautiful people from the Lower Mainland's burgeoning movie industry vanished from the resort's ballroom without a trace in the space of fifteen seconds, never to be seen again. It had been the sensational sort of story that generated headlines worldwide for months afterward and fed the ever-hungry National Enquirer and Weekly World News for years to come. And it was also a story that Austin had always wanted to know more about someday.

Working as a local realtor at the time, Ray Chance, and his business partner, then city councillor Bob Nichols had been fortunate enough to be in the right place at the right time. They picked up the Lawless ski resort for a rock-bottom, fire-sale price. Both men were made wealthy many times over during the ensuing decades that they operated the ski hill.

But by the turn of the century, it had become exceedingly rare to see snow at the resort and even rarer down in Lawless itself. The town usually got a good dump or two each year at the valley bottom, but most of the time it stayed high up in the hills, well beyond the ski lodge and all but the highest of its runs. For those adventurous enough, though, like snowmobilers, and cross-country skiers, there was still plenty of deep snow to keep them happy at higher elevations on the ridges and benches that ringed the bowl-shaped valley.

After suffering a decade of significant revenue losses from the lack of snow and encroaching fog, Chance and Nichols decided to revamp things. The ailing ski hill was closed down, and the partners applied for a casino licence. They were given the go-ahead from the Province of BC the very next year, and the face-lift began almost immediately.

Ray Chance was the brains behind the resort during the renovations. But he was a man lacking in the idea department and decided that flattery was indeed the most sincere form of compliment. Chance figured that a miniature version of Las Vegas was what customers needed to see when they approached the resort from the road. And that is precisely what he did, commissioning the construction of duplicates of some of Las Vegas's most iconic doppelgangers from around the world, but on a much smaller scale. They included the Sphinx, the Great Pyramid of Giza, and for those with more European tastes, a one-tenth scale Eiffel Tower. Now, before starting the drive up the twisting road to the main village, guests were greeted by these highly detailed recreations. Impressive in their own right, they had become a bit of a tourist attraction, drawing people from all over the interior of the province to see them and then hopefully dine and gamble at the buffet and casino. It truly was one of the last things you'd expect to see at a resort nestled in the rugged Cascade Mountains of British Columbia.

Giving his head a shake, Austin unravelled himself from his web of memories and backed the large SUV from the garage, turning it around in a short pullout in his driveway. He and Alex lived on a small acreage halfway between the casino and the town of Lawless itself. When Austin's wife, Patricia had been alive, she'd enjoyed having nothing but nature surrounding her, as had he. It was not that 'big city' life in

Lawless was too hectic for them, far from it, but they both loved the solitude and serenity that the countryside provided.

Austin slowly navigated his way down the lane. The fog seemed impenetrable this morning. Suddenly, the ditch across the road from his driveway was rapidly filling his mist-covered windshield. He hadn't realised was as far down the lane as he was, and said, "Whoa! Eyes wide open, today, man!" Cranking the wheel away from the ditch, he pointed the Honda toward Lawless. First stop: the local Timmies. At the drive-thru, Austin ordered two large double-doubles for himself and Chris, and an extra-large triple-triple for Trip, including a box of doughnuts (heavy on the honey crullers, please). And finally, for himself, he ordered a four-cheese bagel, heavy on the cream cheese (please and thank you).

Driving the remaining three blocks to the Works yard while chewing on his bagel, Austin glanced at the Pilot's digital dashboard clock and saw that it was almost six — he was right on time. The Lawless City Works truck sat idling as he pulled into the yard, already loaded with the equipment for the day. The snowmobiles on the truck's heavy-duty sled deck were most likely primed and ready to go, knowing Trip's attention to detail.

Speaking of Trip, the man of the hour was sitting in the passenger seat of the Silverado, waiting patiently. Austin knew his friend and co-worker wouldn't want to drive this early in the morning in order to give his full attention to the boxful of honey-glazed lovelies, and he was okay with that. Pulling to a stop next to the Chevy, he saw Trip with an expectant look on his face. His expression reminded Austin of a Basset Hound he'd once had as a child which had always looked a little bit sad and always very hungry. Austin didn't have a problem driving them around the valley today as he preferred not to have Trip eating and trying to pay attention behind the wheel. And more to the point, Austin didn't want to drive the truck after Trip's morning snack, only to find his hands sticking to the wheel every time he turned a corner.

Climbing into the driver's seat, Austin said, "Morning, my friend!" He handed off the cardboard tray of coffee cups to Trip, who grabbed them willingly.

"Morning, Boss!" Trip glanced quickly at Austin as he spoke, but then locked his eyes back onto the box of fresh doughnuts still held in Austin's other hand.

Taking pity, Austin said, "You can hold the travelling rations here, and as usual, feel free to dig in!" He held the box out and it was quickly nabbed by Trip's needy fingers.

"Thanks, Boss! You are awe and some!" Trip said. He put the coffee on the console between the seats and eagerly peeled back the lid of the cardboard box to survey the treasures inside. Looking as delighted as a kid at Christmas, his eyes lit up, and he said, "Oh—my—God."

Concerned, Austin asked. "What is it, buddy?"

Trip stammered excitedly, "T-the staff at the doughnut shop put seven crullers into the box today, instead of the usual six! We have a bonus cruller!"

Glancing over, Austin smiled slightly, thinking he detected small tears of joy in the corner of the other man's eyes as he gazed upon the glazed goodies. He fastened his seatbelt and drove them down the block and around the corner to the Conservation Office. Pulling into the rear lot, he found Chris's pickup waiting, engine running to keep her warm inside. He rolled down his window as he came to a stop next to the truck, saying, "Good Morning, Chris!"

Lowering her window, Christine poked her head out and said, "Good morning, Austin! Good morning, Trip! Looks like another lovely day here in the valley!"

Trip waved at Christine from the passenger seat through Austin's open window, unable to talk as he was already wrapping his lips around his second cruller of the morning.

"I thought we could all go in one vehicle this morning, Chris, just to simplify things, if that's okay?" Austin called through the swirling mist.

"That sounds great! Let me grab my stuff first." Christine reached into the rear seat of her cab, grabbing her backpack. She lithely jumped down from her vehicle, holding the pack in one hand. The alarm chirped and the doors locked as she pressed a button on her key fob, then placed it in her pack. Rounding the Works truck, she saw Trip already on the job, standing at attention and holding the door to the rear seat open for her. He brushed at several dozen cruller crumbs that had fallen from his beard onto his tan coveralls. The tops of his cheeks glowed an even brighter shade of red when he looked up and caught her taking in his performance. He smiled broadly through his beard at her. "Thank you, Trip," she said, smiling lightly in return as she entered.

Trip mumbled, "Welcome," cheeks now so red they looked ready to catch fire.

Christine threw her pack on the empty seat next to her. Once she'd situated herself, Austin reached over and offered her a coffee, saying, "Thought you could use one."

She gratefully accepted, saying, "Thanks! I didn't bother making one for myself, yet. I've just had a tea so far today."

Reaching over from the front seat, an encouraging look on his face, Trip offered Christine a doughnut, making sure to give her the end of the box without the crullers. "Thank you, Trip, but I'm okay." She pulled a high-protein, organic snack bar from an inner parka pocket and flashed it at him.

Trip's face fell slightly, perhaps disappointed that Christine didn't share the same passion for doughnuts that he did, and said, "Your loss." He appeared to recover quickly, however; his grin returning as he gazed back at the box once more, seemingly mesmerised by the doughy delights it contained.

Christine smiled at Trip's enthusiasm for the pastries, then stifled a small giggle when she glanced toward Austin in the driver's seat and saw him rolling his eyes good-naturedly at her in the rear-view mirror. With a contented sigh, Trip went to work on yet another of his new pastry pals.

Winding the Chevy Silverado up the mountain road toward Gold Ridge, Austin noted with a sigh how much longer the trip was taking than it normally would; the thickness of the fog making it dangerous for him to drive anything faster than as slow as hell.

"This is unbelievable!" Christine said, shaking her head as she looked out at the swirling grey. "You say it's like this quite a lot here in the winter now?"

"Seems like almost every day, to one degree or another," Trip said.

Austin nodded his head in agreement. "Sometimes, for weeks on end."

"I can see how this would have affected the local ski hill's business." Christine shook her head.

"Yeah, it definitely didn't help — that and the lack of snow," Trip agreed, brushing a fresh batch of crumbs from his beard.

Austin squinted through the windshield, his mouth a grim line as he peered into the blankness ahead, saying, "It's sad what passes for daylight in winter around here these days."

Christine added, with a slight chuckle, "Maybe you should start calling it 'greylight' instead of daylight."

Austin snorted in amusement, then squinted harder through the windshield. After a few moments, he decided it wasn't his mind playing tricks on him — the fog actually was beginning to thin, hinting at the possibility of blue skies making an appearance. Ten kilometres from the ridge, they found the white Dodge Ram 3500 with its rented snowmobile trailer parked in the same spot from the day before. Austin turned the Works truck around in the unplowed cul-de-sac, facing the nose back toward town. "End of the line kiddies, we'll be sledding from here."

Christine stepped down from the truck, blinking slightly in the brightening greyness. "Well, this is a lovely sight. I almost need my sunglasses up here."

"Yeah, when you get up high enough from the valley bottom, sometimes the sun begins to poke through," Austin said. He looked upward, smiling toward the hazy orb of light in the sky, hoping the sun would soon burn away more of the inversion's valley cloud.

Christine looked about and said, "That's kind of strange, though. I thought you mentioned yesterday that the local police were going to be up here to meet us as well. I don't see any sign of them and that truck over there sure doesn't look like it just pulled in."

Closing the passenger door of the Silverado, Trip said, "Nope, that truck belongs to the sledders."

Austin agreed, "Yeah, that is a little odd. When I talked to Fred Paulson at the station yesterday, he promised me that someone would be out to investigate first thing this morning."

"Maybe they slept in?" Christine offered.

"Could be, but we'll just have to see if they show up later. Maybe there's a crime wave happening that we're not aware of. Whatever the reason, we can't wait for them." Austin adjusted the backpack on his shoulders as he spoke, then climbed onto the sled deck. Revving the Cat's engine, he began backing the first snowmobile off the deck.

Guiding Austin down the ramp, Trip concurred, saying, "Yeah, let's get goin' while the gettin's good, folks! Light's a-wastin'!"

From behind the controls of his sled, Austin said, "As you probably noticed, Chris, we only have the two snowmobiles, so you'll have to double up with one of us."

"I figured as much," Christine said, looking at the size of the seats on the snowmobiles. On Trip's machine, she wasn't sure if there would be enough room for her, Trip and Trip's belly. Austin, despite his backpack, might be a more comfortable ride up the mountain, she decided. "I'll ride with you, Austin, if that's okay with Trip?"

Trip shrugged his shoulders and said nothing, but Christine could see that he looked a little bit disappointed that he wouldn't have the pleasure of her company. Feeling bad, she said, "Maybe on the way back, I'll ride with you, Trip." Her words seemed to have an effect, and Trip climbed onto his snowmobile with a slight spring in his step.

"Hop aboard m 'lady, your chariot is about to depart." Austin gestured toward the empty seat behind him on the sled. Christine jumped on behind Austin and held tight. The engines of the snowmobiles growled to life, shattering the quiet day as they began the next stage of their ascent toward Gold Ridge. The fog thinned further and further until brilliant, blue sky dazzled Christine. Clinging tightly to Austin's back, she soaked in the beauty of the snow-frosted countryside as it glided past. Murphy seemed a man confident in his abilities as he steered them up the mountain, piloting the sled with a practiced ease that belied the skill involved.

When they eventually rolled to a stop, Christine pulled a much-needed pair of blue-mirrored sunglasses from an inner pocket in her parka. She slid them onto her nose, tucking several stray strands of long, blonde hair behind one ear as she did. Stepping off the sled, she saw a fresh layer of ice from the previous night's freezing fog had settled over the area, and it had not fared well. She was concerned that the icy build-up might affect her examination of the spoor after the milder temperatures from the previous day, making it more challenging than usual.

Christine crunched across the glittering frosted surface toward the collapsed tent. Kneeling near the torn tent fly, she pulled it aside, revealing a deep impression that had been partially obscured by the fabric. "Oh, my Lord! This thing must be enormous!" Taking out her Canon Rebel, she started snapping numerous pictures of the animal's spoor but knew she needed something with better definition as the current track appeared somewhat distorted.

From over her shoulder, Trip said, "That track must have expanded quite a bit in the last couple of days since it happened."

Christine nodded, "It could have been affected by daytime warming. We'll have to find another one to be sure."

Austin said doubtfully, "It must have expanded. I mean, there aren't any animals around these parts that could leave a print that big, are there?"

Standing, Christine said, "None that I'm aware of, but that's what we're here to determine. This print makes it really hard to say." She snapped another shot with her camera and looked back to see from which direction the prints tracked. Moving slowly toward the fire pit, she shook her head in wonder as she approached. "This is nuts!"

Something had come directly through the fire itself. Remnants of partially burnt logs, some as thick as her torso, were scattered several metres away from the now-cold bonfire. The power it must have taken to plow through that amount of firewood, especially if it were aflame, was insane! She crouched next to the cold embers and let out a low whistle, saying, "Most of the other prints weren't usable, but this one, this is a different story." Brushing aside some ashes covering the print with a small sable brush from her pack, Christine gaped at what she saw. Clearly outlined in the frozen mud near the edge of the fire pit was one of the most immense bear tracks she had ever seen in her ten years as a conservation officer. It was located next to a thicket of green holly bushes awash in red berries. The plant's foliage had kept the paw print shaded from sunlight in daytime and provided a protective canopy from ice frost at night. "Unbelievable!" she said in wonder. "The size of this thing is crazy! I hope I brought enough dental stone with me to cast a print for something so large."

"I know, this is definitely into WTF territory, isn't it?" Austin commented from behind, peering over her shoulder. "I think Trip and I will have a scout around while you do that." Standing next to Austin, Trip craned his neck this way and that, as if looking for any sign that the creature that left the tracks might be coming back their way.

"Sounds good, I'll be at least a half an hour," Christine said, reaching into her pack and removing a bag of dental stone and assorted accessories.

"Okay, just watch your back, who knows if that thing is still nearby looking for seconds," Trip said, head still swivelling like a radar dish.

"Thanks, I'll make sure I keep a look-out." Christine knelt and began dusting the immense print with dental stone.

With Christine tending to her casting, Austin and Trip followed the misshapen, frost-covered tracks in an attempt to see from which direction they originated. Working their way back from where they found Jerry, they determined that the creature had come into the campsite from the direction of the Golden Nugget Resort and Spa.

"Now that is interesting," Austin said. "According to Chris, the raccoon Ray Chance hit also came from a direction that would have lined it up almost perfectly with the resort."

"You're right, the casino is just about a dozen klicks that-a-way, as the crow flies," Trip said, pointing over his shoulder with his thumb.

After a bit more poking around, the pair returned to the campsite to find Christine testing the dental stone's firmness and preparing to remove the casting from the fire pit. Austin said, "Well, we found the direction our creature came from."

Christine stood, saying, "Don't tell me, it came from the resort, right?"

"Well, it didn't come from the Black Lagoon," Austin said, chuckling at his reference.

"Huh?" Christine looked puzzled.

"Sorry, making a little joke there. Probably before your time."

With a slight shrug, Christine added, "Anyway, the area around the resort certainly looks to be a bit of a hot-spot for our four-legged freaks of nature wandering around out there, that's for sure."

"Well, barring the possibility that Ray Chance rented out part of his resort to Victor Frankenstein, which I think is a bit of a stretch, whatever else remains, however improbable, must be the truth," Austin said.

"Indubitably, Watson," Christine said with a smile. Kneeling next to the now solidified dental stone, she began gently prying at the edges with the blade of her pocketknife.

The high-pitched drone of two snowmobiles approaching broke the quiet of the morning air as the Lawless Police Department pulled onto the scene. The blue and white paint job on the sleds contrasted sharply against the red-tinted frost that ground beneath their treads as they stopped.

Austin knew there was going to be a problem from the moment he saw who was piloting the lead snowmobile. The officer in question got off slowly, his ample size causing him a moment of distress as he attempted to disengage his fleshy buttocks from the seat of the sled. He plodded toward them, a dour expression on his face. Behind the gloom was none other than Chief of Police, Reggie VanDusen.

Almost falling off of the second snowmobile in his hurry to catch up to the chief, Constable Oscar Olsen trailed behind, doing his best sycophantic scurry. Slipping and sliding, the man attempted to rush across the ice-crusted snow to catch up to his boss but met with little success and stumbled several times.

Reggie VanDusen had been with the Lawless Police Department ever since he'd graduated high school, starting first as a rookie constable and eventually working his way up to the lofty position of Chief of Police. Austin remembered Reggie as a child. They had both grown up in the same neighbourhood in Lawless. Back in the day, VanDusen had been the neighbourhood bully, and not much had changed since. As he'd grown more comfortable working for the police, advancing in rank over the years, his abuses of power had grown exponentially with his promotions. Now, he was a bully with a badge and had found his place in life. Reggie's aggressively belligerent attitude allowed him to fit right in with the rest of the police force that Mayor Bob Nichols had hand-picked over the years to protect his investments at the ski hill and now casino.

"Howdy, Austin," VanDusen said, curtly. "Isn't this a little outside of your jurisdiction? Did somebody's kitty-cat wander away from home out here? Or are you into some off-road maintenance now?" He nodded in Christine's direction with a wink.

"Actually, I was helping our new conservation officer here, Officer Christine Moon." He gestured toward Christine, who was still kneeling near the fire, unfolding a large empty plastic bag to contain the dental stone casting.

Austin continued, "I wanted to make sure she could find this site. Plus, I wanted to be here to cover any questions she may have or any that you might have about what happened here at the camp, including the rescue of the survivor. We believe we have an idea where the thing that attacked the campers came from as well."

"Hold on, hold on!" VanDusen said. "What do you mean, attack? Nobody said anything about an attack happening here!"

Bewildered, Austin asked, "Didn't Fred give you my statement?"

"Yeah, I read the report you filed, Murphy. But whether there was or wasn't an attack up here is for Lawless Police Department to determine, not you!"

"Take a look around, Chief; it's pretty obvious something happened here," Trip interjected.

"I wasn't talking to you, Williams," VanDusen said, looking at Trip with thinly veiled contempt.

Trip put both of his hands up in front of his chest, palms out toward VanDusen as he backed away, saying, "Okay, fine." He realised his input was neither desired, nor required, and went to check on the snowmobiles.

VanDusen walked around the campfire, looking at the tracks left behind by the creature as he went. He ended his journey standing behind Christine, who was still kneeling next to the cold ashes. The chief watched as she opened the top of a large transparent plastic bag to contain the casting beside her on the ground. As she reached to pick up the casting, VanDusen put his hand softly on her shoulder and squeezed it gently, as if giving her a light massage. "Well, well, whatcha got there, little missy? Are ya makin' a mud pie?" His voice dripped with condescension.

Christine's shoulders tensed as soon as VanDusen touched her. Carefully laying the casting down on top of the opened bag, she stood upright. Turning, she gave the chief a withering stare. "First of all, it's Conservation Officer Moon to you, not 'Missy'." Eyes burning brightly, she stepped toward the police chief and poked him in the chest with her index finger. VanDusen backed up a step, a look of surprise on his face.

"Second of all, it's a dental stone casting of spoor left behind by a possible man-eating apex predator, not a mud pie!" She stepped toward him once more as she spoke and VanDusen backed up again.

"And thirdly, if you EVER touch me again, I'll have you charged with sexual harassment and I'll have your goddamned badge! You got it?" She emphasized her last point by firmly poking the centre of VanDusen's silver badge with her right index finger, pushing the circle-wrapped star deeply into his flabby chest. He backed away yet another step as Christine explained this last fact to him.

Austin observed the confrontation, a small smile playing at the corners of his mouth. It always brightened his day to see someone take Reggie VanDusen down a notch or two.

Trip was also paying rapt attention to the conversation between Christine and Reggie, but his eyes betrayed the lack of emotion hidden by his beard — the twinkle of joy as he watched VanDusen get poked in the badge was undeniable.

"Well, excuuuuse me!" the chief sputtered, backing up one more step away from Christine, perhaps fearing another poke in the badge. But he didn't look where he was going and tripped over a log, going down hard on his back and landing in the semi-frozen slush of blood and mud that surrounded the cold fire pit.

"Jesus Christ!" VanDusen shouted from the ground, trying to get to his feet. He wallowed around like a turtle on his back for a moment as he tried to turn over. Eventually, he managed to roll over and get an arm out to support himself. But his hand slipped in the red-tinted mud as he tried to stand and he went down once more, this time face-first.

VanDusen shrieked, "Goddammit, Oscar! Get the fuck over here and give me a friggin' hand!"

The silent constable hustled over, reaching his hand down to VanDusen. The chief grabbed the proffered appendage and pulled. But Olsen didn't have solid footing on the ice either, and when VanDusen yanked with his full weight to stand, he only ended up pulling his equally portly constable down on top of himself. The chief squawked like a duck as the air was knocked out of him.

Austin had to turn around and pretend to be doing something else for a moment before he burst out laughing at their predicament. Eventually, after several more outbursts of colourful metaphors on VanDusen's part, the pair found their feet.

"Son of a bitch!" VanDusen shouted.

Christine watched Lawless's Finest waddle back to their snowmobiles, no doubt to find something to wipe the worst of the bloody slurry off of themselves. She turned to Austin and Trip as the two police officers began to clean themselves, saying perkily, "I think I might have made a new friend!"

"That's for sure! And thanks for the comic relief! Larry, Moe and Curly would have been proud. But seriously, you'd better watch your back around them, especially VanDusen," Austin said in a low voice.

"Oh, I will. Don't you worry about me, I've been dealing with assholes like that my entire life."

"I can believe it. You handled yourself quite well." Austin nodded over toward VanDusen, "Maybe next time he'll think twice about any of the old touchy-feely stuff." He smiled when he saw the chief and his constable still in the middle of grooming each other like a couple of primates out of a Jane Goodall documentary.

Finally wiping most of the mud and gore off of their trousers and parkas, the chief and his constable returned to the scene. This time they circumnavigated the muck around the fire pit. Instead, they examined other areas of crimson interest, with VanDusen snapping numerous photographs and Olsen taking samples of the blood they found at various spots around the site.

Christine picked up the now-bagged casting and stood, holding it up in front of her face for all to see. It was so large, it obscured her entire head, including her hat. She figured the footpad alone was over thirty centimetres across with claw impressions extending another twenty centimetres past the edge of the pad.

As VanDusen approached to see what she held, Christine thrust the imprint toward his face saying, "This is what attacked the camp!"

"I don't see any evidence of an attack," VanDusen said, looking the casting up and down with a frown. "I see a lot of blood scattered around the area, but that could have come from animals that these guys had hunted illegally, gutted and then skinned."

"You know as well as I do that it isn't hunting season for anything in this area at this time of the year. There is no way that blood is animal blood!" Christine said, frustrated.

"We don't know anything of the sort, yet," VanDusen said. Holding up his bag of samples. He continued, "We'll get this analysed at our lab and then we'll make a final determination." He turned to Austin, "That 'survivor' you brought into the hospital is still unconscious, but when he wakes up maybe he can shed some light on this situation. But until you can show me a body, or a piece of one and not some moisture-swelled goddamned footprint," he pointed at the casting Christine still held up, "this case is on hold, pending further evidence of a crime," he finished tersely.

"A crime?" Christine questioned; her brow knitted in confusion. "It's not a crime scene; it's the scene of an attack by an unknown predator that might still be hungry for more! You need to alert the public that there's something out here killing people!"

"We're not going to start jumping at shadows here," VanDusen said. "We have no proof at this point…"

"Proof! What other proof do you need?" Christine interrupted, holding up the casting in front of his face once more.

"There's no proof that thing was involved in any of what happened up here. For all we know that animal may have wandered through the camp after these guys bugged out, once they were done cleaning their kill, then ate the remains the hunters left behind," VanDusen ended his sentence nodding toward the casting.

"Their tent's still here as well as their snowmobiles! Are you blind? They didn't bug out! They were eaten!"

"We'll see, little missy, we'll see…" VanDusen said as he turned and walked back toward his snowmobile. Constable Olsen circled around behind the chief, like a satellite in orbit, dabbing at his boss's jacket with a muddy rag as VanDusen repeatedly swatted him away.

"I think that went well," Christine said, exasperation in her voice.

"I think they'll change their mind when they get those blood samples analysed." Austin observed.

"This has got to be what killed those men, and it's still out there somewhere," Christine said, inspecting the casting once more. The creature's claws were so long that they projected from the top of the bag. They looked almost as threatening in dental stone as they no doubt were in real life, she thought with a scowl.

Glancing at the sun, which was getting precariously close to the edge of the western mountaintops, Trip said, "I don't think we want to be out here when that sun sets, just in case you're right. So, we'd best get goin'."

"You heard the man, Chris, let's saddle up."

Remembering her promise, Christine handed the casting to Austin who carefully strapped it onto the back of his sled's seat, securing it for the ride back down the mountain. She climbed onto the back of Trip's snowmobile for the return leg of her journey, saying, "Looks like you're my chauffeur this time, Trip."

Trip smiled and said, "Yes, ma'am," then blushed beet red as he started his sled. With a gentle twist of the throttle, he guided them into the tracks left behind by the Lawless Police Department, manoeuvring them back toward civilisation.

Austin paused for a moment before following the others, looking over his shoulder at the abandoned campsite one last time. A sense of dread scuttled across the back of his neck as he watched the remaining daylight melt into the mountain peaks in the distance. The waning daylight cast a blood-red halo around the sun as the first, thin wisps of ice fog curled off the Kootenay Glacier in the distance. Revving his engine, Austin fell in line behind Trip and Christine, his disquiet a silent passenger all the way down the mountainside.

CHAPTER FIFTEEN

"Hey, Dad!" Alex said from the living room floor, greeting his father as he entered the house.

"Hi, buddy! How was your day?" Austin stepped inside, the thick mist from the lengthening evening trying to follow him through the open doorway. After the long day at the campsite, he was looking forward to some quiet time at home with his son as well as a hot meal. As he closed the door behind him, he took a deep breath and knew that his son already had things under control in the food department.

Austin entered the living room and saw his son sitting cross-legged on the floor in front of a thick-legged, glass-topped pine coffee table. "It was okay, pretty boring. I'm just finishing up my homework." Alex scribbled a sentence in his notebook as he spoke, then glanced up briefly and smiled before diving back into his homework.

"Awesome! Say, something sure smells good." Austin hung his parka and Lawless City Works ball cap on a hook near the front door.

"Yeah, I thought you might be a bit late, so I put some spaghetti and meatballs on for us."

"You're the best, bud," Austin said to Alex, ruffling the boy's wavy brown hair as he went through into the kitchen.

It appeared Chef Alex had been busy. On the stove, two pots steamed from beneath gleaming chromed lids. Austin peeked inside of the first pot. It contained a deep red pasta sauce with over a dozen pre-cooked meatballs simmering merrily away. If the empty jar and box sitting next to the stove were anything to go by, this evening's epicurean delight was courtesy of Catelli Super Vegetable Primavera along with President's Choice Angus Meatballs. However, Austin knew the sauce was not just regular Catelli Primavera. No, this sauce contained Chef Alex's favourite go-to ingredient when he cooked things, Frank's RedHot Sauce. The bottle of Frank's next to the pot was looking rather low, and Austin realised he was in for another night of fiery after dinner shenanigans in his gastrointestinal tract.

Thanks to Alex's mother, Patricia, the boy had a penchant for all things spicy, just like she used to have. Austin's breath hitched slightly at the sudden thought of his wife, and he stirred the sauce and meatballs a few times, placing the lid back on top. He moved on to the pasta pot. Inside, thin strands of spaghettini roiled in tangled coils, turning over lazily in the gently boiling water. The digital timer displayed on the stove counted down the two and a half minutes remaining. With cooking abilities learned from his mother, Austin knew that the boy's pasta would be a perfect al dente.

Stepping over to the sink, Austin turned and faced the large kitchen window. On a clear day, it looked out onto a covered deck and expansive yard beyond. Tonight, he saw none of it. With his back to the living room, he closed his eyes, resting his hands on the edge of the sink for a moment. He smiled, wanly, feeling love and sadness mix together all at once. They coursed through his heart in a surge of emotion, overwhelming him as he thought of his son.

The boy's kindness, wit and confidence constantly surprised Austin, but he realised they were just a few of the many things he'd inherited from Patricia. There was that, but the boy also had a keen intelligence and wisdom that sometimes seemed far beyond what someone his age would typically possess. He was immensely proud of his son and loved him more than life itself. Like most parents, Austin would move mountains for the boy, if needed.

After both of Alex's remaining grandparents passed and then his mother, all within a year and a half, Austin was now the only anchor the boy had left in this large, lonely world. His son was helping so much around the house, sharing the chores, and Austin was grateful. It had been a challenge at first for both of them. They had been through the wringer, emotionally, and needed time to process the shock and grief. But little by little, each day, they relearned once again how to carry on with their lives, despite the vast black hole at the centre of both of their personal universes.

Almost greater than the pride for his son was the sadness, however. It dwelt behind every fond memory, tinting them with grief. Each time he stumbled across another of Patricia's belongings that he'd missed sending to the thrift store, it would reopen the wound still fresh in his heart — a sense of utter desolation and loss that cut through to the very core of his being. He stood motionless, his eyes still closed at the sink, adrift in a sea of melancholy. There were so many things he missed about Patricia — her hugs and kisses, her gentle caresses, her musical laughter, and the warmth of her body next to him in bed at night. But above all else, it was Patricia's smile he missed the most. Her radiant, glowing smile that always flooded his heart with joy each time he witnessed it, even after twenty years of marriage. A rush of memories assailed him suddenly, and he leaned heavily on the edge of the sink, bowing his head deeply.

When he had moments like this, reflecting on the past eighteen months, it was as if all the events of their life together were jumbled up, playing over and over on a looped track inside his head. It took him on a rollercoaster ride, twisting him up toward peaks of joy as he remembered their loving moments together and then rocketing him toward lows of gut-wrenching sorrow when he thought of her premature passing.

The symptoms had begun just after Patricia's forty-fifth birthday. At first, she forgot the odd appointment. It didn't seem like a big deal. Not something that concerned either her or Austin very much. She put it down to stress caused by her job as a nurse at the hospital and her exhaustion from some of the long hours she put in there.

But over the next few months, she started forgetting more critical things, like Mother's Day, Father's Day and then eventually Alex's birthday. One evening, Austin had talked her into getting herself tested, his concern growing deeper each passing month. He'd watched the changes in her demeanour. She'd once been so easy to laugh and smile. His day had always been elevated every time he had the pleasure to witness either one. Leaning heavily against the sink, his shoulders heaved again.

Everything changed just after Thanksgiving the previous year. Patricia grew more and more impatient and irritable, less able to shrug off the caprices of life when they arose. The smiles came fewer and farther apart until one day, they stopped altogether. It had seemed as if the part of her that experienced joy and happiness was now gone, forever lost in the vast labyrinth of her deteriorating mind.

Then the diagnosis came back. Patricia and Austin had been dumbstruck — Early-onset Alzheimer's. Over the next dozen or so months, his wife fought long and hard against the disease's debilitating effects. Austin could never remember exactly how many months that it had taken for the disease to kill her because they were all a jumble of raw emotion. The one thing he recalled clearly, however, was that there were not enough of them.

Ultimately, Alzheimer's left her pale, thin and bed-ridden at the hospital's extended-care wing, tended by the same people with whom she used to work. Near the end, when Austin would visit, she would ask if she knew him. He would smile and tell her that he was her husband. She often seemed surprised at this news as if she were unsure if he were telling her the truth or not.

However, for the longest time, there was always one person that she never forgot, and that was her son, Alex. He had been a golden ray of sunshine — a beacon of clarity and lucidity, in an increasingly cloudy mind. Whenever she saw him, her eyes brightened from the dimness that was encroaching upon her, love flooding her face at the sight of her beautiful, amazing boy.

But eventually, even Alex receded into the fog that now comprised her mind. She no longer spoke, her face a blank slate, not responding to anyone or anything. One cold evening in February, as Austin held her frail hand, talking to her about the highlights of their life together, he knew things had changed with Patricia. She now only stared at the ceiling, her eyes empty and unblinking, breathing shallowly. The spark of recognition that sometimes danced near the corners of her eyes had gone.

Alex talked to her next, his eyes heavy with tears, telling her of his latest academic achievements and of his making captain on the junior hockey team. But there was no recognition of any of this from Patricia. She continued to breathe shallowly and stare at the ceiling. It seemed her body had only been a shell, and the vibrant, beautiful woman inside was now long gone.

Austin received a call at home later that night. He remembered feeling numb as he told Alex. They had both been devastated by the news. Though they knew it was coming, it was still a shock. The anchor of love in their life was gone, leaving them both emotionally adrift.

Little by little, over the ensuing weeks and months, they had started to heal. Alex gradually began to resemble the boy he'd been before — as if sensing, though his mother was no longer physically with him, she would always be there for him, in his memories and his heart. But he had also been changed by his mother's death. A new maturity and thoughtfulness seemed to permeate his person, like he needed to be more than he was, to heal and also to honour her memory.

Austin usually kept most of his emotions in check, not wanting to burden the boy further. Some days, he felt such a sense of longing and loss that he had to mentally slap himself and tell himself to get a grip before he was overcome by emotion once more. He'd been coping reasonably well, most of the time. But every once in a while, it caught him off guard, and he had to stop and take a slow, deep breath. He stood a moment longer at the counter, still not looking out the window, but looking inward, his closed eyes feeling heavy with unshed tears. Taking the edge of his shirtsleeve, he wiped at the corners of his eyes for a moment, not wanting Alex to see him like this.

"You okay, Dad?" Alex's voice gently inquired at his shoulder, making him start.

"Yeah, just had something in my eye," Austin lied, still rubbing his sleeve against the corner of one closed eye as he smiled at the boy.

"That sucks, doesn't it. I hate it when that happens." Seemingly satisfied, his son gave him a small pat on the back, then continued to the stove to dish up the dinner. Alex placed a couple of empty bowls down at the kitchen table. He knew his dad was having a hard time some days and he was trying his best to help out wherever he could. Sometimes it was by cleaning the bathroom, and other times it was by doing the laundry. Tonight, it was cooking dinner so that when his dad came home from another long day, they could relax and watch the hockey game together.

Alex drained the pasta into a colander in the sink, then dumped the sauce and meatballs into the pasta pot and poured the spaghetti back on top. He stirred the meal for a little bit and said, "So what's new out on the roads, Dad? I didn't get a chance to ask yesterday." From the counter, the boy handed his father a spoon and knife, adding, "Sorry, the forks were all dirty."

"I think I'll manage, thanks." Sitting down, Austin placed his cutlery on the table in front of himself. "Well, we had another scratch and sniff yesterday, a messy one."

"Really? What happened?"

"Ray Chance hit a raccoon."

"What? How much of a mess could that possibly make?" Alex inquired, eagerly.

"Well, it was the size of a black bear."

"No way!" Alex's eyes went wide.

Austin related the incident with the raccoon, meeting Christine, and the tale of Geraldine Gertzmeyer's turkeys. He left out the part about the slaughter at the campsite since he didn't want his son to worry, or for word to get out and cause a panic until they were confident of the threat.

This was exciting news to Alex. "Wow, a raccoon as big as a bear? How is that possible? What do you think it ate to get that big? Do you think it's some sort of mutant caused by radioactivity and it got into some illegally dumped toxic waste barrels, or something like that?"

Austin smiled. Thanks to Patricia, his son had a passion for old horror and sci-fi movies from the fifties and sixties, and this seemed like a reasonable assumption for the boy to make. "I don't know about that," Austin responded. After a moment, he continued, "According to Chris's colleague down on the coast who's a zoologist, that sort of animal hasn't been seen around these parts for about fifty-thousand years."

"Whoa! Really?"

"Yeah, I know, how's that possible, right? The conservation officer sent some samples down to Vancouver to have them analysed. Perhaps when she hears back, we'll have a better idea of how this thing survived for so long."

"Well, Dad, despite this conversation about exploding mutant raccoons from beyond time and scraping them off of the highway, I think I'm feeling pretty hungry right now. How about you? Are you ready to eat?"

"You bet, son," Austin said, smiling at the helpful person his son was becoming and knowing that Patricia would be proud.

Alex gave his dad a thumbs up and was just about to lift the pot of spaghetti and meatballs from the stove and bring it to the table when the phone rang. He detoured and picked the faded yellow handset off the wall instead, saying, "Hello, Murphy Residence, Alex speaking." He listened for a moment, then said, "Yes, he is. Just a moment, please." He quickly handed the receiver over to Austin with a concerned look on his face.

"Austin speaking, go ahead." As he spoke, he attempted to untangle the twisted, coiled cord that was attached to the old, princess-style handset but gave up after several frustrating seconds.

"Hey Austin, it's Trip."

"Hi, Trip! What's shakin'?" Austin could hear loud music thumping in the background of Trip's phone call.

"I'm just down at Frostbite Fred's," Trip said, speaking loudly.

"I know, I heard!" Trip was at the local sports pub on the main highway, one of his favourite after-work haunts.

"Sorry, it's a little loud here, it's open mic night!" Trip raised his voice a little bit more to be heard. "Anyway, so check this out; the door flies open and in staggers Willy Wilson Junior blabbering away about a monster trying to eat him. He was white as a sheet. Looked like he had some pretty severe frostbite on his hands and probably his feet as well."

"Really? Did he say when or where this happened?"

"Well, the only thing I caught was that he'd been out in the bush somewhere, something about a cave, and I think he said his dad, Willy Senior, got attacked and eaten by some kind of creature. Said he was almost killed, too, but got away while it ate his dad. He was pretty incoherent."

"Jesus! Did you get a chance to talk to him?"

"No, but I saw the shape he was in and got on my cell right away to call Emergency Health Services. Anyway, as the kid was talking, Oscar Olsen, who I neglected to mention was off duty and having a few drinks at the pub as well, gets on his cell phone right away and starts having an animated discussion with someone on the other end. I thought maybe he was calling EMS, too. The kid was still rambling pretty badly at this point."

"If it wasn't EMS he called, then who was it? The station for an on-duty member to respond?"

"That's the thing. After Olsen gets off his phone, he saunters up behind the kid, slaps his cuffs on him and drags him off to the manager's office saying he's high on drugs and disturbing the peace. The really interesting part about all this was ten minutes later, instead of the on-duty cop responding, it was Chief VanDusen himself who showed up!"

"Now that is interesting!"

"Yeah, I thought you'd like to be kept up to speed about the latest developments. So anyway, Olsen directs VanDusen to the manager's office where the kid was stowed. The Chief goes in to interrogate him, but a few minutes after he gets into the office, the paramedics that I called show up. They mosey in and sedate the kid and haul him out on a stretcher. I don't know if VanDusen found out many details about whether it was that thing from the ridge or not."

"Very interesting. Okay, thanks very much, Trip. By the way, the weather office said the fog is supposed to be a little thinner in the morning, so I'm hoping to do some boom-boom with Baby tomorrow. I'll see you at around 0700 at the yard, okay? But if you could clock in a little before that to hook her up, that'd be great."

"You bet, Boss. I'll catch you on the flip-side."

"Tomorrow, my friend," Austin said, ending the call.

Alex, overhearing part of the conversation, said, "What's happening with Uncle Trip, Dad? Something about the raccoon?"

"Something like that. I'll know more in the morning, hopefully. Let's eat our grub and then catch the game," Austin said, referring to the hockey game that was coming on in a few minutes.

"Awesome!" Alex said, dishing out mounds of spaghetti. With a final ladle of pasta on top of the mountain already on Austin's plate, one of the meatballs made a break for the edge of the table.

Austin caught the meatball lightly in the palm of his right hand just as it was rolling off the precipice toward its doom. "Almost like the song there for a second," Austin said with a laugh, placing the ball back on his plate.

"Sorry?" his son inquired. Then sudden realisation dawned on Alex before Austin could respond and he laughed, saying, "Almost rolled off the table and out of the door, and nobody even sneezed!"

Austin laughed again, but as he did, he noted the meandering, red-sauced trail the ball of meat left behind on the white Formica kitchen table. Without warning, his memory flashed scenes of the gore-coated ground at the campsite onto the back of his mind, and his appetite suddenly took a rain-cheque for the dinner that sat on the table before him.

CHAPTER SIXTEEN

Despite the fog, the Bonanza Buffet at the Golden Nugget Casino and Resort had hosted a Friday night dinner crowd that kept things jumping in the kitchen all night long. Time had gone quickly for Dan Lewis, but he was still glad the kitchen was finally closing down for the evening. This was his last garbage run, involving a large bucket of used oil from the deep fryer he had to run out to the reclaim barrel. When he was done, he had places to be and new worlds to conquer. Visions of himself kicking back and kicking ass suddenly filled his head. In his car sat a new MMORPG that he'd picked up at the Gas 'n' Gulp on his way to work. Now, he just wanted to get things done and was in a hurry to get home, play the game, and ruin his friends.

Pulling open the metal door leading to the back parking lot, Dan surveyed the shifting grey void before him. "Damn, this shit is thicker than pea soup, man," he said, unconsciously paraphrasing one of his Grandpa Frank's favourite expressions. The fog was indeed so thick this evening that he could barely see the reclaim barrel down at the corner of the building.

The heavy metal delivery door creaked in its frame as it settled against the faded yellow Dairyland Milk crate Dan wedged underneath the bottom corner. The last thing he needed right now was for the door to slam into his ass and have him make like the Exxon Valdez all over the place again. It was a trick he'd learned on his very first shift, just after he'd had to clean the slippery slop off of the ground, the walls, and himself.

Turning, he grabbed the handle of the hefty white plastic pail behind him and dragged it forward, then paused for a moment before continuing on his final journey. He momentarily enjoying the warmth of the oil steaming between his legs before venturing into the chilly evening.

Somewhere across the mist-filled parking lot sat his 1981 Turbo Trans-Am, invisible for the moment, veiled by the shifting greyness. He thought about the video game sitting on the cracked leather passenger seat of his car and smiled — he'd be transported to another world soon enough when he was done in this one.

Dan's smile oxidised as he thought of the bodywork he still had to do on the rusty Trans-Am. He'd been slowly restoring it, telling everyone how he was going to make it better than new. He hoped by summer he'd have most of the work done and all of the rust patches fixed so that he would no longer have to suffer the indignity of having Chef Murray call his classic ride, 'tetanus on wheels'.

As if on cue, perceptible for a few brief moments through a gap in the swirling mist, the car appeared. Dan ran his eyes lovingly over the sweeping curves of the vehicle's distinctive outline. It sat bathed in a golden halo by a single, humming, sodium-vapour light cycling on and off high above. After burning brightly for a minute or so, the ailing light would fizzle and pop as its ancient circuits overloaded, causing it to dim to a level more appropriate to a corner table in a romantic bistro rather than the primary source of lighting for an entire darkened parking lot.

Next to Dan's Pontiac, its box-like shape no less distinctive in the swirling fog, sat a large, green garbage dumpster. Being the new guy in the kitchen, Dan had the honour of getting assigned the crappiest parking spot on the lot, which just happened to be located right next

door to the puke-coloured refuse bin. He was more than happy his
current cargo was not across the treacherous, black-iced lot.

He inhaled, then slowly exhaled and leaned forward. With his
shoulders hunched, he gripped the bucket's handle in both hands and
lifted it with a grunt. Laden pail dangling between his legs, Dan waddled
toward the reclaim. Every few metres, his feet would lose traction on the
large, unsanded patches of ice underneath the eaves of the building.
Puddles of water, formed by the daytime melting of icicles hanging from
clogged gutters overhead, froze into unintended skating rinks at night.
They rarely saw any sand or salt — it was just another excellent example
of Ray Chance's budgetary cutbacks.

"This is slippery as shit, Ray!" Dan observed out loud as he slipped
and slid his way along the side of the building. Arriving at the reclaim,
the light overhead started spazzing out, threatening to extinguish itself at
any moment and leave him in the dark.

"I'm batting a thousand tonight!" he said, shaking his head. Dan
noted with annoyance that the oil reclaim barrel shared something in
common with the garbage bin across the way; they both had a shitty,
piece-of-crap light overhead that Ray Chance was too cheap to replace.
Some nights, when he ventured out into the poorly lit parking lot, a pail
of oil or bag of garbage in hand, Dan wondered if it might be his last.

Up until last October, he used to joke that his biggest fear was that he
might get jumped by some starving forest creatures for the food scraps
he was carrying — perhaps duped by a cunning coyote, or maybe rolled
by a pack of rummaging raccoons.

The previous fall, however, Dan discovered the reality of the situation
to be quite a bit different. It did a lot to remind him of where he was
working — in a restaurant in the woods, in the middle of nowhere,
pouring more delicious smelling refuse into a garbage bin already

overflowing with remnants of smorgasbords past. It was something that was bound to attract the wrong kind of attention, eventually.

**

The late October evening had been just like any other at the kitchen, apart from it being a particularly busy one. After a rather frenetic evening, Dan had been slogging the last bag of still-warm scraps and slop out to the battered garbage dumpster to add it to the other bags he'd deposited several hours earlier. As he slid the huge, black bag along the ground, it left a slimy trail behind on the asphalt, as if an enormous gastropod had just dragged itself across the darkened parking lot during one of the sodium-vapour light's intermittent down cycles. "It Came From Beyond The Dumpster," he said, ominously, laughing at his own joke.

Dan paused for a moment before reaching the bin, the big bag resting next to his legs. He pulled out his pocket vaporiser. Tonight, it was loaded with a particularly potent strain of West Coast Indica shatter that Dan liked to wind down with at the end of the evening. He inhaled deeply and felt the high-THC concentrate flood into his bloodstream from his lungs, swimming into his head and giving him the floaty feeling that he liked so much. With his vaporiser, he was able to get there in seconds, as opposed to minutes with a joint — joints being so twentieth century of course. It was not lost on him that the easy convenience of such a high-potency drug was not something particularly conducive to his retaining gainful employment, and Dan's spotty work history could attest to that.

Exhaling a cloud of vapour, Dan sighed, grabbed the no longer steaming bag and dragged it the last few metres to the bin. Everything was as he'd left it, sort of. He thought he'd locked the bin, or at least put the security bar down, yet there it sat, one of its thick metal lids in the up and open position. There was also a slight chance that some of the potent marijuana may have clouded his memory and he may have forgotten to lock it, but he was pretty sure he'd closed it at the very least.

He shrugged.

Bending down, he hefted the heavy bag with both arms, its semi-liquid contents gurgling and squelching near his face in a most alarming manner. He silently prayed he hadn't put a hole in the bag as he'd dragged it along the pavement. As he was about to tip it in, a sound came from inside the container — a cracking noise, like somebody popping their knuckles. Slowly placing the bag back on the ground, he stood on tiptoes to take a gander inside the open lid.

The flickering light of the sodium-vapour high overhead was now almost at its peak, much like Dan. Two sparks of glittering light were reflected back at him from within the darkened dumpster. Looking more closely, he suddenly realised the sparks were a pair of gleaming, brown, close-set eyes. They blinked once, and another loud crack reverberated from within the dumpster.

Dan jolted back, choking down a scream. He tripped over his feet and went down hard on his buttocks. Not looking or caring where he was going, he scrambled backward like a crab at low tide, his eyes never leaving the open lid of the bin.

Inside the dumpster, sitting atop a small mountain of spoiled food was a rather large black bear. It poked its head out of the bin momentarily, as if curious to see what all the ruckus was about. Hanging from the corner of its mouth was a bone from the previous day's prime-rib roast. It blinked its beady brown eyes at Dan a couple more times, then sat back down inside the bin to continue its evening repast. A new series of snaps and cracks emanated from inside the bin as it enjoyed the bone's marrow.

What Dan didn't realise was that the bear was currently more interested in eating the big pile of tasty garbage it was sitting on rather than chasing him down and ravaging him. Nevertheless, he leapt to his feet, spun a one-eighty that would have made Tony Hawk proud, and tore his skinny ass back toward the main building.

"Antoine! Antoine!" The heavy metal door collided against the concrete wall as Dan flew through the kitchen entrance. He stumbled to a stop, turned and slammed the door shut. As he locked the door, he shouted over his shoulder into the room, "There's a huge fucking bear in the garbage bin! I don't know how it got in there, but it's eating the garbage right now, and it almost ate me, too!"

Kitchen manager Antoine DePascal stood, rubbing his head and listening to the kid. He had just been cleaning out the deep fryer when the kid exploded into the room. Not a man prone to being jumpy, thanks to his large size, he'd nevertheless cracked his head a good one as he'd jerked back involuntarily, startled by the racket. And now Dan stood before him, an expectant look on his face, still panting slightly, his messenger job done and his near-death experience related.

Taking his oversized hand from the growing lump on the top of his head, Antoine briefly scratched his fingers through his bushy, black beard and asked, "Finished?"

"W-w-what do you mean?" Dan stammered, still nervous from his recent encounter.

"Is that it? Are you sure there isn't anything else you'd like to tell me?" He cocked one of his thick eyebrows slightly.

"N-no!" Dan looked away from Antoine's penetrating gaze, feeling the guilt surge in him as he suddenly remembered not locking the bin. And then he remembered why; it was the same reason he usually forgot to do things each shift at the kitchen and elsewhere in his life, and the reason he had gone through six jobs in the last twelve months.

With a heavy sigh, Antoine grabbed a ladle and an empty cast iron frying pan off of the stove. He unlocked the back door and marched out into the faint, flickering light that bathed the isolated parking lot.

Holding the frying pan aloft over his two hundred and five-centimetre tall head, Antoine began clanging the ladle against it. He boomed out, "Get the fuck out of here, you big, ugly, hairy bastard or I'll make a goddamned fur coat out of you!"

As Dan watched, he realised he wasn't sure how hungry the bear might be and didn't know whether or not it might challenge Antoine if it were starving.

DePascal advanced toward the bear in the bin, continuing his performance. He was a hard-muscled slab of a man that you'd be a fool to reckon with. Most sensible people would cross to the other side of the road if they saw Antoine approaching them with anything other than a smile on his face.

Dan remembered wondering at the time, how anyone, or anything, wouldn't be running like hell, upon seeing Antoine advancing toward them so menacingly while shouting at full volume and whacking a frying pan with a ladle as he was.

With the sound of claws scraping against steel, Dan had his answer. The black bruin's head popped out of the high, green bin, not unlike an oversized bear-in-the-box, no cranking required, Dan thought with a giggle.

Upon seeing the spectacle of this black-bearded man-mountain coming toward it and making such noise, the hungry hairball decided to conclude its evening buffet and move on to greener dumpsters.

Scrambling out of the bin, the bear balanced on the lip for just a moment before tumbling forward and landing on its head, temporarily stunning itself.

This brought a roar of laughter from Antoine and Dan's smile suddenly faltered. Somehow, the sound of Antoine's delight was even more terrifying to him than the discord of his aggressive shouting and noisemaking toward the bear.

After a brief moment, the animal sat up and shook its head, gaining its senses as well as its feet. It bugged out without a backward glance, shooting up the mountainside behind the resort faster than a Greyhound with a hambone to bury.

Seeing that his ear-ringing display of bravado was a success, Antoine lowered the frying pan and ladle to his side and watched the bear scamper off, a grin faintly visible through his thick black beard. He turned to Dan and said, "And that, young Padawan, is how you get rid of bears!"

Still shaking slightly from the adrenaline that coursed through his body, Dan said, "Thanks a lot, Antoine! That was amazing! That thing scared the shit out of me!"

Holding the frying pan at his side and using the ladle to scratch the middle of his muscular back with the other, Antoine said, "And exactly how do you think that bear got into the dumpster in the first place, Dan?"

Realising that the jig was up, but still not wanting to admit fault, Dan sputtered, "I locked it, I swear, really!"

"Hmm… I see," Antoine rumbled as he turned back toward the kitchen. Over his shoulder, he said, "Bears out in the forest are packing lockpicks now, are they?

***

Since that evening, Dan had been religious in his locking of the bin. But half the time he was doing it in the dark due to the malfunctioning sodium-vapours. And despite Antoine's requests for upgrades to the electrical out back, Ray Chance hadn't responded, and neither light had seen any maintenance over the winter. Dan had left an anonymous note to Chance as well, after his close encounter in the fall, saying reliable lighting in the staff parking lot would be a fantastic thing, but nothing had been done. Now, whenever he went out there, he was never really sure what was happening with the lights. Sometimes, they appeared to be performing another feat of electrifying psychedelic wonderment for his amusement. But at other times, he wasn't sure if they were going to crap out entirely and leave him in the dark as they finally shuffled off this mortal coil and joined Tesla in the Great Electrical Hereafter.

Not wearing a jacket, Dan shivered from the cold, moist air that swirled about him. The ageing sodium-vapour over his head suddenly crackled and buzzed, jolting him back to the present. He looked up at the light with loathing — God, how he hated that buzz. It sounded as if a hive of hungry mechanical bees had colonised the sodium-vapour and were now waiting impatiently to suck up the next delivery of dirty oil being delivered to the barrel. Ever since that thought had first popped into his head when he'd started working at the restaurant last fall, his skin crawled whenever he heard that psychosis-inducing sound.

Dan was still smart enough to know that whenever he had to go out back, he usually found time for a quick blaze with his vape behind the dumpster, and that definitely wasn't helping his paranoia. Maybe the pot was making him schizophrenic, too. He'd read about that happening to some people. He shrugged. Whether it did or it didn't was of little consequence, doing little to dissuade him from maintaining his buzz and personal goal of staying higher than the CN Tower at all times. He took another hit off his vape, rubbing his thumb lovingly over a recent engraving of the iconic Toronto building on one corner.

In addition to dealing with the shitty lighting, there was one other reason Dan loathed dumping the used oil into the collection drum at the end of his shift. It seemed he would inevitably spill some of the crap all over his kitchen issued whites. More times than not, even in the brightest, clearest of daylight, he would invariably screw up and accidentally pour some of the oil all over his shirt, pants and shoes.

And he didn't need to catch hell from Antoine, again tonight — the man was already cranky enough because of the broken cooler. When Dan had left the kitchen on his latest oil run, Antoine had been cursing away in Quebecois, doing a final wipe down of the malfunctioning cooler unit. Only recently discovered, it had broken down the day before and gone unnoticed, until earlier this evening. Antoine was not happy about this and had let everyone still on shift at the time know it.

Inside of the cooler had been over ninety kilograms of room temperature, organic prime-rib roasts, dripping blood and juices from their brown, butcher paper wrappers. No, Antoine was not a happy man at the moment. Not only was it a smelly, sticky mess to clean, but Dan knew DePascal hated having to throw out that much expensive food. Just a half-hour ago while helping with the clean-up, Dan had lugged two big bags of the spoiled meat along with wads of blood-soaked paper towel out to the dumpster. Happy now to be smelling old cooking oil instead of garbage bags full of rotting meat, Dan sighed and heaved the heavy bucket of oil up to the edge of the reclaim barrel. He paused for a moment and then started to pour the oil carefully into the drum.

Over his head, the ageing sodium-vapour suffered another electrical overload and dimmed to somewhere just above the level of dead.

"Shit!"

It was what Dan Lewis called 'Lewis Luck'. Somehow, the old sodium-vapour had chosen this very moment to do its imitation of the dark side of the sun, right in the middle of his pour — it was typical, really. He continued pouring blindly, his only illumination now provided by the other failing sodium-vapour over the garbage bin across the foggy lot. Finishing up as best he could, he put the bucket down, stood and tried to scope out his clothes for oil spots in the dim light, but it was too dark to see.

"Can't see a goddamned thing," he muttered, shaking his head. He pulled out his cell phone, set the camera flash to torch mode and then scanned himself from head to toe. Tonight, it would seem, he was on a roll. Despite his blind-pour of the used oil, when he stepped back from the barrel and checked himself out, he was surprised to see that he was still completely oil-free. It looked like he wouldn't be degreasing himself for a half-hour after work tonight because of another disastrous pour.

"Fuck yeah!" New confidence filled Dan's voice. This had to be a good omen for his upcoming video game marathon. His buddies were going to be in for a rough night if his newfound 'mad skills' at oil pouring were any indication.

Bending to grab the empty white pail, Dan took one last, longing look in the direction of his car, faintly outlined in the fog by the light of the remaining sodium-vapour lamp. The more he looked, the more he realised that something didn't seem quite right about the foggy silhouette of the garbage bin located next to his car.

In fact, it seemed all wrong.

He tilted his head back and forth, trying to dope things out from a distance. The light over the bin suddenly flared, going supernova, then dropped down to a deep amber glow, emulating its dim twin over his head. Out of his own mental darkness, Dan's internal light bulb flickered on, and he finally tumbled as to what was different about the dumpster.

The lid was up — and that was impossible because he'd locked it — he knew that for a fact.

"What the hell?"

From where he stood, peering through the shifting fog, one half of the lid appeared to be standing wide open. Maybe somebody had cut the lock, popped the cover, and scrambled into the bin, searching for some tasty treats, perhaps? With a slight snicker, Dan hoped that whoever they were, that they enjoyed the smell of spoiled meat.

His grimace suddenly flatlined, and his eyes widened as he remembered the video game he'd left sitting out in plain sight, naked and exposed on the passenger seat of his car. The more he thought about it, the more freaked-out he became, thinking about his game being stolen by potential garbage/video game thieves. He decided he needed to check things out before heading back into the kitchen. But he was torn — part of him reluctant to venture across the foggy lot to see what had been screwing around with the garbage bin. His sense of self-preservation was now standing up on its hind legs and baying, trying to make him pay attention to it.

Despite his reluctance to do so, Dan moved hesitantly across the slippery lot, dragging the empty grease pail behind him. The closer he got to the garbage bin, the more he saw what was wrong with it, and he felt his newfound confidence level begin to fade like the overhead light only moments before.

As if welcoming Dan to the scene, the sodium-vapour began brightening, awakening from its recent slumber. Dan saw that the lid wasn't actually open but was in fact still closed. The security bar was down and in the locked position, the hardened steel padlock still securing it.

Dan dropped the grease bucket. It wobbled around on its bottom rim for a moment before falling over and rolling toward the green dumpster, stopping just as it lightly brushed the closest corner.

"Holy shit…" Dan Lewis stood motionless, looking in stunned disbelief at the back corner of the steel bin, his mouth hanging agape. The thick metal lid had been peeled back like a sardine can from the rear corner near the hinge. It jutted up, creased at an almost perfect ninety-degree angle. The dumpster's guts hung from this mortal wound; bag after heavy-duty garbage bag torn asunder, their tasty innards picked clean and the rest scattered across the icy lot. Definitely not the work of dumpster divers.

From taking machine shop in high school, Dan knew it took tremendous force to bend a sheet of twelve-gauge steel like the bin's lid without a press or pneumatic ram. And yet something had folded back the entire corner of the quarter centimetre-thick lid as if it were only a flimsy cardboard pizza box from his refrigerator at home — torn open during some half-stoned, way-too-early-to-be-straight, Sunday morning feeding frenzy.

What in the hell could have done this? His breath hitched in his chest as a thought suddenly occurred to him. Dan held his breath for a moment, listening intently. He could hear the cartilage grinding in his neck as he slowly panned his head back and forth, but there was no other sound apart from that.

In a moment of panic-primed perspicacity, he realised how isolated he was, surrounded by fog on all sides in the middle of an ice-slicked parking lot, with not another living soul in sight. He decided that he didn't want to stick around to see if the thing that had ripped open the bin was going to come back for another snack of garbage. He grabbed for the car keys stuffed in his front pocket, thinking it best to burn some rubber as he fled this popsicle stand at very high speed, ASAP.

And then he paused. Job security, combined with his desire to eat food on occasion, told Dan that he'd better let Antoine know what had happened. Pivoting on one heel, he fell face-forward over the now-forgotten grease bucket, slamming his knee onto the ice as he landed. The bucket went spinning across the ice and vanished, swallowed by the billowing fog.

"Bastard!" Dan said, trying to stand, but felt his knee give him a shot of white-hot pain and he slipped back to the ice once more. After several tense, slippery seconds, he finally regained his feet, his breath coming in ragged gasps. He was no longer trying to hear anything, and hoped not to hear anything, as he limped, slid and stumbled back toward the relative safety of the kitchen and its thick steel door. He didn't care if anything heard him either; he just wanted to get back to safety.

Dan shrieked as he scrambled through the still-open delivery door. "Antoine! There's a problem out back! Oh, holy shit, do we have a big problem!" He spun and slammed the heavy door shut, twisting the deadbolt home with such force that it seemed he might break it off.

Antoine DePascal stood slowly from the cooler, rubbing the back of one blood-smeared hand along the side of his equally blood-smeared forehead. He sighed. Standing before him was the kid, a wild look in his eyes, again. He knew he was going to have to deal with some more of the kid's shit and sighed a second time, then said, "What the hell did you do? Spill the grease bucket all over the place, again?"

"N-no! Some thing broke into the garbage bin!"

DePascal frowned, "What do you mean; some 'thing' broke into the bin? How do you know it wasn't a bear again?"

Still short of breath from his running and shouting, Dan paused before replying, "T-That's what I mean. It must have been some 'thing' that broke into the dumpster, because of all the bending of the metal, don't you understand! There's no way it was a bear! And there's garbage all over the place!"

"Did you forget to lock it, again?" Anger growled in his DePascal's voice.

"No sir — I mean yes-sir, I locked it!"

Antoine furrowed his heavy brow. "How could something get into that dumpster? Those things are bear-proof! You must have forgotten, and some starving coyote got in there or maybe a dog."

"No, sir! I remember locking it one hundred percent just after the first seating clean-up!"

This evening, he definitely remembered putting the security bar down and locking it. Since his encounter last fall, he'd decided he didn't want to attract anything wilder than himself when he was taking out yet another bag of smelly garbage to the trash.

He continued, "And you still don't get it! Like I said before, it's STILL LOCKED!" he shouted at Antoine, his voice a mixture of fear and frustration. Dan finished, "The lid's been bent over at the back corner near the hinge — just ripped open like a tuna can!"

"You mean sardine can? That's impossible!" Antoine folded one blood-smeared arm over the other and stood, poised in doubt.

"It's true! Go and see for yourself then!"

"Can't you see I'm still busy?"

"But…"

"The garbage bin lid was most likely defective; you know how old that thing is getting. It's just about as rusted as your goddamned car and probably falling to as many pieces!" Antoine couldn't resist a barb at the expense of the kid's rust-bucket of a ride. He concluded, saying, "It was probably damaged during the last garbage pickup, but you were just too damned stoned to notice! Did you ever think of that?"

"Well…" Dan doubted this line of reasoning but knew there had been times in his life where he'd forgotten a thing or two or didn't notice something because of his pot use, but this wasn't one of them. "I'm super sure…"

DePascal held up a hand and interrupted Dan, saying, "The only thing I want you to be 'super sure' of right now is your ability to pick up the garbage you said is strewn all around outside! Now get the fuck back out there and cleanup the goddamned mess this bear made!"

Dan stared at him, incomprehension clouding his face. "But Antoine!" A tremor of fear filled his voice, "I told you it couldn't be a bear! And what if it comes back and it's still hungry?"

DePascal grumbled, "You'll be fine. It's probably miles away from here by now."

"Can't I just…"

"Yes, you can!" Antoine said with feigned enthusiasm. "Look, here's a flashlight!" DePascal grabbed a magnetic emergency light plugged into one of the kitchen wall sockets and shoved it into the kid's hands. He finished the conversation, saying, "Now, if you don't get the hell out there right now and clean up that mess, you can go ahead and hang up your apron."

Dan knew that his boss didn't mean he'd be done for the day; and that he could hang his kitchen whites up in his locker and go home and relax while Antoine cleaned the mess. No, he knew that it meant he'd be fired. And that meant no more car repairs, or video games or mind-altering substances.

DePascal took only a handful of steps on long legs to cross the kitchen and unlock the door, opening it wide. Still limping slightly from his fall, Dan Lewis moved slowly through the doorway, reluctantly heading outside once more. He turned to look back. DePascal stood behind him in the doorway, watching him go. "You'll be fine!" he shouted encouragingly, then slammed the heavy door shut.

Dan sighed and slowly angled across the ice-glazed parking lot toward the large, green dumpster. Shining the light about, he could see nothing in the greyness that surrounded him and clicked it off again.

The sodium-vapour light overhead crapped out just as he arrived at the bin, leaving him standing in dim, jaundiced-yellow light. Dan held his breath again and repeated his imitation of a radar dish, tilting his head this way and that, as he listened for any sign of something lurking out there, just beyond sight.

There was no sound. Dead silence was his new companion.

Though the mist impaired his sight, Dan's other four senses were working overtime, and he felt more isolated than ever. The freezing fog settled onto his exposed skin as he stood listening, making him shiver. After many seconds, feeling ready to burst, he exhaled all at once then took in great coughing lungfuls of air. He gagged on the dense mist that filled his mouth, throat and lungs. The combined taste and smell of rotting meat remnants from the scattered trash bags at his feet was nauseating. He gagged once more, feeling ready to hurl.

"Son of a bitch! Why is it, every gig I get, I'm the low man on the totem pole stuck doing these shit jobs," he wondered aloud to the swirling fog. "Goddamned Lewis Luck," he concluded. Placing the flashlight on the ground next to the damaged half of the garbage bin, he pulled out his keys. He removed the padlock and pulled the security bar down, then opened the metal lid covering the other side. Crouching down to pick up the slimy buffet scraps, Dan grabbed one disgusting chunk after another. He tossed them over his shoulder into the bin without looking, presuming they'd make it inside as he worked his way around.

"Shit, shit, shit," he muttered.

Scowling as he tried to pick up a particularly slithery piece of gristle, Dan felt a drop of liquid hit his neck but wiped it off and continued work. After a moment, another, more substantial drop splashed onto his neck. He looked upward at the anaemic glow of the sodium-vapour and screamed, "Shitty freakin' light!"

It seemed that when the light wasn't making him play Stevie Wonder in the darkness, it was making like Niagara Falls and dripping water down his neck. And it wasn't just over at this light with the water, no, it was a problem over near the reclaim barrel as well. He almost always got a splash of water down his neck from the leaky rain gutter when he was over there, too. Just one more thing fanning the flames of his job dissatisfaction, he smiled ruefully. He just couldn't win, and wherever he went, Lewis Luck was all around him. He couldn't seem to shake it — anything that could go wrong did go wrong.

"This is it, I'm so done with this job," he groused. But he kept working, crawling around on his injured knee, feeling it throb as he scuttled about on the hard ice, picking up the last few scraps off the ground. Soon, he found himself on the other side of the garbage bin, well away from the reach of the dripping light. Still on his knees, he reached out, his hand closing on the edge of the last shredded garbage bag. Another dribble spattered down onto his neck, quickly followed by a small torrent of liquid. It was as if the light had moved over top of him while he wasn't looking in order to dribble all over him again. He touched the fluid — warm and slick to the touch, not how the water from melting ice and snow off the lamp usually felt.

As if reading his thoughts, the sodium-vapour overhead crackled and buzzed, surging to life once more. The garbage bag still grasped in one hand, Dan turned and looked up into the light, and his stomach shrivelled into a small, hard ball.

A mountain of matted, grey, fur stood behind him. Thick-muscled shoulders supporting a massive, sharply sloping head peered hungrily down at him through the fog. The beast's mouth flew open and long stringy ropes of saliva splashed down into Dan's upturned face. He stared dumbstruck, frozen to the spot like a deer caught in a car's headlights. Row upon row of spittle-slicked razor teeth gleamed in the now-brightening light of the sodium-vapour, once again surging toward overload.

"Mother-fu…"

The creature's jaws cracked shut, engulfing Dan's upper body. His legs spasmed briefly only once as his thorax and head were ground to paste between powerful jaws. With its prey finally stilled, the beast began to feast.

***

Wiping the last smear of blood from the cooler, Antoine DePascal noticed that Dan still hadn't returned from garbage detail and looked at his watch. The kid had been gone almost half an hour. Enough was enough, he decided. He'd had his fill of the lazy little slacker! If that kid wasn't finished picking up the garbage by the time he got out there, then the little bugger was going to be out of a job!

Antoine stormed out of the kitchen, one of his size fourteen feet booting open the delivery door as he went. It smashed into the red-bricked wall behind. Pausing, he kicked a yellow milk crate out of the way and watched with some satisfaction as it spun across the ice before disappearing into the mist.

The heavy steel door behind him suddenly slammed into its frame as it swung closed. In spite of his size, DePascal flinched at the sudden noise. The kid had been really freaked out about the garbage bin, and it was making him jumpy now that he thought about it. Entering the fog, he began to wonder if maybe there might have been something to what the kid was saying after all.

The bin materialised out of the greyness in front of him. He glanced around, but there didn't seem to be any sign of the kid. The flashlight lay on the ground at the side of the bin. He bent down and picked it up, turning it on — still operational. It looked like the little bastard had buggered off, skipping out on the clean-up job.

"That's fine, play it that way, kid. You're gone!" he shouted. He glanced into the bin to see if the kid was inside, playing hide and seek. God knows, he wouldn't put it past him, but it was empty. He peeked around the corner of the bin, the fog swirling around him as he moved. No Dan there, either. Turning around, he called into the fog, "You never were the brightest bulb on the tree, anyway, you little slacker!"

As if in agreement, the sodium-vapour climaxed toward brilliance once more, then gutted out, suffering another near-death experience.

"Son of a bitch…" Squinting into light the colour of concentrated urine, Antoine saw that the steel lid of the dumpster was indeed bent back, just like the kid had said. It had to have been the work of vandals. But why would they do something like that? He shook his head in disgust. Kids these days.

Speaking of kids, it looked like Dan had missed quite a bit of shit as there still looked to be an awful lot of little bits and pieces scattered about. No garbage bags left on the ground at least, just a quite a few pasty, white scraps. So typical of the half-assed job the kid usually did.

"Lewis! Where the hell are you? Why didn't you finish the job?" he inquired into the fog. "I swear to God, if you're screwing around out here and toking up, then you'll be looking for another job pretty fucking quick because your ass is going to be grass." He smiled into the darkness, thinking the kid's ass was already full of grass.

But Antoine realised it wasn't surprising that Dan had missed some of the garbage back here since the light in the rear lot was dim even when it wasn't foggy, making things pretty easy to overlook in the semi-darkness. This was one of the reasons why he'd been on Chance's ass to get those damned security lights fixed out here over the last few months.

Strangely, the kid's car was still here, parked next to the bin. It looked like he'd recently touched up some of the rust with some sort of new primer, but he'd splashed it all over the side in a very haphazard manner. Sloppy at work and sloppy outside of work was the kid's credo, apparently. Antoine shook his head. But if the kid had screwed off already, why did he leave his car? Then it dawned on him. He probably had a stoner friend of his pick him up because the rust bucket next to the bin wouldn't start, again.

"Didn't even have the decency to quit to my face, the little prick!" DePascal huffed, kneeling down. With a sigh, he tentatively picked up a couple of scraps that the kid had left behind, flicking them up over his head and into the dumpster.

He paused a moment, bathed in the dim, yellow light and bent over further to get a closer look at one of the more significant bits of gristle and bone stuck to the frozen ground. It didn't look like anything that

Chef Murray would have bought and trimmed, or even thrown in the garbage for that matter. As the kitchen manager, Antoine knew the chef would never approve such unappealing cuts of meat. Usually, they carried only prime cuts at the casino kitchen — meat with manly names like Angus or Kobe, nothing at all like this stringy crap on the ground.

"Where the hell did all of this shit come from?" And the stench! It was everywhere. It didn't seem possible the meat could have turned so quickly. Was that goddamned kid dumping his shit from home out here? "Seems like the kind of stunt the little fartwad would pull," he muttered. Suddenly, he felt his back muscles begin to cramp. He was going to have to call it quits for now.

"Well that's it, he's goddamn well fire…" He stopped, and froze, looking more closely at what was stuck to the ground in front of him. It came easily from the ice after a brief tug, and he held it up in front of his face. Turning it over in his hands, he examined it: a long stringy looking chunk that appeared for all the world like…

DePascal dropped the scrap to the frozen parking lot with a gasp of disgust. He backed up, tripping over feet that suddenly seemed far too large and ungainly and he landed on his ample buttocks. He slid backward on the ice, staring in revulsion at the thing he'd touched, but unable to look away. Once he'd put a little distance between himself and the scrap, he stayed sitting on his ass, unable to move, shuddering. Antoine took in deep breaths of ice-cold fog, feeling like he was going to hurl.

On the ground near the dumpster, was not a piece of gristle or meat from the kitchen at all, but a long white thread of tendon, the tip sporting the index, forefinger and thumb of a human hand.

"Jesus Christ!" DePascal said, scuttling farther back into the fog.

A low noise from behind vibrated through his outstretched hands and into his arms, making them tingle where they touched the frozen ground. It was a low bass rumble like Antoine would have felt coming from the subwoofer at home when he watched a movie on his big screen.

He turned and froze. The fog now had teeth and claws. His eyes widened, and he tried to crawl away from the abomination towering over him.

A ponderous weight suddenly came down on top of him, stopping his movement and forcing him into the ice. He wanted to scream, but his vocal cords had been crushed along with most of the vertebrae in his neck. He had been paralysed and rendered mute within a space of two seconds.

Random thoughts shot through his brain as it shut down from the sensory overload. The bones of his skull cracked, splintered and ground against one another, collapsing from crushing external pressure. The pain came in white-hot waves that flooded away all conscious thought, leaving him to drown in a searing sea of misery.

**

Several minutes later, the sodium-vapour light flickered back to full brightness, and the fog thinned momentarily. An empty trash bag blew across the ground, scuttling along on a current of air. It moved over top a large pool of crimson next to the bin, and stuck when it made contact. The edge of the bag fluttered down, covering most of a silver vaporiser lying next to the puddle, leaving only a small picture of the CN Tower exposed on one corner. Two words were engraved on its side: Forever Higher.

CHAPTER SEVENTEEN

Swirling the scotch in his glass for a moment, Mayor Bob Nichols downed the remainder with a loud gulp. He primly placed the heavy lead crystal tumbler onto a circular cork coaster atop his gleaming oak desk. Satisfied it was centred on the coaster he turned his attention to the other side of the desk, adjusting the green glass shade of an antique banker's lamp. Though it was very bright, it did little to illuminate the room, the rich umber-coloured wooden panelling on the walls and heavy drapes absorbing most of the light the small lamp cast. His aged, high-backed office chair creaked in protest as he settled back into its well-worn leather and cleared his throat. "All right, Reggie, carry on with your story."

Chief of Police Reggie VanDusen watched the mayor's fastidiousness, noting with some amusement that he hadn't offered him any form of libation as usual. Of course, after the bad news he'd given His Honour the last time regarding his pay increase, and how poorly the mayor had taken it, it wasn't surprising. Yes, that news was definitely cutting into his fringe benefits. Apparently, the first thing off the list was free booze. He was going to miss that, but not this early in the morning. Reggie reflected with contempt that the man sitting across from him was as much of a lush as his partner, Ray Chance.

VanDusen squinted into the lamp's bright light, having a hard time seeing the mayor across the desk, and blinked several times. When the mayor had adjusted the angle of the lamp, Reggie was pretty sure he'd angled the edge of the lampshade up in just the right way, on purpose. That way, it blinded the person sitting across from him, effectively giving them the third degree as they conversed. It was typical of Nichols, Reggie thought, as the man always wanted to have an advantage over anyone else in the room. He had to give it to the mayor; the man loved his power almost as much as he did.

When VanDusen failed to respond to his prompt right away, Nichols noted the slight smile on the Chief's face and added with annoyance, "And what the hell do you have to smile about, Reggie?"

VanDusen blinked once more and said, "Just thinking of lollipops and rainbows, of course, Mr. Mayor. So anyway, as I was saying, Constable Olsen was at Frostbite Fred's having a drink after work last night, and in staggers Willy Wilson Junior."

"You mean one of the two people that you promised me were officially missing and supposedly taken care of?"

"Yeah, that's them. Anyway, it seems that half of the problem has been 'taken care of', at least."

"Meaning, what?"

"I'm gettin' to that. So, in staggers Junior, frostbitten and rough looking. Must have been wandering in the bush for a while cause it has to be at least fifteen klicks from the cavern down to Fred's."

"And?"

"Olsen says the kid started talking a-mile-a-minute about monsters and stuff. Just freaking out about an animal attack, and how his dad, Willy Senior, is now dead from this thing. Kept going on and on about teeth and claws and blood — Olsen said he just couldn't stop talking about the blood. At any rate, that was starting to freak the customers out as you can imagine. It's at that point that Olsen decided to lock him away in the manager's office for his own good, and ours as well."

"He made no mention of the gold while he was babbling?"

"Nope, he never got that far, just talking about this animal that attacked them before he got carted off to the manager's office by Olsen. All the barflies thought he was strung out on drugs."

"That is good news." The mayor smiled.

"Yeah, that's what I thought. So anyway, since Olsen wasn't officially on duty, he quickly phones me and tells me I'd better get my ass up there to do some damage control before the kid spills the beans about our little mining operation at the cavern." VanDusen hefted his bulk into a more comfortable position, the antique wooden chair protesting his decision.

"So, then what happened?"

"So, I got there about ten minutes later and found the kid still sequestered in the manager's office, ranting and raving to himself."

"Nobody had talked to him?"

"Nope, but just as I started interrogating him, finding out a few interesting tidbits about the operation, I discovered that some goody-two-shoes in the pub had called EMS. In waltz the paramedics and they start to treat the kid's frostbite with some heat packs, which is fine. But then, to treat what they're calling his 'delirium', they dose him up with that damned ketamine cocktail they like to use, effectively shutting down the interrogation."

"And where is he now?"

"In a private room at the hospital recovering. I greased a few palms and told them to keep him sedated until further notice, so you don't have to worry about him for now. At any rate, that's not cheap, as you can imagine, so that's another reason I'm upping my cut, Mr. Mayor — expenses keep going up!"

"Then learn to budget your cut better!" Nichols snapped back.

VanDusen ignored the mayor's outburst, saying, "I don't see why I should be forking over some of my cut to protect the security of the gold in general since you and Chance are getting the lion's share of it. That just doesn't seem quite fair, does it?

"We'll talk about what's fair and what isn't at a later date."

"I'll hold you to your word, Mr. Mayor. Anyway, just before the paramedics got there and doped the kid up, I read him the riot act and told him that if he said anything about the mining at the cavern to anybody, it would be the last time he said anything to anyone. Told him I'd be dropping him down one of those holes in the floor of that cavern and that shut him up pretty quick. A good threat is all it takes to calm a person down, sometimes. Although come to think of it, in the kid's case, I think I'll carry through on the threat — that kid is goddamned annoying! It'd be a treat to hear him screaming for a few minutes on the way down one of those bottomless pits." VanDusen's smile returned brighter than ever. He really liked this new thought of taking the kid on a little road trip back up to the cavern once he was well enough to travel again.

"Reggie, what are you grinning about now? Let's focus for a moment here! Whatever you want to do with the Wilson kid is fine. Now, what other 'interesting tidbits' did he relate to you?"

"Well, as I was telling you until you interrupted me, according to Willy, there's something else up there at the cavern along with the gold. It's sort of a two-for-one deal."

"Really? What else is up there? Is it valuable?" Nichols leaned forward in his chair in anticipation.

"Depends on what kind of value you put on something with lots of teeth and a big appetite. As I mentioned, the kid said something ate his dad, and almost got him, too."

"Do you think it could have been that same thing that Chance hit with his Rover?"

VanDusen sighed, still trying to get comfortable. "Don't know, could be."

"If that's the case, there's nothing to worry about! It's dead! Now we can get things back on track."

"Yeah, that's what I was hoping. But there was one more thing."

"Go ahead, spill it!"

"There was an attack up on the ridge near the cavern a couple days ago."

"Do you think it was that thing with the teeth and claws the Wilson kid was going on about?"

"Maybe, but we don't know for sure — it's a big forest! And we're still waiting for the lab results. But that new conservation bitch pulled a print from the ground there and is convinced it was an attack by some unknown predator and that we'd better warn people about it. Austin

Murphy and his sidekick, Williams were there with her yesterday as well."

"This conservation officer, what did you say his name was again?"

"HER name is Moon! The bitch's name is Christine Moon."

"A female conservation officer?

With a barely concealed sigh of contempt, VanDusen said, "That's what I've been trying to tell you. You met her down in the lobby here at City Hall last week. I was there with you, don't you remember?"

"That sounds vaguely familiar. I thought she was just a new secretary that Carl had hired and didn't pay any particular attention to what she was saying. But I do remember her being very easy on the eyes, however."

"Uh-huh, tell me about it, but she's still a bitch. Anyway, so she was there with Murphy and Williams who'd discovered the campsite the day before when they rescued a possible survivor of this attack. And they're the ones who brought that conservation bitch up there with them!"

"Is the survivor from the camp talking yet?"

"Nope, he's lapsed into a coma for now, though this one is not medically induced like the kid's, yet. But I might add that he is also conveniently located right next door to the Wilson kid." Reggie smiled at the thought of having both his birds in the same bush and his hand in a pot of gold.

"How convenient. And how far away was the attack from the cavern? Is it close enough that they might find our little operation if they start looking about for this beast?"

"Well, it must be about at least five or six clicks away, as the crow flies. Hard to say." VanDusen stood up, his chair groaning with relief. "Well, I can't say that this hasn't been fun, Mr. Mayor, cause it hasn't, but there is one other thing..."

"If it's a problem, I'm sure we can get rid of it," Nichols added, confidently. "What is it?"

"It's that woman, Moon; she's started pushing for a public announcement that we have a killer animal loose in the area."

"Do you think that would jeopardise the extraction?"

VanDusen leaned on the back of his chair and looked down at the mayor. "I was thinking about that for a bit — and actually, it might not. If people are leery of going into the bush, that will keep things under control out there for a while. We could put the entire area into an outdoor activity prohibition lockdown for safety's sake. Then we wouldn't have to worry too much about anybody else stumbling onto our little mine site at the cavern."

"You're right! Just like the avalanche advisories! It may give us a bit more breathing room so that we can ramp up the extraction. Let's go with them on this; if it buys us some time, it could only be a good thing. We'll just have to make sure everyone is extra vigilant in case Ray didn't get lucky with his Rover, and there's still something skulking around in the dark up there."

"All right then, I'll keep an eye on them and let you know what's going on at the cavern."

"Very good! Let them announce the bear story if they want, but you know what to do if they get too close to the truth."

"Absolutely, there's still lots of room up there. I think I can arrange the other three a personal showing if need be. If they accidentally fell down a hole or got caught in a cave in, that would be such a tragedy." VanDusen laughed and turned, trundling out of the office.

"Problem solved." The Mayor of Lawless, British Columbia, sat back in his chair and tented his fingers under his chin, a contemplative smile playing at the corners of his lips.

CHAPTER EIGHTEEN

The fog was quite a bit thinner this morning, and Austin hoped it boded well for the day ahead. It was a few minutes before six o'clock when he rolled his Honda Pilot into the yard. The 105mm howitzer sat attached to the back of the white and green City Works Silverado. Trip had been true to his word, as usual, and got there early to hook up everything. As Austin parked, Trip was making the final adjustments to the safety chains and cables on the gun's trailer.

Hopping out of the Pilot, Austin said, "Good morning and thanks, Trip! I see Baby's all ready for her grand day out."

"Morning, Boss. Yes, she is." Trip said absentmindedly, still playing around with a reluctant safety chain.

"Excellent! Then I'll go get the diapers and formula."

Trip finally looked up from the chains as Austin headed for the shop, his only response, a confused, "Huh?" He went back to work, shaking his head slightly.

Austin Murphy was the only person with the key to the howitzer's ammunition cabinet. Being in charge of such a destructive weapon was a responsibility that he didn't take lightly. He kept the key closely guarded at all times. If something ever happened and the weapon was stolen along with the ammunition, he was on the hook big-time. Entering the workshop, he unhooked a thick ring of keys from his belt as he walked. The shells were kept in a locked gun safe in the rear section of the building with ten-centimetre-long bolts holding it firmly attached to the concrete floor. Even without the bolts, Austin didn't think there was much chance of the safe going anywhere thanks to its four-hundred-kilogram weight. In addition, each of the two dozen shells inside of it, when assembled, weighed in at over forty kilograms each. All together it was over a metric tonne of steel and high explosives. Anybody thinking about liberating the gun and the ammunition safe might want to check themselves for a hernia when they were done, he thought with a smile.

With the safe unlocked, he pulled over a small wheeled cart and loaded five each of the shells, propellant and explosives onto it. There was just a little over two kilograms of military-grade Comp-B, an explosive much more powerful than TNT, ready to be inserted inside each shell. Gently handling the charges, he bedded the gun's deadly diet down in its padded travel case. They didn't keep the shells pre-assembled due to safety concerns during transportation and all of the components travelled in separate cases. Once at the location, they assembled the projectiles just prior to firing. Austin knew all of the safety procedures inside and out. In order for the City to operate it, he'd needed to take an extensive training course covering its safe operation last year before the gun could be purchased.

After a quick transfer to the waiting truck, he rolled the cart back to the shop and secured the roll-up door. Being a Friday, Clara wasn't in until a little after eight, due to her aqua fit class at the community pool. He left a quick note on her desk, outlining his plans for the day, then locked up the shop when done.

Hopping into the Silverado's driver's seat, Austin observed, "Hey! I see we don't need to stop at Timmie's today." Sitting on the console between the seats was a box of doughnuts and two coffees. Trip had sprung for their morning kick-start today. Austin grabbed a chocolate long-john from the box and took a bite, then glanced over, seeing the coffee untouched. Before grabbing the first cup he saw, he made sure to double-check the lid before opening it and taking a sip.

A white grease pencil had been used to write on the top of each cup's dark-brown lid. Thelma, down at the Tim Hortons, was just following standard operating procedure at the restaurant chain. But something that wasn't SOP were the cute little things that Thelma drew and wrote on the lids of the cup she knew Trip was getting. Today, off to one side of the 3C3S on top, sat four little hearts that formed into the shape of a flower with a smiley face in the middle. "Awe, I love your cup today, Trip!" Some days it was flowers, other days a pair of birds (the love kind, presumably). She was really quite a good artist. Now that Austin knew which coffee was the eye-openingly sweet one, he popped the tab open on his own slightly less saccharine cup, labelled with a simple '2C2S', also known as a double-double.

Powering down a cruller, Trip said nothing, only knitting his brows together slightly and blushing harder than usual at the tops of his white-bearded cheeks. He chewed for a moment. "Yeah, she really is kind of keen on me, isn't she?" As he spoke, the crumbs from already consumed crullers settled into his bushy beard like swallows returning to Capistrano.

"You don't know the half of it, brother" Austin said cryptically. Trip raised his eyebrows in question.

Austin didn't elaborate and took his first sip of the hot, bracing brew. Putting the truck in gear, he pulled out of the yard. "Okay, Trip, two places for boom-boom with Baby today. First, we'll be hitting the mountain range near the entrance to the valley."

"That's a good spot, it's usually pretty heavy up there," Trip agreed, tearing into another cruller.

"Yeah, there's some crap I spotted the other day that I want to bring down before it gets too concerning and creates an avalanche risk."

Trip nodded in agreement, still chewing. A small avalanche of his own occurring as cruller crumbs spilled out of his beard and onto the lid of the coffee cup in his hand.

"After that, we'll be heading up to Gold Ridge to bring down a little bit of the frosty, white goodness hanging around that neck of the woods, weather cooperating that is."

Trip continued to nod, chew and sip his coffee. Austin saw he was down to serious business now and not prone to talking when deep into enjoying a fresh cruller.

"We'll be working with traffic control on this, as usual. Clara contacted Lenny over at Ruby Roads yesterday to be standing by this morning to cleanup whatever comes down on our side." Ruby Roads was a local excavating company that the City worked with whenever they needed to move a bunch of snow, dirt, or rocks quickly. This was especially true when the City of Lawless's heavy equipment resources and workforce weren't sufficient for a larger job like this. Turning the wipers on to wipe away some of the light mist on the windshield, Austin asked, "You remembered the walkie-talkies, right?"

"Gob 'em, Boff" Trip mumbled, speaking around a mouthful of cruller and unleashing another small torrent of crumbs. With the thumb of his cruller-free hand, he pointed over his shoulder to the back seat of the truck where he'd stowed the radios.

"I'll take that as a big ten-four, good buddy!" Austin said. Trip, still chewing, gave him a thumbs up.

On the drive up to the first avalanche control station on the far side of the valley, the fog was indeed thinner this morning, Austin noted with some hope. He pondered the day ahead as he wound the truck up the meandering snow-covered road. If they could get the first ridge knocked down and cleared in the next couple of hours, then they should be good to clear the spot over Gold Ridge with plenty of daylight remaining.

Out of the haze ahead, their destination appeared. It looked like Larry had been on top of things and the concrete platform from which the gun was fired had been scraped bare by his plow. Austin pulled the truck around and backed the trailer up to it.

Trip climbed down from the truck and walked around to the trailer. He dropped the stabiliser legs and engaged the wheel locks on the howitzer at the same time. Thanks to his previous test sessions at the quarry with Austin, he knew it was imperative the gun didn't move when fired. The thing kicked harder than a bull moose in rutting season, and he didn't want it going anywhere. Stepping back, he took a moment to get a better look at the howitzer. He still didn't think they should be calling this thing a 'gun'. It was more like a cannon, what with the high explosive-tipped shells and deafening noise involved when it was fired. Nope, Trip thought, a gun, this thing ain't. He returned to the cab and grabbed the ammo locker that contained the explosives while Austin off-loaded the shell casings. Working together off of the reinforced tailgate of the truck, they assembled a projectile.

Austin placed the brass casing upright in a specially designed holder attached to the top of the ammo locker, saying gently, "Time to get Baby's formula ready."

Trip rolled his eyes and placed the Comp-B propellant inside the casing.

"Okay now, let's put your hat on so you don't catch a cold," Austin said, carefully screwing the explosive head onto the long brass cylinder. When done, he said, "All right! Let's feed Baby!"

With a long-suffering sigh, Trip said, "Let's lock and load," and cracked open the breech of the gun.

Austin inserted the assembled shell and Trip locked it down. They were primed and ready to go. With a high five, Trip said, "Like a well-oiled machine, my man! Boo yeah!"

Smiling enthusiastically, Austin said, "Okay, time to piss some people off!" He pulled a radio from his belt and called Ruby Roads. "Lenny! It's Austin. Over!"

"Hey, Austin! How's it going, big shooter? Over," came the crackled response from the radio's small speaker.

"We're ready to rumble, Lenny! Over!"

"You got it, bud, one traffic jam coming up! Over and out." Traffic would be unable to move through the pass temporarily while they waited to see the volume of snow that came down in the controlled avalanche. The heavy equipment would have to come in next to clear it, usually resulting in wait times of over two hours.

Looking through the thin fog, Austin aimed the gun's sight at the mountain peak in the distance and dialled in the coordinates he'd made a note of the previous day at the forest lookout. It was all a matter of degrees when shooting a weapon like this, and you had to be precise. His instructor had told him that if you were off by even a fraction of a degree, due to the distance the shell had to travel before it hit its mark, you could miss your target by several kilometres. And Austin didn't want any errant explosive shells raining down from the sky anywhere other than on the exact spot at which he was aiming.

They were ready for their first official use of the gun. Donning their ear protectors, Austin flipped Trip a quick thumbs up and shouted, "Fire in the hole!"

Standing well off to one side, Austin pulled the lanyard attached to the firing lever with a quick jerk of his hand. Despite his training and previous testing with the howitzer, and knowing what to expect from the gun, he was still shocked by the noise and vibration that pulling that one small piece of synthetic rope had unleashed.

With a burst of blinding brilliance and a bone-rattling bang, Austin felt every fibre of his being vibrate from the gun's concussive blast.

Standing on the other side of the Howitzer, Trip felt the fillings rattle in his mouth and his vision blur for a split second as the gun's shockwave battered him. If he and Austin had not been wearing their ear protection just now, they would have surely been deafened.

After a couple of seconds, faintly visible through the light fog and cloud, the shell hit the peak, and a plume of snow erupted from the ridge. Milliseconds later, an enormous BOOM echoed across the valley as the sound of the projectile's explosive payload washed over their position.

Austin grinned as the shell landed precisely where he'd aimed, but his smile faded when nothing further happened. There was no sign of any snow moving down the side of the mountain, except for a small trickle where the shell had hit.

"Okay, then, round two!" Austin said, adjusting the gun's sight a fraction of a degree to the right. Trip began preparing another round as Austin sighted the gun. With the recalibration complete, everything was locked and loaded once more.

"Fire in the hole!" Austin shouted, tugging the rope. The gun's blast battered them once more, and they watched the mountain peak in the distance with anticipation. The shell struck the hard-packed ice and snow on the ridge, and this time it found its mark. A large sheet of snow broke away from the mountaintop and rumbled down the mountainside, coming to rest amongst some trees near its base.

"Woo-hoo!" Austin said, high-fiving Trip with his gloved hand. That was precisely the result he wanted to see, and he was more than pleased. The new howitzer was a success, providing a much better outcome than the old air cannon. He was confident that they wouldn't have any issues this winter with snow closing the road down as had happened in previous years — barring any more earthquakes, that was, part of his mind thought darkly.

"Okay, my friend, let's pack it up here and head to Gold Mountain. Hopefully, the visibility there is as good at the ridge as it was here."

"You got it, Boss." Trip began retracting the stabilisers and locking the gun back down for transport.

Austin looked at his wristwatch; it was 8:55 A.M. "We're doing great today! I'll radio Lenny and tell him we're done here. Once he and his crew have cleaned up, I'll let them go home. We can't use them at Gold Ridge today since they can't get to any of the snow that we bring down in the backcountry up there."

As Austin spoke, Trip looked toward the resort and the glacier that lay beyond it. He wondered what the remainder of the day would bring — more revelations, or revulsion. The way things were going right now, they had a fifty-fifty chance of either, he figured. "More of the first and less of the second, I hope," Trip muttered under his breath, his mouth a grim line beneath his beard.

CHAPTER NINETEEN

With a yawn, Christine rubbed some stubborn sleep from the corner of one eye. She squinted groggily at her cell phone's bright, white screen. She yawned again. Midnight oil had been burned late night last night while she'd gone over some of the information that Zelda had sent her from SFU. This morning, she'd decided to sleep a little later than usual to try and make up for the loss. A quick review of her inbox showed several new alerts pending from Ms. Wolowitz. Didn't that woman ever sleep?

Tea was the first order of the day, Christine decided. Taking the half dozen steps from her bedroom to the galley-style kitchen of her small rental house, she put the kettle on to boil. Opening her email to see what kind of information was upcoming, it appeared several new emails were waiting from her friend. All of them contained multiple exclamation marks. "Looks like the game is afoot," she said, smiling, still thinking of Sherlock Holmes, thanks to Austin.

She sipped her tea as she got ready for the day. Trying to decipher the sometimes-incoherent zoological taxonomy of her friend as she dressed, it all seemed quite astounding. Apparently, the photos of the predator's print from the campsite and the casting she took were a big hit.

Now in a hurry to get going, Christine was eager to delve into the data further on her computer system at the office where she could see things on a bigger screen. Grabbing what she needed for the day, she rushed about the house. After going over the new intel at the office, she was planning on heading up to the resort to see if she could track this carnivorous predator further. Because so many indicators seemed to point in that direction, she figured it was the best place to start in her hunt for its lair.

When the beast was located, they were going to have to kill it, she was certain of that. An animal that had a taste for people as this one already did was never going back to a diet of dumpsters and dirty diapers. And judging by the carnage she had witnessed thus far, this apex predator had already advanced well beyond that stage.

Finally, good to go, Christine stepped out of her house, pleased to see things might be looking up in the fog department — it seemed a bit thinner this morning. Of course, that was subject to change at any time around this area, she thought with a smile.

She climbed into her truck, the cold, grey metal of her Remington bolt-action .30-06 glinting in the weak morning light. The rifle was not one of the highest-powered out there, but she knew what counted most wasn't the stopping power — that was something she'd learned when she'd first started her training.

Harvey Callahan, the officer that had mentored her firearms training, had been a long-time veteran of the forestry service. After thirty years, he'd been getting ready to retire and had seen it all, so to speak. He told her that one of the most important things to remember was that it wasn't always the stopping power of a rifle that counted in the end. You could have just fired the most powerful weapon in the world, but if your shot didn't hit a vital organ, you might only succeed in pissing the thing off that you're trying to kill. He'd also told her a single well-placed shot with a .30-06 was just as capable of bringing down a bull moose or seven-hundred-kilogram grizzly, as a high powered .416 magnum was, as long as the shooter was accurate. And accuracy was something that Christine excelled at, scoring top marks in her class at the target range.

With plenty of time to do so, she mentally ran through her agenda for the day as she slowly drove down her lane into the anaemic daylight now leaking through the fog. The five-kilometre drive from her house into the town of Lawless was going to take a while longer today. The density of the fog varied in consistency between cotton candy-like wafts of fluffy mist, to full-on 'can't see your hand in front of your face' fog banks. There was only so much that the high-intensity fog lights attached to the top rack of her truck could do, and in the daytime, they were practically useless.

Rounding a corner, Christine found herself face to face with a pair of coyotes standing over a small, unrecognisable piece of roadkill in the middle of the highway. She braked hard, and the two scavengers disappeared into the mist like ghosts as if they'd never been there at all. Thoughts of the occupant in her chest freezer sprung to mind. The coyote's enjoyment of their roadkill repast was the reason for the freezin' of the carcass at the shop, she thought with a small smile. The door to the garage couldn't be left open all the time to keep the remains frozen as she had on the first day. The last thing she needed was to attract the pack of coyotes living along the shores of Kokanee Lake, only a kilometre or two from the city's downtown. These compact predators regularly prowled the garbage cans and dumpsters of Lawless in addition to stalking the local pet population in the dead of night. She certainly didn't need to attract them or anything else lurking out there in the fog.

Lawless was having a problem with coyotes just like other areas in the province, and she knew they were high on Austin's list as animal control officer for the city. It was going to be a hard go and she knew it might be necessary to cull some of the pack. She recalled the coyote problem in Vancouver that one of her instructors had told her about while she was training.

There were literally tens of thousands of coyotes living within the city limits of Vancouver. Most residents were utterly oblivious to these unseen, silent predators. In fact, many people would be shocked at the surprising locations that some of these urban scavengers had made their homes. Sometimes all that was needed for a family of coyotes to move in was a small opening in a crawlspace underneath an abandoned house or a thicket of bushes in an empty lot. Many of the unexplained disappearances of cats and dogs in the Lower Mainland could be attributed to coyotes, rather than the commonly held tropes of petnappings or low budget restaurants opening in the neighbourhood.

When the freezer arrived the other day, she'd been glad to put the carcass on ice. Though she usually had a reasonably high tolerance for offensive smells, the stench from this creature was overpowering. Once she'd finished the deep freeze internment, she'd cracked open three lavender air fresheners she'd also purchased to celebrate having an odour free shop once more.

After several more minutes of foggy navigation, Christine finally pulled into the rear lot of the conservation office. She unlocked the shop door but didn't immediately enter. Instead, she stood in the darkened doorway, listening. After a moment she smiled, pleased to hear the freezer humming happily away in the corner of the shop, keeping its precious, smelly cargo frozen and safe.

Enjoying the pleasing floral scent of the air freshener next to the door for a moment, she flicked on the lights and walked through to her office. The first order of the day was to check her answering machine. Looking at the flashing message indicator, she was pleased to see there was only one message. At least Geraldine Gertzmeyer hadn't inundated her with calls again. Playing the message back, she discovered it was from the maintenance man at the resort, Bill Watkins. He said there'd been some damage to a garbage dumpster that might be bear-related and asked if she could come out and take a look at it. Christine wondered if it might be their new large-footed friend. She pulled out her notepad and wrote it at the top of her to-do list.

Sitting down at her computer, she brought up her email. To her surprise, her inbox was even closer to bursting than before, thanks to a series of new emails from Zelda. Apparently suffering a zoological nerdgasm, the girl had inundated her with another wave of information — there were over a dozen different emails now.

Taking a sip from her travel mug of tea, Christine opened the email marked 'raccoon summary'. This email provided a point by point breakdown of the vital stats on the raccoon that Zelda had told her about over the phone yesterday. She shook her head in amazement. It was still mind-boggling that the thing could have existed all these years without ever being in contact with civilisation.

But it was the casting of the print from the other, larger predator at the campsite that really intrigued Christine the most, and she was curious what Zelda could tell her about it. She clicked on an email entitled, 'OMFG!'.

Over the years, Christine had encountered more than her fair share of bear tracks. The accepted method of measurement was to base the calculation on the square-shaped front paw, rather than the elongated rear. The rule of thumb to size a bear from its print was to take the measurement of the bear's forepaw, add an inch and you generally had the length of the bear in feet. Doing the math based on the print in the earth near the fire pit at the camp, she didn't think her answer could possibly be correct. She thought it better to wait for verification from Zelda before saying anything to anyone for sure. After all, some expansion must have occurred to the print in the mud she surmised, because there was no possible way any living bear could be that large! She was sure that Zelda would have something to say about it, and she did.

The OMFG email opened on her screen just as she started to take a sip of tea from her mug and she choked slightly, the cream seeming to clot into a solid lump in the back of her throat. After several moments of intent study, Christine sat back and digested everything she'd just read. She picked up the printouts of the paw impression on her desk and looked at them long and hard. In the pictures, she'd included a ruler in the shot to get a sense of the scale of the impression. But she was sure she'd never have any problem remembering its dimensions as they were burned into her brain — from the back of the heel to the tip of the claw, the paw print measured almost seventy-five centimetres. The beast was a behemoth, and Zelda had now corroborated that fact. The track belonged to Arctotherium Angustidens, an unusually large, nasty, bear species found predominantly in South America, but not any time in recent memory — it had gone extinct over one hundred thousand years ago!

Taking into account the pressure points of the animal's pad and the depth it had imprinted into the earth, Zelda calculated that the creature currently stalking Lawless weighed-in at over two metric tonnes and it could look a two-metre tall human being directly in the eye. Walking fully erect on its hind legs, it could easily look into the second story window of any house, as it would be just a hair over five metres tall! Her blood ran cold as she thought of the size of the creature now that it had been corroborated.

She was stunned by the information on the screen in front of her and sat back in her chair. "Seriously? Where have you been hiding for the last ten millennia or so? Shacked up with my stinky little friend?" She nodded her head toward the humming freezer in the other room.

My God, she thought, what kind of monster is this thing? She knew she'd need to get some warning signs together and post them around the area. But first things first; she needed to inform Chief VanDusen of the situation. Once he was up to speed and on-board, then she'd get the signs out and start warning the population.

Christine picked up the phone handset on her desk and punched in the number for the LPD. It was picked up after two rings, "Lawless Police Department, Desk Sergeant Paulson speaking, how can I assist you?"

"Good morning Sergeant Paulson!" Christine said brightly, "This is British Columbia Conservation Officer Christine Moon calling, may I speak to the chief, please?"

"Officer Moon! Absolutely! Always a pleasure to hear from you again! Just one moment, please." The line clicked and she was treated to some light jazz for her listening enjoyment.

After what seemed like an interminable wait, Chief Reggie VanDusen finally picked up the phone, saying, "Well, well, Officer Moon, hope you weren't waiting long."

"Not too long," Christine said, wanting to say more, but didn't. She needed his help and wasn't about to burn any more bridges with the man, yet, especially after the muddy incident at the campsite yesterday.

"That's good. Listen, we're pretty backed up here right now. What is it that you need?"

"It's not what I need; it's what Lawless needs! We need signs up around town saying there is a dangerous predator on the loose!"

"Now, you know there is no proof that there's any such thing…"

"Yes, there is! I just got confirmation from the zoology lab at SFU that the thing that ate those snowmobilers…"

"May have eaten, we have no evidence…" VanDusen interrupted.

"Evidence? I'm sure we'll have more than enough, once that thing starts defecating human remains all over the place!"

"Until our lab gets the results back to us, you can't go around screaming, 'Killer bear on the loose!'"

"Look, whether anyone was actually eaten or not is irrelevant. Even if we allow for your supposition that the blood around the campsite was left behind by hunters gutting their kill, we still need to let the public know that there is the possibility of a large carnivorous predator skulking around in the fog. They need to be told to keep out of the forest until we find this thing and kill it! The newspapers and radio need to be informed as well!"

"Listen, officer, once I've heard from our forensics lab is when I'll make the final determination about what the danger is and who to contact, and not before! But fine, go ahead if you want, put up some of those nice, friendly, yellow 'Bear in Area' signs around the place. Will that make you happy?"

"No! This thing is going to keep attacking now that it has a taste for blood! This thing exists! It's a reality, and it is still out there! It hasn't gone anywhere! And whether you want to admit it or not, there is an excellent chance it's already killed several people and many more could die unless we do something about it. I'm on my way up to the resort right now to check out some damage to the property last night that they think might be bear-related."

"Then I'd suggest you put out your little warning signs and then get out in the forest and find the goddamned thing!" VanDusen slammed the receiver down, ending the conversation.

"Bastard!" Christine said, still holding the dead receiver to her ear.

"All right," she said aloud, slamming her own receiver down, "if that's the way you're going to play this, fine." She picked the handset up once more and began dialling.

CHAPTER TWENTY

The thin mist that graced the Golden Mile pass on the eastern side of the valley did not extend to the western side, much to Austin's chagrin. It was far too thick for him to see anything beyond a few metres, let alone fire a howitzer shell into the nebulous, grey unknown hoping to hit a mountaintop at the backside of the valley. It appeared the thickening fog was going to put the kibosh on his plan to knock down the build-up on Gold Ridge near the glacier.

Austin pulled the truck over at the valley bottom, just before Highway #3C began to wind up Gold Mountain toward the resort and Gold Ridge beyond. He looked over to Trip in the passenger seat then out the windshield at the grey void and sighed. "Well, we might as well go all the way up to the resort and see if there's any clearing higher up," Austin said, putting the truck back in gear.

Trip squinted into the greyness surrounding them. "Sounds good, Boss." He grabbed the last cruller in the doughnut box and slowly bit into it, relishing the last of his morning sugar fix.

The Gold Mountain Casino and Resort sat at the top of a series of switchbacks that wound back upon themselves — each curve so close to the next that sometimes it seemed they might swallow their own sinuous tails. The lack of snow over the past week had laid the road bare except for a thick crust of frozen slush on both sides. On their drive up the hill,

Austin could see the thorough sanding job that Larry had done overnight — all the curves in the road were well gritted to provide extra traction and make them as safe as possible. Impatient as he was to get to the resort, Austin had to grit his teeth on a journey that seemed interminable at times as he piloted the truck through bank after bank of fog.

Trip looked glumly into the empty doughnut box in his lap. He was currently preoccupied picking out the last few crumbs and bits of glaze from the bottom of the sticky cardboard container. Austin suddenly tapped the brakes, and Trip glanced out of his window. His heart wedged itself into his throat when a large, dark shape suddenly thrust out of the fog into his peripheral vision. His hand moved toward Austin's arm, ready to warn his friend, but he stopped short at the very last moment.

The distinctive noseless face of the Sphinx resolved out of the mist as the truck continued to roll along. The one eighth-scale Egyptian oddity stared blankly back at him through the window as it stood guard duty at the entrance to the Golden Nugget Casino and Resort. Towering next to the Nile Cat, its spire disappearing into the mist over ten metres up, was the one-tenth-scale Eiffel Tower. Trip knew that when driving in the fog, it was sometimes difficult to judge how far along a road you were, until all of a sudden there's a replica of a big-ass Egyptian human-cat hybrid right there next to you. He chuckled to himself.

Observing Trip's reaction, Austin laughed lightly from the driver's seat, saying, "What's the matter, Trip? A little jumpy?"

"Yeah, just a bit on edge, Boss, not knowing where that thing is out there."

"I getcha. That and even knowing WHAT that thing is out there."

"Uh-huh, that, too. But this fog certainly doesn't make it any easier. It's like the mist is helping this thing stay invisible and move about unseen. As far as we know right now, it could be standing five metres from us in this fog, and we'd never know it. It's like it doesn't really exist since nobody's actually seen it, yet." Trip hoped the supposition he'd just stated regarding the beast's current location was incorrect. Nevertheless, he swivelled his head back and forth, looking intently into the fog as Austin slowly drove through the main gate of the resort.

Austin added, "Nobody that's lived to talk about it, that is."

"Exactly, nobody except for that that Wilson kid last night at Frostbite Fred's, and maybe the guy we rescued, Jerry. Any word on him yet?"

"Last I heard, he was still in a coma, but you just made me wonder how Christine was making out with that casting of the print from the campsite yesterday. I hope she's had some word by now."

Austin pulled the truck around to the back of the resort to access the service road leading up to the avalanche control platform. As he turned the corner, a familiar amber trouble light strobed faintly away in the mist ahead. Out of the swirling vapour, Christine Moon's blue Ram 3500 appeared, parked next to a rusty, battered garbage dumpster.

"Well what do you know, I guess you can ask her right now," Trip said as Austin stopped the vehicle.

***

Christine Moon backed up a bit more, trying to get a better shot of the dumpster, but the fog wasn't cooperating. "Damned clammy crap!" Even at a distance of three metres, the visibility was cut in half by the swirling mist, and she was getting nothing of any clarity. She had to be satisfied with a series of close-ups of the various spots of interest near the dumpster.

When the breakfast crew had shown up for work early this morning, a mess had been discovered near the garbage bin. Thinking it to be just a bear problem, the staff contacted Bill Watkins. It was his decision to call the Conservation Office asking if someone could come up to the resort to check things out.

When Christine arrived, as soon as she looked at the bin, she knew it had to be the work of the valley's newest resident (or oldest, depending on your point of view), Angustidens Arctotherium. Definitely not 'just another bear problem', that was for sure. Christine stood and stared for a moment. The lid was sitting at such a weird angle; it looked like something straight out of an M.C Escher print. An entire corner of the sheet steel cover was bent neatly back like something enormous had been fishing snacks out of it — as if the lid were nothing more troubling than the cardboard top to a box of Crackerjacks and something had been digging for the prize inside.

She tried backing up a little bit more, attempting to get a better shot, but she could see it was now impossible, as the fog seemed to have decided it wanted to foil her photographic endeavours completely. "Dammit!"

A voice at her back commented, "I think we're both going to need a clearer day to get a better shot."

She turned and saw Austin Murphy smiling behind her.

"Hi Austin, I'm so glad you're here," she said, smiling back. "I've got news on our predator! I was going to call you in for an update, but I got called out here first."

"No worries. So, you finally heard back?"

"Yes, I did. First of all, it's rather large as we already suspected." To prove her point, she stepped aside and said, "Look what it got into last night." She gestured over her shoulder with her camera toward the garbage bin in the mist behind her.

Trip walked up behind Austin just as she stepped aside, and Christine watched with mild amusement as both Austin and Trip's jaws dropped in unison when they saw the state of the dumpster lid.

"Holy crapoly! What happened? Garbage truck damage the bin again?" Trip asked.

"Hey, Trip! Nope, I believe it was our new resident to the valley, our huge friend who left the prints at the campsite. Can you think of any other creature that could fold back a sheet-steel garbage bin lid like that?"

"Bigfoot?" Trip queried.

"Nope." She shook her head in the negative, her ponytail bouncing around at the back of her hat as she did.

"The Abominable Snowman?" Austin suggested, raising his salt and pepper eyebrows in askance.

With a slight tilt of her head and a pout on her lips, Christine said to the two men, "No, I'm sorry, only contestants from the fossil record can play today."

"So, it is on the fossil record, then!" Austin said, sounding intrigued.

"Yes." She nodded, smiling.

"Okay then, what is it?" Trip asked.

"And how much of a monster is it?" Austin finished his friend's thought.

Figuring she'd kept them in suspense long enough, she said, "Arctotherium Angustidens, is his name, or Angus for short. According to my zoology colleague Zelda, our new voracious friend from the campsite went extinct just a little over one hundred thousand years ago."

"What?" Austin stood with his mouth agape once more.

"Man, he's doing really well for someone his age!" Trip observed, nodding his head lightly in admiration.

"You're right, and he's not a lightweight either. He weighs just over two metric tonnes, and his shoulders are at least as high as the top of your six-foot-two head," Christine said, looking over at Austin.

"Six-foot-three, actually," Austin amended.

Christine smiled at Austin's correction and continued, "And if it stood on its hind legs it could look into your second-story bedroom window, right before it scooped you out with its half-metre long claws and started jamming you into its mouth."

"I live in a bungalow," Trip said, sounding both anxious and relieved at the same time.

"That's crazy! How is this possible? First, that weird raccoon from the past, now this bear. What's next, a dodo bird?" Austin asked.

Christine continued, "And I don't know if this is something either of you might have thought of, but didn't this raccoon, and now bear, show up just after the seismic event here?"

"Something like that, I suppose," Austin responded with a nod.

"What if all that shaking somehow woke these things up?" Christine asked.

Nodding toward the bin, Austin said, "Like a giant alarm clock for very, very sound sleepers, huh? Well, they must have hit the snooze button right after the shaking because that was several weeks ago."

"Well, I don't know why the delay, but somehow I think these three things are related. The shaking, then the raccoon shows up, then the bear."

Looking down at the ground around the bin, Trip said, "Looks like Angus made a bit of a mess, too." The snow around the container was dark with frozen blood, great sprays of it painted over the side of the dumpster as well as a rusty Trans Am sitting next to it.

"According to Chef Murray, he found the bin like this. He also said the kitchen wasn't completely cleaned when he came in, either. It was like the evening crew had just left without finishing their duties."

"More missing persons?" Austin asked.

"They don't know at this point. Possibly two people at least. They're still trying to get ahold of the kitchen manager, one Antoine DePascal, as well a busboy, Dan Lewis, who had been on duty last night before closing. No luck so far, though. But speaking of which, I had more of the bad variety this morning, actually."

"Bad luck?" Trip asked. "What happened?"

"I met Ray Chance for the first time today."

"Oh, that is unfortunate," Austin said in commiseration.

"Yes," Christine said, wrinkling her nose in remembrance. "He doesn't work anywhere near an open flame by any chance, does he?"

Austin Laughed, "No, but he does enjoy the odd cigar from what I've seen. I guess he just hasn't reached his maximum saturation point with that brandy he's always drinking. But someday..." His smile faded away as he trailed off, looking at the garbage bin once more. "Did the police show up yet?" Austin inquired.

"I contacted them, and they said they'd send a car up. But that was a couple of hours ago. And knowing how beloved I am with the LPD, I'll be lucky to see them show up before I'm done here," Christine replied.

"Doesn't look like anyone was very lucky here last night, at least not outside the casino anyway," Trip observed.

"Still speaking of luck, we're out of it ourselves," Austin said, pointing his hand vaguely in the air at the swirling fog. "At least when it comes to doing any avalanche control in this part of the valley. Can't see a blasted thing to shoot the gun at."

"Is the avalanche risk bad?" Christine asked.

"Not too bad, at the moment. There's just a bit of stuff at the top of Gold Ridge holding on for dear life. Should be okay unless we get more fresh snow, or if it gets any warmer. We'll just have to wait a couple of days and hope that it clears up so we can get a shot at it."

"That's great! Then in the meantime, do you think you might be able help me?"

"Always ready to help, ma'am," Trip replied with a brief salute, a slight smile and two very rosy cheeks.

"Well, I've got a mess of 'Bear in Area' signs I've whipped up in the back of my truck. And I need help putting them around town so that people are aware of the threat."

"Sure, give us some, Christine," Austin said. "We'll plant them on our way back to town."

"Great, thanks!"

"No problem! We'll just be a few minutes here first. We have some temporary storage for the howitzer on-site at the resort. We'll drop Baby off here until tomorrow when we can hopefully knock that build-up down if the fog clears."

"Baby?"

"It's a long story," Trip said, shaking his head.

"I'll have to hear it sometime. Anyway, you guys are awesome! Thanks so much!"

"No worries," Trip said, looking at his boots and blushing even more profusely.

***

After loading several dozen signs into the back of their truck, Austin and Trip bid Christine goodbye. Climbing into the City Silverado, Austin said, "Let's get the howitzer bedded down for the day and then plant some of those signs. It should only take a couple of hours, and then I'll treat for lunch at Frostbite Fred's. Sound good, my friend?"

In spite of the half-dozen crullers he'd already consumed within the last couple of hours, Trip's stomach growled in anticipation as it thought of lunch at his favourite watering hole. "Well, if you're going to twist my rubber arm…" he said, trailing off as he climbed into the passenger side of the truck.

Austin heard the celebratory snarl of hunger from Trip's stomach and knew his friend was well motivated for the morning's work ahead. Still shaking his head in wonder and smiling, he hopped into the driver's seat and started the truck, saying, "Let's go put Baby to bed!"

CHAPTER TWENTY-ONE

"Greasy little bastard!" Ray Chance spat. "I knew I couldn't trust him as far as I could throw him!"

"I'm sorry, Mr. Chance, I don't know what happened at the cavern last night," Watkins said, his toque bunched worriedly in his hands. "I went up there at first light to check on Mr. Oritz this morning like you wanted and he was gone. The snowmobile you lent him was still there, though. I called out and searched the cavern a little bit, but there wasn't anybody there, and I don't know where he is. It seems like everyone who works up there disappears."

"Not all of them." Ray Chance glowered across the desk at Watkins.

The fumes from the brandy were more powerful today, Bill noted, queasy from the sharp smell of alcohol. The colour of Chance's mid-morning beverage was much darker than usual. He knew Chance usually cut his brandy down with club soda. Seeing the deep shade of the liquid in the glass, he realised there was no soda in his snifter this morning. For some reason, Chance was drinking the brandy straight up. This couldn't be good news, Watkins thought, then asked, "What do you mean?"

"According to Chief VanDusen, Willy Wilson Junior, that son of your no-good cousin, is now in the hospital in a medicated coma to stop him from talking about what happened up there!"

"What?" He squirmed in his seat as he realised his prediction had come to pass. This was bad news, indeed.

"I just got off the phone with VanDusen a little while ago. He said the kid wandered into Frostbite Fred's last night babbling about monsters, teeth and claws. We're lucky he was incoherent enough that nobody was really paying attention to him, and that he didn't say anything about the gold. The paramedics pumped him full of drugs and hustled him off to the hospital before he could speak about what happened. If he does wake up and try talking, VanDusen is going to drop him off in the cavern."

"Sorry, Mr. Chance, I thought…"

"I don't pay you to think! And what the hell happened behind the kitchen here at the resort? There's blood all around the garbage bin, and the lid's been bent back like it was tin foil! Was this that goddamned bear you were going on about?"

"I don't know sir. It could be." He felt that familiar sinking feeling again.

"All right, then, I want you up at that cavern tonight with a rifle to keep an eye on the place!"

Watkins cringed. The hits keep on comin', he thought morosely.

Chance continued, "If your goddamned bear, or whatever it is shows up tonight, sniffing around, you can take care of it!"

"But Mr. Chance..."

"Shut up! I'm still talking here! Now here's the deal," Chance's voice dropped to a conspiratorial level. Watkins leaned forward to hear, his eyes watering instantly from the brandy fumes. Chance continued, "If things don't start shaping up, or if there are any further problems, I'll call in Chief VanDusen, and he'll help you deal with things." Chance sat back in his chair with a pleased expression on his face.

Best day ever, Bill thought. "Mr. Chance, really, you don't have to do that," he said, and he meant it. He definitely did not want to work alongside the chief of police if he could avoid it — there was something about that man that scared him shitless. This seemed especially true after their recent, one on one, hush-hush 'information sessions' which the chief told him not to mention to Chance. Interrogation sessions, Bill called them.

"And we're going to have to scrape up a few more able-bodied diggers — people more trustworthy." He emphasized the last word then chugged more brandy from his snifter. He continued, "Anyway, this might take a few days. So, starting tonight, and for the next little while, I need you up there watching that goddamned place, so you'll be head of security and chief of mining operations!"

"But sir, I had an evening planned with the misses tonight."

"Go buy her a fur coat then. She'll understand!"

"But there's also maintenance scheduled on the…"

"No buts! You're doing it tonight. That maintenance can wait and so can your wife, and that's that! Now go get some rest, you're going to have a long night!"

Watkins sighed and turned to leave the office, his hand on the doorknob, about to open it, when Chance spoke again.

"Oh, and one other thing, Watkins." Ray smiled when he saw the maintenance man's shoulders draw together, visibly flinching from the sound of his voice, but he didn't turn around. Yeah, it was good to be the boss. Still smiling, Chance continued, "I'm going to be coming up there soon to see what's what. And if things aren't being taken care of…" Chance left the rest of the sentence unfinished.

Still facing the door, Watkins said, "Yes, sir, good-bye, sir." Watkins quietly pulled the inner office door shut behind himself.

Roxanne was currently occupied at her desk filing down a sharp corner on one of her fingernails. "Is everything okay Mr. Watkins?" she asked, her voice betraying her lack of genuine concern.

"It was until now," he said, smiling glumly.

Roxanne's beautifully arched brows knitted together with concern, "Oh, really? That's too bad, Mr. Watkins."

"Yes, yes, it is," he said, shuffling out of the office. He pulled his toque down over his ears as he departed.

***

Crouching near the pungent dumpster as she placed her camera back in her pack, Christine heard the service door from the kitchen open and close. With toque pulled low, a man trudged past her in the fog toward a battered Ford Bronco located just past the garbage bin. It was the maintenance man, Watkins. She recognised him from her earlier encounter with him that morning when she'd arrived. He'd been the one that had pointed out the damaged dumpster to her. After their quick meeting, he'd excused himself, citing a meeting with his boss, Ray Chance. It appeared the meeting was now over, and it looked like he was getting ready to leave for the day.

"Mr. Watkins!" she called out.

Hands stuffed in his pockets with his shoulders hunched forward, the man continued to walk toward his truck for a moment. He paused and turned slightly, looking quizzically at Christine over his shoulder.

She approached him, saying, "Sorry to bother you again, Mr. Watkins, but I need to ask you a couple more questions about what happened here if that's okay?"

"Sure thing, but call me Bill, please," he said, smiling tiredly. He turned the rest of the way toward her, pulling the toque off of his head to speak.

"Thanks for taking the time to talk with me, Bill," Christine said encouragingly. She noted that the tip of his right thumb was missing as he clutched his hat.

Seeing the direction of Christine's gaze, Watkins stuffed the hand back into his jacket pocket, saying, "Old high school woodshop injury." He smiled painfully at the memory. "Listen, Officer Moon, I don't want to appear rude, but I don't have much time since I have to go home to get some sleep for a work shift later tonight."

"Really, well, I won't keep you. That's going to be rough, having to come back here again tonight for another shift, won't it?" Christine queried, wondering what maintenance he would need to do here at the casino in the middle of the night.

"No, it's not here, it's at another of Mr. Chance's properties."

Christine wondered at that. Maintenance at night at another of Chance's properties? Doing what? Cutting his grass? At night? In late January? She smiled, regardless, saying, "I see, thanks. Listen, Bill, I was wondering if you could tell me if you've had any other problems like this regarding wildlife in the area?" As she spoke, she nodded toward the garbage dumpster, barely visible through the fog.

Watkins looked over toward the blood-stained bin, his gaze lingering there for a long moment before answering. He turned back to Christine and looked briefly into her eyes before averting his gaze, saying, "No, ma'am. There was an incident at the dumpster last fall with a black bear, but since then, nothing else has happened, here."

Christine noted his emphasis on the word 'here'. She tilted her head, asking, "You're obviously aware of the need to keep this garbage bin locked at all times."

"Absolutely. I don't know what happened here last night." He glanced over at the bin briefly once more, then returned his gaze to his balled-up toque, now held in his left hand.

"Well, I won't keep you. If you think of anything, Bill, please let me know," Christine said, handing Watkins one of her cards.

"I'll do that. Thank you, ma'am." Putting his toque back on his head, he took the proffered card in his left hand, then gave her a dull smile. He placed the card in his jacket pocket without looking at it, then turned and shuffled tiredly back toward his equally tired-looking truck.

Christine wondered what other things were going on up here of which she, or anybody else for that matter, wasn't aware. Regardless, after questioning Watkins, she decided to do a little poking around to look for Angus's tracks.

After about a quarter of an hour of legwork, she located a set of tracks heading up the mountainside that had been left behind by the massive predator. She stood at the edge of the darkened forest that backed onto the corner of the resort. The mist swirled past her face as she unslung the Remington .30-06 from her shoulder and checked its ammo. The magazine was fully loaded — this time, she was armed and ready.

Pulling her GPS unit from her parka pocket, Christine marked her current location before she began following the tracks up the mountainside through the dense fog. Eventually, the tracks came out at a power line access road. She followed this for another kilometre before seeing the tracks veer back into more thick brush.

Soon, a dense stand of Douglas Fir trees towered above her. The pungent scent of decomposing conifer needles hit her nostrils as she moved forward. The massive fir trees blocked most of the daylight trying to filter through, leaving the way ahead only a dim, grey limbo. Progressing into this gloom, it appeared that the dense network of branches not only blocked the daylight but moisture as well. Very little precipitation had penetrated through to the ground during the winter months, leaving it spongy and thick with moss and needles. Underneath the thick forest cover, it appeared as if it might be spring already. She admired the canopy of trees for a moment, or at least what she could see of it overhead, due to the limited visibility.

Her breath suddenly caught in her throat.

Three metres up the trunk of one of the towering firs, barely visible through the fog, four huge furrows had been carved into the ancient tree trunk, each one over a metre long. There was no doubt in her mind that the gouges in the tree trunk had been left by the huge beast using its sword-like claws to mark its territory.

"My God, Angus," she said in a slightly shaky voice. "You truly are enormous!"

But disappointment followed her shock once she started to examine the ground around her, looking for more prints. The dark, mist-filled forest stretched into the greyness in all directions, and she was at a loss to find any further signs of the creature in order to continue tracking it. Once the beast had started to move through this area of soft, springy moss and decomposing needles, it seemed to have vanished.

The thickness of the fog suddenly became too much for Christine, making her feel boxed-in and claustrophobic as she moved slowly forward. Visibility was down to less than two metres all around her now. She stopped and listened, straining to hear any sound, but heard only the slight drip of melting snow as it fell from the thick branches high above.

"Dammit!" She was frustrated that she couldn't follow the beast any further. But there was some good news; she now knew the general direction the animal was coming from thanks to her portable GPS unit. She was glad she'd brought it along as she would have surely been lost in the fog on her return journey without it. She turned to head back down to the resort when a twig snapped in the mist behind her.

Her body became wire taut, her breath held as she listened intently.

Nothing more happened for several moments, and then came the crack of a second twig breaking under the weight of whatever was approaching her in the fog. Mindful of being silent, she unslung the Remington from her shoulder and brought it to bear in front of her, chambering a round in the process. Releasing the rifle's safety, she froze in place and waited.

There was only more silence.

Standing tensely, she felt the rifle feel getting heavier and heavier the longer she held it out in front of herself anticipating another sound. Her attention became laser-focused when a third twig snapped, this time much closer to her current position. Another followed it in short order. Whatever was out there was approaching her directly from the front.

She lowered the .30-06 to hold it at chest level. There was no point in trying to use the sight since she could hardly see past the tip of her nose, let alone her rifle at the moment. If she had to shoot, it was going to be from chest level height at point-blank range.

Ready to fire, she was literally vibrating, both from tension and the stress of holding the weapon for so long.

A dark shape stepped out of the fog directly in front of her.

Her finger came within millimetres and milliseconds of pulling the trigger, but she hesitated at the last moment and said, "Well hello, deer."

Like an ethereal spirit, a tall, graceful creature came out of the fog, seeming to float toward her. It stopped and looked at her, tilting its head.

Little more than an arm's length from her rifle's muzzle stood a fawn, its large, brown eyes reflecting back Christine's tense, ghostly-pale face in the weak daylight. The beautiful animal stood frozen in front of her. It was most likely as startled as Christine to come across something else so close by of which it was unaware in the fog.

Christine lowered the rifle and re-engaged the safety, speaking softly to the animal so she wouldn't startle it. "You might want to watch your back in these woods for the next little while. There's a big, nasty-assed bear out here in the fog that likes to eat sweet little forest creatures like you, and big city folk like me, amongst other things. So, you'd better run along now and find a safe place to hide, deer."

The creature looked intently at Christine as if listening to her words. Once she'd finished speaking, the fawn nodded its head slightly, seemingly in acknowledgement of her advice, then turned back and disappeared into the fog.

"Well, that was a rush," she said quietly, slinging her rifle back over her shoulder. She pulled her GPS device from her pocket, tagging her current location and selected the resort as her new destination.

Many foggy minutes later, she climbed behind the wheel of her truck and texted Austin that she'd like to meet up with him later for a coffee, her treat. She decided she wanted to go over some maps of the area when this day was done to see if, together, they could possibly figure out the location of the creature's lair. Smiling, she saw Austin text back almost immediately. He agreed that it would be a great idea and said he'd meet her at the conservation office after dropping Alex off to hockey practice at 6:00 P.M. He also attached an emoticon showing a thumbs up and a steaming cup of coffee at the end of the message.

With a small smile, she said, "Well, I guess it's a date then."

CHAPTER TWENTY-TWO

"Sleep well, little one," Austin said, turning out the light and pulling the sliding steel garage door shut. The howitzer was now safely stowed in its second home at the secured storage shed at the resort. Standing behind Austin, Trip rolled his eyes, then pulled out his keys to secure the lock.

"Time to go sow some signs, my friend!" Austin said, patting Trip on the shoulder as he headed to the truck.

After planting several 'Bear in Area' warnings around the main buildings of the resort, they made sure to stop at the entrance to the property and inter a few more of the yellow signs there. Working next to the Sphinx and Eiffel Tower, Austin held the stake as Trip pounded it into the frozen ground.

Austin looked at the black silhouette of the bear on the diamond-shaped sign as they worked, thinking how it needed to be much, much bigger. He figured if anyone was silly enough to go wandering around out in the fog, maybe they'd at least bump into one of the neon-yellow warnings as they toddled off the property and perhaps rethink their foggy perambulations.

"Do you think Chance will leave these here?" Trip asked, tossing the sledgehammer he held into the back of the truck.

"Well, if he does remove them, there's a fine from the Ministry of Conservation, or so Chris told me," Austin said, climbing into the passenger side of the truck.

"I guess if anybody can afford a fine, it's Chance," Trip observed.

"You've got that right," Austin said, nodding in agreement.

With Trip behind the wheel, they made their way back down the mountain road toward Lawless. They stopped every half-kilometre or so to place another bear sign along the way, with several near the entrances that accessed cross-country ski and snowmobiling trails. It went without saying there would always be those adventurous souls who chose not to heed the avalanche hazard warning still in effect.

Driving through the drab, grey twilight that passed for daytime in Lawless this time of year, they listened to the local radio station. After a series of predictably similar pop songs ended, the noon newscast started. Austin reached over and turned up the radio.

"This morning, the Ministry of Conservation issued a bear alert for the citizens of Lawless and area. There is a large predatory bear in the vicinity that may be responsible for at least two disappearances that have been deemed suspicious and are being investigated by both local and provincial authorities. The Lawless Police Department and the British Columbia Conservation Officers Service are advising residents to use extreme caution when out in the surrounding forests. This warning includes the Lawless city limits and extends to the Gold Mountain resort area as well. Once again, residents have been advised to use extreme caution when…"

Austin turned the radio back down. "Well, it looks like Chris was able to get the go-ahead for a radio announcement."

"That's great news," Trip said. "At least with all the signs and the radio, we should be able to keep most people out of the backcountry until we can find this thing and deal with it." He squinted through the mist-covered windshield as he spoke. The intermittent wipers made another pass, and suddenly Frostbite Fred's resolved out of the greyness. "Looks like lunch!" he said. He mentally ran through the menu in his head. Thanks to several hundred visits to the pub over the past few years, he had memorised the establishment's menu. Trip was, as owner, Norm would say, 'a repeat offender'. As soon as he pulled the truck into the parking lot, his stomach began to snarl at him, and he mentally chided it, telling it food was coming soon.

Frostbite Fred's was a public house located halfway between Gold Mountain Resort and Lawless. When it first opened, it had primarily catered to skiers, but now, the tourist trade from skiing had dried up, and the business's clientele had changed. These days, it was mostly mill workers and local foodies. But in winter, thanks to its large, utility trailer-friendly lot, they also saw quite a few hungry cross-country skiers and thirsty snowmobilers stopping in to refuel after an adrenaline-filled day of alpine adventuring. These regular and seasonal customers were the reason Frostbite Fred's was doing more than okay. And it certainly didn't hurt that they served some killer in-house smoked roasts and ribs, along with lip-smackingly good micro-brewed beer and cider.

Before breaking for lunch, they planted several signs around the pub's property. It was a quarter past twelve when they finally finished, and both men had worked up a sizeable appetite. They pushed through the heavy pine doors into the heavenly smelling interior. Freshly baked bread and the scent of slow-roasted, baby back pork ribs assailed their nostrils. Trip felt his salivary glands begin doing their old Pavlov's dog schtick and he discreetly sucked back some of his surplus saliva.

Mathilda, one of the owners, waved and called out, "Hey Trip! Hey Austin! You boys can sit anywhere you like, and I'll be right with you!"

The tip of her white-haired head was just visible over the top of an archaic-looking Bunn coffee maker near the kitchen.

"Great, thanks, Mattie!" Trip said, waving back. After successfully reining-in his salivary glands, he now felt his stomach doing its usual 'Feed me, Seymour' routine, which invariably started mere seconds after he walked through the front doors of Fred's.

Austin and Trip took off their parkas and placed them over the backs of a couple of swivel stools bolted to the floor in front of the gorgeous, antique mahogany bar and sat down. The stools, like all of the tables and chairs in the pub, were bolted to the floor in order to stop the patrons, once in their cups, from hitting each other with them.

Back in the day, the pub had a reputation as being a bit of a rowdy place, as there was usually a donnybrook either in the bar itself or out in the parking lot almost every night. The blue and white cars of the Lawless Police Department were a regular visitor to the bar, more often than not, their emergency lights flashing merrily away as one patron or another was escorted off in handcuffs to the warm, welcoming confines of the Lawless drunk tank for the night.

Fred's owners, Mathilda May (Mattie to the regulars) and her husband, Norm were both pushing seventy if they were a day. They kept themselves young running Frostbite Fred's Public House, just like they always had for the past forty-plus years since they'd opened the doors for the first time. Not being night owls, they had a shift of younger people working in the evening who were more patient and able to handle the rowdy types that sometimes 'came out of their shell' after a few too many drinks. Mattie always said, "It may be a small town, but they've got a powerful thirst and a short fuse!"

After a couple of minutes, Mattie, ambled over to see what she could get them to eat. "Afternoon Trip, Austin, how are you boys doing today? I hope you're good and hungry."

"Always," Trip said, earnestly, still unobtrusively hoovering back more saliva, his stomach growling ever louder, as if eager to corroborate the fact.

"I'm still surviving, but some of your delicious food would hit the spot," Austin said with a smile, listening to the gastrointestinal concerto currently performing in Trip's stomach.

"Great! What can I get you boys today?"

"Well, I'll start with a coffee and the menu, please, Mattie," Austin said.

"Make that two coffees and one menu, please," Trip added. As much as he would have loved a beer at the moment, he was on duty and took his position with the City of Lawless very seriously so coffee it was for now. He knew he would be back later that evening for a wobbly-pop or two (as he liked to call beer), so he was content to wait until then.

"That's right; you never use the menu, do you, Trip?" she smiled. "All right, that sounds good then. I'll be back before you know with the 'Joe'," she turned and walked sprightly away toward the coffee station.

"Thanks, Mattie" Trip said, righting his overturned, white ceramic coffee cup in anticipation of the upcoming java. That done, he lined up a half dozen sugar packs next to it, along with an equal number of plastic cream capsules from a nearby dish.

While Mattie was occupied grabbing the coffee pot and a menu, Austin and Trip began to discuss the bear situation. When Mattie came back, as she carefully poured the coffee for the boys, she said, "I'm sorry to interrupt, fellas, but I saw you putting those signs around the property before you came in for lunch. And just a little before that, I heard a warning on the radio. Now I hear you talking about some bear out in the forest. Do you mind telling me what's happening?"

"Not at all; it looks like we have a bear on the loose that's extremely dangerous — possibly a man-eater." Austin said, pouring cream into his cup from several plastic capsules he'd already opened. "Might have attacked at least two people, maybe more," he concluded. He added another cream to his steaming cup. The coffee was so dark and thick that he thought it might be in danger of being mistaken for chocolate pudding.

"No! You don't say! Anybody local?" As she poured Trip's coffee, Austin noticed Mattie's hand shaking slightly as if nervous at the thought of what might be lurking out in the forest behind the pub, being located out in the middle of nowhere as they were.

"No locals that we know of for sure at this point, but maybe a couple of snowmobilers visiting from the coast," Trip replied, opening more cream for his coffee. In addition to the six sugars, he'd upped his creamer count from six to eight when he'd seen the consistency of Austin's coffee as Mattie poured it. As the old expression went, he reflected with a smile; you don't go to a bar for its coffee.

"My, that's just too bad!"

"Yes, it is," Austin replied, using a paper napkin from a dispenser on the counter to mop up a small puddle of spilled coffee around the base of his cup.

Putting the coffee pot down, Mattie put her hands on her hips and turned to Trip, "Jenny Smith was waiting tables last night and told me you were here when that poor Wilson boy came in raving about monsters and all?"

"Yes, ma'am," Trip nodded.

"Is he all right?"

"We don't know. Apparently, he's in a drug-induced coma in the hospital right now. I think he came unhinged by whatever he saw. Might have witnessed his dad getting killed, which could have been pretty traumatic. I hope Willy's going to be okay — he's a good kid," Trip replied.

"Let's hope so. Jenny said the poor dear looked like he needed some help for sure. Now, on a lighter note, what'll it be for lunch, boys?"

Turning to the sandwich section of his mental menu, Trip ordered one of his favourites, a triple-decker clubhouse on white bread, saying, "And could you ask Norm not to skimp so much on the mayonnaise this time? At least four tablespoons, please. And no crusts! Oh, and one more thing, no lettuce or tomato, either, thanks."

"One triple clubhouse! Certainly, Trip," Mattie smiled. She turned and hollered over her shoulder toward the kitchen cut-out where Norm was busy prepping something or other, "Albino club, Norm! Slop it, crop it and drop it!"

Smiling at Mattie's description of Trip's sandwich tweaks, Austin ordered the closed-face, hot roast beef and gravy sandwich with mashed potatoes of which he was so fond. Patricia used to cook the most tender, mouth-watering prime rib that he had ever eaten. But now, with just him and Alex to feed, it was rare he would attempt cooking a roast, and when he did, it was never with the same level of succulence as Patricia's.

Due to this prime-rib shortage in his life, Austin always looked forward to ordering roast something-or-other whenever he ate out. As Alex always said to the servers when out at a restaurant with his dad, "Just give him the roast beast," knowing no matter what the beast was, his dad would most likely have some. And it seemed that locally,

Frostbite Fred's was about as close as he could come to tasting food that was like some of the excellent home cooking he missed so much. At Fred's kitchen, Norm, along with their whiz-kid, meat smoker-extraordinaire, Max Renaud, the meat never came out of the kitchen anything less than melt-in-your-mouth tender. He was a sucker for the way Norm's in-house baked bread sopped up the thick, rich gravy that covered Max's succulent roast beef sandwiched in the middle. The thirst of the patrons for the micro-brewed beer was one thing that kept the business afloat, but also, it was the excellent food prepared by the wizards in the kitchen that kept the people coming back.

After a short wait, Mattie dropped the generously sized plates of food off to the men. She said, "Enjoy, boys!" then walked away, smiling. It always seemed that once she'd placed the food in front of her customers, they grew silent as they savoured the delicious meals before them. As most people do, they preferred to enjoy their food while it was hot rather than chatting about topics they could easily discuss later and let their tasty meals get cold.

Twenty minutes and a piece of apple pie later, Austin felt a contented burp threatening to erupt from his mouth as he paid the bill at the till. He said to Trip, "I'll get this, and you can spring for lunch next time, buddy."

"Thanks, Boss!" Trip said, trying to scoop the last bit of ice cream from his à la mode pie off of his plate with a spoon.

"Give my compliments to Norm and Max," Austin said to Mattie. "You can tell Max the roast was delicious as always and so tender that it seems like it's been pre-chewed! But I mean that in a good way! And Norm's bread? Two words: Mind and blown."

"Thanks, Austin, I'll pass that along." Turning to Trip, Mattie said, "And I guess I'll be seeing you tonight for the game on our big screen?" She was referring to the television broadcast they would be playing of the hockey game that evening between the Vancouver Canucks and Toronto Maple Leafs.

"You can count on it, Mattie," Trip said with a smile. Though his stomach was full from lunch, his taste buds came alive at the thought of sampling some of the micro-brewed goodness on tap at the pub.

Bidding goodbye, the men exited the building, feeling the now-familiar damp caress of the fog wash over them.

"Man, is this clammy crap ever going to let up?" Trip asked as they walked to the truck. As he spoke, he searched for something in his parka pockets.

"Don't get your hopes up, buddy," Austin said, climbing into the passenger's side of the truck. "They're calling for ice fog down at the valley bottom once the temperature inversion clears in a day or so."

"Ice fog? Oh great! It just never lets up!" Trip knew that once that extra frosting of ice hit the local roads, it would be slicker than a kindergartner's nose on the first day of school. He also knew that he and Larry would have to be extra vigilant in their sanding duties. Suddenly, his eyes lit up when one of his hands located the object of his parka pocket probe.

"Okay, let's head back to town and get the rest of these signs up," Austin said.

"You got it, Boss," Trip said, pulling out a king-sized Snickers bar. He ripped the wrapper off and took a huge bite, then offered it over to Austin, holding it under his nose.

Austin smiled slightly, saying, "No thanks, my friend. But I appreciate your thinking about me."

"Whazzat?" Trip asked around a mouthful of chocolate, nougat and nuts.

"Nothing, warp factor one, Mr. Williams!"

"Aye, aye, Captain." Trip said, tearing off another considerable chunk off the chocolate bar. He chewed for a couple of seconds while he adjusted the seat belt around his ample belly. Once satisfied his safety harness was secure, he jammed the tail end of the candy into his white-bearded mouth and placed the truck into gear.

As they slowly edged forward into the fog. Trip held the steering wheel in one hand while rummaging around in his pocket with the other, presumably on a quest for something more to eat.

With a concerned smile, Austin made a mental note to drop Trip's cruller ration from six doughnuts to three in the very near future.

CHAPTER TWENTY-THREE

High above the fog, the daylight slowly faded, the sun melting behind the snow-capped mountains. In late January, Lawless missed out on quite a bit of sunlight due to the angle of the sun and the closeness of the surrounding valley. By three o'clock in the afternoon, the sun was down behind the mountains, taking the remaining daylight with it. There were several spots in the valley that didn't see sunlight all winter long and remained in the shadow of the glacier the entire season, making for a permanently slippery situation on the roads in those areas. The fog, while varying greatly in consistency throughout the day, began to settle in for another dark, impenetrable evening.

Austin sighed and tore his gaze from the insidious grey mist wafting outside his kitchen window and looked back to the task at hand. Ripping the top off of a small white pouch, he placed it on the countertop next to one he'd already opened near the stove. Tonight, it was going to be another quick throw-together dinner for himself and his son consisting of a true Canadian favourite, Kraft Dinner macaroni and cheese, or KD as it was known in Canadian parlance. To make the upcoming meal a bit more nutritionally sound for the boy, he'd tossed in some frozen mixed vegetables and a half dozen all-beef hot dogs. After adding the prerequisite milk and a dollop of butter, he sprinkled both pouches of the orange powder over top of the mixture and stirred it all together.

This had to be a quick meal because he had to get Alex to hockey practice for six o'clock and then get himself over to the conservation office to meet Christine right after that. He was very curious to see what she had put together and looked forward to going over the map of the area so that they could try to chart the bear's territorial advances.

"Okay, buddy, come and get it!" Austin hollered into the living room.

Alex was finishing his homework while watching a game between the Boston Bruins and the LA Mighty Ducks. Austin didn't know how the boy managed to get his homework done while watching something as fast-paced as hockey, but get it done he did, and done correctly, so Austin didn't mind. His son had been on the honour roll for the past year now since his mother passed away. It seemed like he felt compelled to do better in school now in order to make himself someone of which his mother would be proud. And that was just fine with Austin since it made his life so much easier knowing his son was excelling in school, handling the mourning of his mom's passing in such a constructive and healthy manner.

"Be right there, Dad!" Alex called back. Zipping his backpack, the boy walked through the arched kitchen entrance a moment later. He hung the pack on a hook at the side door near the garage. Come Monday morning, he'd know right where it was and wouldn't have to panic, running around the house looking for it like the proverbial decapitated chicken his dad was always going on about.

The boy was growing like a weed, Austin observed. Only six months ago, he'd been four inches shorter than he was now, and Austin had been buying clothes for him like they'd been going out of style. At first, Austin thought that perhaps it was the washer or dryer shrinking the clothing. But it soon became apparent that the real cause of the 'incredible shrinking clothes mystery' was because his son was in the middle of a huge growth spurt. At fifteen, Alex was just two inches short of Austin's 6'3" height. In hockey, other players on the opposing teams who were a little later to blossom than Alex were no match for the boy's size and speed. It allowed him to basically cruise through the smaller kids like an unstoppable force of nature. And as captain of his hockey team, he played a fantastic game to boot. Austin wouldn't be surprised to see his son in the NHL some year if his performance was anything to judge by this early in the game, no pun intended.

Austin loaded up Alex's plate with almost one and a half boxes of the KD and most of the diced-up hot dogs. The boy would need all the fuel he could get tonight for his upcoming hockey practice. And it wasn't just before hockey that the boy pounded the food back. Along with his growth spurt, the boy's appetite had increased exponentially with his size, and now he easily out-ate Austin regularly at the dinner table. But that was okay; it made Austin proud and happy to see his son shovelling the macaroni and cheese into his seemingly hollow legs, growing bigger and stronger each day. After about three minutes, the feeding frenzy appeared to be over, and the boy's plate was clean.

With a smile, Austin said, "Remind me never to get between you and your dinner plate, okay, buddy? I wouldn't want to lose a hand or something!"

Alex smiled back and said, "Ha-ha, you're a regular Russell Peters, Dad!"

"Thank you; I'll be here all week and please don't forget to tip your waiter!" He held his hand out as if expecting a tip, and Alex gave him a low-five palm slide instead. "Close enough," Austin said, laughing.

With dinner out of the way, Alex grabbed his hockey gear and stuffed his large, black hockey bag into the back of their Honda Pilot. As he did that, Austin quickly picked up the mess in the kitchen then threw on his jacket, following his son out the door to the garage, locking it behind himself.

The drive from their house to the Lawless Community Sports Complex was usually only fifteen minutes, but the fog, once again, decided to compound things and ended up adding an extra ten minutes to the travel time. By the time they arrived at the downtown sports arena, it was only a couple of minutes before six o'clock.

When business had started turning around in Lawless thanks to the new casino, the mayor and city council approved an upgrade to the sports complex. It now housed an Olympic-sized swimming pool with water slide, conference rooms and a large NHL-sized hockey rink with seating for almost two thousand people. Usually, Austin would have loved to stay and watch the practice, but he needed to meet up with Christine within minutes.

"Sorry I can't stay and watch tonight, buddy, but work beckons. As I mentioned, I have to go over some things with Christine." '

Alex said with a grin, "Sure thing, Dad, whatever you say." He'd heard his father talking about the new conservation officer lady several times over the last couple of days. Despite his meagre fifteen years on the planet, the boy's' powers of observation were well developed. He'd noted that whenever Austin started to talk about Christine Moon, he couldn't seem to say anything negative about her. In fact, from the way he was going on about the woman, Alex could see his father was obviously smitten with her and he'd decided a little good-natured ribbing was in order.

"That's all. It's strictly professional," Austin protested in his defence.

"Uh-huh, you bet, Dad," Alex said, laughing as he pulled his hockey bag out of the Pilot's back hatch. "All right, love ya, Dad! I'll see you at eight-thirty!" Alex slammed the hatch closed before Austin could respond.

Smiling, Austin saluted the rear-view mirror and said, "Aye-aye, Captain!"

The conservation office was only a couple of blocks away, but the thickness of the fog made it difficult to see, even with the Pilot's fog lights probing the way through the murk. He pulled into the yard next to Christine's truck and walked to the back door of the shop. She'd told him to just walk in when he got there as she might be in another part of the building. Canadian manners overriding everything else, he still knocked on the door and popped his head inside before entering, saying, "Hello?"

From the other side of the shop, Christine called out, "I'm over here, Austin, glad you could make it!"

Austin stepped into the shop and saw Christine finishing work on something near a full-sized chest freezer in the far corner.

"Thanks, wouldn't have missed it. Freezing some leftovers, are you?"

"Sorry?" Christine questioned, as she walked over, her brow furrowed. Then realisation dawned, and she laughed at Austin's comment. "No, just checking to make sure our smelly little friend is still nice and solid."

"Yeah, he did stink up the place in here, that's for sure. And you can't very well leave him outside on his lonesome either" Austin commented, sniffing the air in the shop. He was pleasantly surprised to note that it currently had a delightful lavender scent.

"You're right; it's not cold enough with the door closed and the heat off. And it's also impossible to leave the door open to refrigerate the room, especially with the coyotes running around the area. "

"And let's not forget Angus skulking out there in the fog as well."

"Oh, I don't think there's any way I'll ever forget him! We definitely don't need anything attracting any more scavengers or predators."

Christine had been busy before his arrival. Laying flat on top of a metal worktable in the middle of the shop was a large topographical map of the surrounding area. Several yellow stick pins sprouted from it like miniature flowers. Plotted on its surface were the Gold Ridge campsite attack, the wild turkey massacre at Geraldine Gertzmeyer's, the garbage dumpster incident at the Casino and Ray Chance's messy run-in with the raccoon. Even though the turkey killing didn't appear to be done by the bear, he realised, just as she obviously did, that it had to be part of the same mystery and could see why she had decided to include it on the map.

"This is interesting," Christine said, pointing to a spot she had plotted near Gold Mountain.

"What's that?" Austin asked, sidling next to Christine at the table.

"Well, at this point, it looks like most of the attacks are situated around the Gold Mountain Resort, as you know. But it seems like Angus is covering more and more ground with each attack, exploring and expanding his territory at the same time."

Still finding it strange to refer to the monstrous beast as Angus, Austin asked again, "What was the full name of this creature again?"

"Arctotherium Angustidens." Christine chimed.

"Yeah, I suppose Angus is a little easier to say." He pointed to a spot a couple of kilometres from the resort that Christine had marked with a pin. "What's this here?"

"That's where I found some claw marks up in the tree where Angus decided he was going to mark his territory. You should have seen them; they were at least a metre long. That thing must have claws like swords."

"Remind me to bring some hedge clippers when we find him," Austin commented. His ears were treated to something he wasn't expecting as Christine laughed at his joke. The musicality of her laughter so reminded him of Patricia that he felt momentarily consumed by a feeling of sadness and loss. But these negative thoughts were also accompanied by something new — an energizing mixture of light and joy also surged through him. However, he was working at the moment and had no time to reflect, so he took this new, complex brew of emotions that he found in his heart, packaged them up, and shoved them deep down inside himself, meaning to examine them in more detail at a later date.

Still smiling from Austin's joke, Christine said, "Maybe a hacksaw might be more appropriate. But seriously, if we can figure out what area it may be branching out into next, maybe we could give people a better warning and save more lives, right?"

"I agree one hundred percent." Austin leaned over the map as if hoping to summon forth some sort of inspired guess as to the monster's lair. "I certainly don't like the way it's getting closer to Lawless."

"I know, it's moving through its territory, spiralling outward. If that pattern keeps up, it'll most likely end up here in town," Christine said, frowning. "And there doesn't seem to be any pattern to what it's attacked, either, apart from the territorial expansion. People, garbage bins and probably more things that we aren't even aware of, yet, I'm sure. But it certainly seems like it's moved up the food chain, and people are at the top of the menu." She stepped back to get a better look at the map.

She continued, "Once an apex predator like this has tasted human blood, it will target people more and more and the other animals in the forest less and less. The way it's starting to look, people are now making up the majority of this animal's diet. And it certainly does seem like it's being drawn toward civilisation," Christine pointed at the city of Lawless on the map.

"Do you think it might be killing for sport, too?"

"It's hard to say, but if this creature were to encounter any large numbers of the population, we'd have a bloodbath on our hands. It would look at the bumper crop of bodies like a smorgasbord. If he's eaten his fill, he may just decide to play with his food, but from what we've seen, his appetite seems to be insatiable, so I doubt that. And I haven't seen a trace of bear feces anywhere near the attacks. You would think for something that big, that there'd be evidence of it voiding its bowels somewhere out there."

Austin added, "I'm sure it would be a pretty substantial pile."

"Yes, and if we can find where it's been defecating, at least we could verify what it has attacked and eaten."

"If a bear shits in the forest, does anybody step in it?"

"Sort of along the lines of 'If a tree falls...', huh?"

"I see you grasped my unsubtle attempt at humour," Austin chuckled.

"Was that what that was?" Christine said with a smile, and then added after a moment, "Oh my goodness, I almost forgot the coffee I promised you!" She walked over to a small counter off to one side.

"You didn't have to go to all that trouble, Christine."

"No trouble for Mr. Tim Horton," she said, turning and holding two double-doubles, one in each hand.

"You are a lifesaver," Austin said, taking one of the proffered cups of the still warm, creamy caffeinated beverage.

Raising her cardboard coffee cup to Austin's in a toast to luck, Christine said, "Here's hoping we'll save more lives than just one."

"I'll second that," Austin said, touching his cup to hers. Together, they sipped their coffee, and Austin observed Christine Moon over the rim of his paper cup. Her smooth forehead was now knitted in concentration as she leaned over the map, trying to extrapolate the beast's future movements. Several strands of long, blonde hair spilled from her loose ponytail down the side of her face. As he drank, a part of him felt something that he hadn't over the last several days, or even the past year: he felt a renewed sense of hope.

CHAPTER TWENTY-FOUR

Firelight from the blazing hearth gleamed in Mayor Bob Nichols's eyes, reflecting the heat of rage he felt as he fumed over the situation at the cavern. Sipping his third scotch of the evening, he felt ill at the thought of how much gold might have been stolen so far by the incompetent, greedy morons that Chance had been hiring.

"Why haven't I heard anything back from that son of a bitch, Oritz?" he asked aloud. He was more than just a little perturbed about the lack of communication with the man. Initially, he'd been more than pleased when he received a phone call from Oritz learning he'd have his assistance up at the mine instead of the incompetent lackeys that Chance had previously hired. After doubling Chances offer, Bob had rested easy, knowing things were in good hands, technically speaking, but definitely not morally speaking, seeing as Oritz was as crooked as the day is long, he thought with a smirk.

He took another sip of his scotch and started fuming once more. As of right now, it'd been almost twenty-four hours since he'd heard a goddamned peep out of Manny Oritz, and he was royally pissed. It seemed to him like there was a pretty good chance that the son of a bitch may have decided to grab some of the gold himself and make like a little butterfly, fluttering off to Mexico or Spain or wherever the hell the crazy bastard was from.

With Oritz now AWOL, Chance had called saying he'd sent his maintenance man up the hill but added that he figured they needed to get up to the cavern themselves to see what in God's name was happening, and soon. Nichols agreed but said they sure as hell weren't going there alone. After contemplating the crackling fireplace for several more minutes, he picked up the phone and punched in Chief Reggie VanDusen's private number.

He endured what seemed like interminable ringing before VanDusen picked up the phone. With more than a hint of exasperation and condescension in his voice, the chief of police said, "Yes, Mr. Mayor, what seems to be the problem now."

"That goddamned Oritz hasn't checked in with me at all today!" Nichols almost shrieked.

"Okay, calm down, calm down! Maybe he's busy doing some mining or exploring the cavern? Did you ever think of that?"

"It's not what he's doing up there, it what he's not doing that's pissing me off! And that's keeping me in the loop!" Nichols made a gulping sound as he took another slug of his scotch in exasperation.

VanDusen said, "If he's at the back of the cavern, he might not be getting any reception on his cell. Remember, the lack of repeaters around here makes the reception kind of spotty at the best of times."

"He was supposed to check in this morning and never did! I've been trying to get in touch with him all day long and so has Chance!"

"So?"

"So, tomorrow, I want you to take Chance and myself up there so that we can see for ourselves what the hell's going on!"

"Look, I've got a lot on my plate at the moment, Mr. Mayor with that goddamned bear and all. I don't know if I'll…"

Nichols cut VanDusen off. "No, what you're going to do is this; you're going to pick us up at the resort tomorrow at noon, and we'll go up there and get things sorted out!"

There was a silence on the other end as VanDusen mulled over some possible responses to Nichols's demands. After a moment, he settled on, "Roger Wilco, over and out," and hung up the phone before the mayor could finish everything he wanted to say.

"Goddammit!" Nichols roared, throwing his nearly empty glass into the fireplace. With a pop and a brief flash of flame, the crystal tumbler exploded against the back wall of the hearth, a fleeting rainbow of colour briefly bathing the study's walls as the alcohol ignited.

***

VanDusen placed the receiver back on the cradle and regarded the phone for a moment as he pondered things. Nichols was getting way too worked up about this gold, but then again, that was understandable. With possibly hundreds of millions of dollars just sitting up there at the cavern, waiting for someone to come along and scoop it up, it could make a guy go a little bonkers. And then there was that 'partnership' between Nichols and Chance which certainly didn't help things.

Back in the early '80s, when they'd first partnered up to purchase the ski hill from the lawsuit riddled Sinclair Corporation, Bob Nichols and Ray Chance had been the best of friends. Over the years, the pair had worked on several real-estate deals around town and earned quite a reputation for themselves as vibrant entrepreneurs who were more than willing to do their part to revitalise the city of Lawless.

But, since that time, there'd been quite a bit of animosity and in-fighting between the pair as they grew more familiar with each other and their respective shady business practices. Now, it seemed that the situation had devolved to the point that Nichols didn't trust Chance at all and vice versa. And that was just fine with Reggie. It was something that most definitely worked in his favour. He was more than willing to dip his own little treasure bucket into this bottomless well of gold, so to speak, and collect what he viewed as his fair share of proceeds scattered about the cavern.

Smiling, Reggie turned his attention back to the person lying next to him in bed. He'd bought some of the finest champagne for them to drink so they could celebrate all of their hard work ripping off their mutual employers. Things had worked out very well for them — their little caper had netted them five sacks of nuggets of their very own, weighing in at over twenty kilos each. It was worth almost seven million dollars Canadian, according to Reggie's calculations. And that was separate from the two dozen other sacks in his root cellar that he'd also be taking a share of as payment for his work.

Since neither Chance nor Nichols realised how much gold was up at the cavern to start with, he had been free to help himself to as much gold as he wanted, for the moment. But he wasn't greedy; skimming another twenty percent or so that Chance or Nichols knew nothing about seemed more than fair to VanDusen, seeing as he was doing all of the dirty work. And it was the icing on the cake to be supplied with information by the young woman next to him, who was both beautiful and devious — definitely his kind of woman.

A sparkle of mischief in her eyes, Roxanne Rooney dropped a single whipped cream-covered strawberry into Chief Reggie's VanDusen's waiting mouth. He watched as her red lips slowly licked the residue off of her long, crimson-tipped fingernails, and he smiled. Yeah, life was good.

CHAPTER TWENTY-FIVE

Friday and Saturday nights were usually the busiest nights of the week at Frostbite Fred's. Trip thought the parking situation this Friday evening could certainly attest to that.

Almost full to bursting and threatening to spill out onto the highway, dozens of pickup trucks were crammed into the lot's confines, along with the odd SUV scattered throughout. Some of these trucks had decks on their beds, and others with trailers attached, but they all shared the same cargo; gleaming snow-chariots sitting primed and ready to go for a round of high-speed fun the next day. Trip wondered how many of the revellers inside the pub were aware of the avalanche and bear advisory now in effect which would be putting a damper on their wintertime fun the next day.

Not all of the pickups belonged to sledders, though — some were dirty, weathered and meant for work rather than recreation. Trip nodded in recognition at some of the vehicles as he wandered through the foggy lot toward the pub. The usual contingent of millworkers had also gathered at Fred's tonight, seeking to quench their thirst and lubricate their dust-covered throats.

The vibration from the driving bass inside the pub tickled Trip's spine before he could even pull open the thick pine doors. Every Friday night was the start of live music playing all weekend at Frostbite Fred's Public

House. The live bands at the pub on weekends were almost always top-notch local talent, but Trip only wished they issued some foam earplugs at the door. However, since there was no cover charge, he wasn't going to complain. The upcoming hockey game was going to be playing in the background on the big screen on the rear wall of the pub, but he wouldn't be able to hear it because of the music. He was okay with that — he'd brought along his earbuds so he could listen to the game streamed through his cell phone on the pub's Wi-Fi network.

Inhaling deeply, Trip filled his lungs with foggy evening air, then pulled the door open and felt the sound waves wash over him. He exhaled explosively, then took another deep breath, this time of the air inside the bar. Pausing for a moment, he relished the smell of beer-soaked sawdust and peanut shells that assailed his nostrils. But even more than that, it was the mouth-watering scent of pork ribs and roast beef lingering on the air molecules that intrigued Trip's olfactory senses the most.

"Honey, I'm home," he said, a grin threatened to burst through his beard as he plunged into the crowded pub. A rainbow of colours washed over him from flashing neon signs announcing some of the numerous beers available from gleaming brass taps jutting from the beautiful mahogany bar. A massive mirror covered the wall behind the bar with row upon row of exotic spirits reflected in its spotless surface.

Dozens of dusty millworkers were desperately trying to TGIF some of the cellulose from their souls with Fred's house-brewed, small-batch, beers and ales. Scattered amongst the lunch-pail bunch were at least a dozen groups of snowmobilers as well, laughing and giggling to themselves, their gaudy neon snowsuits sprouting like Gore-Tex flowers amid a meadow of drab, sawdust-covered plaid.

Many of the patrons were grooving along to the music from the live band that the bar had provided for the evening's entertainment. This week, it was HipBone on stage, a rockin' local group of kids from the neighbouring Kootenay town of Castlegar, located about a hundred kilometres from Lawless. Trip had heard them when they'd played at the bar a few months back and rather liked their sound. They were in fine form tonight, playing covers of some classic rock songs, with most likely a few country favourites thrown in to keep the line-dancing contingency in the far corner happy.

A low stage ran along one wall of the pub. Behind it, a plate-glass window provided a magnificent view of the mountains in the daylight, when the weather was cooperating. The lead singer of HipBone, a thin young man with long, stringy, brown hair, stood with his back to the large window. The kid was so gaunt that every time he turned sideways, he almost disappeared. And even if the singer had been more substantial, tonight, there was no view for him to block. The only thing visible through the window behind him was a wall of multi-coloured, glowing mist, illuminated by the spotlights outside the pub. It created quite a dramatic effect. But apart from that, nobody was missing much.

The stringy-haired kid wailed away into the microphone. Apparently, his line of reasoning went that louder was always better. Trip winced slightly — it seemed the current volume level of the music was already just a hair shy of 'OMG! My eardrums are bleeding!'. Yup, he'd definitely have to bring up the earplug idea sometime in the near future, but in the meantime, he stuffed his noise-cancelling earbuds into his ears and smiled with relief.

Trip knew the one thing that owners, Norm and Mattie, always prided themselves on was keeping their customers happy. And by God, if loud music was what they wanted, Mattie said, then that was what they were going to get! Conveniently, neither of them was in the building when it was time for the music to begin. They were usually done their day shift by five o'clock, and he figured they were probably relaxing at home right now, eating dinner and watching Wheel of Fortune.

Max Renaud, the reigning Kootenay God of smoked meat, was in attendance at the bar's kitchen tonight, like most nights. Trip watched the tall Quebecer heading from the bar toward the kitchen, working his way through the crowd, most likely going outside to tend to some smoking meat. Trip's stomach growled. Was it baby back ribs? Slabs of hearty beef ribs? Or perhaps it was one of his massive chunks of Angus prime-rib roast? Trip brought up his internal image of Frostbite Fred's menu and decided he'd have the number thirteen tonight, the Carnivore Combo, which included all three of the delicious delicacies. They were probably just getting to the 'fall off the bone and call me delicious stage', as page three of the menu proudly proclaimed.

Trip sidled slowly through the crush of people, nodding to several of the locals he knew along the way. On their plates were heaps and heaps of the melt-in-your-mouth meats. As he passed, the face of one patron ignited into a flash of joy as the server, Jenny Smith, placed a steaming plate of succulent ribs onto the table before him. They glistened under the neon lights, taunting Trip's poor belly with a come-hither look that made it bay like Lon Chaney Junior at the moon.

Jenny Smith was looking rather harried and overworked tonight for some reason. Then Trip looked across the room and suddenly saw why. Working alongside Jenny was Carlene Boseman. Although, 'working' was a rather strong word for what Carlene was currently doing. The girl stood there, chatting away with a group of her friends on the other side of the room while Jenny flitted from table to table, hustling her butt off, as usual.

Arms folded, watching the difference in work ethics between his two servers was bartender and shift-supervisor, Greg Canton. At the moment, Greg was frowning very thoughtfully in Carlene Boseman's direction.

Trip bellied up to the bar, squeezing in between two city-folk. They appeared to be fresh in from the coast, sporting matching neon-yellow snowsuits that made Trip wish he'd brought his Raybans with him from the truck. "Evening, Greg," he shouted, "I see you're in the middle of a work dispute."

"Yeah, you're right." He continued to glare in Carlene's direction. "I'm currently disputing the amount of work I want to continue to give to Carlene in the foreseeable future."

Trip laughed and ordered a pint of Frostbite Fred's Amber Ale. Several moments later, his eyes lit up as he took his first delicate sip of the small, but creamy head left atop the pint by the affable Australian's exceptional aesthetic abilities. Trip complimented the bartender on his professional pour and asked him to add the pint to his tab. Greg gave him a quick grin, thumbs up and a "Good on ya!" in return.

With a smile, Trip began to negotiate his way through the crowded pub, his treasured mug of steam-brewed, barley-infused gold clutched protectively to his chest. He moved toward his favourite spot; a small, round table tucked into the far corner near the fireplace. A large red reserved sign sat on top of this minuscule table. Trip placed the sign face down and relaxed with a grunt on the single, comically petite chair that sat behind it. Taking an almost reverential sip of his fresh brew, he peered over the rim of his mug at the throng of people around him.

***

A smile from a recent generous tip turned into a frown of frustration as Jenny Smith looked Carlene Boseman's way. She fumed at the table-waiting arrangements this evening, having to work opposite the other woman. Jenny had no doubt she was going to be run ragged most of the night as Ms. Boseman was not the sort of person that gave her 'all' to a job. Jenny knew from back in high school that Carlene was a person who tried to give her 'least' to a job if anything. The girl coasted along in life, fluttering her thick, black eyelashes at anyone who would pay attention, forever trying to get away with doing the bare minimum at whatever she was doing, and hoping that somebody else would pick up the slack for her. Well, that wasn't going to happen tonight, Jenny thought, especially not with the packed house they had this evening. They needed everyone here doing their job to the best of their ability. Looking toward Carlene again, she shot daggers from her eyes at the girl.

Gliding through the patrons with her empty drink tray toward the bar, Jenny was sure they were over capacity tonight and had mentioned that earlier to Greg, but there'd been no attempt on his part to do anything about, so she'd let it slide. After all, it wasn't coming out of her pocket if they got fined. As she waited for a drink order from Greg, she overheard several of the mill workers at the bar talking about some sort of animal attacks. And just a few minutes before, a group of sledders commented to her that the thought of a predatory bear in the area was making them think about cutting their weekend adventure a bit short.

Concerned, Jenny scanned the crowd. Sitting in the far corner was one of her favourite regulars, Mr. Trip Williams, and he was looking toward her. Now there was a man that could answer some of her questions, she thought. She smiled at him in recognition. It appeared he was just finishing off his first pint of the evening of Fred's Amber Ale. Seeing he'd caught her eye, he waved and pointed down to his almost empty mug, making a sad-sack face. Jenny smiled again and giggled a bit at this, giving him a thumbs up in return. Despite the busyness of the evening, it was the regulars that made the job bearable. She found it pleasant to be serving someone you'd known for years, instead of some pushy out-of-towner with a snowmobile in the parking lot that still had the price sticker stuck to its windshield.

After waiting for Greg to pull several more pints at the bar, Jenny wound her way through the horde of patrons, delivering to several tables along the way. Eventually, she made her way to the corner to drop Trip's second beer off to him.

"Here you go, sugar," Jenny shouted in Trip's ear, placing the beer on the tiny table in front of the grateful looking man. Just as she set the pint down, the band ended their current set to take a ten-minute break, dropping the decibel level in the room from one-hundred and ten to sixty in an instant.

"Thanks, Jenny. You're a lifesaver!" Trip hollered back before realising with some embarrassment that the music had stopped. In a more conversational tone of voice, he continued, "I sure worked up a powerful thirst putting those bear alert signs around the area today."

"I was wondering who I had to thank for that!" Jenny placed her hands on her hips.

"Yes, ma'am," Trip blushed. "We want everyone to be aware of the bear!"

"Well, those yellow signs will certainly help! Have they been able to track it down, yet?" Jenny inquired.

Trip took a long pull of the flavourful golden-hued beer, then said, "Not so much. The fog isn't helping things, though, that's for sure."

"I'd imagine not. What are they going to do?"

"Well, luckily, the new conservation officer, Christine Moon, is on top of things. I think she's going over the territory that the bear's covered with Austin this evening to try and zero in on its lair."

Jenny watched Trip's eyes light up as he spoke of Christine and could tell he was soft on her. "And you and Austin are helping out with trying to catch it, huh?"

"Sort of. But it'll more likely be kill than capture. That thing is bad news all-round. Anyway, we sort of got involved from the start because we found the site of the first attack and rescued one of the survivors."

"My goodness! So, you're a hero, then?" Jenny asked, smiling.

"I helped, yes, ma'am," Trip said, his cheeks above his beard blossoming a lovely shade of pink.

"Well, then, this one's on the house," she said, pointing at the already half-empty mug in front of Trip.

"Miss Jenny, words cannot express my gratitude," he said, nodding his head toward her in appreciation of her generosity. He put in his order for the Carnivore Combo platter and thanked her again for the free beer.

"I'll get that order in for you right away! But remember, you don't have to thank me with words, sugar," she said, smiling. "You can always express your gratitude when it comes time to leave my tip!" With that, she turned around pertly, her long auburn hair swinging softly behind her, and waded back through the sea of customers. She wasn't sure but thought when she'd told Trip he was getting a free beer, his eyes seemed to mist up a bit. Well, she thought, it's nice to know that it doesn't take too much to make some people happy. She drifted back through the boisterous crowd toward the bar for her next tray of drinks, taking orders and empty plates as she went.

Her excellent mood soured quickly when she glanced toward Carlene on the other side of the room, serving some customers. As Jenny got closer, she saw that the only things Carlene was currently 'serving' were more yuks, and her 'customers' were just another group of her friends. Carlene stood there, flapping her gums, ignoring all of the actual paying customers that surrounded her, trying to get her attention.

Jenny arrived at the bar and nicely pointed out Carlene's dereliction of duty to Greg. He nodded to her, saying he was already aware of Carlene's lower-than-normal work ethic this evening and had been keeping an eye on her. Turning toward the server in question, he put his finger to his lips and gave one of his best and most piercing 'Hey, you!' whistles.

With the music temporarily suspended for the break, everyone in the bar stopped whatever they were doing and looked Greg's way, including Carlene. He pointed at the girl and waggled his finger back and forth to signal her to come over to the bar. The smile she'd had on her face from relating another funny anecdote to her friends crumbled away when she saw she was in trouble with Greg once again.

As Jenny moved away from the bar to deliver another round of drinks, she smiled sweetly at Carlene as they passed each other. The only thing Jenny received in return was a scowl. Jenny thought it was most unfortunate she had to hustle more drinks right away and miss out on most of the conversation between Greg and Carlene. From the brief snippet she'd heard as she walked away, it sounded like it was going to be a good one, too. Phrases such as, 'last chance', 'no more', and the ever popular, 'or you're fired!' were directed at Ms. Boseman and suddenly, Jenny's mood began brightening again.

CHAPTER TWENTY-SIX

Revelling in the smell of smoking pork ribs, Max Renaud lifted the hinged lid of his custom-built smoker. Its name was brightly splashed across one side in half-metre high, neon-red lettering, proudly proclaiming it to be The Midnight Toker. Max looked into the smoking maw of his metal beast and poked and prodded with his tongs for a moment, checking the status of his latest batch of melt-in-your-mouth meat.

He lived to cook roasts and ribs, and he cooked them very, very well. So well, in fact, that Frostbite Fred's had gotten a reputation around the valley as THE place to go for a mess of delicious prime rib and baby back ribs that were so tender, they practically fell right off the bone and into your mouth.

When Max had first started working at the pub, owners Mattie and Norm weren't sure if they wanted to have such a monstrous contraption out in back. The last thing they needed was something else cutting into their limited parking space. Ultimately, it wasn't Max's enthusiasm or blueprints for the smoker that finally changed their minds. What swayed their opinion was the marinated, slow-roasted oven-baked ribs that he made without the aid of any smoker. Doing it old-school in a kitchen oven was, as Max had put it, like slow cooking ribs without having the time to slow-cook them. They would be good, he told them, but what they were going to taste from the oven couldn't compare to the smoked delicacies he would be able to craft in a real smoker.

That afternoon, three racks of pork ribs came out of the oven at Fred's, slathered with Max's secret recipe sauce, and they were OMG delicious. Mattie and Norm were instantly sold. Max had smiled as he assured them that the ribs and roasts he'd make for them in his smoker would be even more delicious and that he'd be able to cook many, many more at one time for them to sell to their hungry patrons.

Norm and Mattie decided to fund Max then and there to assemble the monstrosity that came to be known as The Midnight Toker. An elaborate contraption standing almost three metres high, it consisted of several steel oil drums welded together at strategic angles that only Max seemed to comprehend. He said that the angles were needed to stabilize the temperature and maximize the airflow of the hot smoke around the marinated meats slowly cooking inside.

Almost ten years later, Norm and Mattie couldn't be happier with Frostbite Fred's current reputation in the area as a smoked meat Mecca. Now, Norm liked to say quite proudly that Max was their 'Prince of Pork'. And although Norm liked to take his fair share of the credit for the ribs at the bar, both he and Max knew who the true star of the show was once the swinging galley doors to the kitchen came to rest.

Max liked to have several batches of ribs on the go at the same time as they were always in demand, and he wanted to keep the customers happy, just like Mattie and Norm. The latest batch of ribs would be coming out of the Toker in another half hour or so. Currently, there was nothing else he could do outside, so he closed the smoker and crossed the foggy compound. He double-checked the latch on the side of the tall, heavy wooden gate. Pulling down on the three-centimetre thick steel latch, he nodded to himself — everything was secure.

The entire structure at the back of the pub, including the gate, was constructed from ten-centimetre thick Douglas fir trees, which Max and Norm had felled together from the surrounding forest. The fence had been built to last. Holding it all together, a framework of 4x4 posts and cross-members made the inside of the yard a veritable fortress, keeping wandering bears, cougars and coyotes away from the smoker. Strings of razor wire ran along the top of the fence, keeping out smaller, more agile woodland denizens, such as squirrels and raccoons. It reminded Max more of a penitentiary courtyard than an outdoor kitchen compound. He always liked to say, when the zombie apocalypse finally came to pass, it would be one of the safer spots to be in Lawless.

In addition to protecting the Toker, the thick, wooden fence kept the staff safe when going about their refuse disposal duties. The garbage, recycle bins and used oil reclaim barrel were also located inside the fence in the far corner, away from the smoker. The enclosure was constructed so that the dumpsters were also accessible through a gate on the other side of the high fence so that the waste disposal trucks could empty them on their weekly rounds.

Max had seen the signs out in front of the pub and heard the radio broadcasts, and he knew there was a bear in the area. But he was confident there was no way some 'niaiseux' bear was getting anywhere near his beloved Toker and its precious cargo of delicious, smoked pork and beef.

As he moved toward the kitchen entry, though he didn't think it physically possible, the volume of the music seemed louder now that the band was back from their break. He smiled as he envisioned them stepping onto the stage, turning their amps up to the mythical number of eleven. Usually, when back in the kitchen, he was spared the brunt of the blasting music from the live bands, but not tonight. Pushing through the heavy steel door, the sound of hammering bass guitar oscillated in his eardrums. The gang from HipBone just might require some hearing assistance in their very near future, and perhaps himself as well, he thought with a frown.

Glancing toward the grill, it seemed line cook Harry Cartwright was keeping extremely busy. Six hamburgers sizzled on the grill. On the counter next to him, three plates sat piled high with prime rib, heaps of mashed potatoes at their side, all awaiting their glistening crown of gravy. After slathering some delicious, house-made BBQ sauce on a platter of ribs, Harry shoved them under the heat lamp on the wide stainless-steel ledge at the passthrough window. He smashed the bell twice to signal to Carlene there was another order up for her to deliver. This seemed to be in addition to the previous two orders that had already accumulated there, awaiting her reluctant attention.

Max jumped into the fray and dolloped gravy on top of the prime rib platters. He frowned as he looked through into the pub. After what seemed like forever, Carlene finally sauntered up to the window to retrieve the ribs and other meals. Max shouted over the music to her, "A little more speed would be appreciated next time, Carlene! Things are dying here under the lamp before you can even serve them!"

"I'm run off my feet out there, Max!" Carlene snapped back. "Give me a break!" She blew a few loose strands of hair from her face as if to prove her point, then loaded the waiting orders onto her outstretched arms and wandered back into the crowded pub to deliver them.

Max watched the girl through the pickup window. As soon as she'd dropped the plates of food off to the appropriate patrons (or at least he hoped they were), she strolled right back over to one of her tables of drink-nursing cronies and proceeded to visit with them once more, ignoring the thirsty and hungry paying customers all around her. Shaking his head, Max exited the kitchen and approached Greg at the bar to regale him of the continuing saga that was Carlene Boseman.

As he moved through the crowd, he glanced toward the stage. The lead singer reminded him of Shaggy from Scooby-Doo. Earlier in the evening, when the band first entered the bar, he remembered peering through from the kitchen to see if Fred, Daphne and Velma were also going to make an appearance. But when they didn't show, he figured maybe they were still outside in the parking lot at the Mystery Machine feeding some snacks to Scoob.

Max sidled up next to Greg and pointed toward Carlene. "Oh, tell me about it! That little Sheila is a real no-hoper!" Greg hollered back, his thick Australian brogue bursting through as he spoke.

His mouth only inches from Greg's ear, Max said, "She just doesn't seem to get how it's supposed to work, does she? It's supposed to be she does her job, she gets some pay. Not, she visits friends, she gets some pay. If that were the case, I'd look for a job like that myself!" He shook his head for emphasis.

"I know, mate! She's a regular bingle!" Greg bellowed back, deftly pouring two beers at once.

Max sighed, "Where's the work ethic with kids these days?" As he said that, he glanced at the Kokanee Beer sign on the wall behind the bar, and he was surprised to see that almost a half-hour had elapsed since his last visit to the Toker out back. Where did the time go? Another batch was ready to be taken out and devoured, and he knew he'd better get his ass in gear. He eased his way back toward the kitchen, his lithe, muscular form slipping easily between the galley doors, barely disturbing them as he passed through.

"Harry, comment ça va?" Max yelled to his line cook. Harry looked over and grinned toward Max, bobbing his head up and down in time to the music as he cooked. He gave a big thumbs up and hammered the delivery bell three times to signify there were orders for Jenny Smith to pick up. Max smiled and nodded back, feeling lucky to find a cook that handled pressure so well and one so easy going to boot. He continued through the kitchen, pushing on the heavy delivery door and walking out into the misty-grey void that was the compound.

Max moved through the thick, cloying fog toward the hazy glow of the bright, white security lights that were located over the Toker. Even after the thousands of kilograms of meat that had gone through the smoker over the years, he always looked forward to pulling the latest batch of his trademark, mouth-melting meat from the hulking hotbox.

At first, he didn't notice anything out of place thanks to the shifting nothingness that surrounded him; then, he saw the mess and knew he had a major problem. All of his grilling equipment lay scattered on the ground around his feet — prized meat tongs snapped in half, his bowl of secret sauce crushed and smeared across the frozen slush.

Where the towering smoker had been located was now only empty space. Max shuffled forward a little bit more, blinking his eyes in disbelief. The concrete blocks on which the smoker sat were the only thing left. Through the swirling mist, he saw the fence beside it had been compromised as well.

"Tabarnak!" His heart began to trip-hammer in his chest.

Compromised was actually not quite the right word to describe the fence, he reflected. A more appropriate word would have been 'non-existent'. It had been reduced to kindling, the thick posts now splintered and broken on the ground. Barely visible beyond, one of the Toker's steel drums lay partially crushed on the slushy ground outside the remains of the fence, steam rising from residual heat still trapped inside.

Priding himself on not being a stupid man, Max decided that the best course of action at this point would be to go directly back into the pub, do not pass go, do not collect two hundred dollars, and do not go off exploring stupidly into the fog. Suddenly feeling very exposed and vulnerable, he backed slowly toward the kitchen, wishing his head could swivel three-hundred and sixty degrees like Linda Blair's in The Exorcist. Max did not want to meet whatever had done this damage to the Toker. He was in disbelief that what had happened to his beloved smoker was real — it had to be some sort of fevered dream.

Harry jerked his head up from the grill as the delivery door slammed open. He frowned in confusion as he watched Max stumble into the kitchen in a panic, then quickly turn and ram the heavy door shut. Twisting the deadbolt home to secure the door, Max leaned heavily against it for a moment, his face white.

Harry shouted over to him, "You look like you've seen a ghost, man!"

"I think we have a major wildlife problem," Max yelled back numbly. His fingers fumbled as he grabbed for the phone next to the door. Yanking the receiver off the hook, he dialled the local number for the Lawless Police Department posted on the wall next to it. He needed to speak to somebody in the immediate area right now, not some centralised dispatcher in Kamloops.

The phone rang once at the other end, and went directly to voicemail, "You have reached the Lawless City Police Department," Fred Paulson's recorded voice said soothingly. "If you are listening to this recording, we are currently unavailable and serving other residents of Lawless. Please leave a message at the tone, and we will get back to you as soon as we can."

"Merveilleux," Max muttered as the message played. After the beep, he shouted into the handset, "Hey! This is Max Renaud out at Frostbite Fred's! I think we may have some major problems out here. Something broke into our compound in the back to get at the smoker and then trashed the place! We're here until midnight if you get this message, and want to take a look, thanks!"

The music was so loud now that he was forced to use what he called his 'manual digital volume control' and stuck his fingers in his ears. He hustled through the crowd toward the bar, glancing toward the stage as he went. Shaggy was still howling away into the mic.

Jenny Smith, working a table next to the bar, smiled at Max as he approached. She rolled her eyes over toward Carlene, who was back chatting with her friends next to the stage where the band was rocking out. When Max didn't return her smile, she frowned, figuring something was up.

With his mouth to Greg's ear, Max said, "We've got a big problem, mon ami!"

"I know, mate," Greg responded irritably, looking toward Carlene. "That little Sheila's humpin' the dingo when she should be bouncin' 'tween the tables like a joey!"

Max scratched the back of his head as he tried to translate the bartender's Aussie metaphors. Greg's West-Australian brogue was not helping his comprehension. When Max finally followed Greg's line of sight with his own, he hollered, "No, not her! We have bigger problems out back!" Max's frustration was now ascending his emotional mountainside toward the peak of panic.

"Bigger problems? Like what?"

"The Toker is gone!"

"What do you mean, gone, mate?" Greg asked, incredulous.

"As in it's not there anymore, along with half the compound fence!"

"What? That's impossible, that fence could withstand a bloody bulldozer!"

"I don't know what to tell you; you'd better start looking for some rib-eating bulldozers, then!"

"Jesus, I guess we'd better call the feds!" Greg said, picking up the phone from under the bar.

"I already did," Max shouted above the music as he looked over at the stage. Still wailing away, Shaggy gyrated his hips like some anorexic Elvis Presley. It sounded like the band must have found the number twelve on their amplifiers since the music seemed even louder than before.

Greg yelled to Max, "Better make an announcement, then." He started to bring his fingers to his lips for another ear-piercing whistle.

The keyboard player was winding down the set with a remarkably faithful rendition of Sweet Home Alabama's last few honky-tonk piano riffs when the plate glass window beside him exploded. Razor-sharp glass shards rained over the band and crowd nearest them, slicing into exposed skin wherever they struck.

Shaggy turned to face the window just as claws as sharp as straight razors whisked through the shattered window frame. They carved through the man, slicing his abdomen in half. His lower torso was raked forward off the stage into the screaming audience below while his upper body flew across the room, smashing into the mirror-covered wall behind the bar. Bottles of liquor exploded from the impact along with Shaggy's remaining internal organs, showering everyone nearby with sparkling, scarlet shrapnel.

Carlene, screaming next to the stage, took the full brunt of the creature's strength as it tried to squirm its powerful shoulder farther through the broken window. The massive paw caught her on the rebound, and in a blur of motion, she was backhanded across the room, her body slamming into one of the large, hand-hewn support columns that dotted the interior of the pub. The force of the blow wrapped her backward around the thick wooden beam, snapping her spine with a dry crack.

Jenny saw this and shrieked. She dived behind the bar next to Greg who was hunkered down in the sticky glass shards, loading shells into the magazine tube of a sawed-off Mossberg pump-action shotgun. The Mossberg was kept under the bar for times when the pub had some extra-rowdy customers who needed to be settled down, fast — Greg figured this was one of those times.

Another crash added to the deafening discordance as the remaining band members dropped whatever instrument they were playing and abandoned the stage like rats fleeing a sinking ship.

The paw was withdrawn, and a gargantuan head now filled the window frame. Piercing fangs and sickle-teeth snapped and slathered as the beast roared at the huddled patrons inside. Their screams reached a new crescendo, ratcheting up from loud to ear-splitting in only a millisecond.

Max covered his ears from the deafening cacophony and began backing toward the relative safety of the kitchen. The beast's energy level surged to new heights as it sensed the fear of the huddled masses inside. Worming its way farther into the broken window, it suddenly managed to get one shoulder through the frame as well its head. It howled and gnashed its teeth, raking its free, gore-covered paw across the floor, the claws gouging huge furrows into the hardened maple.

Trapped in the corner next to the ruined window, the bass player had nowhere to go. He tried to dive off the stage out of harm's way, but his foot snagged on a cable, and he went sideways, falling face-first onto the stage instead. Quick to capitalise on the man's misfortune, the predator slammed its huge appendage down on top of the now 'ex' HipBone bass player, spraying his essence across the shrieking customers nearby.

Trip knew a rock and a hard place when he saw one. But even worse, sitting behind his petite table in the corner of the room, he realised he was now stuck between an insane, ravenous bruin and a blazing-hot fireplace. Thanks to the dangerously long reach of the massive bear, he was cut off from the rest of the room. After seeing the bass player become bear-pâté, he wasn't too keen on trying to get by the crushing paw himself, so he was biding his time, looking for an opening, but he knew time was growing short.

The bear roared once more, its mouthful of knife-edged fangs glistening with blood, but not from eating any patrons that Trip could see. Its muzzle appeared torn and bloody, with bits of swollen skin and singed fur hanging from its mouth as it roared. Looking at the wound, he wondered if the beast might have been attracted to Max's Midnight Toker out back and decided to try snacking on the metal contraption. Yeah, Trip figured, trying to swallow hot steel would certainly be enough to piss that thing off and make it crazier than it already looked.

While the monstrous beast tried to further its journey through the window frame, the remaining customers who hadn't already stampeded toward the main entrance decided that now would be a great time to do so. An elderly couple who were already moving toward the door were pushed aside by three burly sledders, getting trampled by the men as they fled.

Angered that it couldn't reach more of its fleeing prey, the beast roared once more and renewed its efforts to drag itself through the window frame with its one free paw. It flung its head back and forth in a frenzy, snapping its mouth open and closed with a cringe-inducing crack each time it did. It was as if it hoped to snag someone stupid enough to be wandering by its open mouth at the moment. With another mighty pull, it inched itself into the pub, shredding the maple floor with its talons as it moved. The thick timber in the window frame began to creak ominously, threatening to tear loose.

Greg popped up from behind the bar and levelled the Mossberg at the beast. He began pulling the trigger and jamming the pump back and forth in rapid succession, blasting at the demon from hell across the room. The stock of the gun dug into his shoulder as the ear-ringing blasts erupted from the short-barreled weapon. After each brief flash, a burst of steel buckshot sprayed toward the beast. But the distance was too great for the shotgun's pellets to have any effect and only peppered the bear in the side and shoulder. This served to anger the creature even more, and it renewed its efforts to gain entry into the pub.

Greg hopped up onto the bar, spinning his legs over it as he moved. His heavy-booted feet dropped to the dusty floor on the other side, and he strode toward the beast. Fire erupted from the shotgun's muzzle as he pulled the trigger and rammed the pump back and forth repeatedly, trying for a killing shot until pulling the trigger only resulted in a metallic clicking noise. He was out of ammo.

The bear continued to shriek and roar, wriggling its way through the window frame. Almost all of the customers had finally fled the scene, abandoning their drinks and meals in favour of a chance of seeing the light of another day. Most of them were quite sure Fred's would be comping their meal this night.

Trip was in an even tighter place. Halfway through the window now, the bear's muscular bulk and powerful hindquarters were the only thing impeding it from gaining entry into the pub.

Greg jammed a handful of shells from his pocket into the magazine tube of the Mossberg and took aim once more, approaching the beast from the front this time.

The bear renewed its insane shrieking howls as it struggled to pull itself through the window frame. It swiped its paw ineffectually, trying to reach Greg, tearing chunks out of the wooden floor. With one mighty stretch of its limb, the predator reached in just a little bit more and snagged the corner of a heavy redwood dining table with one of its hooked claws. Revolving like a top, the table spun around and slammed into Greg's hip, sending the Aussie flying backward into the bar. The shotgun clattered from his hands and spun across the floor, skidding to a halt only a few metres from Trip.

Trip Williams knew he had a decision to make; he could wait for the monster to get the rest of the way through the rapidly deteriorating window frame and devour him and anyone else unlucky enough to be still inside the pub, or he could make a grab for the shotgun and try to save himself, and hopefully others.

He had to make a choice, and he had to make it now.

CHAPTER TWENTY-SEVEN

Austin sat down on a rectangular plastic bench inside The Lawless Community Complex. It was 8:30 P.M. If everything had gone as it usually did, he knew the practice should have ended, and his son would be in the shower by now. While he waited, he passed the time chatting with some of the other hockey parents who were also waiting for their children.

Alex came bustling out of the locker room several minutes later with his hockey bag slung over one shoulder. He waved to his father from across the gleaming, white lobby. "Hey, Dad!" Alex called out as he approached.

"How'd it go, buddy?" Austin stood but resisted the urge to ruffle the boy's hair. It was an old habit that was hard to break. At home, the boy didn't mind, but in public, he was now getting old enough not to want his dad make him look like a little kid when they were out and about. This was especially true if there were any girls from Lawless Secondary School anywhere in the immediate vicinity.

"Not too bad, I scored two goals!" Alex stated, proudly.

"Excellent! Way to go!" Austin held his hand up for a high five, and his son reciprocated this time, but grudgingly, since high fives were still not particularly cool at the moment.

"Ready to grab a bite to eat?"

Alex's face transformed. The slightly embarrassed look it held during the recent half-hearted high five morphed into a beaming grin. "You bet!"

Austin could hear the boy's stomach snarling for food as they walked to his Honda in the parking lot. No big surprise there — the boy's bottomless stomach constantly needed refilling, especially after his high-intensity hockey workouts and even more so after a game. Those nights, Austin usually took his son out for a snack at one of his favourite fast food joints, The Burger Barn. Tonight, seeing as Alex had done so well, and in addition to it being Saturday tomorrow, Austin decided he was going to surprise the boy to a treat of some of Frostbite Fred's mouth-watering ribs. Of course, once they were there, he would be able to indulge in some prime rib for himself, feeding what Alex called his father's 'roast beast addiction'.

Minors in British Columbia under nineteen years of age, if accompanied by an adult, are allowed to eat in public houses and bars that serve food, right up until 10:00 P.M. Austin looked at the dashboard clock and saw it was only 8:35 P.M. right now — they still had plenty of time to get out there and get some tender beef on the table in front of them before the cut-off.

"Then let's go get you some good eats!" Austin said, starting the Honda's engine. He added, "Tonight we're going to Frostbite Fred's!" That comment elicited a 'Woohoo' from the boy as he settled into the passenger seat and fired up his cell phone.

After several minutes of driving through the barely visible, mist-filled streets of downtown Lawless, they finally joined the highway heading toward Fred's. Friday nights were usually a busy time for the pub, especially toward the end of the month. But for whatever reason tonight, the traffic was all going in the opposite direction — car after car, speeding past them on the other side of the road, bumper to bumper in the fog.

"That's strange," Austin said.

"What is, Dad?" Alex asked, looking up from his phone.

"The traffic is all going the wrong way. Usually, on a Friday night, there's a string of cars heading toward Fred's and the resort, not away from it."

And it wasn't just the traffic that was concerning to Austin; it was how they were driving that troubled him as well. As he steered the Pilot around a particularly sharp corner with a yellow, diamond-shaped fifty kilometre per hour warning sign, a Chevy pickup rapidly approached them head-on. The driver had been cutting the corner to maintain control due to his high rate of speed. At the last minute, the reckless Chevrolet driver veered back into their own lane, horn blaring.

"Shit!" Austin shouted. Though he was always on guard for crazy drivers due to his job with the public works department, this one was something special. He'd driven onto the shoulder to avoid the idiot but could only go so far due to the ditch and vertical rockface next to it — if he'd been forced off the road, it was a two-metre drop onto sharp, slush-covered rocks below. Alex's side would have taken the full force of the impact, possibly with tragic consequences. "You crazy bastard!" Austin swore once more, narrowly avoiding the maniac. "What in God's name is his problem?"

"Must be late for his next accident," Alex said, shaking his head ruefully.

Alex's joke made Austin chuckle, feeling some of the tension from the close call dissipate. The boy always seemed to know when a little humour would help a situation, just like Patricia, before Alzheimer's erased that part of her forever.

After several more minutes, the inexplicable conga-line of traffic ended, and they were alone on the highway once more. "That was just plain weird," Austin said. They drove for several minutes in silence until they saw the neon sign outside Frostbite Fred's flashing dimly in the mist.

"We have arrived, but…" Austin peered through the greyness ahead.

Pulling into the lot, Austin stopped for a moment and gaped — it was surreal to see the lot so empty on one of the busiest nights of the week. Had it not been for several vehicles belonging to the staff parked along the far side, it looked like the pub might have been closed.

"What the hell?" He continued driving forward, moving slowly onto Frostbite Fred's lot. Off to one side, Austin saw that one of the remaining vehicles was Trip's battered blue Fargo pickup. This was not unexpected, given Trip's penchant for sports, beer and good food, but that didn't make him feel any better because that meant Trip was somehow involved in all of this strangeness as well.

Just as Austin almost pulled to a stop, he spiked the brakes suddenly, causing Alex to jerk forward, his seatbelt locking in place at the last minute. "Whoa! What's up, Dad?" Alex pulled at the tight shoulder harness, trying to undo it and get out of the truck when the sound of two shotgun blasts rang out.

Austin put his arm across Alex's chest just as the boy released his seatbelt and said, "Stay in the truck and don't move."

"Why, what's going on?"

Austin jumped down out of the truck and shouted at Alex, "Lock the doors and stay here until I come to get you!"

"But Dad!"

"No buts, stay here!" Austin said, slamming the door.

Austin thought he'd seen something large moving around at the side of the pub as he'd pulled into the lot but didn't want to say anything and alarm his son. He cautiously approached the side of the building, then stopped and gaped.

The building's timber construction sat exposed, protruding like broken ribs, as if some gigantic alien creature had burst forth from the pub's chest cavity. The picture window was gone, replaced by a massive hole. He peered inside. Splintered wood and broken glass were scattered everywhere — it looked like a war zone. He now had an excellent idea of why the traffic was in such a hurry to get away from Frostbite Fred's tonight. He stepped through the broken window frame into the pub.

There was no movement inside; the only sound, the hiss of static from an amplifier that had fallen over and was now lying on its side. On the floor near the front door were two seniors, a man and a woman, not moving, but it looked like they were still breathing. Looking toward the stage, Austin felt his stomach do a flip. Smeared all over the raised platform was something that may or may not have been a person at one time, as well as what might have been the lower half of someone else at the foot of the stage across from the hissing amp.

Austin stepped the rest of the way into the pub. His snow boot grinding down onto some shattered glass scattered across the floor.

A sudden metallic 'click' vibrated in his right ear.

The click had come from the hammer of a Mossberg shotgun pointed at his temple attempting to fire on a nonexistent shell, its magazine chamber now fortunately empty.

Trip dropped the shotgun in horror, realising that if he had fired one less shell at the bear, thanks to his famously itchy trigger finger, he would have probably blown Austin's head off just now as he stepped through the window frame.

"Jesus Christ! Holy shit! I'm so sorry, Boss! I thought you were the freaking bear trying to sneak back inside!"

Eyes wide, staring at the Mossberg on the ground, Austin said, "I think I'm really glad you just shot your wad!" He looked back up, his face white, "What in God's name happened here?"

Trip said shakily, "I don't think God had anything to do with this. I just pumped a total of three rounds into that thing, and it only pissed it off more! If it hadn't been for my last shot that blew the goddamned thing's ear off, it might still be in here snacking on me!" Trip blurted everything out in a matter of seconds, one word tumbling over the next, agitated and stressed by the attack. He continued, "Bear came through the window, got the lead singer with his claws first and then squashed the bass player over there. If that thing had been able to get its fat ass the rest of the way through the window into the pub, who knows what would have happened."

"Are there any other survivors?"

"I haven't had a chance to look yet."

"How about the police and ambulance? Has anyone called them?"

"I did!" Max said, poking his head into the room from the galley doors of the kitchen. Seeing the coast clear, he brought the rest of his long-framed body through the door. Max observed the carnage as he approached, shaking his head. "I called the police about fifteen minutes ago when I found the Toker torn apart, along with the rest of the compound. The ambulance I just called a couple of minutes ago."

"What did they say? Are they on their way?"

"I got through to the ambulance on 9-1-1, but I only got a recording from the police, so I left a message. I'll try again now," Max turned toward the phone at the bar. As he spoke, a bottle lying near the edge of the red-spattered bar fell off and smashed onto the ground, making all three men jump.

Jenny Smith peeked sheepishly over the edge of the bar, her brilliant green eyes darting back and forth. She quickly ducked back down again and called out, "Is it gone? Is it safe?" Only her high ponytail was visible as she spoke, bobbing up and down behind the mahogany bar, like part of some alcoholic Punch and Judy show.

"Yes, ma'am, it's gone now," Austin said, gently. The girl slowly stood, her eyes still bouncing around in her head like pinballs as she scoped things out as if in disbelief she was still alive.

As an afterthought, Austin added, "Do you have anything you can put over the bodies? The reason I ask is that I have my son sitting outside in my truck, and I don't want to leave him out there with that thing lurking around. But then again, I don't want him seeing the carnage in here either."

Jenny looked like she didn't comprehend Austin at first, but then things clicked, and she got with the programme, saying, "Yes, absolutely." The girl went running off to the storage room at the back to look for something to cover the slaughter.

"Trip, are you up for checking on survivors while I grab Alex?"

"You bet, Boss."

Normally cool and confident, Trip's voice wavered a bit, still sounding shaken from recent events.

"Great! I'll go grab Alex."

"You got it, Boss."

Austin pushed open the double doors at the front of the bar and walked down the three steps to the parking lot. He scanned the fog, looking for any sign in the swirling mist that the beast might still be nearby. Sighing with relief, he saw his son's wide-eyed face pressed against the passenger side window as he approached the Honda, his breath steaming up the glass. The boy wiped himself a viewing portal in the foggy glass to observe the outside world. Seeing his dad, Alex slowly opened the door of the vehicle and looked cautiously around in the fog as he stepped out.

"What happened, Dad?"

"Remember that bear?"

"The one you put the signs up about?"

"Yeah, it's hurt a few people inside the bar, and some of them are dead. I don't want to leave you out here by yourself, but I don't want you touching anything inside the bar either. The police will be here soon, and we don't want to mess up any part of their investigation."

"I understand, Dad. Hands in pockets, right?"

He smiled at his son, saying, "Right."

Austin pulled his cell phone from his pocket and dialled Christine's number, knowing she would want to be out at the scene as well. After several unanswered rings, it went to voicemail, and he left a message. Knowing the police and ambulance would soon be there, Austin thought it might be best to check things out a bit further. He said to Alex, "Let's get inside." The boy nodded, saying nothing.

Father and son walked side by side into the bar. Austin sat Alex down at a table in a corner seemingly untouched by most of the horror. Tending to the unconscious couple on the floor, Jenny looked up as Austin brought his son inside. She walked to the bar, filled a glass with Coke from the soda fountain and brought it over to the table, placing it in front of the boy. "Thought you might be thirsty," Jenny said, a small smile on her lips.

"Thank you, ma'am," Alex said, blushing slightly.

"It's Jenny, not ma'am," she said gently. "And you're welcome."

"Sorry, ma'am, I mean, Jenny," Alex said, his cheeks grew even brighter as he talked to the pretty young woman before him.

"That's better. Say, I know you, don't I? What's your name again, honey?"

"Alex."

"That's right, you've been here quite a few times with your dad, haven't you, Alex?" The boy nodded at her. "Mind if I sit here with you while we wait for the police and ambulance?" Jenny inquired.

"Sure thing," The boy reached over and pulled a chair out from under the table for her.

Austin smiled and nodded appreciatively at Jenny. She smiled nervously back at him, still obviously quite terrified. She seemed to be holding up well, however, and Austin was grateful for her help.

"I'm going to see what's happened around here. I'll be back in a few minutes."

"Please be careful, Dad." Alex sounded worried.

"I'll be fine. Don't you worry about me, Skipper." Austin said, running his fingers gently through the boy's hair and hoping that would be true. Though he sounded confident, he was deathly afraid the beast was going to regroup and try to get back inside. And here they were, defenceless, with a shotgun that was out of ammo to boot.

Austin approached the broken window frame, and Trip suddenly appeared at this side, rifle in hand. After checking on survivors, he'd run out to his pickup truck to grab his gun, thinking they might still need some protection. "Thought you might want some backup," he said, cocking the rifle.

"I thought you'd never ask," Austin responded gratefully. They stepped through the broken window frame together, the thick fog outside coalescing around them, seeming to swallow them whole.

CHAPTER TWENTY-EIGHT

"Of course, never fails," Christine said, hearing her cell phone ring the moment she stuck her head under the shower. She'd just gotten home a few minutes ago and decided that tonight was the night she was going to shampoo her hair.

"Well, they're just going to have to wait, whoever it is," she said aloud as she started the lathering process. Ten minutes and several litres of hot water later, she wrapped her head in a towel to absorb the excess water still in her shoulder-length blonde hair. She picked up her phone and checked her messages. As Austin's voice played back over the cell's speakerphone, she ripped the towel from her head, tied her damp hair in a loose ponytail, and set a new personal best for the fastest time she'd ever gotten dressed.

Moments later, Christine jammed her hat on her head and flew out the front door, her unzipped parka flapping in the breeze. Locking the door, she pulled her house keys from the lock and they slipped from her hand. They bounced off of her snow boot, landing a short distance away. She bent down to pick them up and felt a sudden hard tug at her shoulder, and realised she'd locked part of her fur-lined hood into the door jam.

"Shit!" She reached to pick up her keys but discovered her arm was not quite long enough. Christine slid the keys over slightly with the toe of her snow boot until her fingertips grazed the metal ring to which they were attached. It was at this point that her hat decided to fall off of her head.

"Double shit!" Keys now in hand, she unlocked the door to extract her trapped parka hood and let out a small laugh. All things considered, she felt lucky she'd dropped her keys when she did. Otherwise, she may not have noticed and walked away from the door with her outerwear still trapped in its frame, tearing her parka. If that had happened, it would have made for a very drafty evening indeed.

Slapping her hat back on her head, she jumped into her truck and cranked the engine. She wanted to get to the scene of the incident at Frostbite Fred's quickly, but she knew it would be slow going as the weather was still not cooperating. Squinting through the windshield, she drove slowly down her laneway into the dark, foggy evening.

***

The Gold Rush of 1895 that struck Lawless was one of the biggest things to ever happen in the area, period. When the rush was in full swing, just before the turn of the century, the townsite boasted a population of over twelve thousand people, consisting mostly of gold-crazed prospectors and their hangers-on. To service the growing population, in a matter of only two years after its founding, the town swelled to fifty-three saloons, twenty-two law firms, seventeen hotels, five banks and four brothels.

Over the ten-year period that the gold rush lasted, over fifty-seven thousand prospectors came through the Cascade mountains in search of their fortune in the gold-filled hills around Lawless. Some came through the lower mainland from Vancouver, and others poured in from south of the border from Washington state. All of those eager fortune-seekers attracted another element that was not quite as law-abiding as the rest of the populace.

Numerous gangs and racketeers also set up shop in the area, and it came to be known that if you were planning on travelling to this part of the interior in your quest for fame and fortune, you were advised to best keep one hand on your gold, and the other hand on a loaded gun. It was a town that got its name for what is was, lawless.

The North-West Mounted Police, a precursor to the modern-day RCMP, was coming off the heels of the North-West Rebellion with Louis Riel. They had minimal manpower available to police the area and had stretched their coverage until it was tissue paper thin. Criminal enterprises were more than aware of this lack of enforcement, and things went from wild to wicked very quickly.

Shopkeepers, bankers and saloon owners in Lawless decided that more protection from crime was required than what the North-West Mounted Police could provide, and the Lawless Police Department was born. For the most part, it did what it was designed to do and brought law and order to the rugged mountain town.

In 1897, the LPD boasted just three members who had their hands full most nights and quite a few days as well. When a rich gold miner blew into town with a thirst for liquor and a lust for the ladies, it came to be known that, despite the name of the town, if you didn't watch your step, a constable from the Lawless Police Department would damn well make sure that you did.

In an attempt to house the local miscreants, a small wooden building was initially built for the local constabulary, with only a couple of holding cells available for use. However, business was brisk, and in a matter of only one year, more spacious accommodations were warranted for the LPD and a larger, more permanent building was erected. The new facility boasted over a dozen holding cells to accommodate wrongdoers and eventually hosted a complement of almost seventy police officers.

The hills around Lawless were a madhouse for several years. Many men and quite a few enterprising women were made very, very wealthy during this time. But after the turn of the century, the deposits of readily accessible ore began to decline, and new strikes diminished dramatically. With less gullible and unaware miners from which to pilfer and suck dry, criminal enterprise in the region went in search of greener pastures. The crime rate tanked, and so did the manpower requirements of the LPD. Now, almost one hundred and twenty years later, the town's current population of seven thousand residents were protected by a police department that boasted a total of seven members, plus one dog.

Constable Oscar Olsen was one of those men. He sighed heavily and adjusted his position in the uncomfortable pressure-moulded orange plastic chair in which he sat. His legs were stretched out to an identical orange chair from the next table over, his feet propped up on the edge. Tonight, he was the officer in charge at LPD headquarters. He sighed once more, this time contentedly, feeling relieved. He'd just gotten back from the most amazing dump of his life. It seemed the big bowl of chili he'd had for lunch today had already begun working its magic. Another noxious gust from south of his beltline reminded him that his work in the washroom still might not be done.

He was currently relaxing in the lunchroom, waiting for his dinner to finish being irradiated. The television on the wall blared hockey scores and league standings on TSN. Oscar watched it for a while, almost drowsing off while he waited, his double chins resting on his ample chest. In the microwave behind him, a family-sized tray of President's Choice Mac & Cheese, the White Cheddar Edition, nuked away, its cellophane overwrap still firmly attached and fusing to the bubbling cheese inside at a molecular level. According to the timer on the front of the oven, Oscar's plasticised cheese-curd-and-wheat dinner was now only one minute and forty-nine seconds away from perfection. He snorted himself awake, then yawned, wiping away some drool that had built up at the corner of his mouth with his shirtsleeve.

Oscar wasn't pleased. He thought of the planned dinner out with his sweetie, Thelma, that was not to be this evening. He'd been showering and getting ready to head down to the local Tim Hortons to see her when Chief VanDusen had called, scuttling Oscar's plans. The Chief told Oscar he was giving himself the evening off and didn't want to be disturbed, so Oscar was going to be the man in charge of law enforcement for the area this evening, thanks to so many officers being down with the flu.

He wasn't a stupid man and Oscar knew by now that being the man in charge meant that Reggie would be in the midst of entertaining his 'special lady friend' again for another evening of carnal delights. On those special nights, VanDusen always made it explicitly clear to Oscar or whoever was on duty that he did not want to be disturbed under any circumstances.

Ever since the gold had been discovered at the cavern, Oscar noticed he'd been experiencing more and more frequent evenings as OIC than ever before. He also knew that VanDusen had been stealing quite a bit of the gold for himself and feathering his nest with the precious yellow metal as well as showering his special lady friend with baubles and furs.

Even though Oscar received his fair share of the proceedings from VanDusen on a regular basis, on several occasions, he had nonetheless decided to mimic the chief when up at the cavern. He'd pocketed dozens of nuggets that he'd come across when the opportunity had presented itself. Being the attentive constable that he was, Oscar learned by example. He'd observed how the mayor was embezzling from his long-time business partner, Ray Chance, with VanDusen's help. When he saw the chief screwing them both over on top of that, well then, logic seemed to dictate it must be okay. Still not being a stupid man, part of him knew if he didn't hide his own gold thievery or turn a blind eye to the chief's misappropriations, he'd be checking out the bottom of one of those pits at the cavern firsthand.

Oscar stretched again and brought both of his size thirteen feet back down to the grey concrete floor. He stood, feeling his bowels begin to gurgle once more. "Guess I might need to revisit the throne," he said with a slight chuckle.

The microwave beeped several monotonous times behind him, and he finally noticed the familiar, but tasty scent of polyvinyl chloride tainted Mac & Cheese in the air. His mouth began to water. He flared his nostrils as he sniffed. "Smells delicious," he said, stroking his belly. It growled back at him in agreement.

Typically, at this point in the evening, Oscar would have headed to the cells to check on the status of anyone back in the drunk tank, or anyone else that they were keeping on ice for whatever reason, legal or otherwise. Fortunately, the 'Reprobate Resort', as it was called around the station, was empty tonight. He'd been on duty for the past couple of hours with no calls or much of anything else happening. When he'd checked the messages before his recent dump, things had seemed pretty chill, just the way he liked it.
But since he hadn't bothered to bring the cordless phone with him while he'd done his deed in the washroom stall, he decided his next stop should be to check for any messages before chowing down.

He removed the still bubbling tray of plasticised pasta from the microwave and looked longingly at it for a moment before leaving it to cool on top of the stained Formica table next to where he'd been sitting.

Sauntering from the lunchroom through to the situation room, he arrived at the reception desk that Fred Paulson manned (and dogged) in the daytime. He looked at the answering machine, and his eyes widened. There were over a dozen new messages. "Holy crap!" he said, pressing the play button.

"Hey! This is Max Renaud out at Frostbite Fred's! I think we may have some major problems out here. Something broke into our compound in the back to get at the smoker and then trashed the place! We're here until midnight..." Oscar pressed 'skip message' on the machine.

"This is Gene Cowan calling! Something's just attacked Frostbite Fred's, it..."

Skip.

"Omigod! There's a gigantic fucking bear out here at Fred's eating people! Get someone the hell out here right now!"

Skip.

"You need to get out to Frostbite Fred's right away. There's a monster..."

He skipped through the messages. One after another, they all played the same, panicked messages about an attack out at Frostbite Fred's. With the other two members who'd normally be on patrol tonight down for the count with the flu, Oscar knew he needed to get someone out there immediately, but also knew he should inform VanDusen as well, despite the warning about not being disturbed. Oscar reluctantly picked up the phone and dialled the chief's private number. It rang several times, and with each unanswered ring, Oscar cringed a little bit more, until VanDusen finally exploded onto the line.

"Jesus fucking Christ, Oscar, how many times have I told you NOT to disturb me?"

Olsen held the receiver away from his head for a moment to mitigate some of the shouting in his ear. "I know, I'm sorry, sir, but...

The chief cut him off. "What the hell did I just say to you two goddamned hours ago when you called me about that plugged toilet? We'll get it fixed in the goddamned morning!"

"It's not about that, Chief, it's…"

"I said, do not disturb!" When VanDusen spoke the last three words of his sentence, they were low, hard and mean.

"I know, sir…"

"And don't you know what that means?"

"Yessir, I do, but…"

"All right, what the hell is it? And it better be goddamned good!"

"There's been another bear attack," Olsen said uncomfortably.

"What? Where?"

"Frostbite Fred's. I'm not sure if anybody is dead or not, but according to the messages I just listened to, it sounded like the thing from the campsite was inside the pub and starting to eat people! Whether they survived or got digested is anybody's guess."

"Dammit! All right, I'll get dressed and see you out there in about fifteen."

"Roger Wilco, over and out!"

"And cut that shit out! Just a simple yessir is sufficient."

"Yessir, over and out!"

CHAPTER TWENTY-NINE

The fog seemed to have a physical presence, and Austin's limbs felt heavy as if he were trying to walk underwater. But he knew it wasn't the swirling water vapour holding him back, it was his reluctance to proceed into the unknown. Next to him, Trip had his rifle at the ready, its stock nestled into his shoulder and finger off the trigger, making sure his itchy digit didn't have any sudden spasms with tragic consequence. Multi-coloured light from the blinking neon signs inside the bar shone through the hole at their backs, bathing them in an ethereal kaleidoscopic glow, adding to the surreal experience.

Austin paused and turned, gawking at the damage to the pub behind them. When they'd been here at lunchtime, Frostbite Fred's had sported a big, beautiful, plate glass window that looked out over the lovely valley below, providing a picturesque view when the day was bright, and the fog was gone. Tonight, it appeared a bomb had gone off next to them — shards of glass and timber fragments lay everywhere.

The pub had been built to look like a large Swiss chalet-style building with signature angled roof and all of the decorative trimmings that went with it. Thick logs encased the building, each over twenty-five centimetres in diameter. Some of the logs now had huge chunks gouged from them by the beast's claws while others had been torn away.

Trip shook his head in wonder. If the walls had been constructed out of the usual 2x6s, plywood and drywall like most new construction in the area these days, the monster would have surely shredded it in short order and rampaged through into the pub. If that had happened, the number of casualties would have been catastrophic.

Pushing through the mist around the side of the building, they arrived at the compound. Speechless, both men stood in stunned silence, looking at the sturdy fence behind the Midnight Toker, or at least what was left of it. Splintered logs lay everywhere, and the monolithic smoker was nowhere in sight, only twisted bits of steel remained where it had been bolted to its concrete base.

In a low voice, Trip said, "Unbelievable!" He suddenly smelled the familiar tang of Max's BBQ sauce and looked down at his feet. He stood in a small puddle of the distinctive reddish-brown sauce sprayed across the frozen ground, looking more blood-like than sauce-like at the moment. His stomach did a somersault in agreement with his assessment. The steel bowl that had contained the sauce looked like a pneumatic press had flattened it.

"We need to find this thing before anyone else dies," Austin said, shaking his head. Trip nodded but said nothing. He moved to the kitchen delivery door and tried the handle, but it was locked. Using the butt of his rifle to knock on the door a couple of times, he gave it the old 'shave and a haircut' routine.

Harry, leaning against the wall inside, jumped almost a metre in the air. He cautiously opened the door, saying, "Holy crap, you just about gave me a heart attack!" Pushing almost sixty, Harry didn't look a day past seventy, thanks to his long, grey ponytailed hair and sallow skin.

Trip smiled inwardly, thinking the line cook didn't look like the kind of man that needed any sudden jolts of adrenaline coursing through his rail-thin physique. "Sorry, Harry, just checking things out back there. Didn't mean to startle you, but the door was locked."

"Maybe you could try the buzzer next time," Harry said, eyes wide, hand held over his heart.

Trip replied, "I'll see what I can do. Did you see anything back here?"

"Just the inside of the walk-in cooler. I headed in there as soon as I heard the screaming." There was obvious pride in his voice as he spoke as if hiding away in a cooler at the first sign of trouble, instead of seeing if he could help, was anything of which to be proud.

Austin nodded upon hearing this, saying, "Okay, thanks. Stay cool, Harry." Continuing their journey of discovery, they pushed through the galley doors into the bar proper. The room now had the welcome addition of strobing red emergency lights from the local ambulance service, giving the fog outside the hole in the wall a crimson cast. The entire fleet of Lawless's EMS appeared to have been called out tonight, with both ambulances in attendance.

Two paramedics were over at the stage looking at the mess that had at one time been the bass player and lead singer of HipBone. One of them stood shaking his head in disbelief, while the other looked somewhat nauseated, holding his hand over his mouth.

Near the door, the other pair of paramedics were looking after the elderly couple that had been trampled in the panic. When Trip had checked for survivors earlier, he'd found the elderly couple unconscious, battered and bruised, but still alive. He'd made sure they were as comfortable as could be with balled up bar towels beneath each of their heads. Jenny Smith had tucked blankets around them as well to keep them warm until help arrived. Both now appeared to be conscious and alert.

Across the large room, Alex sat where Austin had left him, a half glass of Coke remaining, his face buried in his cell phone once more. Nearby, Jenny Smith tended to bartender Greg, now conscious again. The Aussie sat on the floor, his back against the bar, holding his right forearm. He was talking animatedly to Jenny about how he'd shot the bear. She smiled, telling him she'd seen it all, adding it was like something out of a Hollywood action film. Greg seemed to like that image and grinned, settling back against the gleaming, oiled mahogany as the paramedics from the stage approached to take over his care.

Alex glanced up from his phone and smiled, a relieved look on his face when he saw his father approaching with Trip at his side, rifle still in hand. Austin waved to the boy, smiling himself. He was pleased to see that his son had listened and stayed put. As he and Trip approached, Alex said, "Jenny was telling me that this bear is freakin' huge! She said it cut up one guy pretty bad with its claws, and another guy got squished!"

"Sorry," Jenny said, approaching from the bar. "I sort of let slip what happened."

"That's understandable, all things considered," Austin said kindly.

Jenny looked over to Trip, her eyes brightening and said, "There he is! The man of the hour!"

Trip said nothing and blushed at this proclamation of his heroism.

"Really? What happened, Trip?" Austin asked.

Looking down at his boots in modesty as he recalled the events, Trip said, "Well, after Greg got knocked back by the bar there, his shotgun came skidding across the floor and pretty much ended up right in front of me, so I grabbed it and used it!"

"You're far too modest, Trip!" Jenny said. Turning to Austin and Alex, she said, "And you didn't just grab it. In fact, I didn't think you could move that fast! You were like Rambo! I mean, you just dove for the gun, rolled, came up on one knee, and then blam! And then blam again!" she concluded enthusiastically.

"Blam?" Austin said, looking over to Trip.

"Something like that. Wasn't a very good shot, though. I only ended up taking the top of one of the thing's ears off with the last shot, but as I said earlier, I guess it was enough. I think the buckshot in the Mossberg was pissing it off more than harming it because of its thick hide beneath. Part of its muzzle was seared-off from trying to eat the Toker out back. That must have hurt like a son of a bitch. I think by the time the thing found the window; it was probably crazy with pain when it burst through."

"Well, thank goodness you and Greg were here tonight! You're both heroes in my book!" She looked from Trip over to Greg, her voice rising with excitement as she concluded, clapping her hands together, obviously enamoured with the men's acts of bravery.

A wail of sirens and flashing red and blue lights brought the conversation to an abrupt halt — the LPD had finally arrived on the scene.

Stepping into the pub from out of the strobing mist, Oscar Olsen held one of the heavy doors open, glancing toward the stage. He appeared queasy and held back, breathing the fresh air from the open doorway for as long as he could.

"Son of a bitch!" VanDusen said, stalking into the room in disgust. "What in God's name happened here? Is this that same goddamned bear again, Olsen?"

"I think so, sir," Oscar called from behind, making it a point not to look toward the stage.

VanDusen looked over to where Austin and Trip were standing and added, "Oh friggin' great! Here we go again! Look who's already here, the goddamned Lone Ranger and Tonto!"

Austin sidled up to the police chief and said, "Late to the square dance, again, huh, Reggie?"

"I don't think there were many people here who enjoyed this little shindig, Murphy," the chief growled.

"You've got that right. Looks like we have at least two dead with several injuries as well," Trip said.

"When I've assessed the situation, I'll determine how many we have of what, thanks, Williams!" VanDusen said haughtily. "And you better not have touched anything here either Williams, or I'll have you charged with evidence tampering and obstruction! And that includes you and your brat there, Murphy!" He glared at Alex, who was sitting wide-eyed watching the whole conversation between his father, Trip and the chief.

With his authority established, VanDusen turned, almost walking over the top of Oscar, who'd sidled up silently behind him as he spoke.

"Jesus Christ, Olsen! What have I told you about sneaking up on me like that?"

"I wasn't sneaking, sir! I was just making notes!" Oscar said, defensively, clutching his notepad to his chest, looking rather green around the gills.

"Then make more goddamned noise scribbling with your pencil! Or maybe tie a friggin' cowbell around your neck, I don't know! C'mon, let's go check this shit out!" VanDusen barked, stomping toward the abattoir that was now the main stage.

"Yessir," Olsen said. Notebook still in hand, he trailed reluctantly behind VanDusen like a small puppy that thought it was about to have its nose rubbed in some of its own natural bodily functions.

Austin watched this with some amusement. Sometimes, he swore it was like an old Abbott and Costello routine.

Through the foggy hole in the wall, Austin saw the flash of headlights accompanied by the strobe of yellow emergency lights as Christine's Moon's conservation truck pulled into the lot.

**

Christine parked her Dodge next to the LPD car sitting in the disabled parking zone. From what she could discern through the fog, Frostbite Fred's exterior looked normal enough with no visible signs of a disturbance. Pulling open one of the slab-like pine doors, she stepped through and saw it was a different story inside. The carnage was insane and seemed to cover everything in sight. She craned her head around, checking things out. It looked as if several people had been eviscerated judging by the blood and entrails scattered about the room.

Striding confidently toward Austin and Trip's location, her boot heels knocked against the red-smeared floor. She ignored the brooding chief of police and nauseated-looking constable as she passed. With a slight smile as she approached, she said, "I presume you've already been chatting with the Apple Dumpling Gang over there, have you?"

"They do keep me entertained, that's for sure," Austin said, glancing in VanDusen's direction as he spoke. He flashed the chief a quick grin and received a scowl in return.

"So, what in God's name happened here?" Christine asked as she lithely stepped next to Austin and Trip, avoiding a piece of gore on the floor. Her movement toward them carried the scent of her freshly shampooed hair on the air currents inside the bar. Austin noted the floral bouquet provided a pleasant diversion for a moment until its delicate notes were once more vanquished by the coppery smell of blood and entrails sprayed around the large public room.

"It's a mess, as you can see. Come with us for a second, and we'll fill you in on some details." Taking Christine on a quick tour, Austin pointed out several things of note he'd observed since arriving. Then Trip began a vivid description of his evening adventure but trailed off as they arrived at the stage where the local constabulary was finishing up their photoshoot.

Christine stood with her hands on her hips, surveying the scene, then looked over to VanDusen and said, "Do you need any more proof of this thing's existence, Chief, or do you want to wait until you get some more samples back from your lab?"

VanDusen gave her a withering stare. "What I do or don't do is of no concern to you, Moon. I'm not beholden to discuss any pending investigations, especially with you!"

"But you certainly can't deny its existence now!" She shook her head slightly in disbelief at the man's arrogant nature.

"I don't have to do a goddamn thing you suggest!" The chief stomped away with Olsen in tow, moving toward Greg, who was still seated against the bar.

Christine shook her head once more saying, "Unbelievable!"

Austin sympathised, saying, "I don't know what it's going to take to get that man to play ball."

"I'm surprised that nobody has spotted the thing until now," Trip said, changing gears on the conversation.

"Well, I think it's pretty safe to say that this thing is nocturnal. I don't think we've had any attacks in the daylight, yet." Christine said.

"None that we know about, anyway," Austin added. "Plus, I think this fog is certainly helping Angus in the stealth department, that's for sure." He turned to Christine and finished, asking, "So, where does this put us now?"

Christine looked thoughtful for a moment. "Well, we're still waiting to hear if that blood from the campsite is human or not. But then again, whether it is or it isn't is a moot point since we now have a least two confirmed deaths attributed to this creature here tonight. The way the pattern is looking, after what we plotted on the map earlier, I think that we're going to have to prepare ourselves for the eventuality that this monster might find its way into the town of Lawless itself. If that happens…" she trailed off.

"I know, I've thought that myself. What else can we do?" Austin asked.

We need to make everyone in town and the surrounding valley aware that this thing is out there and that it seems to be eating whatever it can fit into its mouth. I'll call the radio station again in the morning once a live DJ is on duty so that they can make a new announcement to remind everyone that this thing is still stalking the area and that it's deadly!"

"Maybe I can get the word out to some of my hunting buddies to keep an eye out as well." Trip added, helpfully.

Christine nodded, saying, "Thanks, Trip, but present company excluded, the last thing we need is a bunch of would-be 'Great White Hunter' types wandering around out in the bush, getting drunk and shooting at anything that moves."

Chuckling in agreement, Trip said, "Yeah, you're right. It'd be just like a regular hunting season then."

***

By the time Christine finished at Frostbite Fred's, it was after three o'clock in the morning. She was almost asleep on her feet when she arrived home but took a moment for a quick snack of cheese and crackers, then brushed her teeth. Just as she lay her head upon her pillow, almost dozing off, she realised she still had several things left to do and bolted upright in bed.

Picking up her cell, she brought up the number for the local radio station and dialled CKLL, or Big Buzz FM as it was known to the locals. The early morning host, Reba Casalino, had just stumbled in the door, sounding almost as exhausted as Christine felt as she answered the phone. After a brief rundown of what happened at Fred's the previous evening, she informed the DJ that she wanted to give people enough information to make them listen, but not enough to cause panic in the streets. Residents needed to be aware of what might lay in wait just outside their door at any moment were they to go wandering off into the fog. They needed to know that their decision for a healthy stroll could be the last decision they would ever make. Reba agreed wholeheartedly, adding that she thought many of them already knew judging by the double-digit number on the station's answering machine currently flashing in her face.

After thanking the radio host for her help and ending the call, Christine fired off an e-mail message to the Conservation Service's head office down on the coast informing them of the latest developments with the bear. At the end of the message, she added that if they wanted to send extra officers up to help track the creature currently stalking Lawless, she would most certainly welcome the assistance.

A quick text to Austin asking if he could put up a few more bear signs around town was the final thing she needed to do before placing her head back upon her pillow. He'd left the pub a little before midnight in an attempt to get Alex home at some sort of reasonable time. Hoping he would have had a short but sound sleep, she texted her thanks in advance, saying she'd contact him when she awoke for a status update.

With a sigh, Christine lay back and placed her phone on the bedside table. Setting her large, chromed, analogue alarm clock to wake her in five hours, she hoped to get some sort of solid sleep, while still not letting the day waste away — it was sure to be a long one with perhaps an even longer night attached.

CHAPTER THIRTY

The sky had cleared overnight, the temperature inversion finally blowing out of the valley. It was a quarter to seven in the morning and the first hint of daylight tentatively probed the edge of dawn, its radiance just starting to dance along the tips of the rugged mountain peaks.

The fact that the weather had changed for the better and the fog was gone did not even register in Ray Chance's brain. His head throbbed and his mind was still cloudy from a couple of dozen ounces of brandy too many the night before. Pulling into his reserved parking spot at the Golden Nugget Casino and Resort, he massaged his temples and frowned, saying to himself, "What in God's name is going on here?"

Back in the day, when they used to have skiers at the resort, all one hundred rooms would have been rented at this time of year. Sadly, those were the good old days, and now, they only maintained half of them for guests to stay in while they gambled their little hearts away. Fortunately, the gambling revenue from the casino more than made up for the lack of room rentals.

But today was odd. For some reason, the parking lot was almost empty. The resort was supposed to be currently booked to half capacity, as far as his spotty memory could attest. If that were the case, he pondered, then where the hell were all the goddamned cars to go with all the goddamned guests that were still supposed to be checked-in here this morning?

Chance stormed into the lobby and screamed at the front desk manager, Al Frisco, saying, "Al! What in God's name happened to all of my goddamned guests?"

Al raised one of his impeccably groomed eyebrows and said, "Well, sir, there was an incident at Frostbite Fred's last night and…"

"How the hell would an incident at the goddamned pub down the hill affect us up here?"

"Well, sir, there was a bear attack."

"What? One little bear attacks and everybody clears out?"

"It was a very large bear apparently, sir, and two people were killed."

"Jesus Christ! Either way, how does that affect us?"

"It seems that there were some travellers from the resort down at Frostbite Fred's last night, sir. According to Melanie, who was on shift last night, these people came flooding back from Fred's and ran straight up to their rooms. They packed their things and then came right back down to the front desk, and she was suddenly swamped with over a dozen people lined up to check out."

"What? Didn't anybody try to talk them into staying? Offer them a free buffet or a twenty-dollar slot voucher or anything?"

"Yes, sir, Melanie made that offer to all of them, but the guests wouldn't hear any of it, telling her they valued their lives more than their vacations. Apparently, the ones that were waiting to check out caught the attention of some of the other tourists gambling in the casino. Once they'd talked to the ones from down at Fred's, there was a snowball effect, and within a few hours, about ninety percent of our patrons were lined up to check out. In fact, I had to help process a few of them myself when I came in early for my shift this morning. Al made sure to emphasise the word 'early' as he mentioned that last detail to Chance.

"Jesus jumped-up Jehoshaphat! What the hell are we going to do now!" Ray bellowed.

"I'm not sure, sir. Perhaps we can run a 'Bear Scare Buffet Special' and put rooms on at fifty percent off to entice customers back up here?" Al added, somewhat seriously.

"Hmpf! Not funny, Frisco," Chance said, stomping to the elevator. He jabbed one sausage-link finger at the call button to take himself up to what he called the penthouse, also known as the second story of the resort to everyone else. Next to the elevator, an ornate wooden stairwell wound up to the guest rooms and his large office located there. In over the thirty-year span he'd been managing the resort, the stairs weren't something Chance had ever considered using, and his rotund physique could attest to the fact. With a ping, the shiny brass elevator doors opened, and Chance stepped inside. He turned around and glowered across the lobby toward the front desk.

Al Frisco smiled blandly back at Chance until the elevator doors closed, then shook his head, pulled out his cell phone and began checking help wanted ads on LinkedIn.

When the elevator dinged open onto the second floor, Chance waddled across the hall toward the frosted glass door labelled, Raymond Chance, Manager, Private. He unlocked the door and flung it open hard enough to rattle the glass, then stormed toward his interior office.

Roxanne Rooney's desk was empty at the moment. Most days, she never showed up for work until almost 9:00 A.M, but Ray was okay with that since she was so very easy on the eyes. Due to the early hour, he wasn't able to receive his morning dose of eye candy and frowned slightly as he gusted through into his office, slamming the door behind himself. Grabbing the crystal decanter on his desk, he poured a couple of fingers of brandy into a snifter next to it then pounded half of it back.

A brand-new Motorola UHF two-way radio base station sat on his desk next to the decanter. Chance powered it up and grabbed the microphone. He'd insisted Watkins bring a radio paired to the station with him when he went up to the cavern last night. After several frustrating minutes of trying to raise the caretaker without success, he gave up.

"Shit! You lazy little bastard! What the hell is going on up there?" To help himself ponder the situation, he finished his first drink then sloshed an entire fist of brandy into the snifter. After a couple of mouthfuls, he picked up the telephone receiver on his desk, punching in Bob Nichols' private number.

The Mayor picked up on the second ring. "Ray, what the hell is going on?" Nichols asked before Chance could utter a word.

"I was going to ask you the same damn question, Bob! Our goddamned resort is empty this morning because of that goddamned bear of yours traipsing around the countryside eating people. We're lucky we've got the gold to provide us with some income to fall back on!"

"My bear? Since when did I take ownership of the thing?"

"Just like everything else in any other small town in the world, when there's a problem, it's always the mayor's problem." Chance chuckled, knocking back the last of his drink in one gulp.

"I see. Doesn't the fact that it was your man Watkins who discovered the cavern make you somewhat responsible as well? Let's split the difference and call it OUR bear, then, shall we? In any event, yes, I heard about the attack. VanDusen called me just a little while ago."

"Well, I don't know what we're going to do now! I can't get ahold of Watkins up at the cavern! I spent forever on the radio trying to reach him this morning, but he isn't picking up."

Nichols smiled thinly into the receiver and said, "All right, here's what's going to happen: I'm going to head up to your neck of the woods around noon today. VanDusen will be up shortly after that, once he's had his nap. He said he wasn't going anywhere without some sleep — being up all night at Fred's tuckered him out, apparently."

"Great! Then we'll grab a couple of snowmobiles from the resort once he's awake, and we'll all head up there together!" Chance said, excitedly.

"That was going to be the next thing I was going to say if you hadn't interrupted me," Nichols sighed. He finished, "So today we shall see what's happening up there and get all of this shit straightened around once and for all! Fair enough?"

"Perfect! I'll be ready," Chance said, slamming the receiver down. He settled back into his leather chair, grabbed the snifter and heavy crystal decanter and slugged himself with another fistful of breakfast brandy.

CHAPTER THIRTY-ONE

Austin Murphy sat on the edge of his bed, rubbing sleep-heavy eyes, a huge yawn threatening to split his face in half. His ageing clock radio, or vintage ticker, as Alex called it, showed the time was just a hair past 7:00 A.M. Blinking at the display, he corrected himself, it was actually two hairs past seven. Yawning mightily once more, he still felt groggy from the late night before, with only five hours of sleep under his pajama top.

He checked his cell phone and saw a waiting text message from Christine and responded to it right away. Knowing she'd probably been up all night and was most likely already napping, he said he'd get onto tackling some more signs as soon as he'd refuelled with some breakfast. Speaking of which, after tying his bathrobe's belt around his waist, he opened his bedroom door to the tantalising smell of eggs, bacon and toast. He wandered into the kitchen, still rubbing his eyes.

Alex stood at the stove, cooking up a breakfast that he knew they both enjoyed. Briefly turning his attention away from the frying pan in front of him, he looked over his shoulder and said, "Morning, Dad."

"Morning, buddy, why are you up so early?"

"I was starving when I woke up this morning! I didn't get my ribs last night, remember? That glass of Coke at the pub and then those two bowls of granola I had when I got home really didn't fill me up very much."

"I'm sure," Austin said, nodding in agreement. "We probably should have poured the whole box of cereal and the entire jug of milk into you. That might have lasted you a couple of hours longer. But then again, with your appetite…"

Alex nodded in agreement and turned back to the task at hand.

Austin smiled, glancing toward the counter behind the boy. An empty egg carton, bread wrapper and the crumpled plastic hide from a pound of bacon sat upon its surface. Man, that boy can pack it away, he thought, then recalled himself at the same age and the distress he'd caused to his own parent's food budget at the time. He smiled wistfully — payback was a bitch. It was not that he begrudged feeding his son, as the boy needed all the calories he could get into his growing body each day. Today, he needed to fuel up big-time as his team, The Kootenay Lawbreakers, had a big game this evening, playing against their main rivals from a few valleys over, the Driftwood Dodgers.

Preparing a quick coffee for himself using the pod coffee brewer on the counter, he turned to his son and said, "So, I've promised Chris I'd put some more 'Bear in Area' signs around town this morning. Did you want to give me a hand?"

"Sure thing!"

"Great! If you can tag along for a few hours, I can put you to work swinging the sledgehammer pounding in some posts."

"Is Uncle Trip going to be helping us?" Alex asked. His son liked hanging around with Trip, whom he affectionately called Uncle, having known the man since birth. With his mother no longer living, it seemed important for him to include other people in his life, especially someone like Trip, who was not only his godparent but his dad's best friend as well.

"No, I told him to get some sleep and that I'd probably be okay today since I knew I could count on you, Skipper!" He flashed a smile at his son. "So, it'll just be you and me. And as an added bonus, I thought that when we're done, we could go to the Burger Barn for lunch and get you one of those triple cheeseburgers that you love so much."

Alex seemed somewhat disappointed upon hearing his uncle was not going to be joining them, but his eyes brightened when he heard the word cheeseburger. He asked, "Can I have yam fries, too? With gravy?"

"I don't see why not."

"Yes!" Alex grinned, pumping his fist into the air in victory.

Austin smiled in amusement. Though his son was just about to eat a sizeable breakfast, he was already looking forward to his upcoming lunch — the teen had an appetite that almost matched his uncle's.

The toast popped up as Alex finished scrambling the eggs. "All right, Dad, looks like our breakfast is ready!"

"Okay, buddy, let's fill up and then get out there and make everyone bear aware!"

***

A dozen kilometres away, Jerry Benson woke screaming.

Behind closed eyes, before he was fully conscious, fangs, claws, and blood sprayed across his mind. In quick succession, Matt, Nick and Tyler all appeared, smiling and laughing around the campfire as they'd reminisced about the good old days. Then, in a flash, he saw them again at the ends of their lives, and the horrors that befell each of them.

He screamed himself into consciousness, sitting bolt upright in bed, another scream perched on the edge of his lips before he opened his eyes. Everything came flooding back in full, living colour, playing over and over in his mind, on a repeat loop in the ultra-high-definition Imax theatre at the back of his brain. Crystal clear in his memory was an image of him speeding off into the night on his snowmobile, driving like a madman. Then came the feeling of knowing the monster from hell was somewhere at his back, coming for him in the fog. Finally, he remembered suddenly flying through the air as the ground disappeared from beneath his snowmobile's treads.

And then there was nothing but darkness — until now.

Looking around, he realised he wasn't cold, wet, or bleeding anywhere, and tucked away the scream ready to spill from his lips, saving it for future nightmares.

It would appear he was now in a warm, quiet, very white hospital room. Next to his bed was a single, yellow flower in a small white vase.

A petite brunette nurse came racing into the room, her white-soled sneakers squeaking on the glossy-white, freshly waxed floors. "My gosh, Mr. Benson, you scared me!" she exclaimed. "Are you okay? You've been in a coma for a couple of days, and we didn't know if, or when, you'd come back to us!"

"What? Where am I?"

"You're at the Lawless Community Health Centre." She smiled and pulled out a digital thermometer, touching the device to his ear and checking his temperature.

"What about my friends?" Jerry started to inquire for a brief moment, and then reality came crashing back down on him once more. He tried to drag himself up on the pillows at his back to sit upright in bed but was thwarted by the cast that he discovered was now part of his right forearm. An IV drip fed glucose from a transparent plastic bag into a vein in his left.

"I'm sorry, Mr. Benson, but you're the only one that they brought in." The nurse saw Jerry's positional predicament and adjusted the bed to an upright sitting position for him. She placed a blood pressure cuff on his unencased arm and inflated it.

"Thank you," he said, feeling more comfortable. He closed his eyes while she checked his blood pressure. All the moments of terror from the campsite rushed back into his mind again. "Oh, God," he sobbed quietly.

"I'm so sorry for your loss, Mr. Benson," the young nurse said, noting his blood pressure on a chart and taking off the cuff. The thick lenses of her black, horn-rimmed glasses magnified the compassion in her pale, blue eyes.

"Who brought me in?" Jerry suddenly realised he had no idea how he'd gotten here.

"I believe it was Austin Murphy from the Public Works Department here in Lawless that brought you to the emergency."

"Could I talk to him, do you think?"

"I don't see why not. I'll try to contact him for you. But it's Saturday today, so I'm not sure if he'll be in, but I'll try."

"Thank you. I'd appreciate it." Jerry smiled tiredly.

With a gentle look, the young woman said, "No worries. I'll contact him as soon as I get a chance. If you're okay for the moment, Mr. Benson, I've got another couple of patients I need to check on. I should ask, though, are you in any pain?"

"Just a little sore, and then there's this," he held his cast up. "But I guess I'll survive, thanks. You've been very kind."

The nurse nodded slightly with a small smile again and glided out of the room. Jerry was left alone with his thoughts. But they were thoughts he didn't want to have — thoughts of the monster and all of the horror and the three best friends he's known his entire adult life who were now gone forever. Why did he survive and not Tyler, or Matt, or Nick?

Perhaps if he could somehow find somebody to help track this monstrosity down so they could kill it, he might feel that his friends would have had some retribution, and he felt better for a moment.

But then, a pang of new and different guilt arose in his mind. What if the monster had followed him back to the campsite from the cavern in the fog? He definitely didn't like this new thought, the one that told him he might have led the creature to his friends and was somehow responsible for their demise.

If he didn't do something about it, he knew the guilt was something that would haunt him for the rest of his life. He hoped somehow, he could help, or find someone to help him. Then maybe he could staunch the horror show that now seemed to be playing behind his closed eyes 24/7. Another separate part of him hoped that, perhaps, Austin Murphy might be the man to make that happen.

CHAPTER THIRTY-TWO

Alex stepped onto the front porch, marvelling at what this new day had brought. "Sunshine!" he exclaimed, his breath steaming from his mouth.

"That's a sight for sore eyes, for sure," Austin said. "And it brought us some colder weather with it, just like the weather office said." His breath curled up into the delightfully clear, frosty air.

Across the valley, over the cusp of the mountains, rich, golden rays shot into the deep blue early-morning sky, ready to spill into the Kokanee Valley below and flood Lawless with something that was a rare commodity in the wintertime, sunlight.

"This is awesome, Dad!" Alex inhaled and exhaled a few more times, watching his breath plume and pretending to puff on an imaginary cigar.

Enjoy it while you can, buddy. Ice fog is in the forecast for tonight." Austin climbed behind the wheel of the Pilot as he relayed the bad news.

"Ah, man!"

Driving down his lane to the highway, Austin enjoyed the fact he could see where he was going for a change — no unexpected ditches popping into sight as he drove. He sighed, "Ah, now, this is living!"

With the clearing at the moment, though short-lived, it gave him some small hope that they might be able to track this monster down once and for all. Yes, things were finally looking up.

At the yard, Austin and Alex were met with yet another pleasant surprise. Leaning on the rear corner of the public works truck, munching on a cruller, was Trip, who had apparently been by Christine's compound already. In the back of the truck sat several dozen yellow 'Bear in Area' signs. Alex waved to Trip as they pulled in, a big smile on his face. Trip gave the boy a quick salute in return.

"Trip, my friend!" Austin said, rolling down his window as he pulled up, "What are you doing here? I thought I gave you the weekend off?"

"You did, Boss. But I remembered Chris mentioning she wanted to put some more signs up this morning. And when I saw the sun coming up, I knew you'd most likely be hard at it helping her — looks like I was right! Plus, I want to see this thing stopped just as much as you do, or at least make people aware that it's out there until we can stop it and kill it, that is." He bit into his cruller; his forehead creased with concern.

"Well, thanks again for being here, my friend." Climbing out of the Honda, Austin turned to his son, saying, "All right, Skipper, I just need to go and grab a few things, I'll only be a minute or two."

"Okay, Dad." Alex jumped down out of the SUV and wandered over to the public works truck where Trip was brushing his latest cruller from his coveralled belly. "Hey, Uncle Trip, how's it going?" Alex asked, jumping up to sit on the edge of the truck bed next to where Trip was leaning.

"Not too bad, little buddy!" Something as rare as the sunshine above appeared on Trip's face below; a discernable smile suddenly beamed from beneath his bushy beard as he spoke. He had known Alex since the day of his birth and was the boy's godfather. The first day he'd seen the boy, he'd always called him little buddy, for some reason. But now, at fifteen, the boy stood just over one-hundred and eighty centimetres tall and sported seventy-five kilograms of solid muscle (the latest stats Austin proudly shared with him last week). But of course, like all things with teenagers, that was subject to change on an almost daily basis. Yes, Alex was anything but little now. In fact, the boy stood five centimetres taller than Trip at the moment and was still growing. Yes, he definitely might have to revisit his choice of a nickname for his godson very, very soon.

"Were you scared last night when the bear was attacking at Frostbite Fred's, Uncle Trip?" Alex asked, wide-eyed.

"You have no idea," Trip said, honestly. "That thing is the biggest, meanest, ugliest looking mother I've ever seen. It really is a monster," Trip added the word monster because he knew his godson was a big movie buff and enjoyed the old horror and sci-fi movies of the 1950s and 1960s.

"Do you think a regular gun could kill it, Uncle?"

"Well, I saw Greg at the pub hit that thing repeatedly in the side with the Mossberg, and it only aggravated the damned thing. When I was able to use that same gun a bit later, I think I only got lucky when I blew the things ear off. And an ear is a small thing, but I think that it must have hurt like hell. "

"How so?"

"Since last night, I've thought quite a bit about it, and I don't think a creature that large would ever have known what real pain feels like."

"What do you mean?" Alex tilted his head quizzically.

"I mean, yeah, it would have had some scrapes and scratches from smaller creatures that it came across and chowed-down on throughout its life, but I bet it was never anything major because I'm pretty sure it's never met anything bigger than itself!"

"That it couldn't eat!" Alex added.

Trip nodded. "Exactly! A creature that size probably wouldn't have had any natural predators and would have only ever dealt-out pain and hurt, never receiving any in return since it was at the top of the food chain. My shotgun blast that ripped its ear off could be the first real pain that thing ever felt in its life, next to when it tried to eat Max's Toker that is."

"Hmm… That's a good point." Alex looked down at his size twelve snow boots for a moment in thought. Looking back up at Trip, he said, "So, how do you think you're going to stop this thing, Uncle Trip? It doesn't look like regular guns are too effective against a bear of this size, from the sounds of it." He contemplated his footwear a moment longer, then said, "Hey! I know! You're a hunter; do you have an elephant gun?"

"Sorry, little buddy," Trip chuckled, "I don't usually hunt too many pachyderms in this neck of the woods."

"Oh yeah, I suppose so," Alex said, sounding disappointed. He brightened again, saying, "A flamethrower, maybe? Or a tank? How about a nuke?"

"I don't think it'll come to nuclear warheads, little buddy, but that animal is huge, and since we don't have any of those handy, I don't know if we have anything that would pierce the hide of that monster!"

Austin walked back into the compound from the office, saying, "Don't have any of what handy?"

"An elephant gun to kill the bear," Trip said with a slight laugh.

"Or a nuclear warhead," Alex added.

"Ah, yes, and here I used my last nuke at the target range last week! That is just too bad. Well, I guess we'll just have to make do with putting some more signs up around the area in the meantime. And you guys can do me a huge favour!"

"What's that, Dad?"

"I just got a call from the hospital, and the guy we rescued, Jerry, is finally awake!"

"Awesome!" Alex said, a big smile on his face.

"Yes, and he wants to talk to me for some reason."

"Really?" Trip asked. "Maybe he wants to thank you."

"Maybe. Either way, I guess I'll find out soon. What I was thinking of doing was this: If you can drop me off at the hospital, I'll stop in and see what Jerry wants while you two go around the city and start putting up some of those signs. I'll call you when I'm done, and then we'll meet up with Chris, who should be up and about by then."

"Sounds like a plan, man! Let's do it," Trip said.

"Yeah!" Alex agreed. "Maybe we can find an elephant gun somewhere, too!"

"Or a nuke," Austin added with a smile as he climbed into the passenger side of the City Works Silverado.

CHAPTER THIRTY-THREE

Austin looked thoughtful as he watched Alex entering the 7-11. His son had always been a boy who looked to the well-being of others around him first. Figuring that Jerry was probably not in the best of spirits, he'd asked if they could stop at the store on the way to the hospital to pick up something to brighten the poor guy's day a little bit. More and more, Austin was pleasantly surprised by the actions of his son.

"He's got a lot of Patricia in him," Trip said as if reading Austin's mind.

"Yes, he does," Austin responded, a wistful expression on his face. "She was always going out of her way to help people in need whenever she could, and it certainly looks like it rubbed off, doesn't it?"

"He didn't just learn that from Patricia, you know. You're almost the same in that respect. But yeah, you're raising a good kid there."

"Thanks."

They sat in silence for a couple of minutes, Trip munching on another cruller and Austin sipping the double-double that Trip had kindly provided, lost in thought. Alex came back shortly, a bag loaded with goodies in hand.

"What've you got there, little buddy?" Trip asked.

Climbing into the Silverado's cab, Alex said, "I picked Jerry up a couple of magazines." He reached into the bag and flashed them a copy of People Magazine and The Weekly World News. "And I also got him these," he said, pulling out a bottle of Coke, a bag of Cheese Pleasers, a Snickers Bar, and last, but not least, a travel-sized toothbrush and toothpaste. He prepared to hand the bag to Austin and added, "Oh, I almost forgot, there's also something in there for Mrs. Plotnikoff!"

"That's awesome, Alex! That should keep Jerry busy for a little while, that's for sure," Austin said, nodding in approval. "And I'll make sure Vera gets your present."

"Way to go, little buddy, I'm sure he'll appreciate those things." Trip wiped his hands on his coveralls, then gave the boy a quick thumbs-up and put the truck in gear.

Despite upgrade projects over several decades, the Lawless Community Health Centre still retained its stately exterior facade. Completely updated inside, the two-story building gave a feeling of permanence and stability to the downtown core and oozed small-town charm. In summertime, a dense quilt of ivy covered its thick stone walls. But the vibrant, green blanket was now gone, and only dark vines remained, twisting and snaking over the cold, grey stone, leaving the building naked and exposed to the world.

Trip pulled the truck into the porte-cochère entrance over the main entry. Stepping down from the passenger side of the truck, bag of goodies in hand, Austin said, "Okay, guys, I'll see you in an hour or so. Keep your phone handy, Trip, and I'll text you when I'm done."

"Will do, Boss," Trip said, pulling out his phone and checking the volume level as he spoke.

"See you soon, Dad." Alex exited the back seat of the super cab, giving Austin a quick pat on the back before jumping into the passenger seat next to Trip.

Austin watched the truck pull out onto the street, his breath pluming around his head in the crisp morning air. He looked down at the bag in his hand, and his heart swelled with pride at the thoughtful, caring young man his son had become. If this kept up, he felt he might just overdose on pride. Shrugging, he figured there were probably worse ways to go. He turned toward the automatic doors, and they whisked silently open as he approached.

The hospital, along with city hall, was a striking example of another building in Lawless that had been financed by the gold that flowed through the town in the past. Both structures had benefited immensely from the town's wealth of precious metals. They had been built to last as well as impress. Their extensive classical architecture seemed almost out of place in the small but modern village which now surrounded them.

Entering the lobby, Austin marvelled at the interior of the hospital. As he wiped his boots on the thick rubber-backed carpet inside the entrance, he looked down and saw the gleaming white walls reflected in the polished, Italian marble floor.

At the beautiful oak reception desk, Vera Plotnikoff scribbled away in yet another crossword puzzle. She was one of the many volunteers at the hospital, helping the small community health centre stay on budget. Almost a permanent fixture in the lobby, the elderly woman had been there since retiring from teaching elementary school, many years before. She'd always had a soft spot for Austin, as he'd been one of her favourite students. But despite the intervening years, and maybe because of the crosswords, she was still sharp as a tack.

Behind the massive desk, she sat doing crossword after crossword while waiting to help people locate their ailing loved ones inside the building. Austin had reconnected with her when Patricia had gotten sick, with Alex almost viewing her like a third grandmother. When Vera saw Austin enter the lobby, she recognized him at once, saying, "Well, well, young Mr. Murphy. What brings you to the hospital on this fine day?"

"Morning Mrs. Plotnikoff, How're you doing?"

"I'm right as rain and fit as a fiddle, thanks for asking! How's that boy of yours doing?"

"Excellent, thanks. Growing like a weed!" Vera Plotnikoff smiled at this news. After a moment, Austin added, "I'm here to visit the man they brought in from the bear attack a couple of days ago, Jerry Benson. Apparently, he's conscious now, and he's asked to speak with me."

"Well, maybe it's to thank you! I heard you saved his life." Vera clapped her hands together in a small round of applause as she spoke.

"Yes, ma'am, Trip and I pulled him out of a pretty bad predicament."

"That was very, very nice of you! You were always one of my better students and such a nice young man. Well, I won't hold you up — it looks like you've got places to go and people to see." Vera scanned the small directory book in front of her and said, "He's in Room 222."

"Thank you so much! Oh, and before I forget, this is for you." Austin reached into the plastic shopping bag and rummaged around for a moment, looking for what he figured Alex had bought the woman. His guess was correct, and he extracted a thick crossword book, saying, "This is from Alex."

Vera's eyes glistened as she accepted the book and said, "Please thank your young man for me. Both of you have a lovely day!"

"We will, and you as well, Mrs. Plotnikoff." Austin nodded with a smile as he moved toward the stairs.

***

Jerry Benson's hospital room was very, very white. This morning, after his return to consciousness, as he lay there, trying not to think, the stark whiteness of it all was one of the first things he'd noticed. It reminded him of the snow at the campsite, before it had been stained with the blood of his college brothers. Now, every time he closed his eyes to stop seeing all the white, just as he dozed off, the enormous grey beast rose unbidden in his mind, bursting through the campfire of his memory and charging at him, wanting to devour him. Then his eyelids would snap wide open, and he'd be staring at the whiteness all over again. Now, just as he felt himself nodding off, the image came to him once more, uninvited by his subconscious, flying to the forefront of his mind, and his eyelids flew apart.

When his eyes opened this time, however, instead of a bare, white room to greet him, he found a man standing at the foot of his bed. He was a tall, angular man with a greying, neatly trimmed beard, holding a plastic 7-11 shopping bag in one hand. He looked vaguely familiar.

"Hi there," Jerry said hoarsely. "Do I know you?"

"Sort of," the man said, smiling slightly. He approached the bed, extending his hand. "I'm Austin Murphy, one of the guys that pulled you up from the edge of that cliff you went over."

"Hi, it's great to meet you," Jerry said, smiling weakly as he shook Austin's hand. The meaning of what Austin said took a couple of seconds to percolate through Jerry's pain-killer addled brain, and he stopped in mid-shake. "Hold on, could you back that up a second? Did you say cliff?"

"Yup, when you went airborne, if you hadn't fallen off your sled and landed on the ledge where you did, you would have ended up at the valley bottom, about six hundred metres down, along with your snowmobile."

"Holy shit!" Jerry's eyes went wide.

"Holy shit, indeed." Austin nodded slightly.

"Well, thanks for the rescue!"

"You're welcome. You just got lucky, actually. I was checking the avalanche conditions from the forest lookout. From what I could see, it looked like there'd been some major problems at your camp, so my friend and I decided to investigate. When we followed the snowmobile tracks, we found you, semi-conscious on the ledge."

"I am in your debt," Jerry said gravely.

"No worries."

"Thanks for coming by to see me. I wanted to talk to someone about what happened to me out there." He nodded toward the mountains visible through the small white-curtained window.

"Haven't the police been by to talk to you since you woke up?"

"Not yet. I don't know if they've been informed. But I suppose they'll want me to give a statement."

"That is strange... Well, maybe I can help you. First of all, do you want to tell me what happened?"

Jerry pushed himself up in bed a bit more before speaking, then cleared his throat, "Yeah, thanks. Long story short, I'm a geologist by trade and my buddies and I usually have a winter getaway each year to someplace or another around the world. We've been doing it for the last fifteen years or so since we graduated college. Anyway, this year, it was decided that snowmobiling was the way to go. When I heard my buddies were coming up here, I was all gung-ho, since the recent seismic activity that you had a few weeks ago was very, very interesting, from a geological standpoint."

"Well, thanks. We do like to shake things up in this part of the world. Speaking of which, that quake certainly caused quite a bit of havoc on the roads around here with avalanches and rockslides, amongst other things."

"I was surprised that you hadn't had any more activity since then."

"No, should we be expecting more?"

"Well, there's a major new fault line running through the north end of this valley. According to the data that my colleagues and I've correlated, you could have another at any time now, and a major one to boot. The last one only caused a small amount of slippage in the fault, but from the data we have, it looks like you might be in line for another one, only this time, much, much bigger."

"That's not exactly comforting news."

"That's only one of the things I wanted to talk to you about."

"What's the other?" Austin asked, pulling up a small wooden chair next to the bed and sitting down.

Jerry sipped water from a waxed paper cup on a table next to his bed before continuing. "Well, we got up there just after noon and set up camp. I told the guys I'd be off exploring some of the rock formations near the ridges to see if I could find any new layers of strata revealed by the quake, and also to try and ascertain the state of the fault." Now that he was talking about something he was passionate about, Jerry shifted into teaching mode. "This area has been a real hotbed of fossil finds over the last couple of decades. As the glacier has melted, whenever there's been a significant seismic event, there's usually fresh fossil evidence due to the backscatter effect — all sorts of interesting things coming to the surface from deep down below. In fact, a community much farther north of here with a similar geographic layout had an amazing discovery, and they found the remains of a woolly mammoth almost one hundred percent intact! So, you can imagine my excitement to be able to check out your area after what happened here. I was hoping to find something similarly exciting."

"Well, at least you were right about the exciting part."

"Yes, but the wrong kind, unfortunately. That kind of excitement ate all of my friends." He paused, his chest heaving as he choked back a sob. After a moment, he continued, "I honestly don't know if there'll be any of them left to bury. Has any trace of them been found?"

"We didn't find any bodies anywhere, just a lot of blood."

"I think that's because that goddamn thing ate every last bit of them. It's a fucking monster!" Jerry's face flooded red with anger as he talked about the beast.

"I know, I've seen it! And we've had other attacks since we rescued you as well."

"No! How many?"

"At least two that we know of. And we just had one last night out at a local pub on the highway."

"Frostbite Fred's?"

"Yup, that's the place. You know it?"

"We drove by it on our way up to the campsite. Tyler said he loved their ribs. He'd been here a few years back in the summer and was raving about them. Said he wanted to swing by there on the way out of town to get some for the road." Jerry's face dropped for a moment as he recalled his dead friend.

"It looks like it'll be a while before they're back in business, there was quite a bit of damage when the creature tried to get into the pub to snack on the patrons."

"Jesus!" Jerry shuddered at the thought, then had another. "But there's something else I should mention."

"About what happened at your camp?"

"Sort of. While I was away exploring the ridge, I came across something very interesting at the source of the fault."

"What's that?"

"I found a cavern. I believe it's only been recently exposed because of the quake."

"Okay, and?" Austin leaned in to hear Jerry, whose voice had dropped to a whisper.

"I think I found a major new vein of gold up there."

"Really? Well, that's not too surprising, given the history of this area."

"I know, but there's something else that I have been thinking about, and it may be linked to that beast killing people down here."

"How so?"

"Well, I think I led that monster back to my camp and then it killed my friends. When I was at the cavern, there was something that didn't register at the time. But it has since then, now that I've had time to think about it." Jerry paused again.

"And?"

"And it was something I noticed on one of the trees near the cavern just as the sun was going down before the ice fog hit."

"What was that?"

"Claw marks. But they were so high up the tree, I almost didn't see them at first, and even then, they didn't really register. I thought at the time, how could something claw so high, right? So anyway, I dismissed them. Now, with everything replaying through my mind as I lay here, I finally remembered them and figured it might be important, so that's why I asked to talk to you. I thought it might help you track it down."

"Thank you. Any information we can get at this point is helpful." Austin suddenly remembered he had a bag in his hand. "Oh, and before I forget, this is for you." He held out the shopping bag to Jerry.

"What's this?" Jerry took the bag and opened it, peeking inside.

"A few things to make your stay here a little more pleasant."

Jerry smiled as he pulled out the contents. "Thanks, this should help pass the time."

"Don't thank me, thank my son, it was his idea."

"Well, then, please thank him for me."

Austin looked at this wristwatch. "I'll do that. Well, I've got to run now and make sure we get more bear warning signs planted. Maybe we can find this thing now that the weather's cleared. Thanks again for the information. Take care!" He turned to leave.

"I will!" Jerry suddenly felt exhausted once more and lay the shopping bag at his side.

Almost as an afterthought, Austin turned back, pulling his wallet out of his pants pocket as he spoke. "Just in case, if you think of anything else, here's my card. Give me a call," Austin handed a business card to Jerry and tucked his wallet away once more. He nodded to Jerry briefly, then turned and left the room.

"Thanks again," Jerry said, turning the card over in his hands as Austin Murphy walked down the gleaming, white corridor. Jerry looked up as Murphy turned a corner, wondering if that would be the man to bring about a resolution to the horror that stalked the local mountains. He examined the card more closely and discovered it had printing on both sides. Apparently, the man wore two hats in this town. One side of the white card informed the reader that he was Austin Murphy, Head of Public Works, City of Lawless, BC. At the bottom were his office and cell phone numbers. The reverse side had the same phone numbers listed, but at the top, it read: Austin Murphy, Head of Animal Control, City of Lawless, BC.

Jerry Benson smiled thinly as he muttered to himself, "I wonder if he's going to be able to control that thing wandering around out there in the forest."

CHAPTER THIRTY-FOUR

Austin exhaled, a cloud of vapour jetting from his mouth and dissipating into the crisp morning air. He stood for a moment under the entrance, checking his messages. It seemed Christine was awake and wanting to see him. He sent a quick reply, telling her that he was at the hospital and going to call Trip to come and pick him up. She replied not to bother Trip at the moment as she would swing by and give him a ride, adding she had something she wanted to show him.

Marvelling about the joys of living in a small town, less than two minutes later, Austin watched Christine's Dodge Ram pull up under the covered entrance. The vehicle's thick, studded tires crunched on the frozen slush as it slowed to a stop.

Reaching across and pushing open the passenger side door, Christine said, "Morning, Austin!"

"Hey there, Chris! How was your sleep?" Austin asked, climbing into the pickup.

"Not long enough." She stifled a yawn with the back of her hand.

"I know how you feel. What did you get? About four hours downtime?"

"Three and a half."

"Ow! That's not enough."

Glancing upward out of the windshield at the dazzling day overhead, Christine said, "Tell me about it. But what about this weather, though? It's amazing, isn't it? It's so nice to see the fog gone!" She sounded as giddy as a schoolgirl on her first day of summer vacation.

As Christine expressed her glee, Austin was struck once more by the musicality of her voice. She smiled broadly as she looked up into the luminous morning. He looked up as well, thinking that the brilliant blue sky reflected in her mirrored sunglasses was no competition for the piercing blue eyes that sparkled beneath. He said, "I agree, absolutely! It's the first sunlight we've seen down here in weeks. Enjoy it while you can, though, because unfortunately, it's not supposed to last."

"What?" Christine put the truck in gear and slowly pulled away from the hospital entrance, heading toward the conservation office.

"I just double-checked with Sam at the weather office before you got here. He said the fog is supposed to pour into the valley again tonight. But with the cold air now here, that means it'll be an ice fog instead of that soggy stuff we had before."

"Ice fog?"

"Didn't Carl leave you any notes about regional quirks and quarks?"

"No, as I think I mentioned, he left rather abruptly a few weeks back." Christine shrugged.

"Yeah. I know it was kind of strange. He'd been talking about his upcoming retirement for months. Trip said, a few weeks back, Carl was telling him about this great new hotspring at this cavern he'd found and saved in his GPS, and how he would be dragging Trip up to it for some exercise in the near future. Then, he just packs it all in and disappears in a puff of smoke! Trip swung by to check on him, and his fifth wheel was gone like he'd bugged out without telling anyone and just blew town! Nobody's seen or heard from him since."

"I was kind of surprised to get the call myself. I knew I was lined up to replace him, but not as quickly as this, so I really had to scramble to get up here in time from the coast. But I don't regret the move; it's such a beautiful area." She glanced up at the sky again. "I can't believe we're going to get more fog. Ice fog this time, you say?"

"Yessum. It's usually constrained to the glacier area. But sometimes, once the inversion clears and the temperature drops, it can come flooding down into the valley in the evening."

Concerned, she asked, "It creates a lot of problems, does it?"

"Well, if it hits like Sam figures tonight, the ground, the buildings, the cars and everything else outside will all be covered in a layer of thick frost by tomorrow morning."

"Sounds slippery."

"You don't know the half of it! It makes travel extremely dangerous."

"It'll probably happen, then. Your Law and all, you know…" Christine said as she pulled the truck into the back of the conservation compound.

"Huh? My Law?"

"Yeah, you know, Murphy's Law!"

Austin groaned. "Gee, never heard that one before!" Smiling, he looked across the yard from where they parked, spotting two cylindrical metal bear traps, both empty at the moment. He said, "So, on a different note, are you going to try to capture Angus if we can find him?"

Still sitting behind the wheel of her truck, Christine looked over at Austin. She said nothing, but tilted her head slightly, a smile tracing the corners of her lips, as if to say, you poor, poor, tetched little thing you.

Seeing this expression, Austin added, a smile of his own forming on his face, "But I don't suppose you have a trap big enough, huh?"

With a laugh, Christine said, "Nope, so unless you're going to throw gas grenades at it like King Kong, I think trapping it is out of the question. We need to put this predator down before it causes any more deaths."

"So, what are you going to use to stop it? Trip said the shotgun he and Greg used only pissed it off."

As they walked through the door into the shop at the back of the building, Christine said, "That's not surprising. According to Zelda, the hide on Angus probably has a layer of subcutaneous fat at least a half dozen centimetres thick. There is no way shotgun pellets could penetrate that, not from the distance that Trip said they fired the buckshot from. A shot with a .30-06 might do it, but you'd have to be very precise. Which brings us to the reason that I was up so early."

"What's that?"

 "I got a call from one of our local courier services with a special delivery, and I had to boogie down here to the office to meet them."

"Did you have something come in from Amazon?"

"I don't think you'll ever get one of these from Amazon," Christine said, walking toward the gun storage locker at the far side of the workshop. She grabbed a set of keys from a desk drawer next to it and unlocked the tall, black gun safe.

"My headquarters was kind enough to ship some extra equipment up to me that I requested." She pulled open the door to the safe. "Meet the Hannibal .577 Tyrannosaur rifle."

Next to Christine's Remington .30-06, a massive rifle sat locked down in the second slot of the storage locker. It didn't look much longer than the Remington, but as Christine removed the gun, Austin could see that the barrel was huge, and it looked much more substantial than your average rifle. He whistled and said, "A Tyrannosaur rifle? As in Rex? It has to be since the bore of that barrel is so huge!"

"Yes, at seven hundred and fifty metres per second, the shells generate almost fourteen thousand kilojoules of muzzle energy."

"Wow, that's impressive!"

"Thanks, I got that from the sales brochure." Christine beamed him a smile, continuing, "This rifle was designed to stop charging rhinos, hippos, elephants and the like. The manufacturer named it the Tyrannosaur, or T-Rex, because it's the only rifle that would be capable of stopping something as large as that dinosaur, were it to exist in our world today.

Austin said, "I'd say our bear qualifies as something existing in our world today, size-wise and thick hide-wise, that is."

Christine took one of the rifle's shells out of an ammo box in the locker and held it up for Austin to see. "The 750 grain, .577 calibre shell from this rifle can stop pretty much anything on the planet." She twirled the ten-centimetre long shell in her fingers. "This shell should be able to go into one side of Angus and out the other, and then impact another bear his size, without barely slowing down at all."

"Sounds like it must have quite a kick."

"You better believe it. This rifle has three mercury recoil reducers built into the stock. But that being said, if you're not well-braced before firing, this thing will take your shoulder right off if you don't know what you're doing."

"Ouch! I guess I'll leave that to the professionals."

"That'd be me!" Christine said. "I've had training on a rifle like this several years back and scored top marks with it at the range."

"Nice." Austin nodded appreciatively.

Christine took the gun back to the locker and placed it inside a soft, Kevlar-based gun case already there. She added a box of shells, then zipped it all up and put it back in the locker.

"What? You're not going to take it with you?"

"No, I want to travel light today and just do some reconnaissance. But I am going to bring my .30-06 because you just never know." She removed the Remington from the cabinet and placed it on the counter for a moment. "So, anyway, I thought I'd keep you up to speed with the weapon update and all since you've been involved with this from the beginning. Plus, with you being head of Animal Control for the City of Lawless, I thought you could appreciate this weapon. And speaking of animals, I have to say, you've been much more helpful than the police in this town."

"Ah, yes, Chief Reggie VanDusen and the ever-faithful Constable Oscar Olsen, amongst others."

"How did a man like VanDusen get the job of Chief of Police in this town, anyway?"

"It helps to be friends with the mayor, apparently."

"He's almost as unpleasant as the mayor, that's for sure. Did one of them rub-off on the other or something?"

"Well, one of them is always rubbing somebody the wrong way."

"I can believe that! When I got into town last week, I bumped into 'His Lordship' at city hall when I was picking up the keys to the forestry office. Your mayor is quite a piece of work, to say the least!"

"Yes, Bob Nichols is a treat, isn't he?"

"That's a very diplomatic way to put it. But a treat, though? I can think of several other words that are not quite so complimentary," As she spoke, she noted some disorder on the worktable and started to square it away.

"What happened? If you don't mind my asking?"

"Not at all. When Carl up and disappeared, the conservation office got locked up, with new locks placed on the doors as a precaution. The ministry contacted the locksmith and asked them to drop off the new set of keys at city hall so that I could pick them up when I got into town." Christine finished straightening a couple of items on the counter next to the gun locker.

"And?"

"And I was picking up the keys to the office from the front desk at City Hall when Mayor Nichols, Ray Chance and Chief VanDusen walked in from the street. I recognised the Mayor right away, thanks to the huge portrait of him hanging in the lobby. So anyway, I approached him to introduce myself." She stopped, grinning and shaking her head slightly from side to side.

"What happened — what's so funny?"

"So, I stick my hand out and say, 'Hello, I'm with the BC Conservation Officer Service. My name's Christine Moon, and I've just been reassigned from the coast!' I added how I'd be serving Lawless and the surrounding area. So, Nichols looks me up and down, pauses for a moment, then says, 'I'm sure you'll do just fine with all that.' Then he adds, 'Tell you what, why don't you just put me down for three boxes of Mint Melties and you can have the girls from your troop deliver them to the front desk here whenever they come in.' "

"That sounds about right!" Austin laughed. "The Mayor is off in his own little world most of the time. Personally, I think he's suffering from dementia."

"I can believe that. So, after the mayor and chief stroll away, muttering to each other, Ray Chance walks up to me. He basically undresses me with his eyes, then says, 'You can come up to my casino anytime, toots, and help me conserve some of my poker chips!' and then he staggers away. But speaking of Ray, I wouldn't want to put him anywhere near an open flame! The fumes that come rolling off of him are incredible!"

Austin laughed. "Ah, yes, the always lecherous and forever fuming Ray Chance!" Austin looked toward the daylight flooding through the window. "Well, I need to get back to the boys and make sure we get the rest of those signs up." He pulled his cell phone out, preparing to text Trip.

"Sounds good! I'm going to head up toward Gold Ridge to try and track Angus. I marked the spot that I tracked him to with my GPS, so I'm hoping I can pick up his trail again while this beautiful sunshine lasts." She flashed another smile at him and concluded, saying, "But I'll drop you off on my way, first."

"Thanks! I'll let Trip know and get their location." Austin started to type on his cell and saw his signal strength meter wavering between one bar and nothing. The building's metal roof and structure were interfering with the phone's antenna. He moved toward the window to try to improve the reception.

Watching him, Christine said, "That reminds me! I almost forgot to show you the other toy I had sent up yesterday!" Christine opened her backpack sitting on the counter and pulled out what looked like an oversized walkie-talkie with an LCD screen. But this was no ordinary radio; it was an Iridium Extreme Satellite Phone. "This will come in handy around here, let me tell you!"

Austin looked up as he finished texting Trip and put his phone away. He recognized the industrial-looking, ebony-hued device in her hand. "Oh, that's awesome! I've been bugging the city to get a satellite phone for a little while now, but they haven't allowed for it in their current budget, yet. Things have been a little tight recently, especially after purchasing the howitzer as well as the added expense of the cleanup from the quake. But until they get more cell repeaters in this area, a satellite phone is practically a necessity if you get into trouble out in the backcountry around here."

"Exactly!" Christine stuffed the satellite phone back into her pack, throwing it over her shoulder. "I can't tell you how much I appreciate your putting more signs up. It'll give me a chance to get out there and try to track Angus while the weather holds. I'd like to avoid further incidents like the campsite massacre and Fred's if we can." She grabbed her .30-06 propped next to the counter and slung it over her shoulder, then began walking toward the shop door.

Austin suddenly said, "Say, that reminds me!"

She turned. "It does? Of what?"

"Trouble in the backcountry! I was going to let you know about our survivor from the attack!"

"Right! I was going to ask you about him. How's he doing?" Christine asked, concern in her voice.

"Well, his name is Jerry Benson, and it turns out, he's doing well. Apart from some obvious PTSD, and a forearm fracture, amazingly enough. But it's what he said about our monster bear that I thought might interest you more."

"Okay, I'm listening." She tilted her head, quizzically.

"He said he thought the bear might have come from this new cavern that he discovered up on Gold Ridge near the glacier."

"Really? A new cavern?"

"Yeah, he thinks it may have followed him back from there to the campsite, and you know what happened next."

"That is horrible to hear! But at the same time, it sounds like that would be a perfect place for a creature like Angus to make his lair. This great news! I'll know where to focus my search now. Thanks!"

"No problem," Austin said, following along behind her. Climbing into Christine's truck, he felt his phone vibrate in his hand. Trip had just texted back that he and Alex were only a few blocks from the conservation office.

A couple of minutes later, Christine and Austin rolled to a stop. Alex was finishing up, pounding another sign into the ground with Trip holding it steady. Alex gave the post one more whack for good measure then looked up at the sound of the approaching truck. He smiled and waved when he saw Christine. She waved back, saying, "That is a handsome young man you have there," then added softly, "He certainly takes after his father, I must say."

Austin blushed slightly and smiled at the compliment, saying, "Thanks, I'm sure Alex would like to know that an attractive woman such as yourself just called him handsome."

Now it was Christine's turn to blush. "Well, thank you." She cleared her throat slightly and said, "I really appreciate your help with the signs and everything, once again by the way."

"Not a problem, we should be done pretty soon." Austin stepped down out of the truck.

"If I can track Angus successfully, maybe I can use my new boom-stick today."

"Just be very, very careful, okay?"

"Thanks, I will. I'm a big girl, you know — with a gun," she reached around and patted her Remington affectionately in the gun rack behind her.

"That's true, but remember, don't get cocky, kid." he said with a slight smile.

"I know. I just want to see if I can locate some more of his tracks now that the weather has cleared. I'll be careful."

"Please do, and don't forget to try and make it back before nightfall." Austin closed the passenger door and walked around the front of the truck. He stopped next to Christine's window, and she rolled it down. Austin concluded, saying, "Remember the ice fog warning."

"Yes, mother," Christine said with a grin. She rolled up her window and pulled out onto the road, tooting her horn and waving to Alex and Trip in the process.

The sun dazzled Austin, reflecting off the truck's rear window. He smiled, thinking the blinding brilliance of the sun overhead paled in comparison to the shining light that radiated from within the woman now driving away.

CHAPTER THIRTY-FIVE

Mayor Bob Nichols wove his Cadillac Escalade SUV through the circuitous curves of Provincial Highway #3C. He was on his way to the Golden Nugget Casino and Resort to see what was what. Scowling at the numerous 'Bear in Area' signs along the way, his bony fingers dug farther and farther into the steering wheel with each new sign he saw. He blew by two more, one on each side of the road. This had to be number seven and eight, at least, since he'd begun his climb up the hill. "Goddamned bear! Scaring all of my customers away and costing me God knows how much money! You big, bastardly, hairy son of a bitch!"

The sun, beautiful and brilliant in the cold late-January sky held no appeal to Nichols. Distracting thoughts whirled through his mind, negating his ability to appreciate the day around him. He gritted his teeth, ruminating on what to do with the theft up at the cavern, and now the issues with this supposed bear. Things had gone from phenomenal to horrible in a matter of only a few days.

Rounding a corner, the Eiffel tower suddenly popped into view as he manoeuvred through the last bend before the resort's entrance. Bob's face brightened temporarily when remembered the frantic, excited phone call he'd received from Ray Chance just after the quake at the beginning of January. The minute his handyman, Watkins, had departed, Chance had been on the phone with the news, saying, "Jesus Jiminy Christmas! I think we're going to be goddamned billionaires, partner!"

Chance told Nichols that he presumed Watkins hadn't known what he'd found up at the cavern was real gold. Bob had agreed, figuring if Watkins had known it was real, he most likely wouldn't have told Chance about it and given any of it to him — of that, he was quite sure. Now, however, as far as they both knew, Watkins was AWOL and making up for lost time and money, most likely on his way to Palm Springs with several bags of nuggets and not a care in the world. "Bastard!" Nichols muttered.

They'd quickly come to an agreement regarding how to deal with the fortune in the gold they hoped to extract from the cavern. Like their partnership, it was supposed to have been a fifty-fifty affair. But Nichols was pretty sure that Chance was probably stepping over the line now, taking his share from fifty percent into the loftier and more profitable sixtieth or seventieth percentiles. Bob knew from years of experience that he couldn't trust that little tub of lard as far as he could throw him, and he knew that wasn't very far.

Under the guidance of Nichols and Chance, the first wave of gold removal by Willy Wilson Senior and Junior had been a great success. From what he'd heard, most of it had been quite easy to extract, given the fact that the majority of it was in the form of nuggets scattered throughout the main cavern's floor. When that ran out, additional effort had been needed to extract the gold ore from the cavern walls itself. But the effort had been minimal, apparently there were several big, beautiful veins of gold running throughout the cavern. It just sat there, glistening in the rock, waiting for two entrepreneurial individuals like Bob and Ray to come along and scoop it up — just like it was meant to be. He smiled to himself for a long moment.

Nichols's good mood had returned, thanks to these new thoughts of golden nuggets dancing in his head. He pulled around the back of the main building and parked his Cadillac in the reserved spot with his name, next to Chance's Land Rover. As he climbed down out of his gleaming, black SUV, he almost fell on his ass. Despite their shared desire to save as much as they could on maintenance around the resort, they really needed to get on top of the sanding around this place. Walking carefully over to the Rover, he stopped for a moment to examine it. It seemed Ray had done an admirable amount of damage to the front end of his vehicle when he'd terminated that raccoon the other day.

"Nice job, Ray," Nichols muttered aloud. "That's going to cost you a couple of pretty pennies." Then he added, "Not that you can't afford it, you cheap little prick!"

Feeling better now after seeing Chance's damaged Rover, Nichols continued inside, humming to himself. The lobby was vacant, with several slot machines scattered near the entrance chiming and pinging happily away to an audience of none. Walking to the elevator, he pressed the large, glowing button marked with a number two and looked about the room as he waited for it to descend.

A contingency of seniors from the Golden Castle Retirement Home, or as Nichols thought of it, God's waiting room, were in attendance today. In the far corner, a couple of locals playing Texas Hold'em stared glumly at their monitors, but that seemed about it. Apart from this ragtag assortment of regulars, the casino wasn't making much money today. "Bastardly bear," he muttered.

A bell dinged, and the beautiful brass-trimmed doors to the elevator opened, revealing a sparkling mirrored interior. He stepped inside and turned around, looking across the lobby. Chance's current front desk attendant, Al something or other, looked over to Nichols and smiled blandly at him for a moment. Bob scowled back and pressed the button labelled 'Two'. As the door slid closed, he looked at his expression in the mirror. Feeling he didn't look as pissed as he felt, he frowned a bit more. No, definitely not angry looking enough. He frowned harder until his reflection looked positively demonic. There, that was much better, he thought, his scowl now perfect.

The bell dinged once more, and the doors slid open. Nichols breezed through the frosted outer door into Chance's office and was greeted by his pin-head receptionist, Roxanne Rooney. "Good morning, Mayor Nichols. Do you have an appointment with Mr. Chance today?" She put down her nail brush for a moment, her red-taloned hand reaching for the intercom button as she spoke.

"Always," Nichols said, and blew past her desk toward Chance's oak office door.

"Sir! You can't just barge in there!" she exclaimed.

"Sure, I can; it's easy! Just watch!" He pushed the door open and entered Chance's office. Turning quickly, he slammed the heavy door in the receptionist's concerned face.

"Bob! How the hell's it going?" Chance asked. He finished pouring his drink and placed the brandy decanter back on his desk, then glowered across the room at Nichols.

"You know as well as I do," Nichols said in a low voice, approaching the desk. He sat down in the worn leather chair opposite Chance. His scowl now needed no assistance; it deepened as he looked at his waste of space business partner.

"Yeah, I do, just trying to keep up appearances." Chance slugged back a mouthful of brandy from his glass.

Nichols looked at Chance with thinly veiled disgust. Not even noon hour and the man was already half-plastered! "Any word from your man, Watkins, yet?"

"Nothing. Not a goddamned peep!" Chance said.

"Son of a bitch! What the hell happened? Another one of your men just disappears in a puff of smoke in the middle of the night! Rather convenient; don't you think, Ray, especially after the first pair you hired, and now Oritz buggering off as well?"

"What are you trying to say, Bob?"

"That I wouldn't trust you as far as I could throw your tubby little ass!"

"Screw you, Bob! If that isn't the pot calling the kettle black, then I don't know what is!"

Thinking of his little surreptitious arrangement with the chief of police, Nichols grinned on the inside. He was more than pleased how much gold VanDusen had scammed for him from the cavern already, but instead, said, "Whatever! Either way, we still don't know what happened to any of them."

"As far as we know, maybe that goddamned bear of yours ate them!" Ray watched with glee as the mayor scowled harder as he gave ownership of the bear problem to him once again. "In any event, I'm ready to go, where's VanDusen?" Chance asked, sloshing another couple of fingers of brandy into his snifter. "I thought you said he was leading the charge today?"

"As I told you on the phone, he should be along shortly. He was at Fred's all night because of that damned bear and ended up doing a shitload of paperwork with the RCMP. He said he needed to go home and get a few hours sleep first."

"Oh, boo-hoo for him!"

Although he had reservations about Ray Chance's drinking habits, Bob Nichols still had none about his own. It was almost noon — the time civilised people could start drinking. He eyed the brandy snifter on Chance's desk. "So where are your manners, Ray, aren't you going to offer me a drink?"

"Yeah, I suppose so. I guess we'll both need a couple of good stiff shots to warm us up before heading up into the great white north."

Nichols watched with distaste as Ray poured the brandy. He noted Chance's 'couple of shots' was almost a full snifter, while his was only about two fingers tall if he was lucky.

Chance handed the snifter to his long-time business partner. Raising his glass, he intoned solemnly, "To our golden future."

With a slight raise of his glass in return, Nichols said, "To our getting everything we deserve!"

Both men both took a sip, each eyeing the other with suspicion over the top of their glasses as they drank.

CHAPTER THIRTY-SIX

"Absolutely gorgeous!" Christine removed her sunglasses, her eyes devouring the sun-drenched vista of Lawless nestled in the Kokanee Valley below. The majestic Kootenay Glacier gleamed a brilliant white in the morning sunshine, dazzling her as it reigned over the valley below, resting comfortably on its jagged, mountaintop throne.

She turned. The forest beckoned.

Rays of sunshine speared through the canopy of branches high above, their golden shafts piercing the forest floor below. The rich scent of decomposing coniferous needles was heavy in the air. A kaleidoscope of colour blazed through icicles that sparkled from the tips of the trees. She moved forward into a living rainbow that dazzled her senses — like a storybook come to life. Smiling in appreciation, she stole another brief moment to admire the world around her, awed by the beauty of the day. "Good job, mother," she said aloud.

Following her GPS, Christine soon found herself back in the stand of Douglas fir trees where she'd lost track of the bear's trail last time. Now, in the clear light of day, she was able to detect some damage to the flora that she'd missed previously because of the fog. After careful examination, she discerned the direction the bear had travelled, finding tracks leading away from the stand of trees paralleling the backside of the resort, heading toward Gold Ridge.

   With her snowshoes on, after consulting her GPS, she decided to hike a few more kilometres and see if she could get a better fix on the beast's home turf. Though the terrain was steep in places, she was still keen on at least trying; hopefully there was a sign of the monster taking refuge amongst the thick fir trees at the back of the ridge or inside this mysterious cavern located somewhere up along the jagged rockface.

   Christine pushed forward through the deep snow, her snowshoes crunching crisply through the thin layer of ice that lay on top. The snow crystals sparkled like millions of tiny diamonds, shining radiantly as she trekked along. Making excellent time, she arrived at Gold Ridge just after 1:00 P.M. and rested for a moment in the shadow of the glacier. Breathing deeply, her lungs savoured the crisp mountain air. She consulted the altimeter in her smartwatch and saw she was only a couple of metres shy of the twenty-two hundred mark. The watch didn't have a temperature sensor, but she didn't need one to tell her it was definitely colder up here — streams of thick vapour poured from her slightly parted lips into the frigid air.

   Checking her pulse rate on her watch to see where her cardio level was currently sitting, she said, "Not too shabby." After almost two hours of walking in snowshoes, sometimes at very challenging inclines, she had hardly broken a sweat. Her vitals showed no signs of stress, apart from a moderate pulse rate increase created by the climb combined with the higher altitudes. You go, girl, she thought with a smile.

   With the fog gone, tracking the creature had become much easier, but once the tracks hit the edge of the ridge, things changed once more. Deep snow transitioned to a wasteland of sharp scree that had tumbled down the side of the mountain. The sheer volume of irregular-sized rocks scattered over the ridge made any further tracking of the creature impossible.

But at least she now had some options. Surveying the rock face from across the sea of scree, she saw several places where large boulders had come loose and plummeted down the mountainside during the recent quake. From the edge of the ridge, looking toward the valley bottom, she marvelled at the size of boulders that had thundered into the valley — some were as large as houses. "My God, that must have made a hell of a racket," she said, shaking her head in wonder.

Knowing she must be close now, Christine checked her GPS. She was surprised to see she was only about five kilometres, as the crow flies, from the site of the camping massacre two days before. It was just about exactly where the survivor said he'd discovered the cavern. But she'd arrived here from the direction of the Gold Mountain Casino and Resort, not the campsite. Was this the area from which the predator had originated, she wondered? The distance seemed about right.

Reattaching her snowshoes to her backpack, she pulled out her binoculars and examined the ridge ahead. Scattered among the rubble and rock at the base of the cliffside, she spied several dark recesses that could have been cave entrances. As she scanned along the rockface, she suddenly stopped at one particular opening that seemed to jump out at her, and she knew it had to be the one. Plumes of steam swirled up from the ground near this break in the wall of rock. Plus, it looked big enough to house the likes of Angus, and it was close to the forested section of the ridge as well.

"That's got to be it," she said, putting her binoculars away. She scrambled across the scree for several minutes, finally arriving at the intriguing-looking cavern. In a hushed voice, she said, "Well, this does look promising."

The large tear in the cliffside revealed a cave entrance part way up the rockface almost three metres in height and nearly as wide – a steaming aquifer cascaded from its dark confines. A treacherously narrow pathway ran along a ledge leading up toward it, disappearing into the cavern's mysterious depths.

Taking a small Maglite from her pack, she pulled off an errant paperclip stuck to the magnet attached to its side. The small but powerful magnet allowed her to affix the light to any rifle, enabling use at nighttime, or other dark locations, such as this cavern. She unslung the Remington .30-06 from her shoulder and heard a solid click as the magnet pulled the flashlight firmly to the underside of the barrel. She switched it on.

Approaching the entrance, Christine walked slowly and cautiously. The path was mostly wet at the moment, but it looked like it had been quite hazardous earlier in the day. A thin layer of ice coating the ledge now melted in the afternoon sun, alleviating some of the danger. One section that curved along the rock wall near the base of the path had a reddish cast to it that looked very much like dried blood.

Small bits of rock crumbled from the side of the path and splashed into the boiling water below whenever her foot got too close for comfort near the edge, reminding her not to be careless. She certainly didn't want to stumble and spill some rock, making a noise that might alert the bear to her presence, or worse yet, fall into the boiling water below.

Her flashlight's beam played along the first few metres of steamy blackness inside the entrance showing her little of what lay within. "Well, here goes nothing," Christine said under her breath. She thrust her rifle through the veil of wafting steam and walked boldly forward, not knowing what to expect.

Inside the cavern, darkness reigned supreme, swallowing her light. "Omigod!" She craned her head around to take it all in — the cavern was gigantic. The flashlight illuminated a ceiling that stretched over seven metres up into the darkness; long stalactites hung down from its recesses. Below, the cavern floor lay hidden beneath swirling steam from boiling pools and streams that crisscrossed its surface. She walked silently as she moved forward, the sound of gurgling water her only companion.

Someone had erected a tent near the entrance, hidden behind the veil of steam caused by the aquifer. Nice, she thought. A cosy and warm little setup near the hot springs — can't beat that. But if this were the location that the bear was using as its base of operations, why had it not bothered the people camping here, or had it?

She looked closer at the tent and saw it collapsed on one side, looking torn. The tent fly was also shredded, and it seemed like the shelter hadn't seen any occupants for a while. A small stool lay on its side next to a cold campfire, as if the person occupying the seat had needed to vacate the premises in a hurry.

The beam of her light picked up the glint of something glass-like, standing out from the stones at her feet. It was someone's battered iPhone 5, covered in cave dust. She picked it up and tried it. It turned on immediately, but the phone's screen warned of a low battery. She turned the screen off and dropped it into a small baggie, putting the phone into her parka pocket to catalogue later as evidence.

Shining the light farther back into the cavern only revealed more darkness and steam. But there was one other thing that caught her interest in a major way along the far wall. Almost out of reach of her Maglite, an assortment of picks and shovels leaned against the rockface. As she approached, she saw the tools had been used to free some ore from a colossal vein of gold. It stretched along the wall of the cavern, snaking into the blackness beyond. Near the tools sat a stack of empty burlap sacks, waiting to be filled with ore.

Christine was stunned. The amount of gold in this cavern was phenomenal! She could certainly understand how the people doing the mining here would want to keep this little black hole in the wall a secret.

The steam from the boiling pools seemed to ebb and recede, almost like a tide as she moved forward. In spots, it thinned to nothing, but swelled to a depth of over a metre in others, washing over her thighs in thick waves, making it difficult to see her feet. During the times she could see more of the floor, she noted countless numbers of small colourful rocks surrounding her. They ranged from the size of a large grapefruit, down to that of a grape. They were all rounded or oval, worn by time and water coursing over them for countless millennia.

She entered an area containing pools of water that boiled merrily away. Moving very slowly, she parted the swirling vapour with her outstretched leg, being ever so careful, not wanting to fall face-first into one of these pools hidden by the steam. "I don't believe I'll be taking a soak in there anytime soon," she whispered.

Christine played her light around the cavern floor near her feet and suddenly stopped. "Well, well, what do we have here?" The mist swirled around a Glock 17, lying on its side amongst the rocks next to a particularly large pool. The dark-grey finish of the handgun stood out starkly against the multicoloured spray of stones that surrounded it. She picked the pistol up and checked the magazine, finding three shots remaining. On the ground, numerous spent shell casings gleamed in her flashlight's beam. What in the hell happened here? She shook her head as she dropped the Glock into one of the evidence bags from her pack, then placed it into the same parka pocket that contained the iPhone 5.

Turning toward the entrance, she heard the faint wasp-like drone of a snowmobile approaching in the distance. She negotiated her way back across the treacherous cavern floor for a look outside. Peering through the veil of mist, she saw not one, but two sleds — the first, almost to the scree, and another one rapidly approaching in the distance.

Switching off the light on her rifle, she slung it back over her shoulder and moved into the darkness toward the wall of the cavern next to the tent. She was curious to see who this was — perhaps it was the people doing the mining up here? As part of her duties as a conservation officer, she was required to make sure resources weren't being depleted or that the environment wasn't being harmed in any way. Crouching down behind the tent out of sight, she waited to see what would unfold, eyes and ears wide open.

***

The snowmobile ground to a halt several hundred metres from the cavern entrance, where the snowline ended, and the scree began. Piloted by Chief VanDusen, Mayor Bob Nichols sat behind as his passenger. They'd arrived just ahead of Ray Chance, who, piloting the other machine, was now approaching rapidly from behind.

On the way up the mountain, every few minutes, Nichols had craned his neck to look back and see if Chance was still managing to follow them. The mayor was an optimist at heart and hoped that perhaps at some point, Chance might shoot off the path and meet a vertical and grisly demise by driving off a cliff somewhere. But sadly, each time he glanced back, the little lush was still trailing doggedly behind, swerving along the trail they'd left, trying to keep drunken control of his sled.

After two snifters of Napoleon brandy, plus whatever Chance had had before Nichols arrived at the resort, the mayor was surprised his partner could even make it out the door of the casino, let alone pilot a snowmobile this far up a snow-covered mountainside. But Ray had insisted and to his credit, had survived the journey thus far. Bob had to admire the man's determination, or perhaps it was stupidity. Knowing Chance, he decided he'd most definitely have to go with the latter option.

VanDusen cut the snowmobile's motor, and Nichols asked, "All right, Reggie, fill me in again on what happened when you were last up here."

The chief stepped laboriously off the sled and turned to address Nichols. "The last time I was up here was a couple of days ago, just like I already told ya. And that was just before Chance called Oritz in to keep an eye on our little operation. He was supposed to be keeping Watkins in line as well, but I don't know what's happened here since, so your guess is as good as mine."

Chance finally zigged and zagged his way up to the scree and killed his snowmobile's engine. As he tottered toward them, Nichols asked, "Ray, what did you tell Watkins to do, exactly?"

"To get his ass up here and get the hell to work and that someone would be up here to check on things, that's what I told him. And where the hell is he, anyway? Goofing off with that goddamned Oritz?" Chance wondered out loud, taking a swig of brandy from the flask he produced from a pocket deep within his parka.

Nichols sighed, "All right, let's see if we can find somebody around here and figure out what's been going on." The trio scrambled across the scree for several minutes, none having an easy time of it. Arriving at the cavern, with a wheeze, Nichols said, "Reggie, make sure you're covering our backs, and our fronts with that popgun of yours, just in case that blasted bear is around here somewhere."

VanDusen nodded, unslinging a Remington Versa Max shotgun from his shoulder. He clicked the under-muzzle light on and cocked the weapon, taking the lead. Nichols followed, with Chance stumbling along behind.

The chief shone his light back and forth, illuminating the way as they entered the cavern. He played it briefly over the tent at the side of the entrance. Not seeing anything of interest, he probed toward the rear wall where the mining was currently taking place. Carefully scanning back and forth with the high-intensity beam, he was on high alert, looking for any sign of a big, hairy beast.

"Watkins!" Chance hollered, his voice echoing throughout the chamber.

"Chance, shut your trap!" Nichols said in a loud whisper. "If that bastardly bear is in here somewhere, maybe we shouldn't wake it the hell up, okay?"

"Good thinkin'," Chance said, wavering slightly on his feet.

Nichols looked at Chance and shook his head in disgust. He didn't know how many times he'd had to fix a problem that Chance's drinking had caused for their shared businesses. With two DUIs to his name and a colourful history of violence at the casino when in his cups, Ray Chance was quite a piece of work. For such a small, round man, there was an awful lot to detest, Nichols thought, sadly. It really put to the test the adage about good things coming in small packages. Speaking to VanDusen, he said, "So where was most of the ore being extracted after the majority of the nuggets had been picked up?"

"It was back there," VanDusen said, shining his light farther along the cavern wall near the picks and shovels leaning there.

"And at no time was there any mention of anyone seeing this monstrous bear anywhere around here, was there?" Nichols asked.

"Nope, except for that kid. But we don't need to worry about him for the moment since he's a drooling vegetable after we moved him to the psych ward at the hospital. That massive dose of Thorazine we keep pumping into him certainly keeps him quiet. Apart from Willy Senior, whether the bear got to anyone else up here, though, is anybody's guess," VanDusen concluded.

"All right, let's go look for Watkins and Oritz," Nichols said.

"And then we'll grab some gold!" Chance hooted, swigging from his flask.

"Jesus! Would you keep your voice down!" VanDusen said, angrily.

Chance muttered something under his breath to VanDusen about shoving things into places where the sun never shone. Then he burped, his sour, gaseous eruption reverberating throughout the cavern.

The three men moved silently away into the swirling steam. Chance still staggered behind, his flashlight's beam wavering wildly over the cavern walls and floor as he tried to maintain his balance on the rocky, uneven ground. Under his breath he began humming, 'We're In The Money'.

CHAPTER THIRTY-SEVEN

"Die, Dracula, die!" Alex said, holding the post tight as Trip gave it a few final whacks for good measure, driving the pointed wooden stake into the frozen ground.

The last 'Bear in Area' sign had now been planted, and not without some irony, Austin noted, as it was directly in front of the conservation office. He looked at his wristwatch and saw it was well after noon-hour. Placing his hands on his hips, he addressed the troops. "Okay, guys, that was great work this morning. Thanks for all the help! Let's call it lunch for now, and it'll be my treat at The Burger Barn!"

Austin's comment elicited an excited 'Yes!' from Alex and a 'Woo-hoo!' from Trip. They were both starving. Pounding posts all morning had left them with quite an appetite and Austin was sure there'd be a few burgers filling the hollow legs of his son and the empty belly of Trip in the very near future.

All in all, they had put another forty Bear Aware signs around the town. It wasn't just the outlying areas that they were concerned about anymore. The way Angus had been expanding his territory, there was an excellent chance he might find his way into town, so it was imperative everyone in Lawless was aware of THIS particular bear.

Earlier, while the boys had been putting some of the signs up, Austin had been on the phone to the radio station to ensure they were keeping up their warning notices regarding the bear. Reba Casalino mentioned that she'd already been doing so at Christine Moon's direction all morning, but that she'd make sure the afternoon and evening DJs did so as well. Austin thanked her and asked that they emphasise the 'extreme caution' part. After the attack at Frostbite Fred's the other night, Reba said, she wouldn't have any problem doing so.

Trip and Alex were climbing into The Works Silverado when Constable Oscar Olsen pulled up in his police car, flapping his arm out the window, waving at Austin. "Hey, Austin! Come here a second," he called.

"Hey Oscar," Austin said, walking up to the police car. "What's happening?" Oscar looked tired, with large black circles under his small beady eyes. Austin had known the man his whole life, just like the chief of police. They had gone to school together in Lawless from kindergarten to senior high and Austin had always felt a little sorry for the man. His whole life, Oscar had always scuttled along in the shadow of VanDusen, kowtowing to the other man, being berated and belittled almost every day, first in his school life and then in his career with the police force.

"Just finished up processing the scene at the pub."

"You just finished now?"

"Yeah, the RCMP showed up as well, of course, and by the time we got everything documented to their level of perfection, it was almost noon-hour! VanDusen went home to get some sleep at about eight o'clock this morning, but I was there the whole time." His mouth opened wide, and a large yawn escaped.

Austin nodded, folding his arms as he listened, then said, "The boys and girls in red serge certainly do like to dot their 'I's and cross their 'T's, don't they?"

"God, do they ever!" Oscar sighed.

"So, what's happening now?"

"The chief is going to be with Mr. Chance and Mayor Nichols up at the resort, sorting something out there. He said it would take all afternoon, so I'm in charge again." He yawned once more. "We've still got three other members down with the flu that's going around, and two on vacation, so it's all on me right now."

"Well, at least things seem quiet at the moment."

"I hope they stay that way until the Chief gets back." Oscar was never a man to take pressure well and visibly shuddered as he spoke. He continued, "I'm just running out to Geraldine Gertzmeyer's for a moment. She called the station and left a pretty excited message, once again, and I'm just going to check up on her. Maybe some of her little Norberts showed up again."

"Ah yes, her babies! Well, say hi to her for me!"

Oscar smiled tiredly, saying, "I'll do that."

"If you hear any other news, please let me know. Keep the population safe, Oscar." Austin turned to walk away.

"Hey, Austin, one other thing before you go."

Austin turned back, wondering what other news Olsen had. "What is it, Oscar?" He detected a note of trepidation in the constable's voice.

"About this bear." Oscar's face sagged, a look of shame on his face.

"Yeah, it's big, hairy and hungry. What about it?"

"I think I might know where it is, but I'm not supposed to say anything."

"What? What do you mean you might know where it is?" This was big news, indeed.

"Well, a new cavern opened up near the back half of the resort on Gold Ridge, past where the old ski runs end near the glacier. It happened just after that earthquake at the beginning of the month. We've had some problems up there over the last few days. Most of the people working there have been disappearing."

"Working there, doing what?" Austin wondered if gold might somehow be involved.

"I can't say, but I think it could be the bear. I think it might have eaten them."

"Is that what they're checking on now?"

"Yes."

"All right, Oscar, thanks for the info. Let's just keep this between you and me for the moment."

"Absolutely." Oscar sounded relieved as if sharing the burden of truth had reduced his anxiety to some extent. He started the police car back up.

As Austin turned and started walking back toward Trip and Alex, Oscar called out one more time. "Austin!"

He turned back with one eyebrow raised questioningly.

Olsen said, "When you see VanDusen, be careful around him."

"More so than normal, you mean?" What was Oscar so afraid of?

"Yeah, just watch your back." A look of grave concern clouded his face. "Seriously, watch your back."

With that, Oscar pulled away, giving a quick wave to Trip and Alex.

Austin stood there at the side of the road, pondering his recent conversation with Oscar. Watch his back? He figured VanDusen was a couple of nuts short of a jar of butter sometimes, as well as a misogynist, but he didn't think he would ever have to watch his back around the man. It seemed that perhaps things were a little more serious up on the hill than Chance was letting on. Was there gold in that cavern like Jerry surmised? Gold that everyone involved was trying to be so very, very secretive about? So much gold, perhaps, that they were willing to kill for it?

Austin shook his head, clearing the web of thoughts. He climbed into the driver's seat of the Silverado, saying, "Soups on!" A round of cheers came from his work crew, almost loud enough to drown out the noise from their stomachs, audibly growling for burgers and fries.

CHAPTER THIRTY-EIGHT

Set inside the cavern a half-dozen metres, the bright orange tent was erected next to a small firepit. It allowed someone to have a campfire without the flickering light acting as a beacon on the mountainside when the sun went down, if and when the fog cleared for a while.

Hunkered down next to this tent, Christine craned her neck, looking up into the dim light that filtered through the cavern's entrance. A fissure in the rock wall next to her ran up toward the ceiling and disappeared into the darkness. It appeared to turn into a natural vent, allowing for the smoke from the fire to have a place to go and not smoke a person out like a side of ribs at Frostbite Fred's.

While she waited for the snowmobilers to arrive, she'd taken off her backpack, snowshoes and rifle, hiding them inside the tent, allowing her to sneak about with greater stealth. Glancing about her environment, she noted a couple of large boulders just discernible in the dark behind her, farther along the wall. It looked like they could provide her with some additional cover, if need be, and hopefully allow her to blend into the background. She filed the thought away for future reference.

Over the sound of the steaming water gushing from the entrance, she heard male voices conferring with each other and getting closer by the second. Risking a sneak-peek, she leaned forward on her haunches and peered around the corner of the tent, trying to catch a glimpse of the new arrivals to the cavern. As she adjusted her position, she felt her legs starting to cramp. Not now, not now, she thought. Her time snowshoeing was coming back to haunt her exhausted calf muscles. She hadn't had a chance to stretch out before she'd ducked into cover behind the tent, and she was paying for it now.

Her eyes widened at the sight of the first person coming through the cavern's entrance. With rifle extended, Chief Reggie VanDusen slowly probed his way inside, turning this way and that, taking point. What in God's name is he doing up here, she wondered?

The sense of surprise at the chief's appearance was replaced by open-mouthed wonder when she saw who came through the entrance next. A tall, grey-haired gentleman wandered in, looking rather off-put by having to be in such a place. Thanks to her visit to city hall last week, she recognised this man as none other than the Mayor of Lawless himself, His Worship, Bob Nichols. Okay, now, really, what the hell is HE doing here?

Finally, staggering along at the end of this little conga-line was a small, portly man in a loud orange parka. He trailed behind the other two men by a good distance, his path taking wide sweeping arcs as he attempted to walk a straight line into the entrance. When she saw him swigging from a silver hipflask held in one gloved hand, she knew it could be only one person, Ray Chance. Christine could almost smell the fumes coming off the man from her hiding place.

The group paused near the entrance and spoke quietly amongst themselves for a moment. Thanks to the acoustics of the cavern, Christine was able to overhear most of what they said. She knew that this was also a two-way street and that any noise she made could be easily heard by them as well.

She ducked back behind the tent and bit her lower lip, stifling a groan in response to the pain of her cramping calves. She dared not move, just in case she made a noise and alerted the new visitors to her uninvited presence.

"Watkins!" Chance hollered.

In a barely hushed whisper, the mayor said, "Chance, shut your trap!" The men were obviously concerned as to what else might be lurking inside the cavern with them. They talked between themselves quietly a moment longer, then Chance shouted out loud once more, saying, "Go get some gold!"

VanDusen chided, "Jesus! Would you keep your voice down!"

The men started walking toward the back of the cavern, and Christine silently stood in a half-crouch to alleviate some of the cramping in her legs. Massaging her knotted muscles as she moved, she eased herself along the rough wall, settling back down into a more comfortable position near the first of the two boulders.

So that's why you boys are sneaking around up here, she thought. You're the ones having yourselves a little surreptitious gold mining operation going on here. That's certainly a pretty good reason not to tell anyone you might have a bear problem up here as well, she thought with a frown. She pulled out the Iridium satellite phone from her side pocket and turned it on, shielding the screen with her hand to block the light as she did. The signal strength metre on the screen showed minimal connectivity due to the surrounding rock. Hoping it would be enough, her fingers flew across the keypad as she silently fired off a text message into the ether.

The cramping in her left leg intensified, tightening into an even larger and more painful knot. The muscle was now a hard ball, causing her to suck air involuntarily through her teeth as she gritted them together in pain. She was desperate not to make any noise, but as the charlie horse worsened, her leg spasmed heavily, causing it to jolt against some loose stones near her boot. They clattered noisily across the cavern floor, and the sound of low footsteps retreating away from her suddenly stopped.

"What was that?" the mayor asked, sounding nervous.

"I hope it's not that friggin' bear," Chance slurred.

"Just hang tight, I'll check it out," VanDusen's low voice growled.

Christine heard footsteps from the other side of the cavern, crunching across the uneven floor, rapidly approaching her hiding spot. Panicked, she needed a new place to hide and recalled the information she'd filed away in her brain earlier.

In the near blackness, she crept around the first boulder. It looked like it was out just far enough to allow her to squeeze into the recess between it and the second boulder if she were lucky. Staying low and still stretching her leg out in an attempt to mitigate some of the cramping, she tried to pull herself sideways into the gap. But something was already there, blocking her way.

Christine reached her hand in to feel what was stopping her progress. The object was hard, cold, and covered in what seemed like Gortex fabric. Moving her hand around a moment longer to try to get a better feel for the object, she wrinkled her face in distaste and suddenly jolted back in disgust. Her hand was covered in something cold, wet and very sticky. An unmistakable smell wafted toward her nose.

Her world was suddenly filled with a brilliant white light. She heard the distinctive sound of a shotgun being cocked, followed by a voice from the far side of the tent. "Move a muscle, and I'll blow your fucking head off!"

CHAPTER THIRTY-NINE

The Burger Barn was a large, red barn, which, like its name implied, sold burgers. The structure was an actual barn that had been converted into a restaurant back in the late 1980s. At the time, the owners, Ed and Marie Popov, had spent many, many months and an equal amount of dollars fixing the old barn up to make it passable to the public health inspector. And they had done a fantastic job of it. The first thing to go had been that pesky barn smell that just didn't do anything to whet people's appetites. Now, when you walked into the Burger Barn, the only thing you smelled was some of the finest flame-broiled Angus beef burgers this side of Alberta.

Alex entered first and held the door for his dad and Trip.

"Thank you, kind sir. You're a scholar and a gentleman," Austin said as he entered.

Trip followed Austin through the open door, giving Alex a thumbs up and a smile as he passed.

The interior of the Burger Barn was eclectic, to say the least. It looked like Ed and Marie had started the decoration of the restaurant with a western motif but had transformed it into a showcase of whatever they found funny or intriguing.

Some of the colourful collection that lined the interior of the cavernous structure had been brought in by regular customers over the years who loved the interesting mix of bric-a-brac that covered the walls. And they were always looking for something new on display since their last visit. It seemed that part of the draw of the place, apart from the food, was the colourful gewgaws all over the walls and ceiling for people to look at while they ate.

Needless to say, the two-story-high interior walls of the dry, old barn were getting quite crowded. Over the years, Ed and Marie had been inundated by a tidal wave of assorted artefacts from their fervent fans wishing to help them out. As well, the Popovs had added new trinketry of their own to the decor of the barn's interior on a regular basis. Eventually, they had to tell everyone that, though they appreciated the thought when they were presented with some new knickknack or other, they just didn't have room to put everything out on display. As it stood now, the collection was amazing and covered almost every square inch of space on the building's walls and ceiling.

The restaurant boasted a dozen heavy, pine tables that dotted the lower level of the large space. Across from them, underneath the old hayloft, a modern, stainless steel kitchen gleamed. Next to it, a beautiful wrought iron staircase spiralled up into the loft. Up there, adventurous diners could enjoy their burgers and the spectacular scenery if they wanted, or maybe go up there just to see more of Ed and Marie's assorted oddities.

These days, the old loft boasted a hay-free dining area, and the only hay you'd find up there now was coming from the patrons. It seemed, as customers took their first bite of a Burger Barn Angus Double-decker Cheese and Bacon Burger, some of them would invariably say, "Hey! This burger's delicious!" So, one day, since it seemed like it was a regular phrase coming out of people's mouths, Ed decided to make it official and ensconced an engraved Douglas fir plaque at the bottom of the spiral staircase that read, 'The Hey Loft!'

Across from the loft seating area and the kitchen, numerous tall, plate glass windows ran up the entire front wall of the building. Each large window was separated by enough wood to ensure the wall's integrity while giving customers a fantastic view of the local mountains on clear days, when they occasionally arrived, such as today. The interior of the restaurant was currently bathed in golden, mountain sunshine that beamed through its sparkling windows.

At the zenith of the loft over the kitchen stood one of the most curious curios of all, a two-metre tall, two hundred-kilogram, wooden indigenous person. In days gone by, the imposing figure would have stood in front of a five and dime store. And in fact, it had done so for many years in the neighbouring town of Driftwood. The detail of the intricately carved figure was amazing, and Ed knew he had to have it the moment he saw it on display at Sal's Sloppy Seconds Store. He relocated it to a special ledge that he'd built at the apex of the barn's high vaulted ceilings, much like the spot where Jesus Christ would sit ensconced on his cross in a Roman Catholic church.

The local indigenous people who ate at the Burger Barn knew that Ed and Marie didn't mean any disrespect to them by having the statue in the restaurant. In fact, the front of their menu stated that Ed and Marie were thankful and honoured to be able to feed all of their amazingly loyal customers. It also mentioned their immense respect for their indigenous customer's heritage, and that they were grateful for being allowed to operate their restaurant on unceded aboriginal ground.

And it seemed the local natives also appreciated the irony. The Aboriginal Peoples of Canada had suffered greatly at the hands of European settlers with their desires to 'save' the Indigenous residents from themselves through Jesus. But through the settlers' use of their relatively 'new' seventeen hundred-year-old patriarchal religion known as Christianity, more often times than not, they did more harm than good.

Now, local Aboriginal band members who came to the Burger Barn took some delight in eating at this 'White Man's Shrine', or the 'Church of the Holy Cheeseburger' as most of the local tribe members now facetiously called it. They sat there along with all of the other patrons, enjoying their delicious Angus cheeseburgers in the sunlit 'Hey Loft', while high above, the cigar store Indigenous Jesus blessed the room with his dime-store kitsch.

Looking up at the carved, wooden figure high above his head as he entered, the word came to Austin. Treasures, he suddenly recalled, that's what Marie called the bric-a-brac on the walls sometimes, just like Patricia had. Once more, he felt a pang of loss and loneliness and buried it deep down inside his psyche, meaning to examine it further at a later date.

Austin stood underneath an unusually large and toothy 'treasure' at the moment, one that had been brought in by a local hunter many years back. Affixed to the wall over the main entrance was a sizable grizzly skull, forever frozen in mid-roar. These days, the only thing caught between its fangs were the brilliant rays of sunshine that streamed through the restaurant's dozens of windows. The skull was mounted in front of an old convex mirror, just like they used in convenience and grocery stores back in the days before closed-circuit TV took over the job of a clerk's eyeballs and refracted light. Witty as ever, Ed had engraved another wooden sign similar to the one next to the stairs of the 'Hey Loft' and hung it below the skull. It read: Warning! Animals In The Forest May Be Closer Than They Appear!

As always, when they walked in, Alex had to stop and marvel at the bleached skull. "Just look at those teeth, Dad! Those things are wicked sharp!"

Austin craned his neck to look up at it, saying, "That they are, Skipper." He thought of the creature that currently stalked the residents of Lawless and shuddered slightly, wondering how much bigger the mouth on the beast in the wild must be compared to the one over his head.

As if reading his mind, Alex asked, "So is the bear you guys are looking for a bit bigger than that?"

Austin responded, "Just a bit."

"Something like at least three times the size, I'd say," Trip added.

"Holy shit!"

"Language, Alex!"

"Sorry, Dad, but that is one humongous bear!"

"That it is. Tell you what, why don't we order some lunch and then we can discuss it a bit more, okay?"

Marie Popov was in attendance at the till today. When the three men approached to order, she said, "Afternoon, gentlemen! What's your pleasure?"

Austin smiled, saying, "Hey there, Marie! How's your day going?"

Marie nodded her greying head perkily, saying, "Not too bad, but a little slower than normal, there doesn't seem to be as many people out and about here today."

"I think a lot of them have been noticing the signs that we planted around town," Trip added from over Austin's shoulder.

"Well, I guess that'd do it! You guys will just have to order extra food today to make up for it!" Marie replied semi-seriously, a small smile playing at the corners of her lips.

"Okay, Alex, what's it going to be today? The usual?" Austin asked.

"Yes, please, Dad!" Alex said, holding his stomach to help muffle some of the extremely loud growls that were currently coming from it thanks to the discussion of food choices. It apparently decided that now was the time to remind him how hungry he really was after all the work he had done pounding the stakes into the frozen ground with Trip this morning.

Marie said, "That'll be one bacon, triple-cheese with extra ketchup, hold the onions, hold the pickles. An extra-large yam fries, a side of gravy and a quadruple-thick chocolate milkshake on the side, right?"

"That's right! Thanks for remembering Mrs. Popov!" Alex beamed with delight at his order being remembered, and also the thrill of having a 'usual' somewhere. He felt very grown up.

"I know what my regulars like," Marie replied, with a grin. She and her husband, Ed, had been selling burgers to the residents of Lawless for almost forty years now. After that length of time, she pretty much knew the order of every regular customer that walked through the door. And there were plenty of regular customers, as the burgers at the Barn were some of the finest in the area. Despite the out-of-the-way nature of Lawless, the restaurant drew in burger connoisseurs from as far away as a hundred kilometres, bringing in customers from neighbouring communities such as Driftwood, Silvervale, and Sagebrush on a regular basis.

"What about you, Austin, the usual?"

"No thanks, Marie. I think I'll skip the double cheeseburger today and branch out in a new direction. Today, I'll have a chicken burger, extra cheese, please! But pair it with the usual Coke, fries and gravy on the side, of course. Thanks."

"I would never forget your gravy, Austin!" Marie said, merrily. And what about you, Trip?"

Holding his own gurgling belly, Trip said, "I'll have the usual, Marie, thanks."

"One Quadruple Bypass Combo, extra pickles, onion rings on the side. You got it, Trip." The Quadruple Bypass Combo, or QBC, as it was known in the area, was one of the more popular items on the menu. It consisted of four, five-ounce Angus beef patties, four slices of aged cheddar, two strips of applewood smoked bacon between each patty and finished with a fried egg on top. Marie rang this last item into the till and then Austin paid with his credit card.

"Thanks very much, Austin, here you go," Marie said, handing him his receipt and a small, red plastic sign, tented in the middle like a miniature sandwich board. A white number three was on both sides of it. "It'll be about ten minutes; I'll bring out your orders out when Ed has them ready."

Austin nodded in gratitude. He looked briefly around the dining room but didn't see any other customers at the moment and wondered why Marie would need a number to find their table. Just habit after all these years, he supposed, and smiled, thanking her.

The three men moved to one of the sizable pine tables scattered around the main floor of the restaurant near the tall, plate-glass windows.

After taking their parkas off and getting comfortable, talk of the latest scores in the NHL became the topic of interest, with all thoughts of the bear temporarily forgotten. Alex's passion for the game became evident as he dutifully listed off all the winners and losers, including their final scores over the last several weeks.

Less than ten minutes later, Marie was at their table with the food, saying, "Here you go, boys." She placed the meals on the table in front of the hungry men. She also made sure to leave the stainless-steel cup in which Alex's milkshake had been blended on the table in front of him. The cup contained the excess shake that wouldn't fit into the tall glass of frosty chocolate heaven that Marie slid in front of the boy's wide-open eyes. She knew that one of the perks that drew people back to the Burger Barn, again and again, was an attention to detail that some of the bigger places missed. It was amazing how such a little thing as a couple of extra ounces of milkshake, that may have otherwise been thrown away, was able to bring such a huge smile to this young man's face.

"Wow, thanks, Marie!" Alex exclaimed, eyeing the tall, delicious-looking shake glass with the moisture beading on its sides. "You're the best!"

"Not a problem, Alex," she said with a laugh, "Just trying to keep everyone happy. Is there anything else you boys would like?"

"No, thank you, Marie, I think we're all good." Austin flashed her a quick okay sign as he spoke and picked up his crispy chicken sandwich with obvious delight.

Trip smiled, nodding in agreement with Austin's comment to Marie, then attacked his QBC, extra pickles bulging from between the patties, with a fervour that only a true carnivore could appreciate.

Watching the boys tearing into the food seemed to trigger something in Marie's memory, and she said, "Austin, one other thing before I leave you boys to devour your food. About that bear they were talking about on the radio today. Is it really as dangerous as they're saying?"

"Well, after what happened at Frostbite Fred's last night, I'm more than prepared to answer that with a big 'Yes.' It's huge, and it is deadly. Not something you'd want to meet skulking around out in the fog."

"Oh, my gosh!" Marie clucked, shaking her head.

"Yeah, and I almost saw it last night!" Alex enthused.

"Really? Were you scared?" Marie asked.

"Nah, I was okay, my dad was there," pride evident in the boy's voice.

"Well, you guys still be careful if you go out in the woods, then, okay?"

"We will, Marie. Thanks for the great food, as usual," Austin said.

Marie smiled and left them to their meals. Austin watched as she stopped at a table near them to give it a quick wipe with her cloth on the way by, no doubt seeing a speck of something that didn't belong on a table that was already immaculate and gleaming. He had to hand it to Marie and Ed; they kept the place spotless.

As they were finishing up their burgers and fries, the faint but familiar honk of a hockey air horn and the crowd going wild came from Austin's parka draped over the back of his chair. Recognising the distinct alert sound his father had set for his phone to notify him of incoming text messages, Alex said, "Looks like you scored another one, Dad!"

Austin smiled as he pulled out his phone, the email notification now winding down with several bars of the old Hockey Night in Canada theme song at its end. He read the message on his screen, and his smile faded away with the song. It was now replaced by a look of concern.

Picking at the last crunchy little bits of his yam fries on the red-checked paper covering the wicker serving basket from his lunch, Alex watched his father's expression darken and said, "What is it, Dad?"

Trip brushed an abundance of bun crumbs from his beard, also noting Austin's change in demeanour and asked, "Yeah, what's shakin', Boss?"

Austin looked up; his brow wrinkled with concern. "Christine's in trouble. We need to get up to Gold Ridge." Austin stood, starting to put on his parka.

"Is Christine okay, Dad? What did her text message say?" Alex asked, standing and grabbing his jacket from the back of his chair, concern heavy in his voice.

"All she typed was, 'At cavern on Gold Ridge. Need help NOW!'"

CHAPTER FORTY

The click of a weapon being cocked behind her head was more than enough incentive for Christine to do as the voice told her.

"Stand up slowly and put your hands in the air! Don't do anything stupid, or I'll blow your fucking head off!"

"Yeah, thanks," Christine muttered under her breath, pulling back from the cold, wet, slimy thing into which she'd just stuck her hands. "I caught your sales pitch about that the first time you said it, Spanky."

Standing with her back to the light, she raised her hands near her face in compliance with VanDusen's 'request'. She wrinkled her nose in distaste, what she suspected was all over her hands was indeed correct — the coppery smell so distinctive, she had known what it was before she could even see it. They were covered in blood. The ultra-white light of VanDusen's beam illuminated the gore on her hands, making them appear as dark and sticky as if covered in blackstrap molasses. Bile rose in her throat.

VanDusen kept his light trained on Christine's back. Before she turned, she looked to the spot where she'd been trying to hide, and in the stark light saw what it was she'd been trying to snuggle up next to in the cosy, dark little nook.

Someone had tried to crawl into the small gap between the boulders to hide from whatever had been chasing them, but only got halfway in and then got stuck, unable to go any further. It seemed the poor unfortunate soul had gotten their arm wedged between the rocks as they tried to hide and had been unable to free themselves.

Whatever had been after them apparently decided to snack on the part of their body it could reach and gobbled it up, leaving the top half wedged into the recess. Several bright, white vertebrae from their spinal column protruded from the remains of their chest cavity, along with a few bits of intestine and internal organs, but nothing remained of their lower torso and legs.

One of the person's hands peeked out from between the boulders at an odd angle due to the broken arm still wedged into the rock. Its fingers were splayed, as if the person were waving goodbye, saying, 'Hey! It's been fun! Gotta go!' as they had been devoured alive from the bottom up. The hand was missing the tip of its right thumb, most likely from an old high school woodshop incident.

Her disgust so all-encompassing, Christine had forgotten about VanDusen until he spoke from behind her once more. "All right, keep your goddamned hands where I can see 'em and step out from behind the tent!"

"Calm down, Reggie, it's me, Christine Moon, from the conservation office." She slowly turned, crimson hands held high.

"You! What in the hell are you DOING back there?" VanDusen shouted in surprise, his advice to Chance to keep his voice low seemingly now null and void. The chief gestured the flashlight on the end the Remington toward Christine's raised hands, illuminating the blood.

"Finger painting?" Christine questioned. She sidled out from the gap between the tent and cavern wall, gore-coated hands still raised high.

"Move," VanDusen said, gesturing off to one side with the muzzle of his gun. She obliged and moved over a couple of feet. The chief shone the light into the gap between the boulder and the wall and said, "Holy shit!"

Chance stumbled up next to VanDusen and surveyed the scene. He turned his head and spewed most of the contents of his stomach all over the cavern floor, spraying the police chief's pant legs in the process.

"Jesus Christ! Would you watch that shit, Chance!" VanDusen said, jerking his foot back and trying to shake some of the steaming, bright yellow mess from his uniform pants.

Chance turned to Christine, wiping the sleeve of his parka across his mouth, saying, "Holy Christ! What in God's name did you do to that poor bastard, lady?"

"Seriously? Does this look like something a woman would do to another person?" Christine asked.

"Maybe, maybe not. Then again, you've never met my ex-wives!" Chance slurred. "Plus, you never know what a person is capable of when there's gold involved!"

"Gold?" Christine inquired.

"Yeah, gold," Nichols said as he crunched up on the uneven stone floor behind VanDusen. "There's no harm in her knowing now."

"Bob," VanDusen started, "What are you doing? Don't…"

"Don't what? Tell her we have a shitload of gold ore here? Don't tell her we've been keeping it quiet by bumping off anyone who might spill their guts about it? Don't bother being discrete, Reggie, our lovely, young friend here won't be leaving this cavern anytime soon to tell anyone about this."

VanDusen remained silent and gestured the end of his Remington toward the middle of the cavern, pointing Christine away from the wall.

Christine complied, holding her sticky hands high above her head. VanDusen stepped in behind her, his finger resting lightly on the trigger should she try anything funny.

"Just shoot her!" Chance shouted.

"Why don't you just shut the hell up, Ray!" Nichols said. He turned to Christine, waving his flashlight in Christine's face and scowling slightly. "I know you, don't I?"

"Yes, we met last week, Mr. Mayor. I lead that Girl Guide troupe, don't you remember? I was just passing through here and thought I'd stop in to see if you wanted any more cookies," Christine said. She was trying to think of a way out of her predicament and recalled Nichols's absentminded comment when he met her the previous week.

"That's right. I did see you at city hall. Well, this is most unfortunate, as I enjoy a nice Mint Meltie on occasion. And I'm really going to hate myself in the morning for having to dispose of a woman as attractive as yourself. But it's nothing personal; it's just business." He shook his head slightly, frowning sadly.

"That's bullshit, Bob! She's with the Ministry of Conservation. Snooping around, no doubt, trying to ruin this operation." He jabbed his gun toward her as he finished his sentence.

"Well, I see you've at least found my damned maintenance man!" Chance said, shining his light over toward the boulders.

"Yes, and I think he was attacked by that bear you refuse to believe exists!"

"Oh, we believe it exists all right," Nichols said. "Conveniently, it'll probably be blamed as the reason you're no longer going to exist in the very near future." He smirked slightly as he relayed this news to Christine.

"Wait! Isn't there some way we can work this out? I swear I won't tell anyone!"

"That's exactly what Carl said!" Chance squealed in delight, then giggled merrily.

VanDusen joined in with a cackle of his own, then looked over to Chance, saying, "Yeah, you're right, Ray! She's just like Carl!"

"W-what do you mean?" Horrified, Christine knew precisely what they meant. Carl had never bugged out, deciding to retire early as everyone thought. These men had murdered him and had no qualms about doing the same to anyone else that stood in their way.

"What do you mean?" Chance said, mimicking Christine, then added, "Isn't it obvious?" He grinned wickedly, wiping some drying vomit from the corner of his mouth. "Maybe you can say, 'Hi' to Carl on your way down!"

Nichols cleared his throat and said, "Well, young lady, the only way this situation is going to resolve itself is with you at the bottom of one of those pits at the back of this cavern, just like your predecessor, as Raymond observed so obliquely just now. In fact, when I say bottom, that is a bit of a misnomer, because as far as we know these pits don't have any bottom! Isn't that right, Reggie?"

"That's right! I don't rightly know how far down they go, but they sure do come in handy for getting rid of busybodies like you!" He poked his shotgun toward Christine.

"Look, I swear I didn't see anything."

Nichols sighed, as if upset at the decision he had to make. "Yes, yes, I'm sure you didn't. However, it is most unfortunate that you overheard some of the things we said."

"But I won't say anything to anybody!"

"Yeah, you probably won't. It's hard to speak and scream at the same time when you're falling down a hole!" Chance enthused drunkenly, clapping his hands together while practically capering with glee.

"I'm sorry, young lady. Reggie, would you show her the way, please?"

VanDusen thrust his shotgun in Christine's face, ending any further conversation. He tilted his head toward the back of the cavern, saying, "You heard the man, now move!"

CHAPTER FORTY-ONE

Geraldine Gertzmeyer loved only one thing more than her prized wild turkeys, and that was her late husband, Norbert. But even then, it was a close call. This morning was day four of her vigil. A quilt over her legs to ward off the chill, she sat on her front porch, waiting patiently. A hot cup of tea lazily steamed on the table beside her. Ol' Bessie lay across her lap.

Back when Norbert had been alive, Geraldine had said the turkeys were like the children they never had. In fact, thanks to the distinct lack of feathers atop their bald little heads, not to mention their wrinkly little faces, the turkeys were almost a spitting image of Norbert in his later years. Geraldine sometimes watched them after Norbert passed, talking to them, and giving each one a name. She almost felt as if her late husband were still with her, the gaggle of little Norberts, clucking and gobbling about the yard so comforting as they were to her.

When she'd tottered along her porch to the back corner of her house to check on the 'children' several days ago, her heart had almost broken. All of her lovely little babies had been torn apart and scattered across her backyard, blood and entrails everywhere.

Though Ol' Bessie had the name of a dog, this particular dog's bark and bite were much bigger than that of an average canine. Its dark steel coat gleamed against the hand-sewn quilt in Geraldine's lap. In her gut, she knew that the thing that had eaten her little Norberts wasn't finished. And when it came back looking for more, she and Ol' Bessie would be ready for it.

Ol' Bessie had been Norbert's elephant gun. It glinted in the bright sunlight, well polished from many years of regular use. A souvenir of a long-ago vacation to Africa, it came from a time when she and Norbert had both been much younger and much more adventurous. Neither she nor Norbert had ever actually shot an elephant with the weapon, but instead used it to scare off assorted varmints and pests of a much smaller stature around their beautiful acreage.

Though Norbert had been fascinated by the stopping power of the large rifle, he was more interested in the noise the gun made when it was discharged instead. But they'd never used it to kill anything. Sometimes, it had been used to frighten off some mangy coyotes that came sniffing around their livestock and pets. Other times it had been used to scare off a hungry bear ready for hibernation looking for a meal of rotting apples still on the ground, left behind after the fruit had been harvested.

Since the purpose of the elephant gun was for noise more than force, most of the time, it had been loaded with two hundred grain, sixty-gram shells. They'd always found the lower capacity shells more than loud enough to scare things away, yet still manageable enough for a smaller woman like Geraldine.

Sipping her tea, she sat waiting on her porch like she had every day since she'd found her little sweeties slaughtered. She waited for the thing to come back that had taken away her last joy in life. And when it did, it would regret its decision.

For the last several days, each morning, she'd bundle up in her winter coat and gloves, then place Mongo on her head. Mongo was a large, furry hat that Norbert had always installed on his big, bald head whenever the weather got cold. Apart from the warmth it provided, for

Geraldine, it was a souvenir of happier winter's gone-by from which she couldn't bear to part. Bundled up in her parka, with the oversized fur hat on her head, she'd grab her large mug of tea and Ol' Bessie, then settle into her rocker on the front porch to wait.

This morning, she'd woken to sunshine streaming through her bedroom window, and it had been a lovely surprise. The winters in the valley around Lawless were so grey with that blasted fog most of the time now, sapping any ambition or motivation a person might have. It just made you feel like you wanted to stay indoors, buried under your comforter for the entire winter. Yes, it was a feeling Geraldine knew all too well.

But not today, the sun was shining, and it looked like a day of renewed hope was on the horizon. Despite the bitter cold that accompanied the sun, the golden rays warmed her face. Geraldine felt that this would be the day she would finally avenge her little Norberts.

She reached for another sip of tea only to find the mug empty, just a couple of loose leaves floating in the bottom of the cup. With great care, she stood from her rocker, feeling her knees pop. She put her quilt aside and shuffled along with her walker back inside the house to get another mug of tea.

Several minutes passed, and Geraldine returned with another fresh 'cuppa', as Norbert had called a hot cup of tea. Steam coiled from the ceramic mug into the frigid morning air as she stepped outside. She stood at her walker, looking for the finches that had been flitting back and forth in the branches of the trees near the front porch all morning. It seemed that the sun had enlivened the small birds as much as her as if they sensed that this long winter might soon be coming to an end.

There were a half dozen bird feeders near the front of the house, kept well-stocked all winter long. Rather than going south, the little finches spent the winter living in the numerous small birdhouses that Norbert had put up in the trees many years before. She loved to watch them hopping from their houses out onto the branches and back into their little homes once more. Never seemingly happy in one location, they were always flapping back and forth from one place to another. At one point, some squirrels had been part of this morning's festivities. They'd chirped away in the higher branches of the trees, then scampered quickly down to the feeders now and again, sneaking the odd larger nut that Geraldine put into the mix just for them which she knew the birds couldn't eat.

On sunny days like this, the finches were usually all over the trees, literally bathing in the seed at the feeders, their chirping like music to Geraldine's ears. But now, neither the finches nor the squirrels were around at the moment. In fact, there was no sign of her forest friends anywhere in sight — either around the feeder or up in the trees. For some reason, it seemed they'd all disappeared as if in a puff of smoke in the few moments she'd been inside the house grabbing another cuppa. Where did they all go? She had never seen it so quiet in the forest surrounding her home. Her legs creaking, she slowly sat in her Adirondack rocker, looking around the yard for signs of her friends, winged or otherwise, but there were none. She shook her head and pulled her quilt back over her knees, then placed Ol' Bessie across her lap.

Despite her years, Geraldine had excellent hearing and eyesight. Now that the musical sound of the birds tweeting had stopped, the clear January day took on a sharper, more menacing air. It was as if the entire forest had cleared out since she'd gone inside to get her latest mug of tea. She picked up the ceramic mug from the table next to her chair, her swollen knuckles looking skeletal and white as she cupped the mug in her hands to take a sip. Her arthritic finger joints appreciated the warmth as she put the mug to her nose and inhaled deeply, breathing in the wafting steam and savouring the citrus smell of bergamot in the Earl Grey tea.

As she sipped her cuppa, Geraldine was able to see the entrance to her property where it met the highway, just visible through the winter-drab trees. A vehicle turned into her lane, coming to pay her a visit. It was a patrol car from the Lawless City Police Department. The lane dead-ended in a cul-de-sac that lay directly in front of her stately old home. The car pulled up in front of her steps, and she was pleased to see it was Constable Oscar Olsen behind the wheel. She had called the police department earlier that morning and left a rather excited message, asking if they might have some news on what had killed her little Norberts.

Olsen slowly extricated himself from behind the wheel of the car, his stomach getting him temporarily tangled in the seatbelt. After a brief moment, he liberated himself, hitching his pants up with one gloved hand and ambling toward the porch steps. A look of surprise crossed his face when he saw Ol' Bessie.

Geraldine set her tea down and smiled sweetly at the constable. "Afternoon, Oscar."

"Hey there, Mrs. Gertzmeyer! How're you doing today?"

"I'm doing about as fine as a person of ninety-three can be! Thanks for askin', young fella. I sure hope you've got some news about my sweet little dead Norberts."

"Sorry, ma'am, your sweet little dead whats?" Oscar looked flummoxed.

"I apologise, Oscar, I'm forgettin' myself, the wild turkeys I mean. They looked like my late husband."

Oscar hitched his pants once more over his enormous belly and looked thoughtful for a moment. With a slight chuckle, he said, "I suppose I can see the resemblance. Actually, you are correct, ma'am, that is exactly the reason I'm here; to let you know about the predator that killed your turkeys. It's sort of a good news, bad news kind of thing."

"What's the good news?"

"The predator that killed your turkeys is dead."

"That is great news! But what's the bad news?"

"Turns out we have another one in the area as well. A big one!"

"Well, if it comes sniffin' around here, I'll be ready for it." She patted Bessie in her lap.

"Yes ma'am, I can see that," he said, nodding toward the gun.

"Yep, I thought I'd keep her handy in case the turkey-eater comes back, then I'll show it a thing or two."

"That's understandable, ma'am. You do know how to use that, don't you?" He nodded again toward the elephant gun.

Geraldine looked down at the weapon in her lap, then back up at Oscar and said, "Oscar Olsen, my husband and I were scaring coyotes and bears away with this gun before you were even a bulge in your daddy's BVDs!"

"I'll take that as a yes," Oscar laughed. "Maybe I'll just take a quick look around then. How would that be?"

"That would be much appreciated, Oscar! It happened round the back."

"Okay, sounds good, Mrs. Gertzmeyer," Oscar said as he moved down the porch steps to ground level once more. He nodded briefly once more then turned back to his patrol car.

Geraldine called out, "I haven't had the heart to go back there again since that pretty new conservation officer took some casts of the prints a couple of days ago. It should be easy to spot the scene of the massacre, either way."

"Thanks, ma'am. I'll have a quick walk about the property here just to make sure everything's okay."

"You do that, Oscar Olsen, and when you come back, I'll have a hot cup of tea ready for you!"

"Thank you, ma'am, that'd be nice." Oscar tipped the brim of his hat to Geraldine. He reached into his cruiser for the Benelli Nova pump shotgun secured between the seats. Unlocking it, he pulled it out and chambered a round, making sure it was loaded and ready to go. With a satisfied grunt, he checked that the safety was on and slung it over his shoulder. Tipping his hat to Geraldine a final time, he proceeded around the side of the house toward the backyard.

"Such a nice young man," Geraldine said to the empty rocker beside her. It creaked slowly back and forth in the January breeze, but apart from that had no opinion to voice one way or the other.

Oscar Olsen rounded the house and found the scene of the turkey attack right away. Mrs. Gertzmeyer had been correct; it was easy to find. So much blood, though! In the report the conservation officer had cc'd to the police department, Oscar didn't remember her mentioning so much carnage. He followed a trail of blood and feathers embedded like ancient fossils in the now solid mantle of ice and snow. The refreeze overnight had left a hard, frozen crust of slush on the ground that was solid enough not to break underneath Oscar's weight.

Near some bushes, he spotted white powder dusted around a print in the frozen yard. He knelt for a moment near the impression and examined the dental stone residue. It must have been from the very same creature Ray Chance had subsequently terminated via his Land Rover. Oscar looked about noting the smaller boot prints left around the scene by the conservation officer. They went everywhere. Boy, she must be thorough, he marvelled. Her prints followed a trail down toward the back of the acreage.

It looked like the raccoon had dragged some of the turkeys down this trail during its impromptu banquet, or perhaps after it killed them. He followed the path for a moment, then stopped — it branched in two and he now had a choice to make.

One path continued up the mountainside, winding into the forest beyond. Going that way, he could access Gold Mountain Resort's property or go up toward Gold Ridge, where the cavern lay somewhere among its rocky edifices. This path appeared to be a likely candidate for the bear to access the valley below if it were in the area. Oscar was pretty sure Christine Moon would have gone that route, hoping to track the beast further.

The other path gradually dropped down toward a dark, age-stained barn and large, fenced acreage beyond. The barn's dilapidated appearance belied its solidity. Oscar had been out to it several years before when Geraldine had been having a problem with some vandals at night. He knew the unassuming building's cellar also housed the acreage's workshop, which contained the tractor and also played host to a huge root cellar.

To feed their animal wards, the Gertzmeyers had grown all of their own hay and organic vegetables on the acreage. Thousands of kilograms of potatoes, turnips and cabbages had been stored in the root cellar, along with hay in the loft above. Since Norbert's passing several years back, Geraldine hadn't used the building or cellar below for much of anything. She seemed to be leaving it to whatever fate decided for an ageing barn on an untended acreage in the rugged Cascade Mountains of British Columbia.

Oscar took in the beautiful landscape before him for a moment. It dawned on him that he should make it look good for Mrs. Gertzmeyer and figured he'd better choose a path and have a quick stroll in the sunshine, pretending to investigate to at least to keep her happy.

He weighed his two choices: to his left, the steep, rugged path winding up into the thickly forested mountainside beyond. To his right, one hundred and two wide-open, rolling hectares of beautiful Kootenay loveliness stretching off into the distance. If he went that way, he knew he'd be able to see anything coming to chow-down on him from kilometres away.

Smiling to himself, he ambled toward the weathered barn. It hadn't been a tough call, he always liked to go with wide-open spaces, if possible — it gave him room to manoeuvre his bulk. Who knew, maybe he'd encounter a deer or an antelope playing together on his way to the barn.

Despite the faded red paint on the old barn, it was still solid and dry, yet looked like it was ready to fuel somebody's wood stove for the winter. Arriving at the structure, Oscar looked up to the hayloft door overhead the main doors, and his stomach rumbled, perhaps thinking of a different 'Hey Loft', instead.

Checking the two, tall main doors of the barn, he noted the heavy padlock that lay across them, slightly rusty, but still secure. To his left, double storm doors leading to the cellar of the barn lay firmly closed against the base of the exterior wall. He wandered around to the back of the building and stopped. The rear access door was swung inward, open most of the way. This door was a single affair, but still quite large, measuring almost two metres wide by three metres tall. Strange it wouldn't be latched, Oscar thought as he looked at the lock. It wasn't broken, just popped off the door, like some ponderous weight had pressed against it and pushed it open, rending the heavy-duty lock from the aged wood.

Sweat beaded on Olsen's brow, despite the frigid temperature outside. His forehead steamed as he stepped toward the open door. Unslinging his shotgun, he took the safety off and moved to the entrance of the darkened barn.

"This is Constable Olsen with the Lawless City Police Department. I have a weapon aimed directly at your location. I need you to step out of the barn and identify yourself." He walked in a little way, barely able to see anything after being dazzled by the sunlight outside. Reaching to his belt, he grabbed a small flashlight clipped there and removed it, turning it on and shining it about the room. Satisfied there were no immediate threats, he attached the magnetized light under the barrel of his shotgun, and reluctantly moved deeper into the bowels of the barn.

Rusty chains hung from dry, solid beams, dangling next to equally rusty saw blades. They were complemented by a lovely coating of dust and cobwebs. Oscar cast the light about — everything seemed fine on the main floor. He shone it up into the murk where the loft was located. A narrow ladder led up into more darkness. He was disinclined to climb it and check on the loft at the moment, thank you very much.

Against the far wall of the barn, another large door opened onto the old root cellar that Norbert had dug into the foundation. It was a large opening, almost as large as the main entrance, in fact. When he'd put the cellar in, Norbert wanted to make sure that he'd have enough room to drive their old tractor and its attachments right down into the workshop located in the cellar. Very handy when he had forks loaded with a bin of potatoes and a trailer full of apples or whatever else they wanted to keep chilled in Mother Earth.

The root cellar door opened inward as well, and was currently standing open, flung back inside the darkened room. Oscar didn't think there was anything in the root cellar anymore, but he walked toward it to take a quick peek inside. Perhaps there was a jar of Gertrude's tasty canning left on one of the pantry shelves that he could sample. He licked his lips at the thought of some canned peaches or pears. That was something that would really hit the spot right now.

The floor of the barn ramped down a short tunnel into the cellar below. At the bottom, it opened into a spacious storage room and shop, with a separate cold room off to one side to store apples, potatoes and other hardy root vegetables. On two of the walls, shelves meant to house canning and other preserves sat empty.

Oscar frowned, disappointed and feeling slightly nauseous. The stench down here was eye-watering. It smelled like something had crawled up and died in a corner somewhere.

The far wall contained an extended workbench and a man-sized, storm door exit. In one darkened corner, the ancient tractor rested, draped in a tarp.

A huge mound of old burlap sacks sat piled in the opposite corner across from the tractor. Oscar thought it strange for Geraldine to be so messy, knowing how neat and organised she usually was after so many calls to her property over the years.

He stepped closer, exploring with his flashlight's beam. The sacks were a filthy grey colour and...

They suddenly moved.

He stepped/stumbled backward. "What the hell?"

Oscar began backing away, farther and farther until suddenly he felt a jolt against his spine and heard the tools hanging on the pegboard jangle behind him. He had backed up as far as he could go.

The mound was not made of burlap sacks, he could see that now. Something huge slept in the darkened corner. Thick, ropey muscles rippled beneath a matted, gore-smeared pelt as the beast awoke and became aware of his presence.

Moving sideways along the workbench, Oscar's eyes never left the creature. His every sense was now focussed on the thing across the room. He was unable to look away.

Thanks to Oscar's penchant for speaking aloud to himself, the monstrosity that inhabited the pelt was now alerted to the interloper in its private domain.

Angular and lean, the beast slowly turned its head toward him. Most ursine species have layers and layers of fat off which they can subsist when times are tough, or during hibernation, but this massive carnivore had none. Cut like a bodybuilder, its hard-muscled back and sides flexed as it stood. It looked into Oscar's eyes, bottomless hunger sparkling in his light's beam. Now standing on all fours, the stump of one blood-crusted ear grazed the ceiling of the root-cellar, almost three metres up. Its other uninjured ear lay back against the side of its head, like a cat getting ready to pounce on its prey.

Oscar couldn't look away. It was if the beast was devouring his soul as it stalked slowly forward, gorging on his fear and never taking its eyes off of him. With maximum effort, he broke the creature's gaze.

Salvation suddenly gleamed over his head.

A short flight of stairs led up toward the dual storm doors over his head. Crisp daylight leaked through their seam.

In one fluid motion, the creature charged from across the cellar toward him.

Olsen stumbled quickly backward up the stairs. Overhead, the double doors looked firmly sealed.

All at once, he remembered the Benelli in his hands. He aimed the shotgun and pulled the trigger.

**

The boiling water steamed into the teapot as Geraldine filled it up. Placing the near-empty kettle back onto the stove, she decided to add a couple of extra cookies to the plate already on the trolley. Oscar was such a nice boy. She remembered his affinity for her chocolate chip pecan cookies the last time he was here to check on her, and she didn't want to disappoint him. This time, there was an entire dozen of the ten-centimetre wide cookies on the plate, unlike the half dozen last time which hadn't seemed to be enough for a growing boy like Oscar.

Placing the cosy-covered teapot next to the cookies on the tea trolley, she wheeled it into the front parlour. She turned and grabbed her walker, heading out the front door to let Oscar know the tea was ready.

Wheeling around to the rear corner of the porch, Geraldine looked about for a moment, then said aloud, "Where has that boy gotten to?" The last she'd seen him; he'd been heading toward the barn after investigating around the property like a regular Columbo.

But he was nowhere in sight at the moment. Thinking maybe he had gone around the house the other way, she turned to head back toward the front to see if that were the case.

Behind her, the silence of the mountain air was shattered by a series of shotgun blasts coming from the direction of her barn. She lost her grip on her walker temporarily and almost fell to the porch floorboards from shock.

Turning as quickly as she could, Geraldine looked toward the barn. The storm-cellar doors burst open, and Oscar flew up the steps. It seemed he'd shot the doors all to hell to get out of the cellar quickly for some reason. Oscar seemed to be in a hurry as if he couldn't wait to get to his tea and cookies fast enough.

He sprinted toward her, arms and legs pumping, yelling something now at the top of his lungs. She couldn't hear what he was going on about since he was still too far away. She tisk-tisked to herself with concern. All of this exertion couldn't be good for a boy of his size. Whatever it was, it must be important.

As he ran, Oscar looked over his shoulder toward the barn. The main doors suddenly exploded into slivers as if made of balsa, wooden shrapnel flying everywhere.

Geraldine now saw the motivation behind Oscar's storm door shenanigans emerge from the barn. She gaped at the monstrosity emerging from the structure, blinking her eyes rapidly in the bright sunshine, hoping that what she was seeing was a trick of her tired old eyes.

It seemed the heavy padlocked doors of the barn had not slowed this creature's pursuit of Constable Olsen. He turned for a moment, and then stumbled forward once more, continuing to sprint toward Geraldine as fast as his beefy legs would carry him.

Pausing for a moment to assess the situation, as any good predator would, the beast looked toward the main house. It locked eyes with Geraldine on the porch, then looked back to its prey, watching it flee for a moment, and looked no further. The beast began loping casually toward Oscar, saliva pouring from its mouth. It didn't seem in any particular hurry, as if the creature somehow sensed that its prey could never outrun it.

Constable Oscar Olsen ran toward Geraldine, waving his arms as he went. She finally heard what he was shouting, "Bear! It's a goddamned bear! Get inside! Lock yourself in the house!"

"No shit, Sherlock!" Geraldine clucked. She turned her walker around and shuffled rapidly in retreat. Ol' Bessie was currently sitting just inside her front door, where she'd left it after making tea. She cursed her stupidity for coming back outside without the elephant gun.

Looking over his shoulder, Olsen saw the beast now focussed solely on him. It surged toward him on long, powerful legs.

Oscar turned back toward Geraldine, faltered for a moment, then suddenly found his second and third winds all at once, and his legs came alive.

Geraldine was moving like she hadn't since she was a spry eighty-year-old. In her peripheral vision, Oscar began to overtake her. She pumped her walker as it had never been pumped before, renewing her efforts to get to Ol' Bessie and help the constable.

Olsen's attempt to win the First Annual Lawless Bearathon was ultimately doomed to failure — the beast was fast, lean and ravenous while Oscar was slow, fat and delicious.

Out of the corner of her eye, Geraldine saw Oscar brought down by the monster. Razor claws tore through his back as he was flattened into the frozen earth.

Geraldine put her head down and focused on putting one walker-wheel in front of the other, pumping and pumping. Her sole reason for living now was to make it to her front door and have this thing from hell suffer a reckoning at the muzzle of Ol' Bessie —payment for her little Norberts and now Constable Olsen.

Arriving at the door, she leaned slightly backward and pushed the unlatched door open with her bottom. She grabbed the large gun and heaved it up, cocking it in the process. With the barrel of the gun on the front edge of her walker, she braced the stock against the door frame at her back.

The creature quickly finished its appetiser of meat and assorted by-products that had previously been known as Oscar Olsen and looked toward the house. Eyes still wide with hunger, it spotted the woman on the porch and strode confidently toward her.

Geraldine stood defiantly on her porch in front of the beast, Ol' Bessie straining to be unleashed.

The monster had almost reached the first step. Three metres, two metres, one metre...

Leaning forward into her walker, Geraldine pulled one of Ol' Bessie's triggers. The muzzle flashed a brilliant white as the gun ruptured the quiet of the day.

It had been quite a while since she'd used the gun, and she'd forgotten how loud it really was. Aiming in the general direction of the monster, she'd hoped to wound it or at least scare it off. However, her ability to target the gun was somewhat limited after so many years of inactivity, and she only grazed the animal.

The concussive blast did have an effect on the bear, and it halted in its tracks, startled by the noise as much as the pain. The beast shrieked, the side of its face stinging from the rock salt charge the elephant gun had drilled into its skin. Its brown eyes locked onto the woman's once more, its wounded ear twitching back and forth, and it rumbled deep in its throat.

Geraldine fell backward through the partially open door, slamming it back into the wall and denting the plaster. She landed on the thick, occasional carpet that covered the gleaming hardwood, Ol' Bessie landing on top of her. Her spine impacted the floor, and she shrieked in agony as her arthritis reminded her of who was boss around here.

The bruin lunged up the steps toward Geraldine and jammed its head into the open doorway. Pressing into the frame, the wood creaked and groaned as the creature's jaws ratcheted open and closed in quick succession, snapping like a castanet as it tried to grab her and drag her back outside.

Geraldine kicked her heels down hard on the maple floorboards inches from the creature's slavering mouth and pushed with all of her might. She slid the thick carpet backward over her immaculately polished hardwood floor. This gave her some breathing room, temporarily moving her further away from the snapping, drooling jaws of the predator.

Its mouth wide open, the beast roared and tried to ram its head all the way through the doorframe. It reared back and then dove forward once more, head down as it ducked under the roof that lead up to the porch. The beast's massive shoulders buckled the log posts that held the doorframe in place. Above its head, the heavy, reinforced sheet metal roof began to fold back like an accordion as the creature surged forward and back, again and again. The door frame and attached logs started to creak and groan alarmingly as the monster smashed its way into its prey's burrow.

Recoiling in fear, Geraldine snatched her feet back once more from the gnashing teeth. She suddenly recalled the antique shotgun she still held protectively in her arms, and what it contained — she had one shot left.

Pulling back the second hammer, she pointed the gun at the massive head in front of her and pulled the trigger. Ol' Bessie roared, and the sixty-gram bullet blasted out of the elephant gun's barrel, temporarily deafening Geraldine from the resounding blast.

The rock salt peppered through the creature's injured ear and it shrieked and pulled back, sounding as if all the damned souls of hell had finally been freed from purgatory.

Angry at its inability to kill this insignificant little creature, the predator raged at the small morsel that had dug itself into its burrow and managed to cause it such pain. It lunged toward her again, smashing its head into the doorway repeatedly as it tried to grab the food in front of it. With every impact, little by little, the frame, along with the thick wall to which it was attached began to shift inward ever so slightly, the porch roof groaning in complaint.

Scuttling backward a bit more, Geraldine slid up against the wall on the other side of the entry. She now found herself jammed up against the bottom of the staircase.

Pulling back again, the beast reared up to its full height and drove both of its massive paws downward into the porch steps, smashing the wood to splinters.

The protective metal roof that ran along the second story over the front porch had been severely weakened by the animal's previous actions. As the beast dove forward into the doorframe once more, the heavy canopy collapsed, dropping down onto its head with a crash.

Geraldine hoped this would squash the bastard, but her hope was short-lived. Within seconds, the ugly son-of-a-bitch reared up through the splintered wood and sheet metal, squealing with fresh rage so loud it seemed it might shred her eardrums.

The creature gave one final rending roar of frustration, then turned and loped away.

With a mixture of relief and fear, Geraldine Gertzmeyer watched as the enormous predator disappeared from view. It pushed through into the forest off to the side of the house, moving toward her neighbour's property now, the Gold Mountain Casino and Resort. She felt relieved that she was still alive but also felt fear for any unfortunate soul between here and the resort who might encounter this now enraged, wounded creature.

CHAPTER FORTY-TWO

British Columbia is riddled with thousands of fault lines. The Lower Mainland, along with Lawless and many other towns located in the interior of the province lay directly or indirectly over numerous faults in the earth's crust. Many of these are primed and ready to experience a slip of enormous magnitude.

This was something which would have been news to most people in the area around Lawless, up until recently. Had you asked the average resident if they were in an area that was safe from earthquakes, they would probably have answered in the affirmative, not suspecting the surprising truth.

Provincial Highway #3C travels over a snow-capped mountain pass called the Golden Mile. The scenic highway winds its way down the mountainside through beautiful groves of aspen, poplar and pine, finally descending into the Kokanee Valley which houses Lawless itself.

In winter, the pass is especially problematic to maintain due to numerous weather systems that move through the area. It also has its share of challenges during the other three seasons as well. Several extremely narrow sections are flanked by jagged rock on both sides, continually shedding debris from above like a sheepdog sheds hair. Most years, local rock-scaling crews are kept more than busy from spring through fall. When the snow begins again in late October or early November, it complicates matters considerably once more.

On the fifth of January, one such complication occurred. The earthquake that struck Lawless rattled-open the eyes of everyone in the area, shaking this new earth-moving reality into their complacent little heads. There had been some minor damage to a few of the buildings in town, mostly shattered windows and cracks in some of the foundations here and there, along with a few broken pipes as well. But up in the mountains, it had been a different story. The Golden Mile Pass had been inundated by a mix of snow and rock that came tumbling down the mountainside, blocking access into Lawless and cutting it off from the rest of the world.

Seventy-two hours later, the road had been cleared to limited, single-lane traffic. The Lawless Public Works Department, with the help of Ruby Roads Contracting, worked diligently to clear the blockage, beavering away together on the Lawless side of the slide while the Provincial Highways Department hammered away on the other.

After the highway had finally reopened, the head provincial engineer with the BC Highways Department, Len Maxwell, informed Austin that come springtime, the Province would be back to assist them in doing a full-scale removal of any residual rock up the mountainside that might not have come down in the quake. He also mentioned that the town was lucky that the earthquake had been relatively minor. Anything more significant would have brought down quite a bit more rock — so much more, he said, that they may have been digging Lawless out for about three weeks instead of three days.

Since that time, the residents of the area had been warned to make sure their emergency preparedness kits were kept up to date, with at least two weeks supply of food and fresh water. If another quake were to occur, the Provincial Government would have enough on its plate with all of the other major centres requiring assistance, and Lawless could quite possibly be one of the last places that might receive any help. Austin urged everyone attending the town hall meeting after the January quake to make sure they were adequately prepared.

These thoughts and more were going through Austin's mind as he approached the front door of the Burger Barn. A sudden tingling started in his legs, almost as if they had fallen asleep while he'd been sitting eating his lunch. Very strange, he thought.

As he pondered this sensation, the waxed-paper cups stacked ready for use on top of the soda fountain began bumping into each other. This was quickly followed by a musical tinkling sound as the curios all over the restaurant started vibrating against whatever they were attached to including each other.

Dawning realisation made Austin turn, and he hollered at Trip and Alex, still back at their table putting on their jackets. "Earthquake! Get away from the windows now! Get under cover!"

Already startled by the moving earth, the pair needed little motivation from Austin. Alex's eyes went wide with fear as he heard his father shouting. He ducked agilely under the table he'd been eating at only moments before.

Seeing the boy was safe, Trip followed suit, making his way under the table as well. But due to his size, he had to try more of a wedging technique, rather than ducking to get himself into the same position, but he still got there with surprising speed.

Austin jumped back from the entrance door at the last second as the grizzly skull and mirror above it came crashing down, missing him by centimetres. He dove sideways under the nearest table, situated near the main counter. His concern was more with anyone being hit by falling bric-a-brac than the roof of the solid old structure coming down on their heads.

Across the room, Alex and Trip were braced under the heavy pine table, holding onto its legs as the room shook around them. Alex had a look of utter terror on his face.

The windows on the front wall suddenly imploded, showering down plate-glass that mixed with the dropping debris, turning it into a razor-sharp rainstorm.

Austin shouted across the restaurant, "Hang on, buddy! It shouldn't be too much longer! Stay put with Trip!" Alex said nothing and ducked his head into his shoulder to avoid flying glass.

The quake that hit six weeks before had happened overnight, and Alex had slept through that one. This event was something that he'd never experienced in his fifteen years on the planet. Judging by the expression on his face, it was probably the last time he ever wanted to experience anything like this.

Trip, on the other hand, seemed to be holding up quite well, his face unreadable, showing no emotion. Austin thought he was either very calm at the moment, or completely freaked out and not showing it in order to keep Alex calm as well. Either way, he appreciated it and gave Trip a thumbs-up. Trip raised his eyebrows slightly and returned the thumbs-up to Austin to signal that he'd keep Alex safe.

At the front counter, Marie had taken refuge in the archway that lead into the kitchen, placing both of her arms across the door jamb to brace herself. She yelled for her husband, Ed, to get away from the stove and deep fryer.

With an alacrity that would have put an Olympic hurdler to shame, Ed leapt onto the potato prep counter and huddled under the cover that its steel shelves provided.

High above them all, Ed's admirable job of shelf building could no longer withstand the vibration from below and the sturdy, reinforced ledge where the Aboriginal Jesus rested tore loose. The hand-carved two-hundred-kilogram statue swan-dived off of its crumbling perch and plummeted headfirst through the middle of the Hey Loft dining area below. It tore through the ceiling of the kitchen, pounding into the steel vent hood over the electric deep fryer, flipping it forward and spraying its scalding contents out toward the dining area.

Forty kilograms of boiling vegetable oil spilled out of the fryer in a searing-hot, golden wave that raced across the kitchen floor, heading directly toward the table under which Austin Murphy was currently hunkered. All around him, bric-a-brac and gewgaws fell from the walls and ceiling, smashing to the ground near his under-table refuge. A large brass spittoon slammed into the tabletop over his head. It bounced off, landing in the smoking oil that poured toward him. The high-frequency metallic twang the brass container made when it hit the pine temporarily deafened him in the process, and he shook his head.

Austin looked for any other options available for refuge nearby that were better than his current position, but there were none — they all sucked. Decor continued to drop down from the walls and ceiling above his head in a deadly deluge. The next table over for possible refuge was too far away to risk relocating, the shaking so strong now. He doubted he could crawl there, even if he tried.

Only metres away and travelling fast, the smoking-hot oil poured across the hardwood floor, heading directly toward Austin.

He had nowhere to go.

CHAPTER FORTY-THREE

Christine held her hands high in the air and slowly walked toward the back of the cavern, her mind going a million miles a minute as she tried to think of some way out of her predicament.

VanDusen followed directly behind her, his shotgun levelled at her back. "Keep movin'! There's plenty of room at the back of the bus."

"Somebody knows I'm here! You can't just dump me!"

"Sure we can! And that's bullshit anyway!" Chance shouted. "Nobody knows you're here because nobody knows where HERE is!" He staggered along just to the side of Christine. She watched him walk and noted that he was more than just a few sheets to the wind. Then again, she supposed, you didn't have to watch him walk to know how drunk he was — anybody within three metres could easily tell from the alcohol fumes pouring off him. If anyone were brave enough or foolhardy enough to strike a match near the man, they'd be taking their life in their hands.

"Calm down, Ray," Nichols said, off to her other side. "The young lady is obviously trying to buy herself some more time and cause us to have second thoughts about disposing of her."

"You can't just kill me, you know, people will come looking for me!"

"Maybe," VanDusen said, "but people go missing all the time in this huge, wild province of ours. And I can bet this is the last place they'll look. After all, it's a big forest out there, quite easy for someone to get lost, never to be seen or heard from again! And who'd look in a cave? I'd say it's pretty easy for even a seasoned conservation officer to disappear around here."

Chance finished VanDusen's thought, slurring, "But then again, even if they found this place, they'd never find you, since you'll be at the bottom of a frickin' hole!" He giggled at the thought.

Christine felt a tremble in her legs as they moved farther back into the cavern. At first, she thought it was either fear or her tired legs cramping once more from the snowshoeing. It turned out to be much, much worse.

"What the hell is going on…" Chance muttered, his gout-ridden legs feeling the vibration for the first time.

"Jesus Christ!" Nichols cried. Still flanking Christine, he stumbled and went down to one knee on the rubble scattered across the cavern floor. As the shaking intensified, he gave up trying to walk and began scuttling his way across the unstable ground toward the entrance on hands and knees.

The beam from VanDusen's barrel-mounted flashlight wavered back and forth as he tried to keep it trained on Christine's back. He hollered, "Shit! We've got another earthquake! Everybody back to the entrance, now!"

As Christine turned to do as instructed, VanDusen stopped her, his shotgun's light levelled at her chest. "Not you, little missy, you can just stay right the fuck here." He backed unsteadily toward the entrance, shotgun trained on Christine as the earth continued to shake and jive.

From the dark recesses of the cavern ceiling, a stalactite came crashing down next to VanDusen, missing him by less than a metre. He leapt sideways as it impacted, hitting the uneven ground hard with his shoulder. The jolt of pain caused him to loosen his grip on the Remington temporarily. As his hand twitched instinctively to hold onto it, one finger hit the trigger, and the shotgun discharged by accident. There was a flash of light from its muzzle, but the thunder of the falling rock muffled the sound of its blast.

Christine saw the opportunity to make herself scarce and took it, heading off on unsteady legs toward the nearest wall of the cavern, well away from the shitheads, shotguns and stalactites.

Chance and Nichols were halfway to the front of the cavern when vast slabs of rock started slamming down outside the entrance. The massive chunks had broken loose from the cliffs high above and now pummelled the ground with a force and vibration so great that everyone still able to stand inside the cavern was dropped to their knees. Chance curled into a fetal ball, trying to make himself as small as possible to protect against the falling rock. Several more stalactites dropped to the floor next to him, shattering on impact and showering him with chunks of calcite.

The shaking continued unabated, and the daylight that had been filtering through the steam-shrouded entrance became dimmer and dimmer. Boulders, some as large as Christine's Dodge Ram, pounded into the ground outside, filling the entrance until there was nothing left in the world but darkness.

As suddenly as it started, the quake ended. Blackness and silence now ruled over the cavern, its occupants sealed inside as tightly as Tutankhamun's tomb.

CHAPTER FORTY-FOUR

The scorching oil snaked across the floor toward Austin, smoke rolling off its surface. At over two-hundred and thirty degrees Celsius, it would literally melt the skin from his body if it touched him. He looked out from underneath the table, desperately trying to find another sanctuary, but knick-knacks were still raining down from the walls and ceiling above. They smashed into the heavy pine table that protected him in a killing crush of plummeting paraphernalia.

Seeing blistering the oil spreading out toward his father, Alex shouted, "Dad! Look out!"

Austin prepared to take his chances dodging the dropping debris, ready to scramble out from the safety of his table to avoid the sizzling slick, now only an arms-length away from his face.

Suddenly, the oil poured into a metal strip grate in the floor, hissing and steaming as it made contact with the residual moisture in the drain. Because of some debris blocking his horizontal view of the world, Austin hadn't seen the stainless-steel grill earlier, and he heaved a huge sigh of relief as the smoking oil poured into it.

"Stay where you are!" Austin called over, "There's a grate in the floor here catching the oil. I'm okay!"

The grating's purpose was to collect spills near the pop and ice machine to avoid slippery and sticky floors. In this instance, he was quite relieved to see it worked just as well with superheated oil.

Like someone flipping a switch and cutting the power, the earthquake stopped as quickly as it started. It didn't wind down or judder gradually to a stop — it just ended, the ground beneath them now stable and still.

Dead silence laid claim in the building, and no one moved for several moments. Pushing aside a pile of treasures that had built up around their table, Alex and Trip crept out from underneath their pine shield at the same time as Austin extracted himself from his.

"I guess the ride's over!" Trip said, standing on legs that still felt rubbery like there was a little of the quake still vibrating in his bones.

Alex slowly surveyed the damage and whistled. He crunched through the broken glass over to his father, saying in a quiet voice, "Was that an earthquake, Dad?"

"None other, Sport," Austin said, patting his son on the shoulder. Suddenly not feeling the manly shoulder pat to be enough, he grabbed his son and hugged him fiercely as well, thankful he was safe.

"I don't like them." Alex's eyes were wide and unblinking as he looked over Austin's shoulder, then he hugged back, hard.

"I agree," Austin laughed at his son's comment and released him from the bear hug. He looked about the building. It was almost entirely devoid of artefacts and gewgaws now, apart from some old BC licence plates that were still solidly screwed in place, along with one toilet seat. The large plate-glass windows were now mostly scattered across the restaurant's floor, sitting in a drift of broken glass along the front portion of the dining area.

Trip gave out a low whistle. "Looks like now would be a good time to repaint." As usual, his face was unreadable beneath his bushy, white beard. Though his voice seemed unshaken as he spoke, his eyes betrayed how he really felt — they were currently open about three times wider than usual. With relief flooding his voice and a glint in his squint, Trip said, "Glad you didn't get deep-fried, Boss."

"You and me both! I didn't relish the thought of being served with a side of fries."

"Hah! Relish! That's a good one, Dad!" Alex piped up at Austin's side.

"Puns 'R Me, I guess," he laughed half-heartedly. "In the meantime, we'd better check on Marie and Ed."

"You read my mind, Boss," Trip said. They moved toward the kitchen, being careful to avoid the still hot and slippery oil spread across the floor.

With a crash that made all three men jump, Marie Popov unravelled herself from the kitchen pass-through, her face white with shock. Her foot had knocked a plate that had miraculously remained unbroken on the counter. But it now joined its brethren and lay in shards on the floor beneath her dangling feet as she sat upright next to the pass-through.

After abandoning her kitchen doorway sanctuary midway through the quake, Marie had perched safely inside the stainless-steel opening in the wall where Ed passed through the burgers and fries. It had provided excellent protection from the falling doodads and boiling oil. Alex stepped forward and gently helped lower her from the countertop.

"Thank you so much," Marie said as her feet set down on the floor, feeling grateful to the strong young man. She gave Alex a quick peck on the cheek and headed through the swinging galley doors to the kitchen to check on her husband, being mindful of the puddles of oil on the floor.

Against the far wall of the kitchen, Ed was currently blaspheming away in Russian as he extracted himself from the metal shelf underneath the heavy, steel counter that held the industrial potato peeler and slicer. He blinked his eyes and continued his Russian rant, taking off his pop-bottle lensed glasses. Ed called them his second pair of eyes, and never went anywhere without them. He wiped at the thick lenses, removing the moisture. The glasses had steamed up during his cosy curl amongst the potato peelings that piled up on the secondary shelf. Each day, he prepared hundreds of kilograms of fresh, delicious french fries made from Grand Forks grown potatoes, readying them for immersion in the deep fryer situated nearby.

"Glad to see you're okay, Ed," Austin said with concern as he approached. "Watch your step, though; it's a little on the greasy side today."

Ed nodded shakily and replaced his glasses as he stepped around the Indigenous Jesus, now supine where the deep fryer had resided. He peered at his wife as he approached, his dark brown eyes appearing much larger once he'd secured his spectacles, giving her a shocked, moon-pie stare. He asked if she was all right. She nodded and then he took her in his arms as she buried her face in his shoulder.

Alex took the high road and slid Hollywood-style over the chromed countertop where the burgers were assembled, neatly bypassing his dad to assist Ed and Marie. Both seniors looked unsteady on their feet and ready to keel over where they stood. As the boy grabbed Ed's arm, he noticed the man was still vibrating. "Here, let me help you, Mr. Popov," he said, wondering if the man were just jittery from the jarring he'd recently taken or if he had Parkinson's Disease.

"Thanks, young fella." He patted Alex's arm. "I swear If I didn't have a heart murmur before that shakin', I sure as hell do now!"

Marie looked up from Ed's shoulder, her arms still around his waist, her face wet from crying. She said with a sniff, "A little swabbing the deck is in order, that's for sure!" Ed smiled down at his wife, a look of relief replacing his shocked expression now that he held her safely in his arms once more.

"I'm glad you're both okay, but we have to run now; a friend is in danger," Austin said. He turned, leaving the couple to comfort each other. He and Alex carefully navigated their way back across the oil-slicked, treasure-filled floor to the kitchen doorway where Trip was standing by, ready to help.

Marie called out from the kitchen, "Oh, Austin! Could you do me one small favour before you go?"

Almost to the front door, he turned back, saying, "Sure, Marie, what's that?"

Could you flip the sign over to closed? I think we may be down for a few days for some much-needed renovations."

"Will do." Austin smiled, turning the engraved wooden sign on the cracked glass of the entry door from 'Bring on the Beef', to 'Roast Beef Roundup'.

Ed smiled and hugged his wife. He looked at Marie and then around the restaurant, taking in the damage, saying, "I think next time we'll make sure everything is glued to the walls and chained to the ceiling!"

Marie called out to the trio near the door, "You boys best get out there and see if you can help your friend and the rest of this town of ours."

"Will do. We'll check back with you later," Austin said, pressing on the door and stepping out onto the street. As he held it open for his companions, the lower sheet of glass in the door finally gave up its battle with gravity and slid out, shattering on the concrete sidewalk below.

The three men picked their way through the detritus of broken tree branches and downed streetlights toward the truck. Alex said, "What now, Dad?"

"We need to get to the hospital."

"What? Why? Are you hurt?" Alex's voice was filled with concern.

"No, but I think I know someone who can help us find Chris."

"Let's get hustling then," Trip said. He shook his head as they walked. Many of the windows along the main thoroughfare were broken, with cracks visible in the sides of dozens of structures for blocks in every direction. Major upheavals had left stretches of sidewalk across the road protruding into the sky like broken teeth. Other sections of the street had sunk away into the ground, along with several buildings, including the Bank of Montreal. Many parked vehicles had been upended, and the broken asphalt made traversal a very interesting affair.

"This looks like something out of a war zone," Alex said in a low voice, a shocked expression on his face.

The Lawless City Works Silverado Austin had been driving was still next to the curb outside of Verigin's Deli where he'd parked it, but the truck's headlights were now pointing skyward by a half metre, the bed having dropped an equal amount in the back. It looked like it was drivable, once they manoeuvred it out of Main Street's new sunken, angled parking system.

Arms folded as he surveyed the damage, Trip said to Austin, "Why don't you drive."

CHAPTER FORTY-FIVE

The cavern was silent and dark. There was no sound Christine could discern, apart from her own ragged breathing. She didn't know what had happened to the three men in the quake and didn't much care. She had tried to get as far away from them as she could, and thought she'd succeeded. Despite this feeling of newfound freedom, she remained still, crouched low to the ground, not wanting to give away her position if any of them were still nearby. Being optimistic by nature, she hoped that something large and heavy had squashed one or two of them, but she was being cautious, nevertheless.

Christine waited, silently and uncomfortably. A thick layer of rubble had covered the rounded river stones on the cavern floor during the quake. These new chunks of rock were broken-glass sharp and painful to kneel or crouch on for too long.

She continued to wait patiently.

More silence was her reward.

Reaching into her pocket looking for the small Mag-lite that she kept there for emergencies, she was surprised to find the 9mm pistol still in the plastic baggy where she'd placed it earlier and then promptly forgot about. When VanDusen had taken her prisoner, he'd removed her service revolver from her side holster, but he hadn't thought to check her pockets for anything else. After all, why would anyone suspect a female conservation officer to be carrying a concealed weapon?

Leaving the pistol in her pocket, for now, she pulled out the flashlight next to it. Carefully cupping her hand around it to shield the beam, she turned it on and winced at the dazzling amount of light that still leaked through her closed fingers. She tried to close her hand tighter to avoid any more light leakage but felt the rim of the light cutting into her palm and knew she couldn't hold it like that for extended periods.

Christine clicked the light off. She breathed quietly for several seconds, trying to hear if anyone or anything nearby noticed her brief attempt at bringing a ray of sunshine into this dreary underworld. She remained crouched amongst the debris on the cavern floor, perfectly still for a little while longer, her leg cramps now thankfully at bay.

Off to her right side, there was a clattering noise of rocks hitting rocks. Perhaps chunks of quartz loosened by the quake tumbling down from the cavern ceiling above? Or was it someone stumbling around in the dark. It was hard to say.

Almost ready to give up waiting and make a move, her patience was rewarded. Off toward the front of the cavern came the sound of someone moving around.

***

"Jesus Christ! This shit's sharper than my first wife's tongue!" Ray Chance grumbled. He was on his knees, trying to stand up by pushing his hands into the razor-edged rubble for leverage. He gave up and sat on the rough floor instead, his thick parka protecting his ass from the most jagged of the rocks. "Now, where the hell are my goddamned gloves? And where's my flashlight? I can't see a friggin' thing!" He was pretty sure he'd had a flashlight in his hand before the quake but knew as sure as shit that he didn't have one now and figured he must have dropped it during all the shaking.

Reaching into his jacket pocket, he found his errant gloves. "There you are, ya little buggers!" After another moment of silence, Chance continued, "Holy shit! What have we here?!" In his other pocket, his hand had settled onto an old friend, his flask of Napoleon's finest — and it was undamaged. He had to rely on touch at this point because he had no light. But that didn't matter to him at the moment. Nothing did, except for the flask he now found in his hands. The fact that he was effectively blind in the inky blackness that now comprised his world didn't matter. Nor did the fact that God knew what, from God knew where was out there waiting to eat him or that he could be trapped inside this cavern for the rest of his life, it mattered not. Once his fingers latched onto the metal and glass flask, they operated on muscle memory, unscrewing the cap and flicking it aside with his thumb before he'd consciously even considered taking a drink. All thoughts of self-preservation and fear had flown from Chance's mind once he smelled the nostril-clearing vapour of the open alcohol in front of him. Without thinking, he swilled half of the remaining brandy in the flask in one quick quaff. The distilled gold from Saint-Rémy seared its way down his throat, making him wince slightly, even after these many, many decades of alcohol abuse. Despite the painful swallow, he licked his lips after his drink and said, "Oh, mama, that's the stuff."

There was a sudden movement in the rocks behind him. Chance let out a girlish squeal, startled by the noise.

A flashlight clicked on at his back, he turned toward it, the beam dazzling him.

"The pause that refreshes?" Nichols asked at the other end of the flashlight, crouching down next to Ray. During the quake, Chance had held out a brief hope that one of the falling stalactites might have squashed the tall, arrogant prick like the oversized maggot he was, but it appeared that lady luck was not on his side this afternoon.

Nichols reached down to offer Chance his hand for assistance in standing upright, but the smaller man waved it off, saying, "I'm a big boy. I can take care of my own fat ass!"

"Suit yourself." Nichols stood, retracting the proffered hand. He played the light held in his other hand around the cavern walls and stopped when the beam reached the entrance, causing him to say, "Sweet Mother Mary, we're entombed!"

"What the fuck are you going on about? We're not... oh," Chance saw the massive pile of rock blocking the entrance and stopped mid-sentence. "What in the goddamned hell are we going to do now?"

"We're going to have to go spelunking to find our egress."

"Spe-what?"

"Potholing, caving."

Chance's pasty white face looked back at him blankly in the light's high-intensity glare.

"Let me drop it down a notch for you; we'll have to explore the cavern to look for another way out."

"Oh, okay, thanks. What about VanDusen? Have you seen him?"

"No, I'm not sure what happened to our intrepid guide."

***

Christine listened as the two men finished talking and decided she'd better move to a better hiding place than the middle of the cavern floor. Carefully standing, she tried not to make any noise as she moved about on the loose rock. Just as she started to step forward, she suddenly stopped.

A yawning, inky black lava tube lay less than a half metre from where she stood. Thanks to Nichols flashlight in the distance, the opening to the yawning pit had been made briefly visible, faintly outlined in a current of vapour that swirled about the lip of the tube. Had she continued walking blindly forward in the dark, she would have found herself on a one-way trip to the bottom of the pit, wherever that was, doing to herself what VanDusen had only promised. She shuddered at the thought.

Taking a deep breath, Christine started to tentatively move toward the side of the cavern, giving the pit a wide berth.

She suddenly heard the distinctive sound of a Versa Max pump slide once again being cocked behind her head.

"That's about far enough, Missy," VanDusen hissed at her back.

"Shit!" Christine flinched and froze. VanDusen's shotgun mounted flashlight clicked on, and she saw a massive silhouette of herself projected onto the far wall of the cavern.

"Well, well, at least you know that from Shinola! Now get those pretty little red hands all the way up again where I can see 'em!"

Christine reluctantly raised her blood-covered hands. She hung her head slightly forward, giving an air of resignation, hoping to sell VanDusen on her being helpless and in despair. In reality, she was readying herself to pop the safety off the Glock in her pocket and unload it into him, the first chance she got. Perhaps dropping and rolling away in the dark as she grabbed for the pistol.

"You don't need to do this, you know."

"Hell, yeah. I know I don't need to; I want to!"

"What, you get off on this?"

"Get off on it? I never thought of it like that before. Gee, I suppose I do! What do you know, I get off, on offin' people! Hell, yeah! I like the sound of that! I should put it on my goddamned business cards!"

At her back, Christine heard Nichols voice call out as he slowly made his way toward them across the uneven cavern floor. "Well, now, Reggie, I see you've gone and found our new playmate, once again."

"Yessir, Mr. Mayor. Looks like she thought she'd try to hop away on us all quick-like-a-bunny-like after the quake, but I surprised her, didn't I, Missy?" VanDusen emphasized the Missy in his sentence with a hard, driving poke of the shotgun's muzzle into the centre of Christine's back.

She was driven to her knees, feeling the hard quartz dig into her kneecaps immediately after the blow to her spine — a double dose of pain. She grunted aloud from the bruising jolt. The heavy, poly-cotton shell of her parka and layers of clothing beneath protected her somewhat from the brunt of the brutal prod; otherwise, she was sure it would have done some severe damage to her spinal column.

Christine readied herself to launch into her 'Glock 'n' Roll' action plan at the first opportunity she got. It was now apparent to her that all three men were at the very least greedy, and quite possibly, all stark raving mad with gold fever. Here they were, risking their own lives and the lives of others as they sought to carve as much gold from this cavern as possible without having to worry about land or mineral rights that just might belong to the local First Nations band or the Provincial Government.

And then she thought of the insanity of trying to mine this gold while there was a ravenous monster in the area eating everything in sight, their own workers included. Could the lust for gold drive people crazy enough to ignore things like that? Well, she thought, if it does, then here comes two more living, breathing examples of this fever right now. Turning her head slightly, she watched the approaching procession.

Chance walked in the lead, weaving his way toward her, speaking to himself under his breath. He was muttering something about how a certain someone could go ahead and piss off with their potholes and spee-lunking and shove it up their egress.

Bringing up the rear was His Highness, the Mayor of Lawless, his flashlight glowingly illuminating the way ahead of his exalted feet. But in the process, it also had the unfortunate effect of illuminating the top of Ray Chance's butt-crack; it glowed a pale, luminous white like a mushroom in the moonlight.

"Oh, lovely," Christine said, "here come the ladies from the Welcome Wagon."

VanDusen gave Christine another quick jab in the back with the muzzle of his gun again, saying, "Shut your gob, Missy!"

"Or what? You're going to kill me already! What are you going to do? Make me even deader?"

Arriving on the scene, Nichols said, "Reggie, would you stop harassing and poking the poor girl. You're going to leave a mark on her lovely pale skin."

"There'll be plenty more than that on her by the time she ends up at the bottom of one of these holes," VanDusen retorted with a grin, waving his gun toward a nearby lava tube.

"Yeah, let's just dump her and get the hell out of here!" Chance interjected from the mayor's side. The fumes from his breath made Nichols turn his head slightly and gasp for breath.

"Ray, please, would you back up a couple of feet? You're making my eyes water," Nichols said, waving his hand in front of his face and coughing slightly. He continued, "As I was going to say, let's not get too carried away here, Reggie." He turned to Chance, "I don't think we're going to be eradicating our little complication here quite yet, Ray. She may prove invaluable in extricating us from our current quandary."

"Say what?" Chance mumbled.

"She might come in handy for getting us the hell out of this fucking tomb!" Nichols clarified.

"Oh, okay, thanks for dumbing it down, Bob," Chance slurred.

"Entirely my pleasure."

Christine interjected, "Great! Since there's some value to my existence now, would you mind if I stood up? These rocks are getting awfully hard on my knees!"

"Very well. Reggie, if you'd be so kind."

VanDusen stepped back and gestured with the business end of the gun for Christine to stand, saying, "Keep your hands where I can see them! Anything funny and you'll have a hole in your spine the size of a dinner plate!"

"Great, I'll make sure to stop by for the buffet, later," Christine said, slowly standing. Her shoulders were tired from her hands being raised for so long, but her knees appreciated the relief.

"You're a lippy little bitch!" VanDusen said.

"And you're a redneck halfwit, so I guess that makes us even!"

VanDusen turned the gun around, pulling his arm back to jab Christine between the shoulder blades with its stock again when Nichols interceded, saying, "Now, now, children! Let's see if there's another way out of this black hole in the wall before things devolve into another donnybrook!"

"You heard the man, Missy, move!" The chief shoved the shotgun's barrel into his prisoner's spine once more.

With Christine in the lead, hands held high, the group moved toward the back of the cavern. Steam from the boiling pools obscured the ground near their feet on occasion, causing them to proceed with extreme caution. The exit they were looking for was a horizontal hole out this blackness, not a vertical shaft plummeting straight to hell.

CHAPTER FORTY-SIX

The drive to the hospital, ordinarily about two-minutes long, including stops at both traffic lights and the four-way flasher, took Austin at least ten minutes longer than normal. Some of the sinkholes in the roadway were big enough to swallow their Silverado whole, plus another car as well, so careful negotiation through the destruction was imperative.

"Holy crap!" Alex said, gawking at the damage, "This is nuts!"

"Not the easiest of commutes this afternoon, that's for sure," Trip said, shaking his head as he surveyed the work that would be needed to get everything shipshape over the next few months.

Austin remembered seeing pictures of the earthquake in Anchorage, Alaska that occurred on Good Friday, 1964. Downtown Lawless looked like that now. Whole sections of the main thoroughfare were askew, with some city blocks almost an entire storey lower from one end to the other. Dazed citizens wandered the street, being mindful of the new four-metre drop off the edges of some of the sidewalks. It gave new meaning to the phrase, 'Watch your next step; it's a doozy!'

"Just unbelievable," Austin said softly, shaking his head in wonderment.

They passed a dilapidated garage attached to a local auto-body shop where the entire roof had collapsed inward. The walls now leaned into the centre on all four sides, still trying to support a nonexistent roof. Nearing the police station, it looked like a water main had ruptured. The entire road was now a deep, muddy hole the size of an Olympic swimming pool requiring them to reroute through the surrounding neighbourhoods to get to their destination.

About to turn onto the short drive leading up to the hospital, Austin instead accelerated and drove past the entrance.

"Dad! What are you doing?" Alex asked in surprise.

"What do you mean?"

"Yeah, aren't we going to the hospital?" Trip inquired.

"We are, but I just remembered something I need to pick up, first," Austin said cryptically.

"Where to, Boss?" Trip asked, his eyebrows raised in question.

"The conservation office."

"Why?" Alex questioned.

"I'm hoping to bag me a T-Rex."

Much to his surprise, Austin found that he was able to drive the remaining two blocks to his new destination without the need to circumnavigate any significant holes in the road, downed trees or powerlines. The gate was open to the conservation office, and he drove to the rear entrance of the building. Apart from a few cracks in the masonry, nothing appeared out of place or damaged in the solid, one-story cinder block structure.

Stepping out of the truck, Austin said, "Be right back, guys. Hang tight!"

"Are you sure you don't need a hand, Dad?" Alex asked, rolling down the window of the truck.

"I think I'll be okay, thanks, Sport." Austin trotted around the front of the truck, arriving at the gated portcullis attached to the back of the conservation office. He pulled a set of keys from his pocket and unlocked the gate. Using the same set of keys, he opened the shop door. When the locksmith had replaced the locks a couple of weeks ago, just after Carl's abrupt disappearance, he'd also left a set of keys with the Lawless Public Works department in addition to City Hall. There were many times over the last few years when Austin had needed to drop off or pick something up from the rear compound when Carl was out and about. Having a spare key had come in handy, so the locksmith had just carried on the tradition.

Austin flipped the bank of light switches, but there was no power and the room remained dark. Fortunately, daylight from two small windows on the walls proved sufficient for him to see and he made his way into the dim interior.

Finding the keys in the drawer where Christine had left them, Austin unlocked the gun safe and removed the T-Rex rifle. It was still nestled in its Kevlar case along with a box of shells. He hefted the weapon, feeling its weight. Not surprising, he figured, since something able to deliver the level of firepower that this rifle could certainly wouldn't be a lightweight.

After locking things back up, Austin climbed behind the wheel of the truck, handing the rifle case to Trip who was in the passenger seat snacking on a Snickers. Wedging it between his legs, Trip unzipped the

433

case and looked down the barrel of the gun. Raising both bushy eyebrows, he noted the size of the bore on the T-Rex, saying, "Are we going hunting for some wascally wabbits?"

Austin replied, "Yes so be vewwy, vewwy quiet." He put the truck in gear, heading toward the hospital.

In the back seat, Alex rolled his eyes but still laughed at the joke. He enjoyed the easy friendship between the two men, especially during times of difficulty. Their ability to make a joke in order to diffuse some of the tension was a lesson not lost on him.

Arriving at the hospital, Austin was relieved to see the building appeared relatively unscathed by the quake, still standing tall and solid. Then again, he supposed, a handcrafted, stone structure like the hospital was a little harder to shake apart than a modern wooden house or apartment block.

An ambulance sat parked in the emergency entrance, its lights strobing away, no doubt dropping off someone injured in the quake. Mutt and Jeff were on the job, helping the ambulance attendants unload the vehicle's occupant.

Austin pulled up to the main, non-emergency entrance, being careful not to block the ambulance in any way, as he was sure they were more than a little busy right now. After the jolt the town suffered, they'd no doubt be making a few more trips back and forth before the day was out. Putting the truck in park, his work phone began to vibrate and ring in his pocket. He quickly pulled it out and hit the talk button without looking at the caller ID, hoping it was more news on Christine. He put the phone to his ear, saying, "Lawless Public Works."

"Austin! I'm glad to hear your voice, my friend!" It was Len Maxwell, Austin's counterpart at the BC Highways Department.

"Hey, Len, what's shakin'?"

"Hah! Just about everything in your goddamned part of the province, man, that's what shakin'!"

"Really? I hadn't noticed."

"Ever the funny man, Austin," Len chuckled.

"I presume you didn't just call to hear the soothing sounds of my voice, did you, Len?"

"No, sir!" Len's voice suddenly became business-like. "I thought you'd probably have your hands full with everything that was happening up there at the moment. But I thought you'd like to know; you were just hit by a seven-point-eight magnitude quake which stuck about twenty kilometres east of your location. Let me tell you; we felt that one down on the coast here as well."

"Yeah, I can imagine! Things are pretty messed up around here right now," Austin replied, the humour no longer in his voice.

"So just to keep you in the loop, you are officially cut off from the rest of the world."

"What? Again?"

Trip sat up straighter next to Austin, trying to listen in on the conversation.

"Yup, a report just came across my desk. That the slab of rock and snow that we were concerned about back at the beginning of January finally came loose. So, we won't have the pass open for a while, from the looks of things. As you can imagine, other slides are blocking the way which we'll need to deal with first, before we can even get to your neck of the woods. So, I'd say it'd be at least a week before we can start digging things out."

"You've got to be shitting me! How much rock came down?"

"All of it, I think."

"Unbelievable! All right, Len, thanks very much. I'll get things going on this side as soon as we get everything else under control and I'll talk with you then."

"You'd better believe it, brother. Good luck over there. You're going to need it!"

"Thanks again, Len." Austin hung up the phone and said, "Well, that's just lovely."

"What is it, Dad?"

"We're not going to be going anywhere for a while; it seems the pass is closed due to a massive slide. Remember that giant chunk of rock, the one I told you about a few weeks ago?" Alex nodded his head in acknowledgement. "It finally broke loose, and we are officially cut off from the rest of civilisation."

"Again? How long this time, Boss?" Trip asked.

"Len said it'd be about a week before they could get to us and begin digging us out."

"Jeez," Trip shook his head.

"But for right now, I want you to stay with the truck, Alex," Austin said, looking into the back seat toward his son. Alex nodded in understanding.

He turned toward Trip, "I might need you inside the hospital with me."

"You got it, Boss."

Alex asked, "Are you going to be long?"

"Shouldn't be, we're just going to see if we can get some extra help to locate Chris."

"You mean Jerry?"

"Yup. When I was here last, he told me he'd been up near that cavern she texted us from. He said he'd been doing some rock hunting near it the day of the attack. Plus, he had his GPS unit with him, so, hopefully, if he still has it, he can tell us where this cavern is."

"That'd be great!" Alex enthused.

"Exactly what I thought, Skipper." Austin climbed down out of the truck, and Trip mirrored him on the passenger side. The entrance door to the hospital was propped open at the moment, and Austin could see why — the door frame had shifted during the quake, and now the right side wouldn't close completely. "If that's the extent of the damage to this place, we're getting off easy," he said.

"I wouldn't hold my breath," Trip muttered.

"The emergency generator must have kicked in," Austin said as they entered. There was still some illumination inside the building, but not all of the lights were on, and those that were functioning did so with diminished brightness. Glancing around in the low-level light, the lobby looked normal enough, but upon closer inspection, the hospital was in rougher shape than he'd first thought. There was a fresh web of cracks in the plaster at most of the intersections in the walls, as well as chunks that had crumbled off other spots and dropped to the floor. He shook his head. Hopefully, it was only minor structural damage — just another thing they would have to add to the list when the town started cleaning up and repairing the damage to the area in the coming weeks and months.

Looking over to the help desk, Austin saw it was of no help at the moment. It was deserted, and Vera Plotnikoff nowhere in sight. He presumed she was elsewhere in the hospital giving some assistance to people in need of more help than either Trip or himself. "Looks like everyone is just a little busy at the moment. If Jerry's still in the same room, we'll just pop up and pick his brain for a moment."

They decided to take the stairs. The elevator, even if it were working under reduced power levels, would be a perilous proposition at best. The last thing they needed right now was to get trapped inside a broken elevator. Then again, it was only a two-story structure, so it wasn't too much of a strain for either of the men to climb the single flight of stairs.

Austin mounted them two at a time, arriving on the second floor without breaking a sweat. Trip came up behind him, one step at a time, puffing slightly when he arrived at the top. It looked like he was no doubt feeling his six-doughnut-a-day habit catching up with him, finally. Austin hoped his friend would take that as a warning sign and cut back on the mega-meals he was so fond of but held his tongue. On top of everything else, Trip didn't need Austin giving him a nutritional lecture right now.

Walking down the corridor to Jerry's room, Austin noted the damage on the top floor of the hospital wasn't as significant as it had been on the lower level. But judging by the labyrinth of cracks in some of the plaster walls, there would still be considerable work required to bring the building back up to code.

Austin entered Jerry Benson's room ahead of Trip, surprised to see the man sitting on the edge of his hospital bed trying to pull a shirt sleeve over the cast on his lower wrist, with little success.

Approaching the bed, Austin said, "Hey there, Nostradamus! Looks like your prediction was correct!"

Sounding visibly upset, Jerry said, "Yeah, I noticed. Yay for me! First, it's monster bears, then it's earthquakes! Don't you people have anything up here in the interior of this province not trying to kill people? I'm so outta here!"

"Well, don't get too far ahead of yourself, my friend. The pass is closed due to our most recent earth-shaker."

"Seriously? So, you're saying we're trapped in this valley with a man-eating monster from hell for the foreseeable future? For how long?"

"At least a week," Austin said, frowning.

"A week? Unbelievable!"

"Yeah, tell me about it." Trip said, from Austin's side.

Looking over to Trip then back to Jerry, Austin said, "Sorry, you haven't been introduced. Jerry, this is Trip, who helped in your rescue."

Jerry nodded, saying, "Thanks for the hand."

Trip nodded. "De nada."

Austin bunched his toque up in his hands and spoke earnestly to Jerry. "We're here because a friend of ours is in trouble, and you're the only person who might be able to help find her. We believe she's at the cavern you discovered before the attack. And I believe you're correct, that cavern is probably that creature's lair. If we could use your GPS, perhaps it'll point us in the right direction, which would be great. But then again, you've also been up at the cavern as well. It would be so much easier for us to find our friend and help her out if you were assisting us. Plus, we may also have something that might just bring that monster down for good."

"Ah, jeez," Jerry said. He thought for a moment, then continued, "Listen, I certainly want you to rescue your friend and all, but I don't know. I hope to God whatever it is you have will be powerful enough to stop this thing."

"Well, that's what the experts tell us," Trip said.

"Well, let me tell you. It's been so hard for me! I can't seem to get the massacre out of my head! I keep seeing it every time I close my eyes. I don't know if I can bear to see that creature again, no pun intended."

"I can imagine, it must be very hard," Austin sympathised.

"But that being said, I owe you guys big time for saving my ass, so, yeah, I guess I'll help you out. But just so you know, I'm doing so under duress."

"Fair enough," Austin said. "All right! Let's get you out of here, then!" He grabbed the sleeve Jerry had been struggling with and helped him put it over his cast. "Where did you last have the GPS unit?"

"Right! It was in my jacket pocket."

Trip, standing next to the narrow clothes cupboard, opened it up and looked inside. A neon-blue winter parka, its right sleeve slit down the middle, waited on a hook for its owner. He took it out and handed it to Jerry, saying, "Looks like they've already done some alterations for you in the emergency room."

"Oh crap, I guess I'm not returning it now!" Shaking his head, Jerry took the jacket from Trip and said, "Thanks." He felt around in its pockets for a moment and eventually located the GPS receiver. He pulled it out and placed the jacket on the bed. His face suddenly brightened, the thought of them finding the beast and dispatching it from the face of the planet now at the forefront of his mind.

He hit the standby button. Nothing, the screen was dark. On the top side of the unit, he held down the power button instead, hoping to reboot it, but it was still inoperable. His face fell. The device lay cold and unresponsive in his hand — his attempts at digital resuscitation via the main power unsuccessful. "Damn it! It looks like it was either damaged in the fall or else the battery's dead" This wasn't good news; Jerry knew that for a fact.

"Can't you replace the battery?" Austin asked.

"It's a sealed unit, and there's no way to charge it! The friggin' receiver has a proprietary charger, and I forgot to bring it along with me on vacation!"

"Well," Trip said, picking up Jerry's parka from the bed, "Looks like we'll need you for sure now."

"You're the only person who knows how to find Chris," Austin added, grabbing Jerry's boots from the cabinet.

"Yay for me again!" Jerry said half-heartedly, as his new personal valets assisted his getting dressed.

When the three men arrived back down at the Works pickup, Alex greeted Jerry as he pulled the door open to enter the truck, saying, "Hi, Mr. Benson! Are you feeling better?"

"Hi, kid, yeah, I'm doing a bit better." He climbed stiffly into the truck. "Say, thanks for the stuff you picked up for me earlier," Jerry said, acknowledging the goodie bag Alex had bought for him. The boy smiled. Jerry continued, "I heard that you guys have a friend in need, now, huh?"

"That's right, sir, she's the new conservation officer in town, and we think she's in danger."

Jerry closed his door and looked over to Alex, saying with a slight smile, "Danger seems to be a common thing in this area." A small groan escaped from his mouth as he settled back into the seat of the truck. His smile morphed into a scowl of pain, his cracked ribs grinding together as he tried to get comfortable.

Putting his seatbelt on, Jerry noticed the T-Rex rifle propped between the front and back seats of the truck. The large-bore muzzle was pointing up toward the ceiling of the cab. His encounter with the bear came flooding back to him as he looked at its cold, grey metal and he shuddered, saying to Alex, "You're going to need a bigger gun."

"Well, we're hoping this rifle will do the trick!" the boy replied. "My Dad told me, if a T-Rex were alive today, this rifle could bring it down! It's got a .577 millimetre, seven-hundred and fifty-grain shell that can travel at over five-hundred and fifty metres per second!" Alex proudly repeated, parroting the information he'd gathered about the weapon from hearing his father and Trip talking about it earlier.

With a sigh of resignation, Jerry said, "Yeah, well, I guess we'll find out. Once we find that big, hairy piece of shit, that is, pardon my language. Personally, if I had to wager on it being between the rifle and the bear, I'd put my money on the bear."

CHAPTER FORTY-SEVEN

With the natural ventilation provided by the entrance now cut off, the steam and heat created by the hot springs began to build inside the cavern. Christine noticed the effect only minutes after the quake occurred. She hoped that the steam would continue to build and allow her a chance to escape at some point in the haze.

"Son of a bitch!" Ray Chance exploded. He unzipped his parka, saying "It's hotter in here than my second wife's body!"

"Ray, do you really have to equate everything that happens in your life to your ex-wives?" Nichols asked.

"Do you really have to be such a goddamned, nitpicking freak?" Chance retorted.

"That's what I like about you guys, you can really feel the love," Christine said.

"Shut up and get moving!" VanDusen barked, pushing the barrel of the gun into Christine's back, giving her a hard shove. She stumbled a bit, almost going down once more onto her knees in the razor-sharp rock fragments scattered across the cavern floor.

"Keep moving!" VanDusen said, pushing the gun's barrel into the small of Christine's back.

Rocks and stalactites of all different sizes had come loose from the ceiling during the quake and were now strewn across the cavern floor— the path ahead was not direct by any means. They were able to step over some of the smaller debris, while other fragments were so large, they had no choice but to go around.

Soon, they found themselves before the openings to several tunnels. On the right, a man-sized entrance beckoned. In the middle was a smaller entrance that looked more like a nook. And on the left, a much larger opening yawned wide.

Christine stopped once more, saying, "What now?"

"All right, let's see," Nichols said. He stepped in front of the group, taking control of the situation and making a decision using his mayoral powers of deduction. Shining his light into the first entrance, he paused, then after a moment backed up and shone his light into the next. He repeated the process with the third and then turned to them, saying, "I have no frigging idea."

"Maybe our little conservation chickee here has an idea — she's the outdoorsy type!" Chance offered.

"Well?" VanDusen said, giving Christine a poke with the Versa Max for good measure.

Moving to the first entrance where Nichols still stood, she asked, "Can I have your light for a moment, please?"

"Certainly," he said, handing his flashlight over to her and stepping aside.

Christine stood at the entrance to the first tunnel and shone the light back and forth. She then repeated the process at the other two tunnels just as Nichols had and then stepped back.

"Well?" the chief asked.

"This one," Christine said, indicating the entrance on the left.

"How do you know?" Nichols asked.

"Ancient Conservation Officer Secret," Christine said. In reality, she'd been waving the torch back and forth in front of each opening and taking note of the tendrils of vapour curling along the cavern floor, watching them ebb and flow around her legs. In front of the leftmost entrance, she'd noticed a more pronounced, but subtle shift in the movement of vapour, indicating more airflow coming through there, so that was the one she chose.

Still holding Nichols' flashlight out in front of herself with VanDusen's gun pressing into her spine, Christine reluctantly lead the group into the largest of the tunnels. After a short walk, it opened out into a new sub cavern. At just a little over three metres in height, the ceiling in here was not as high as the main one, giving it a more claustrophobic feel.

For several minutes, they pressed forward in silence, making their way around obstacles and following the cavern until it narrowed down into a smooth, natural corridor. They now appeared to be in a dormant lava tube. Fortunately, this one was horizontal rather than vertical like the ones in the main cavern.

The tunnel took several twists and turns, then split into two. The opening to the left remained level, while the one to the right sloped slightly downward. Figuring further exploration down into the bowels of the earth was not the best of options, Christine chose the opening that remained level and entered the tunnel. She played her light around the tunnel as she moved, noting the insane amount of gold that swirled through its smooth walls and ceiling.

"Jesus! More gold! This place is unbelievable!" Chance was beaming, running his hand over the bright-yellow vein of the metal next to where he walked.

The passage ended in what might have been a dead-end in the past, but no longer. A sizeable section of rockface had crumbled away, likely during the most recent quake, or perhaps the one from several weeks before, exposing a new opening. As with most things in this cave system, the entrance to this new antechamber was obscured by steam pouring from it, no doubt from additional pools of super-heated water inside.

"Ladies first," VanDusen said, still stalking behind Christine with his shotgun.

"You're not a scholar or a gentleman," she said, stepping tentatively through the opening.

Waving her hand in front of herself, Christine tried to dissipate some of the mist so that she could better see. Once she was past the initial vapour barrier, the steam cleared considerably. The culprit here was just a small hot spring flowing near the entrance. The uneven floor sloped downward slightly and opened into an immense cavern, stretching out before her into pitch black recesses. Moving forward, she shone Nichols appropriated light here and there as the rest of the gang piled into the cavern behind her.

"Oh, my God!" Christine said, stopping in her tracks. This was truly mind-boggling. Unable to believe it, she now found herself standing on the shore of a sandy beach at the edge of a vast, underground lake. There was only the slightest hint of steam rising from this body of water, and it was obviously not as scalding hot as in the main cavern. Something was moderating the water's temperature here. The mirror-smooth lake stretched out in front of her for hundreds of metres, as far as her light would shine and well beyond.

But there was also something else very interesting that she'd noticed when she'd entered the cavern moments before. Extinguishing her torch, she turned to VanDusen, saying, "Turn off your light!"

"What? Why?"

"Just do what she asks, Reggie!" Nichols barked. The chief complied, and an unearthly pale blue glow filled the cavern. They became still and silent, taking in the incredible sight before them.

The lake was alive with life.

The surface of the water was clear and calm and as smooth as glass. But beneath the surface, vast patches of bioluminescent algae illuminated the body of water from within, filling it with a spectral radiance. The glow descended into its depths for hundreds of metres, wherever the patches of the algae appeared. However, what shocked the group into stunned silence was the internal glow of colour pulsing from the plethora of aquatic creatures darting and swirling before them in the depths of the geo-thermally heated lake.

"Bah, it glows in the dark and has some fish, so what? Still more of the same crap," Chance grumbled.

Christine looked over to Chance and said, "Speak for yourself, Sparky. Why don't you just have another snort since everything's always 'the same crap' to you once you reach the bottom of that flask, isn't it?"

"What do you mean by that?" Chance slurred.

"Figure it out," Christine replied.

"Are you going to let her get away with that?" Chance sputtered at the chief.

A small smile played about the corners of VanDusen's narrow lips. "Yeah, I think I am."

Still acting indignant, Chance said, "I vote we go back to the entrance and dig ourselves out."

"Whoever said you were in a democracy, Ray? There's no voting around here!" Nichols said. "But you go right ahead and do what you want to do. And let me know how it works out for you once you try lifting those house-sized boulders blocking the entrance! Did you remember your hernia belt?"

"Well, it doesn't look like this is the way out with all this goddamned water and glow in the dark fish crap. That's all I'm saying!" Chance groused.

Clicking his Maglite back on, VanDusen said, "Looks like there might be something else in here with us, too. He shone his light on the ground. Skeletal remains were scattered along the shore of the lake. "Hard to say whether something killed these things, or if the carcasses only washed up here on the shore then rotted — its anybody's guess," VanDusen concluded.

But Christine didn't have to guess. "Those aren't new; they've been here for a while." She briefly flashed her light over them — she'd seen them earlier. The bones were faded, off-white, with no sign of any meat or cartilage on any of them. They had either died here on the shore, many years before or been picked clean by other predators. But if they were picked clean by something, then picked clean by what? What else was lurking in this cavern with them, sealed off from the rest of the world for countless millennia? There appeared to be an entire ecosystem at play here, one that had been existing for thousands and thousands of years before they'd stumbled upon it. But what lay around the next corner in this cavern of wonders was anybody's guess indeed.

Christine directed her beam away from the bones and moved it along the corner of the cavern closest to them. A ledge less than a metre wide paralleled the edge of the lake, running along the rear wall for hundreds of metres into darkness.

She stepped forward, wanting to explore the ledge along the back wall further when she felt a familiar poke in her back. Looking over her shoulder toward the chief with frustration, she said, "I know you're pretty excited and all, big boy. But do you think you might be able to pull your little boomstick out of my back for a second or two so I can check things out?"

"I think we can accommodate you, young lady," Nichols said. "Reggie, would you kindly allow our young lady-friend here a bit more freedom to explore?"

"All right, but don't you try anything else funny!" VanDusen jabbed his rifle toward her once more to emphasize his point.

"Don't worry; I think I've permanently lost my sense of humour."

"Watch your mouth, bitch," the chief grumbled.

"Sorry, I can't watch my mouth because I can't see my face. Suck it up, buttercup."

Leaving VanDusen fuming happily away, Christine moved out onto the ledge. Her left hand traced the smooth stone of the cavern wall as she went. There was a section up ahead that appeared particularly intriguing, and she wanted to check it out. It looked to be white marble or something like it, extending for dozens of more metres away from her, running next to the edge of the underground lake.

Being mindful of her step, Christine didn't want to tumble into the lake of glowing bio-life. Warm and inviting though it appeared, she wasn't particularly curious to find out whether or not the lake contained anything of an aquatic equivalent to the monstrosity currently stalking the residents of Lawless in the outside world.

Arriving at the gleaming marbled wall, what she suspected was correct; there was indeed an alternate exit from the cavern they were currently in, but it was entirely blocked by millions of tonnes of blue-white ice from the glacier.

Christine marvelled at the process at work in this incredible cavern. The massive Kootenay Glacier slowly, but inevitably moved past this cavern entrance each day, scraping away bits and pieces of itself against the rock as it progressed. It had probably been doing so ever since the last ice age.

Judging by the what lay on the small ledge at the edge the lake, every once in a while, a large chunk of ice would calve off and fall into the heated, luminescent mineral water. Whatever the ice contained would then begin to thaw in this warm, living lake.

Christine reached down and put her hand into the water next to the glacier — it was nice and warm as she suspected. She shone her light farther along, seeing other creatures that had fallen from the ice as it moved past but hadn't cleared the projection of rock. Their skeletal remains rotted on the edge of this nocturnal lake, never making it into the welcoming warmth of the water so close by, unable to receive their chance at rejuvenation.

The lake looked to be well-circulated with no evidence of any build-up of decaying bio-matter clouding the water. It seemed that whatever was deposited into it was being washed out elsewhere through some method of natural circulation, possibly flushing into an underground river somewhere.

Out along the jutting lip of rock, something rested that appeared to be the size of a German Shepherd. It lay partially submerged in the water where the narrow ledge of rock dipped down to surface level.

Christine sidled toward the creature. Its head was lying on the rock lip at the edge of the pool, facing toward her. The rest of its body still lay in the water as if it had recently crawled out and only gotten so far, before collapsing. She ran her hand along the glacier's blue-frosted surface as she moved along the narrow rim of rock, approaching the thing from the lake with extreme caution.

Kneeling next to the animal, she saw it wasn't breathing, and it definitely was no dog. Judging by the incisors and pointed snout, what she currently crouched next to appeared to be a giant rat.

"This is unbelievable!" Christine murmured, shuddering slightly. Sitting back on her haunches, she processed the information for a moment. Never had she seen a rat so large! As part of her training as a conservation officer, she was conversant on the many types of wildlife indigenous to the province of BC. She knew there were no rodents of any kind as large as this anywhere in North America these days. In the topics they still existed, but this was definitely not one of them. "We're a very long way from South America, and you sure as hell aren't a capybara!"

The creature before her had a long, striated tail that floated in the water, the trademark of the North American genus Rattus Rattus. She stood and stepped over to the other side of the creature for a better look, keeping her light trained on it.

Kneeling once more, Christine reached out hesitantly with one hand to touch the animal's wet, matted fur. As her hand softly grazed its pelt, the creature jolted and spasmed, suddenly drawing air into its lungs, perhaps for the first time in over ten millennia. She jerked her hand away, choking back a scream of surprise at the same time.

The rat opened its eyes and looked at her with fear and shock. It let loose the most ear-rending, discordant squeal she had ever heard and started dragging itself along the rocky lip of the pool to get away from her, moving directly toward the group of men.

"What in God's name is that?" Chance shouted. "That looks like the biggest goddamned rat I've ever seen! Shoot the fucking thing, Reggie!"

Knowing the shotgun would be useless at the distance he was from the rodent, Reggie VanDusen stepped onto the rock ledge. He slung the shotgun over his shoulder, pulling out his 9mm Glock and pumped four rounds into the shivering, quivering creature.

The rat shuddered and squealed as the bullets penetrated its body, giving up the new lease on life it had so recently reacquired.

"What are you doing?!" Christine shouted in surprise. "That could have been one of the biggest scientific discoveries of the century!"

"Now it's the deadest scientific discovery of the century!" VanDusen shot back.

Shaking her head in disgust, Christine looked around, examining further the other material ejected by the glacier. There were branches and rocks scattered here and there as well as skeletons of other assorted creatures that didn't survive their flash freezing and subsequent thaw, forever basking on this midnight shore.

She wasn't sure what would have caused these creatures to become trapped in this glacier but suspected something catastrophic had happened to them all at once, landing them in this ice for almost one-hundred thousand years. But what was bringing them back now, she wondered. It seemed there was much more to this body of water than met the eye. Moving back along the lip of rock, she returned to the relative safety of the gold-crazed assholes.

As Christine steeped down off the ledge, a new noise came from the far corner of the underground lake. Something was approaching rapidly from the darkness along the narrow ledge. A low mewling echoed through the chamber, as if a weak or scared animal were back there somewhere, injured and disoriented, crying out for help. The mewling sound came again, only this time it sounded more like a low, feral rumble, and it was much, much closer.

CHAPTER FORTY-EIGHT

Daylight was always too brief in the mountain communities of British Columbia during the winter, and Lawless was no exception. Within minutes, the sun went from a half-circle of golden radiance dancing on the cusp of the amber-hued ridges to a fading memory of beauty silhouetted by rugged, snow-capped peaks. The first hints of twilight crept around the edges of the afternoon skies as they headed up toward the resort. The day's sudden return of the sun had been as short-lived as ever.

Austin saw none of the afternoon's beauty — his attention was focussed solely on the cracked and broken road in front of him. Some sections dropped several centimetres, while others by several metres. Driving quickly and blindly into a break in the road could be especially problematic, as they might not drive back out of it, or survive the drop if it were deep enough. He needed to monitor both his speed and the road ahead very carefully, in order to avoid these new, earthquake-created depressions.

Fallen trees also lay across the asphalt in many places, forcing them to stop on more than one occasion to cut a path through the timber blocking the road. Some sections of highway were almost completely impassable. Detouring onto the narrow shoulder became a necessity as there was no other way around. But that put them at risk of sliding off the road and plummeting down the steep mountainside. Apart from a couple of hair-raisingly close calls, their sure-footed four-wheel-drive was able to surmount all obstacles with mountain goat-like aplomb.

Austin's concern grew as he manoeuvred along the curving, narrow road. He glanced at the sky through the windshield; the sun was now fully behind the snow-capped horizon — daylight was wasting. When evening fell, the ice fog would roll in and screw everything up royally, as if things weren't screwed up enough already.

They eventually rounded the final corner to the casino's entrance. With the lack of fog, Trip was happy to see that the Sphinx did not scare the crap out of him this time around, unlike his previous encounter.

But it seemed that the quake today had created a problem at the Eiffel Tower. All the shaking had compromised the ten-metre high model's foundation. Now, France's most iconic structure leaned drunkenly, resting the top of its tower on the head of the Sphinx across the lane, as if unable to remain upright any longer due to one glass of wine too many. The Sphinx did not look happy about this and Trip did not blame it. As the truck rolled toward the casino's gaudy, flashing entrance, he said, "Looks like Ray is going to have to do a few repairs around the ol' cantina. He won't be too pleased about that!"

Austin grinned. "You've got that right. Whenever anything costs him some money, even regular maintenance, that's never a good thing." As if to prove his point, the truck hit an unsanded patch of ice and slipped sideways a bit, and Austin smoothly corrected the truck's course. Doing his best shrill-voiced Ray Chance impression, he said, 'Goddamned piece of iron from France is humping my friggin' Nile cat!'" Trip laughed at Austin's uncanny impression and Alex guffawed from the back seat.

"I'm sure he'll be able to find some way to claim it on his insurance," Trip reasoned.

"No doubt," Austin agreed.

Alex glanced toward the resort's main entrance as they passed. He said, "At least the power's still on up here!" His eyes drank in the multitude of coloured, flashing lights as they drove by.

As always, when they came up to the resort. Alex loved the massive sign with the plethora of lights flashing, blinking and strobing away over the high, covered entrance. Austin promised himself that someday he'd take his son to Las Vegas to show him what a REAL light show looked like.

"Yup, they have their own generator up here that kicks in when the local power grid goes down," Trip concurred.

"You'd better believe that's happened on more than one occasion up here," Austin added.

"That way, they don't have to worry about interrupting a customer's losing streak, if the power goes out," Jerry interjected.

"Now you're getting it," Austin agreed.

As the truck pulled around the corner of the building, Jerry noticed only a handful of vehicles parked in the icy lot near the kitchen service area. An early eighties Trans-Am stood out to him for some reason, its rust-covered paint job looking particularly deep and vibrant in the lengthening twilight.

The only other vehicle of note was the brightly coloured 'Golden Castle Retirement Home Adventure Bus'. It appeared that the recreation supervisor of the home was currently allowing its residents the adventure of flushing their money away on the casino's slots and Texas Hold'em tables. The minibus, a bright yellow and blue Mercedes, sat near a large snowbank on the far side of the lot. It had been parked in back after the seniors had vacated it at the resort's gaudy entrance. Shaking his head as he nodded toward the bus, Jerry said, "I'm surprised anyone would still be up here with that monster somewhere in the area."

Trip leaned around, putting his left arm onto the console between the front seats, saying, "Jerry, buddy, you would be amazed at what it takes to disrupt a dedicated gambler's concentration sometimes. I swear you'd almost have to throw a bucket of ice water on some of them to get them away from these damned machines!"

"You got that right, my friend," Austin concurred.

"Yeah, I can believe that," Jerry said, looking into the sky. He noted the blue was much deeper now and craned his neck to look up toward the top of Gold Ridge and the glacier beyond. With the last of the sun now gone, he saw something that made his heart drop, and he closed his eyes for a moment.

Ice fog was beginning to descend from the top of the glacier, just like it had the day of the massacre at the campsite. He knew from experience how quickly the ice fog moved and that it would only be a matter of a few more minutes before they were inundated in a sea of icy greyness once more. Behind his closed eyelids, he saw nothing but quick flashes of teeth, blood and claws. When he could no longer endure any more of the Grand Guignol's Greatest Hits playing on the high-def holodeck at the back of his mind, his eyelids flew open, and he looked through tear-blurred lashes at the road ahead.

"What's the matter, Mr. Benson?" Alex inquired, seeing Jerry's glistening, wide-open eyes.

"Just having a moment is all, thanks, kid. I saw that damned ice fog starting to roll off the glacier and remembered what happened the other day to my friends."

"Sorry about that again, Mr. Benson. I sure do know how it feels when you lose someone close to you."

Jerry sensed the sincerity of the boy's word's as he spoke, and it moved him. He decided that he was glad to be here, helping these earnest people rescue their friend from the same monstrosity that had killed his. Smiling sadly, he said, "Thanks, kid."

Alex nodded. "And the ice fog sucks big time, too!"

"I agree," Jerry said with another smile, this one a little bit brighter, thanks to the boy's enthusiasm and humour.

Austin piloted the truck around a final bend in the lane toward the maintenance area where the snowmobiles were stored.

Taking in the scenery as they drove, Alex looked to the access road that led to the now-defunct ski hill and Gold Ridge beyond. As he turned back to his dad and Trip, trying to catch the train of their conversation, something in the corner of his sharp young eyes caught his attention. "Holy shit! What's that?" Alex shouted, making Jerry jump slightly in the seat beside him.

There had seemed something strange about one of the massive boulders situated along the back edge of the casino grounds. Located almost a kilometre away, they'd been put there as a line of demarcation to separate the resort and casino from the now abandoned ski hill.

"Alex! What's the problem?" Austin asked.

"There! Up the road to the old ski runs we just went by!" He pointed back the way they'd just come. "It looked like something big was moving near the boulders."

Austin stomped on the brake pedal, bringing the truck to a juddering halt on the frozen ground. He threw it in reverse and backed down the lane around the corner, skidding to a halt once more. All four men looked up the hillside. In the distance, with the last of the daylight fading away behind the mountain, they watched as one of the resort's huge 'boulders' moved slowly down the hillside on four large legs, directly toward the casino.

"Jesus Christ! That thing's even bigger in daylight!" Jerry said.

"We've got to warn the people in the resort!" Austin said. Dropping the truck out of four-wheel-drive mode, he cranked the steering wheel and tromped on the accelerator, spinning the Chevy around one-hundred and eighty degrees. The pickup rocketed forward, throwing the occupants back into their seats. Ice and gravel shot out from the rear tires of the truck, striking its undercarriage like hail on a tin roof.

The noise caught the attention of the enormous predator descending the mountain toward them, and it paused, looking their way.

Alex, his face pressed to the window, watched the colossal bruin. It moved slowly and confidently like it had all the time in the world. The beast's head tracked their movement as they sped back around the corner of the building, never once breaking its line of sight with the vehicle, locking them into its predator's vision.

"I think I have an idea," Austin said. Driving at breakneck speed down the remaining half kilometre toward the resort, he slammed on the brakes just before careening into the wall next to the kitchen.

Everyone piled out of the truck, with Jerry and Alex looking nervously over their shoulders up the lane, but there was no sign of the bear, yet.

Austin pitched his game plan. "Trip, you, get this," he said, reaching into the truck and grabbing the Springfield .30-06 from the gun rack. He tossed it to his co-worker. More than once, Trip had used that rifle to bring down an unnaturally aggressive coyote at the dump or to scare off other scavenging wildlife in the area. Austin knew that particular rifle and Trip were old friends.

"What about me?" Jerry asked, hopefully eyeing the T-Rex rifle slung over Austin's shoulder.

"Right! Sorry, I don't want to leave you out, Jerry. Here you go," Austin said, reaching toward the high-powered rifle.

Jerry grinned, his excitement level soaring as he prepared to accept the T-Rex from Murphy.

Austin reached past the rifle's strap to the utility case on his belt. He unclipped a leather holster attached there and reverentially handed it over to Jerry.

Jerry looked down at the object in his hands and opened the case, unfolding the ten-centimetre lock-blade contained inside. He looked up at Austin. "Gee, thanks... I guess."

"Sorry, it's the best I can do at the moment," Austin sympathised.

"It's a good knife, Mr. Benson! I gave it to my dad for Christmas just last year!" Alex exclaimed.

Jerry smiled, not wanting to hurt the kid's feelings. "It is a good-looking knife, kid," he feigned, holding it up in front of his face. "I suppose I can always poke the big bastard's eyes out if I can get close enough."

"That's a great idea!" Alex enthused.

Austin said to Trip, "So here's the plan. I'm heading inside to round everyone up and make sure they're in a safe location somewhere inside."

"Wherever that is," Jerry interjected.

Ignoring Jerry's quip, Austin said, "Trip, I want you to take the truck."

"Got it. Where am I going, Boss?"

"The maintenance shed. It's time to change somebody's diapers," Austin said, cryptically.

"I'm on it, Boss!" Trip climbed behind the wheel of the pickup. He floored the Chevy, spinning it around in the icy lot, and in a flurry of sand, ice and gravel skidded around the corner out of sight.

Jerry had swivelled his head back and forth, watching this exchange between Austin and the now-departed Trip in disbelief. He momentarily forgot his fear. In its place, he found his sense of incredulity and said, "Who do you guys think you are, the Green Hornet and Kato?"

"What do you mean?" Alex asked Jerry.

"Your dad and his buddy there seem to think they're the Marines, Cavalry and Dudley Do-Right, all rolled into one."

"That's not fair," Alex said, defending his dad. "They're trying to help save some lives here since nobody can drive in to help us with the road being blocked from the avalanche. We're on our own here, Mr. Benson! The only other way in or out is by air, and that's not going to happen either, not with the ice fog on the way!" Alex pointed over Jerry's shoulder toward the Kootenay Glacier.

Jerry turned and saw a thick wall of fog drifting down the hillside from above, preparing to coat the resort and valley below in a fresh crystalline blanket. He'd almost forgotten about the fog and was taken aback by the intensity of the boy's speech as he spoke in defence of his father's actions. "Sorry, kid, you're right. My emotions got the better of me there. We need to do everything we can."

"Thanks, Mr. Benson." Alex nodded, satisfied. "What about me, Dad?" The boy sounded eager to help.

Austin appreciated his son's standing up for him, once more marvelling at this kid of his. "Alex, you can come with me to help make sure everybody is safe and secure!"

"Awesome! I'm on it, Dad. You know me!" Alex said, high fiving his father, this time with no reluctance.

Returning the palm slap, Austin said, "I do know, and thanks, Son." He turned to Jerry. "Okay, so we're heading into the casino now to warn everyone we can find that the bear is coming their way and could attack at any moment."

"So, we're just going to warn everyone inside about the bear, and that's all?" Jerry inquired. This plan seemed pretty straightforward.

"Not quite," Austin said. "After that, we're also going to piss Angus off — and then encourage him to follow us and eat us instead! It's simple, see? So, let's go!" He pushed the kitchen door open and barrelled inside with Alex close on his heels.

"I'm pretty sure that thing won't need too much encouragement to eat you," he said to the kitchen door as it clicked closed in his face. "One human tastes pretty much like next, I'm sure — just like chicken." He smiled grimly as he took a glance up the lane toward the bear's last known position but was unable to see anything.

The glittering white bank of fog flowed down the slope toward the resort, the last of the fading twilight glinting off its top layer, giving it an other-worldly look. Everything it touched received a glittering, frosty coating as if an ice queen were enchanting the land and redecorating it to her whim. With a sigh, Jerry hoped that this was one fairy tale he would not have to be part of for very much longer. He turned and hurried inside the kitchen.

CHAPTER FORTY-NINE

"Now what in the hell is that?" VanDusen said, shining the light attached to the end of his shotgun toward the sound. The Maglite offered several brightness levels and beam sizes. The chief currently had it set to wide-angle, floodlight mode, in an effort to spotlight whatever was rapidly approaching their location.

Christine shone Nichols' flashlight about but could see nothing, yet.

The animal sounded nearer now, much louder and thoroughly menacing. Just beyond where the beams of the flashlights could reach, another low growl emanated from the throat of the creature.

As one, the group stepped backward, their inborn sense of self-preservation unconsciously kicking in as the thing in the darkness came closer and closer.

Listening carefully, Christine thought she recognised the sound from somewhere, but couldn't quite place it.

"Just shoot into the darkness, Reggie!" Chance said shrilly in VanDusen's left ear.

"Just shut the fuck up, Ray and let me concentrate!" VanDusen shouted, shouldering Chance aside and taking the safety off the Versa Max.

"Don't waste any of your ammunition until you have something to shoot at," Christine admonished in a low voice from his right.

"Way ahead of you, bitch," VanDusen said. He pumped the slide, putting a round into the shotgun's chamber.

Nichols stood slightly behind Christine and VanDusen. If it came down to brass tacks, he meant to use the woman as a human shield to save himself from whatever was out there. Sorry, my dear, he thought, it's just self-preservation. Christine had her back to Nichols, focussing on what was approaching, apparently unaware of how close he stood.

They were all frozen in place, listening for another sound. The chief slowly tracked his gun back and forth, ready to squeeze the trigger should anything come at them.

Chance turned to VanDusen and barked once more, "I still say you should just pump a few rounds into the darkness and see if you can scare it…" He never finished.

With lightning speed, a shape streaked from the edge of darkness at them. It was frighteningly quick, blurring through both the chief's and Christine's light beams as it rocketed toward their location. Whatever was coming at them was now moving so fast that neither of them could track it as it approached.

The beast launched itself out of the darkness, seeming to fly through the air in a well-timed leap. It slammed into Ray Chance, knocking him backward by several metres into the darkness. Chance made a huge, almost comical 'Oof!' as the air was knocked out of him.

The members of the party scattered. Nichols shrieked and grabbed for Christine, but she lept sideways, away from his grasping hands. She did a quick commando roll along the shore then regained her feet with cat-like agility. She'd been more than aware of the mayor's clumsy attempts to casually sidle up behind her earlier and had figured out the reason why. Despite looking otherwise, she had most definitely been paying close attention to His Highness, and she'd been ready to move. Nichols swore as he stumbled forward, now grasping only at empty air, instead of the woman he wanted to hide behind.

Seeming to come out from his trance of shock, VanDusen brought the Remington to bear on the animal. The sharp, white brilliance of the Maglite cast the scene before him in stark detail. He pulled the trigger.

An empty metallic click came from the gun — it was jammed. "Shit!" VanDusen swore. His panicked fingers attempted to clear the jam, feeling large and ungainly as he fumbled with the shotgun.

The creature tore into Chance. Fangs like swords sliced into his throat and face, shredding him to ribbons. His startled screams devolved into a series of wet gurgles within seconds. Blood flowed from his lacerated body, his hands batting weakly and ineffectually against the beast's muscular chest. With a quick jerk of its thickly corded neck, the animal tore Chance's head from his body.

"Jesus Christ! What the hell is that?" Nichols screamed, backpedalling and tripping over his feet. He went down hard on his ass in a jolt of pain and scuttled away from the repugnance on display before him.

VanDusen gaped in horror. Stringy, white tendons, pumping arteries and slabs of fat splayed out from where Ray Chance's head used to be. The stump of his neck looked for all the world like the reheated spaghetti with way too much Ragu sauce that Reggie had wolfed down for a late breakfast that morning. He thought he might possibly blow chunks but knew that now was not the time to act like a queasy rookie. And yet, he could have sworn he'd just heard someone who sounded an awful lot like him screaming like a little girl. His fingers finally unknotted, freeing the jam in the Versa Max, and he pumped round after round into the creature ravaging Chance.

Christine knew what the beast was and had no desire to stick around to see if VanDusen could exterminate it. As soon as she'd seen it, she'd known she needed to get as far away from their current location as possible. She ran toward the entrance of the antechamber, disbelief crowding her mind, her thoughts awhirl. It couldn't be, but it was — Ray Chance was getting eaten alive by a sabre-toothed tiger!

What was the hell going on around here? First, it was a giant raccoon, then a monster bear, and now a man-eating feline from the Flintstones. It was as if the veil of one-hundred thousand years that separated humankind from these prehistoric terrors no longer existed and its complacent position at the top of the food chain was no longer assured, at least not inside this cavern.

The sound of crunching feet on gravel came from behind Christine, and she looked back. Mayor Bob Nichols was hot on her heels, moving admirably fast for a man of his advancing years. He'd been following the beam of her flashlight as she fled. Picking up her pace, she bolted through the steam-shrouded exit and into the lava tube tunnels beyond.

Christine ran as fast as she dared towards the main cavern. Since abominations from the past had compromised the exit she was hoping for at the rear of the water-filled cavern; it seemed her only choice now was to head back toward the entrance. And seeing as she didn't want Nichols following her to the front of the cavern, she needed to draw his attention away from the direction she was travelling.

Her hope was to provide some sort of diversion for the creature, should it get past VanDusen's shotgun and come looking for more tasty treats. Hell, even if the chief finally killed the cat, judging by what she'd seen so far, there were probably plenty of other primaeval nightmares already stalking around back there, defrosted in the primordial soup of the underground lake. She had no doubt something else would come looking to have either one, or all of them as a tasty, after-thaw snack. Yes, the more she thought about it, the more the 'Honourable' Bob Nichols, Mayor of Lawless, seemed like an excellent diversion.

After a quick burst of speed, she was far enough in front of the mayor so that he'd lost sight of her as she jogged around a gradual curve in the tunnel. There was a fork ahead, and Christine paused for a moment. She knew she needed to bear right, but instead turned to the left and tossed the flashlight several metres down the tunnel where it rolled to a stop in the dust. It was the one they hadn't explored on their way into this steamy hell, and she thought that perhaps it led to more boiling springs and cavernous drop-offs to nowhere.

She hoped against hope that Nichols would be stupid enough to take the torch and run with it in that direction, buying her more time to make good the escape she had devised. She trotted down the tunnel that branched to the right and paused, peering back around the corner.

As if on cue, the hopefully soon-to-be-ex Mayor of Lawless came scampering around the corner of the tunnel, breathing hard as he stumbled after her in the dark. He spotted the flashlight on the ground a little way down the tunnel to the left and trotted over to pick it up. He paused, a slight wheeze of laughter escaping his lips as he marvelled at his good fortune in finding the light. Still breathing heavily, he stood, hunched over slightly, one hand on his knee as he swept the light back and forth between the tunnels, looking unsure which way to go. He was no doubt wondering what the hell had happened to Christine. After hesitating a moment longer, he chose a path.

Christine smiled as she watched the flashlight's beam bobbing up and down the unexplored lava tube, disappearing into the darkness. Bob

Nichols's fate was now up to whatever he found down at the end of that dark, lonely tunnel. Or whatever ended up finding HIM down at the end of that dark, lonely tunnel, which she thought seemed more likely.

Moving around the bend from the branching tunnel, Christine pulled out the iPhone she'd found earlier, turning it on to use its screen as a meagre light. As she'd fled the underground lake, inspiration struck, and she remembered the natural vent she'd seen earlier near the tent inside the main cavern. Maybe, just maybe, that vertical shaft was wide enough for her to shimmy up. She'd done it before. Having grown up climbing some of the West Coast's more challenging, rocky wonders with her father, she knew how to climb a chimney with the best of them.

Christine Moon ran up the tunnel toward the front of the cavern, an ember of new hope glowing brightly in her chest.

CHAPTER FIFTY

Edna O'Toole sat in the smoking section of the Golden Nugget Casino bar. She watched the latest cloud from her nicotine vaporiser get sucked up into the room's ventilation system. The smoking section (or vaping section on some days it seemed) was a bit of a misnomer as it wasn't actually a section located inside the casino but instead accessed through a breezeway that connected it to the main building. Thanks to a decision several years back by the provincial government, there was now no smoking of anything, anywhere in any public building in the Province of BC, including within three metres of any door or window.

This separate 'smokehouse', as her fellow nicotine addicts affectionately called it, was usually quite busy, but this afternoon, Edna had the room to herself. It appeared the scare with the bear had thinned out the crop of regular gamblers and most of the visitors as well.

Then there was that damned earthquake. She'd just settled into the smokehouse for a delicious after-lunch vape when it struck; then all hell broke loose. The shaking had been quite substantial, at least out in the smokehouse.

Stumbling along on unsteady feet, she'd panicked, worried about the seniors and bolted into the casino. Amazingly, none of the Golden Castle residents appeared in any way concerned about their current predicament. They all just sat there, staring into their machines, and pressing the buttons again and again, as if stimuli from the outside world was no longer worthy of their attention, superseded by the colourful graphics on the slot's screens and mindless music blaring from their speakers. Apparently, these hypnotic homewreckers drove all conscious thought of self-preservation from their minds as well as their wallets.

Edna had screamed at the seniors to take cover as the room shook around them.

There was no response. They kept feeding credit after credit into their insatiable one-armed overlords, pulling levers and pressing buttons, utterly oblivious to their current jeopardy. And then, just when Edna had been getting ready to start physically hauling the old farts into doorways and other locations of safety, the quake had ended.

She'd stood there, looking around in disbelief. Stanley Skrill had just been wheeling himself over to another slot machine when she called out to him, saying, "Why didn't you run for cover when the earthquake struck? Didn't you hear me shouting, Stanley? Didn't you feel the earth move?"

With a tone of aged disbelief, he said, "Feel the earth move? I haven't had that happen in twenty years now!" He shook his head sadly.

Thankfully, the resort's renovation at the turn of the millennium had been a quality job as the damage to the building appeared to be minimal. The power had been unaffected, and the slot machines kept on taking money.

Edna shook her head as she thought about it. Then shook it some more as she thought of the call she'd just gotten from Jacquie, manager of the Golden Castle Retirement Home back in Lawless. Along with her narcoleptic bus driver, Skip Buffer and her gaggle of golden-age gamblers, she was going to have to hang tight at the hotel for the foreseeable future. She was told road into town was impassable in places at the moment, to a minibus at least, and nobody knew when it would be open again. So now she had to get a room for the night for each of her geriatric wards. She fumed as she vaped, puffing away on her vaporiser every few seconds. The thought of stepping out into the sub-zero temperatures to give Skip the bad news was something to which she was not looking forward.

Edna looked into the lobby from the smokehouse window. She sighed. This afternoon, apart from herself and the residents of the retirement home (or inmates, as she called them), the place was as dead as most of her clients would be in the next few years.

The excursion had gone reasonably well, initially. After a spot of mid-morning gambling, everyone sat down for their prepared lunch meal in the dining room of the restaurant. Afterwards, they segued into the casino proper for more wild gambling abandon — or as much wild gambling abandon as seventeen cranky octogenarians could muster. Unlike most patrons of the Bonanza Buffet Restaurant at the casino, they did not get to choose their own meals at the smorgasbord. Needing two hands to work a walker or roll a wheelchair and also carry a plate of food at the same time was something far beyond the capabilities of most of the residents of the home. They were allowed to choose between two delicious options: the chicken or the fish.

Edna liked to think of these excursions in more dramatic terms, however — something more along the lines of 'Adventures in Babysitting 2: Seniors Strike Back' would be more appropriate to this afternoon's excursion.

Things had been going swimmingly until Stanley Scrill decided to sample some of the french fries off of Patsy Barrington's clubhouse sandwich plate. Patsy responded to Stanley's digital incursion into her crispy pan-fries by giving him a sound whack on his knuckles with the edge of her butter knife. This caused Stanley to let out the most god-awful wail Edna had ever heard. After that, she'd made sure to separate the two of them, and the rest of the lunch had gone relatively smoothly.

With the meal over, she and Skip had wheeled the inmates that couldn't walk into the slot machine section of the casino. The other, more sentient seniors, or 'Walkers', usually wandered around on their own when they were done, partaking of whatever game they pleased. However, in Edna's experience, it was the Walkers that were the ones that had to be watched the closest. If you didn't constantly keep checking up on them, sure enough, every once in awhile, one of them would wander out the front door into the shivering cold for another winter walkabout, like some Australian Bushman adolescent on their quest for manhood.

The Holy Rollers, now, they were much easier to handle. The wheelchair clients were usually quite happy to be wheeled anywhere other than repeatedly up and down the retirement home hallways. Edna knew she could park Patsy Barrington in front of a Break Five machine and she'd contentedly pump credit after credit into the machine for the next couple of hours with nary a peep.

Edna watched another vapour cloud lazily rise into the air and get gobbled up by the room's always hungry ventilation system. She glanced out the front window of the smokehouse noting the darkening sky, then at her watch. It was just after three o'clock.

When she checked that everyone was doing okay just a few minutes ago, she decided to have a final vape before getting ready to go out into the cold to talk with Skip at the bus. Taking another drag off of her vaporiser, she looked out the front window of the lounge toward Gold mountain and the Kootenay Glacier in the distance. What she saw didn't please her. Waves of white ice fog were rolling off the glacier and pouring toward the casino and the valley below. Great, she thought, not only was she trapped out here at the casino with a bunch of shuffling cast members from the Walking Dead, but now it was going to be as slippery as hell to boot. By the time she finished her vape session, it would be another grey limbo outside.

Tearing her gaze away from the front window, Edna looked to the back parking lot where the Golden Castle Adventure Bus was parked. As the daylight continued to fade away, it became harder to discern the silhouette of the Adventure Bus sitting on the far side of the lot. It seemed Skip had parked next to a large, dirty snowbank.

The driver of the Golden Castle Adventure Bus, Skip Buffer, was a man old enough to be an inmate in the retirement home for which he worked. Skip usually came into the casino for the free lunch provided for the tour bus drivers, and then he'd invariably leave as soon as it was over, heading back to the bus to doze away the rest of the day. That was usually the last she'd ever hear from him until about 4:00 P.M. when he'd stroll back in to help round up his fellow seniors.

Right now, Skip was no doubt napping behind the wheel out in the bus, engine running, heater and stereo cranked. There was no way he would hear his cell phone even if she tried to call him; she knew that from experience. Part of Skip's job description was to help make sure the residents were looked after when he and Edna took them out on excursions. She knew, to be honest, he did sort of help, but only as far as making sure that he got the free meal that was coming his way first. Once Skip helped to make sure everyone got seated, he was off to the buffet to tuck into his complimentary meal with obvious delight. After stuffing himself with his usual prime rib dinner and three trips to the dessert cart, he usually went back out to the bus to sleep it off.

Today had been like any other day, and just like clockwork, about fifteen minutes before the quake struck, Skip had headed back to the bus for his nap. Edna was still surprised that all the shaking hadn't brought Skip running back into the casino, concerned for Edna and his passengers, but there had been no sign of him.

Though she didn't need Skip to come in to start rounding up the inmates at his usual four o'clock load-up time today, she did need him to help get the seniors situated in rooms for the evening inside the mostly undamaged hotel. Taking a long final puff from her vape, she blew a huge cloud at the ventilation duct and sighed again. She might as well get it over with, and let Skip know the bad news and get the ball rolling. Edna was still perturbed at having to go out into the cold and shake Skip awake. She much preferred it when he came inside to help collect the inmates, and then she only had to walk out the front door and into the lovely, warm, preheated bus along with all of her senior charges.

There was a fire exit in the smoking room, but the alarm hadn't worked in a while now. Edna pushed on the release bar with her hip to open the door and stepped outside. The cold air hit her like an open-handed slap to the face. Her breathe swirled around her, clouding her vision temporarily, like a precursor to the vaporous ice cloud descending the mountainside toward the resort.

She stood for a moment outside the door and watched with a shiver as the first wave of ice fog hit the edge of the property. It rolled over everything in an all-consuming wave, swallowing the Adventure Bus, then the rusty Trans-Am across the lot.

Moments later, the fog devoured Edna and the Golden Nugget Resort as well.

Moving blindly forward into the fog, she aimed for where she'd last seen the Adventure Bus parked. She hated the fog as she always got so disoriented and turned around by it. A last bit of fading light remained in the January afternoon, providing some illumination for her, but it didn't help, and she was engulfed in an eerie, grey void.

To help guide her, she listened for the music from Skip's stereo in the bus, but she didn't hear anything, which was very strange. It was usually thumping away. How Skip could sleep with that racket was anybody's guess. She also expected to hear the distinctive sound of the bus's Mercedes-Benz diesel engine, albeit somewhat muted by the fog, but it wasn't running. Had it been, the marker lights for the bus would be shining through the mist, yet there was no sign of them either, and that was even stranger.

"Shit, Skip! Why did you choose today to be the one day you didn't crank the stereo and run the goddamned engine to keep warm!" Edna cursed aloud.

The rusty Trans-Am was suddenly in front of her. She was getting close! Brushing by the car, she looked inside the rapidly frosting side window. On the passenger seat sat a distinctive blue game case for the PS4 video game system. She recognised it because her son played games for the same system for hours on end at home. The title on the cracked leather seat displayed an angry Orc or something like that, saliva dripping from its toothy maw, attacking some poor schmuck with a sword. Nice friendly image, she thought.

Walking past the car, she entered the grey limbo once more.

A large dark shape suddenly appeared in front of her.

The bus! Thank goodness! She knew the fog could get so thick sometimes that you could lose track of your hand in front of your face. Or as Skip liked to joke, made it harder to spot than a pensioner at the casino a week before the government pension cheques came out.

Edna approached the bus, the front-end chrome shining slightly in the greyness — a welcome sight. It appeared Skip had parked the bus right next to a huge pile of snow, plowed up throughout the winter and pushed off to the side. Why in the hell did he park so near it, she wondered. Always cautious with his ride, Skip never wanted some careless motorist to scratch the finish, or to scratch it himself by getting too close to something. He always made sure to keep it well away from anything pokey or scratchy in the parking lots of whatever venue they were visiting. The man was obviously losing it!

There seemed to be something wrong, though. The bus was rocking from side to side and up and down, the mound of snow seeming somehow attached to the large Mercedes. This wasn't a thing that piles of snow were accustomed to doing to tour buses in her experience, at least not in the Kootenays. As she stood transfixed, something seemed to ripple from beneath the surface of the grey mountain of snow at the driver's side window of the Adventure Bus.

She suddenly realised it wasn't snow mounded up, but instead dingy, grey fur. A monstrous creature was trying to burrow its colossal snout into the driver's side window of the bus in front of her. Thick muscles undulated along its back as it pressed its angular head deeper into the vehicle to feed.

Edna jammed the back of her hand into her mouth to stifle a scream. She wasn't the focus of the enormous creature's attention at the moment (Skip had that honour), and she wanted to keep it that way.

The monster's muzzle was wedged into the driver's side window of the Mercedes, filling it completely. It worried away at what was inside like a dog trying to get at a bone full of marrow. It pulled and twisted its head violently back and forth through the shattered window, trying to extract its meal from the bus.

Edna watched in horror as the animal finally yanked the object of its desire out of the driver's side window. With a final huge pull, it freed the gore-streaked bottom half of Skip from the Adventure Bus — the top half no doubt already being digested in the beast's stomach. The huge predator reared its head up into the air and caught the remains of Skip Buffer in its mouthful of stiletto teeth. It crunched and swallowed, chunks of viscera and blood spraying everywhere.

Edna stood stunned, not knowing what to do. Though her WorkSafe BC manual gave great advice about assisting those in peril, nowhere inside did it include any reference to helping extract co-workers from the maws of nightmares made real.

The noise the creature made as it ate was beyond belief. Edna moved her hands from her mouth to the side of her head and covered both ears. She didn't notice the blood dripping down the back of her hand, drawn by her teeth as she'd tried to stop from screaming. Now with both hands over her ears, she backed up, the bile rising in her throat.

Edna O'Toole suddenly wished for a third hand to cover her mouth to stop the spew of vomit and the scream of terror, both of which she felt imminently forthcoming. She kept slowly backing away, hoping the fog would hide her presence.

But she couldn't hold it back any longer, and the scream that she'd been bottling up tore free from her lungs. She was quite surprised by the sound that came out, startling herself almost as much as the bear. It wasn't a scream so much as a high pitched 'Eek' as if she were a large mouse who'd just spotted an even larger cat. It was not overly long, but it was loud enough for the creature to stop in the middle of its last juicy mouthful of Skip and turn its gargantuan head to gaze directly into her eyes; they gleamed with a hunger that seemed infinite.

Edna shrieked again, but this time, much louder, and much, much longer.

Then there was only the sound of her ragged breathing as she stumbled across the parking lot through the mist. She hoped to see the flashing neon signs over the entrance, or maybe the slot machines twinkling away in the bright, heated safety of the lobby, but instead saw only greyness.

Her breathing came faster and faster as she lurched frantically forward, looking for any sign of lights ahead in the murk. Her life might end right here, right now, if she got lost and couldn't find the casino.

There was a deep rumbling noise. It could have been the sound of her own breathing caused by years of nicotine abuse, but she didn't think so. Either way, she knew the beast was coming for her and the thought made another panicked scream well up in her throat.

Salvation suddenly appeared in the impenetrable fog, and the casino's lights shone brightly before her. Like a moth, she flew toward their welcoming glow, but she didn't-couldn't-wouldn't look back, knowing that if she did, it would be the end of the line for Edna O'Toole.

The entry doors to the Gold Nugget Casino were on an electric eye system that opened when a patron approached the door. Edna ran toward those doors, expecting them to open automatically; however, the thickness of the fog combined with the fading daylight had affected their sensors, and they remained closed as she rapidly approached.

She slammed face-first into the glass doors with enough force to crack the glass and then rebounded off them, landing hard on her back.

Ears ringing, she smiled slightly, staring up at the ceiling of the entry canopy, mesmerised by the multicoloured lights overhead that blurred into twins and triplets above her. They looked so very pretty, she noted dreamily.

The ground quivered as something heavy approached where she lay, and terror snapped her from her reverie as she remembered her dilemma. She tilted her head back and looked out into the fog from her upside-down point of view. There was no sign of the beast, yet, but knew she had only seconds before it was upon her.

Without warning, the entry doors whisked open at her feet. She quickly flipped over onto her belly. Still feeling far too dizzy to stand, she used her forearms to turn herself around. She flip-twisted one-hundred and eighty degrees and dragged herself into the airlock portion of the casino's entry vestibule. At her back, the earth moved with each and every step the beast took as it plodded toward her position.

CHAPTER FIFTY-ONE

VanDusen pumped round after round into the giant cat, until his shotgun was empty, the four shells the gun held now only smoking casings on the ground. The cat wasn't moving anymore, thank God, but then again, neither was Chance. Looking down at Chance's decapitated body, he said, "Sorry about the gun jam back there, Ray."

Thanks to the Versa Max's three-plus-one, vented, gas-assisted semi-automatic nature, Reggie was able to rapid-fire the four rounds it contained at the prehistoric furball in less than five seconds. The first round of ammo found its mark and blew chunks out of the cat's hindquarters. Because of the predator's savage movements, the second two shots missed slightly and blew chunks out of Chance instead, but by then Ray hadn't been moving very much anyway, so Reggie didn't feel too bad about his panicked lack of marksmanship. The final round in the Remington hit the cat in the head, removing the top half of its brainpan along with both ears.

Reggie's ears were ringing from the blasts, and the only sound he heard in the cavern now was his own ragged, adrenalised breathing.

But for just a moment, as he took several more huge gulps of moist cave air, with the sound of the last shotgun blast still reverberating throughout the vast cavern, he thought he heard something more.

He paused, listening intently as the ringing gradually faded away. Toward the far corner of the calving glacier, another deep bass rumble echoed from the cavern's darkened recesses. Was it the glacier grating against the rock, perhaps, he wondered? He held his breath, listening to hear more, but the sound didn't repeat.

Breathing a sigh of relief, he felt around in his coat pockets for the box of extra shells he'd brought along for the Remington, but they weren't there. They must have fallen out during the earthquake when he, along with everyone else, had been running for their lives.

"Shit!"

VanDusen didn't drop the shotgun, but instead removed the Maglite from the muzzle, slinging the Remington back over his shoulder. He wanted to hold onto the gun in the event he could find the box of shells somewhere nearby, or as a last resort, use the damned thing as a club.

At the back of the cavern, the low rumbling came again. Definitely not the glacier. He hoped it was some rock, loosened by the quake settling into place somewhere back there, but he knew he'd be lying to himself.

Reaching into his jacket holster, VanDusen felt renewed confidence when he confirmed that his 9mm Glock 17 was still there. Groping along his equipment belt, he felt the two spare magazines still attached that he'd brought along for the Glock. Including the magazine in the pistol, he'd normally have a total of fifty-one shots available, but he'd used four on the rat, so he only had forty-seven shots left. If there were any more surprises in these caverns, this might not be enough firepower to defend himself. The Glock was able to pump out a lot of bullets in a short time, but their stopping power against whatever else might be in this cavern would be minimal, especially if any new surprises had hides even half as thick as the cat's had been.

He retreated toward the entrance of the cavern, the bioluminescent algae on the walls not giving him enough light to see farther back toward the far corner and the glacier. As he backed up, Reggie fitted a rubber combat ring from his utility belt to the barrel of the Glock. He then attached the ring to the back of the flashlight and grasped the 9mm utilising the rubber ring. It allowed for spot-on targeting and deadly accuracy. Now armed and ready, he shone the light toward the back wall of the cavern, as far as it would probe.

"It's like the goddamned black hole of Calcutta in this place," he muttered.

As his light explored the darkness, the rumble came again, followed closely by another, slightly different noise, yet still somewhat similar to the first.

The Maglite picked up a glint of reflections where the glacier scraped against the cavern's wall next to the ledge.

Something was coming his way.

He watched four dancing specs reflected in the beam of his flashlight. Scratch the 'something', he thought, it looked like two things rapidly approaching. The glowing specs became more substantial and brighter, and Reggie felt the blood draining from his face as he realised what was behind the innocent reflections dancing so merrily in his light's beam.

Now almost at the exit to the tunnels, VanDusen stopped, unable to take his eyes or his flashlight from what was approaching. After several more long seconds, his worst fears were realised — coming toward him was not one, but two creatures.

"You've got to be fucking kidding me! Cubs?" he said aloud. "That piece of shit bear is a bitch, and she has cubs?"

Though Reggie had never seen their mother, he was still stunned at the size of these creatures. The cubs were both more massive than any grizzly or polar bear he had ever seen. Each looked to weigh almost a tonne, and they seemed well fed. He wondered if mama bear had been keeping them plump with the little two-legged snacks she kept finding excavating gold about her lair.

The bears were about one-hundred metres from him now, coming around the edge of the glowing lake near the rear corner. They strode confidently, moving like they had a purpose — and he figured he was their purpose. Reggie VanDusen turned and fled into the tubes.

He huffed and puffed as he hightailed it to the main entrance as fast as his flabby legs would carry him. Unfortunately, after several hundred bacon-triple cheeseburgers from the Burger Barn, that wasn't very fast.

Between wheezing gasps, Reggie could hear what sounded like several tons of hungry bruin pounding steadily along on the ground, approaching him from behind as they moved steadily down the tunnel toward their next meal.

Sprinting forward, Reggie looked for a boulder to hide behind or something to climb up on so he could perch safely out of the cubs' reach, but there was nothing.

Ahead was a junction; he had to choose left or right with no time to think about it. He looked down and saw tracks leading in both directions. He couldn't remember which way they'd come and felt his adrenaline surging as he heard the prehistoric nightmares drawing closer.

"Shit!" VanDusen shouted in frustration and chose a direction, taking the tunnel that branched to the right.

Long-clawed feet scraped along the tunnel floor in the darkness at his back, and he surged forward, running for his life. The twin beasts sounded so close that he thought he could almost feel their fetid breath tickling the sweaty folds of his neck fat. Their excited, anticipatory breathing echoed through the tunnel behind him, so loud now it threatened to drown out Reggie's own terrified gasps.

Chief Reggie VanDusen ran as fast as he could. And Chief Reggie VanDusen did not look back.

CHAPTER FIFTY-TWO

Austin and Alex jogged through the kitchen to the casino floor and quickly surveyed the room. There were about a dozen and a half seniors scattered throughout, some on the slots and some playing electronic Texas Hold 'em and blackjack.

Jerry ran past as Austin looked toward the lobby, and he knew the front was taken care of for the moment.

"Alex, see if you can go talk to some of them, and let them know what's happening." The boy nodded and trotted over to a gaggle of senior ladies to tell them of the urgency of the situation.

Moving toward a group of men clustered at some slots, Austin hollered, "Can I have your attention, please!" A couple of white heads turned slowly toward the sound of his voice and then turned away once more. The rest just kept pumping credits into the machines, pulling levers and pushing buttons, utterly oblivious to the tall, bearded man shouting at them in the middle of the room.

Knowing that he needed to get the attention of these people as quickly as possible, and that talking just wasn't cutting it, Austin decided that now was the time to go loud or go home.

Not wanting to injure anyone by firing into the ceiling of the building, Austin aimed the T-Rex at a slot machine located in the far corner, located well away from everybody else. He pointed the gun, secured it against his shoulder and hoped that the internal dampening worked as well as Christine said it did.

He pulled the trigger.

The Tyrannosaur rifle roared, letting loose a blast that cleared all thought of gambling from most of the minds around him, and anybody else within several hundred metres, Austin was quite sure. The machine in the corner exploded into thousands of smoking fragments, tokens flying everywhere.

It had the desired effect. The seniors seemed to react all at once and deaf or not, wheelchair-bound or not, most of them jumped about a metre in the air when Austin pulled the rifle's trigger.

"Holy hell!" shouted a small, white-haired man with a face like a sultana. Startled from the blast, he said, "What in tarnation did you go and do that for, ya jackass? That was one of my favourite machines!"

"There's a killer bear headed this way!" Austin tried to herd the man toward the kitchen.

"What are you talkin' about, ya jackass?" "I don't see any goddamned bear!"

Exasperated, Austin said, "Not in here, outside! And it's coming this way!"

"Well, it'll just have to wait, I still have a dozen credits in this machine!" He nodded toward the slot at his back.

The other seniors nearby had gathered around Austin and Mr. Jackass to see what all the commotion was about. They began to look around in concern for this bear being mentioned.

Austin turned and addressed the rest of the group as a whole. His raisin-faced friend muttered, "Jackass" once more under his breath as Austin turned away.

***

Jerry jogged through the kitchen and found no one in sight. He burst through the galley doors, relieved to see Austin and Alex getting things under control in the main gaming room.

Sprinting toward the front of the hotel, he prepared to tell anyone that cared to listen that the bear was approaching and that they needed to get to the upper floors in case it broke through at ground level.

Across the lobby stood an elderly couple next to a huge, one-armed bandit, the Million Dollar Slots. The man held a cupful of casino tokens, dropping them into its coin slot. His companion stood next to him, ready to pull the plunger once he'd satisfied the electronic behemoth's insatiable appetite. Adorned with so much flashing neon and LEDs, Jerry felt his eyeballs throbbing after looking at it for more than a few seconds, but this didn't seem to affect the elderly couple adversely. They stood next to the machine, feeding it coin after coin, pulling the lever and watching the wheels turn, utterly unaware that they were in mortal danger.

Jerry ran to the front desk, hoping to get some assistance, but the front desk attendant was nowhere in sight.

"Hey! You two!" Jerry shouted at the couple next to the giant slot machine.

Startled, the elderly man and woman looked over toward the dishevelled, unshaven man with the wild eyes yelling at them, and a look of concern finally registered on their faces.

"Yes! You two!" Jerry pointed at the pair. "You need to get upstairs NOW! The bear is here!" Jerry bellowed, pointing toward the entrance.

There was an enormous explosion from the casino portion of the building. Jerry snapped his head over in that direction and saw that Austin had just terminated a slot machine in the corner with the T-Rex rifle for some reason.

Whatever the reason, the concern in the seniors' eyes near the Million Dollar Slots cleared immediately as the blast shattered the casino's peace. The man grabbed his walker, then his companion and started pushing and rolling them toward the elevator across the lobby with a speed that some would have called downright sprightly.

But the little old lady would have none of it and turned back, scurrying over to put several more coins secreted away in her pocket into the machine's slot. At the elevator, the man, reaching for the call button with his cane, looked back in dismay, seeing the woman no longer with him, once more over at the monster machine. He spun his walker around and scuttled back across the lobby so quickly it was surprising his wheels didn't leave skid marks. As she was about to pull the lever, he grabbed the old woman by her sweater sleeve, rolling them both back across the lobby to the safety of the elevators, making sure not to let go of her this time. All the while he guided her, the woman kept looking back toward the slot machine, more anxious about missing out on a huge jackpot win than ensuring their own safety.

Jerry's concern for the elderly couple at the slot machine vanished as soon as he looked toward the lobby doors. A woman, crawling on all fours, was trying to get inside the casino. She had made it through the first set of doors in the air-lock-style entry, but the secondary doors refused to open for some reason. Behind her, a horrific shape surged from the thick fog.

Frozen to the spot, Jerry's terror from the campsite returned, smothering him once more when he saw the thing approaching the woman. He'd witnessed this creature up close only once before, but now, seeing it in perspective next to human-made structures, he couldn't believe its mind-numbing size.

The beast lumbered forward, its bulk filling the three-metre-high doorway that surrounded the woman. She was still on her stomach in the airlock, scrabbling with her fingers at the stubbornly closed inner doors, trying to pry them open.

Jerry flew across the lobby toward her, hoping it was only the fog affecting the external sensor and that the one on his side was working. If he could trigger the doors with his approach, he figured he could grab her when they opened and drag her safely into the casino.

"Please help me! For God's sake, help me!" she screamed at Jerry through the glass. Her face was terror-stricken, and tears flooded her cheeks. Looking over her shoulder at what was almost upon her, she let out a low whimper.

Leaping toward the entrance, Jerry discovered, as he'd hoped, the internal sensor was working, and the doors began to slide open from his rapid approach. He reached out with his good arm toward the woman, ready to pull her to safety.

The bear arrived behind the woman at the same time Jerry reached her front. The beast thrust one of its log-like arms into the airlock and pounded it down onto the lower half of the woman's body to stop her forward movement. This immediately ended her cries for help. The force generated from the paw slapping down on her lower body squeezed everything from below her waist forward all at once. Her head and upper body became engorged with blood and fluid as her internal organs ruptured from the pressure. It was as if her head were a balloon with the face painted on beforehand, only revealing itself as it was inflated. Her body was punched forward into the thick, partially open glass doors.

The airlock doors contained a safety release mechanism that freed them from their track in case of emergency. If someone pushed hard enough on the glass to flee the building during a crisis, it would swing outward into the parking lot, allowing them to escape, even if the power were off. Unfortunately for the woman in front of Jerry, since they did not release inward as well, she was plowed into the doors, bursting like an overripe tomato as she hit the glass.

Jerry's view through the door was suddenly obscured as blood and viscera from the woman sprayed inside the airlock due to the paw's immense pressure. The metal door frame tore from its bottom safety track, the edge hitting Jerry broadside, throwing him across the lobby. He landed on his back, spinning along the highly polished marble floors, and slammed into the base of the Million Dollar slots. The bells on its top jingled loudly as Jerry jarred it. Lights flashing the machine beeped and booped, and the wheels began to spin. Each prize on the display locked into its final position, all five now showing dollar signs. A red light started strobing at the top of the machine, and its bells and sirens began ringing and blaring. A series of clunks and whirs came from the unit, and suddenly the payout tray was filled with one-dollar tokens spilling out onto Jerry's unmoving feet and legs where he lay slumped unconscious.

Unfazed by the flashing lights, or the bells and sirens from the slot machine, the monster slid its paw back out of the airlock, the remains of Edna O'Toole still squashed into its pad. Dragging its catch-of-the-day onto the icy cobblestones of the courtyard, the beast began scooping the woman's dripping crimson remains into its ravenous, salivating maw.

***

491

Now that he had everyone's attention thanks to the T-Rex's blast, Austin shouted once more, "Your attention, please! There is a killer bear on its way here! You need to get to the second floor or into the kitchen coolers for safety!"

The seniors still looked at him questioningly. One bald, oblong, prune-like man shook his head in disbelief, saying, "What're ya talkin' about? Are ya drunk, sonny?"

A resounding crash came from the lobby, and all heads turned toward the main entrance. Jerry was on his back next to a machine labelled, Million Dollar Slots, tokens pouring out of its coin tray onto his prone body.

Visible through the central archway were the entrance doors. Through them, most of the seniors in attendance were able to see the drama unfolding as the massive beast dragged something under its paw back out of the blood-drenched airlock and began to eat it.

The temporarily mute gaggle of white-hairs shrieked and moved all at once. Like birds in a flock separating from each other, half a dozen seniors swarmed toward the elevator doors and another contingent branched off toward the coolers in the kitchen, with Alex guiding the way.

The first part of the flock arrived at the casino side of the elevator doors, finding them closed. They hammered at the call buttons, and the doors pinged open only to reveal the elderly couple from the Million Dollar Slots hiding inside, holding onto each other tightly. Mild though the earthquake had been at the casino, it had created enough havoc to throw the elevator off its pneumatic ram, and it no longer rose to the second floor.

Seeing the elevator out of commission, Austin yelled, "Shit on a cracker!" He glanced to the front doors and saw the beast trying to worm its way inside the entrance, pressing into the metal frame, the steel straining around the creature's muscular body. He needed to do something, and he needed to do it now. Turning, he began to run from the room.

"Dad!" Alex shouted, "Where are you going?"

Pausing, Austin shouted back over his shoulder, "Stay here with these people! I'll be right back! Try to get everyone into the coolers in the kitchen if you can! The elevator is out!"

Austin sprinted from the room, hearing one final word uttered at his back as he ran, "Jackass!"

CHAPTER FIFTY-THREE

Mayor Bob Nichols stumbled in panic down the tunnel toward what he hoped was safety. He didn't see the girl anywhere and presumed she was somewhere up ahead. When Chance got jumped by that alley cat from hell back there, all conscious thought had flown from his mind. The only thought he'd had was to get the hell out of there as quickly as possible. If he were lucky, the cat would be kept busy eating Chance, and he'd have the time to hide or something. Hearing VanDusen's shotgun blasts echoing through the caverns as he fled, he'd hoped that the chief's aim was true.

Finding the flashlight at the junction, he'd scooped it up and shone it around, unsure of which way to go. Perhaps some other horror had attacked the girl, and she'd dropped the light as she was dragged away, or maybe she'd just dropped it in a flight of panic herself. As he moved, the light's beam flashed back and forth. Reflected in its glare, yet another vein of gold swirled through the tunnel walls. He scowled as he ran by the precious metal, sorry that he'd ever become part of this.

The ground began sloping downward quite noticeably in spots as he progressed. Suddenly, the passage opened out into another cavern before him. He felt relief, hoping there might be something to defend himself with inside or at least a place to hide temporarily. The sound of running water echoed inside the cavern, and the space seemed free of steam, likely the boiling aquifers didn't extend this far. He could see quite a ways into the distance with his light and shone it carefully around. Fortunately, there didn't appear to be any creatures wandering close to the entrance.

Nichols walked slowly into the cavern in wonder, his fear currently on the back burner by what he saw before him. The ceiling was immensely high, the tips of the closest stalactites barely discernible to his probing light. He directed the beam toward the sound of rushing water.

There was an opening on the far side of the cavern wall that looked to be an outflow from the lake above. Water flowed from this gash in the rockface in a high-pressure stream, jetting out and spraying down into a black void far below. Bob wondered if the gushing water was a result of the recent quake, or if it had been pouring through this gap for millennia.

He glanced off to his right. There was a solid rock wall that ran for about thirty metres then ended in the same precipice the water shot over on the opposite side. Walking to the edge, he shone his light down into the chasm's depths — there was no bottom in sight.

He was at a dead end.

Looking for someplace to hide, he turned in a full circle shining his light all around. There were a few smaller boulders scattered here and there, but nothing of any appreciable size that would hide a man of his stature. He walked back toward the cavern's entrance, beginning to tentatively move up the tunnel's incline in the direction he'd come. As he moved along, he stopped and carefully peered around each corner, just in case something was lying in wait for him.

Nichols noticed the angle of the grade more now that he was going back the way he'd come, and his breathing became laboured and ragged. He paused for a few deep breaths and then rounded another corner, stopping dead in his tracks.

Approaching from the blackness at the end of the lava tube, four dancing dots of light moved down the tunnel toward him. Rescuers, he thought at first. Hallelujah, I'm saved! But just before he called out to the sparkling lights at the end of the tunnel, he looked more closely and realised the dancing lights were not flashlights at all. They were the reflection of two pairs of predatory eyes moving in his direction, gleaming back at him in the light of his torch. Bob began slowly backing up, then turned and fled toward the cavern as fast as his arthritic hips would carry him.

Though he knew there was nothing back there that could help him, he didn't care, and only wanted to put some distance between himself and whatever in God's name was now coming down the tunnel.

Back at the dead-end cavern of wonder, it felt like his heart was threatening to pound its way out of his chest. He ran to the edge of the precipice, sweat pouring from his panicked brow. It dripped into his eyes, stinging them and blurring his vision. Turning back from the void, he blinked rapidly to clear his eyes so he could see what had followed him down the corridor.

"Jesus Christ! Just bugger off and leave me alone!" He rubbed at his eyes and shouted at what was emerging from the darkness into the cavern. When his vision cleared, and he was able to discern what was stalking him, his heart skipped a beat and almost stopped.

About one hundred metres from him, twin bears stood, framed by his spotlight. Much larger than an adult grizzly, these bears still looked like cubs. He surmised that they had to be related to that thing stalking around the forests of Lawless, though not quite fully grown, despite their massive size.

Nichols snapped his head left and right, looking for something, anything, with which to defend himself. Grabbing a chunk of rock, he threw it at the bears as they approached. The fist-sized rock bounced off the shoulder of the cub on the left. The beast didn't notice the impact in the slightest and kept plodding toward him, its sibling at its side.

Standing at the brink of the drop, Bob felt the gaping blackness pressing against his back. The bears approached slowly, seeming in no apparent hurry, now that they knew their prey wasn't going anywhere.

Nichols looked backward over the edge of the cliff, his mind registering what he'd only glimpsed as he'd tried to blink the salty sweat from his eyes. There was a secondary ledge just below where he was standing. It looked to be about a metre wide, situated about three metres down. He could drop down onto it out of their reach — of that he was sure!

The twins were now about ten metres from him, and Nichols knew if he were going to do something, he'd better do it soon, or he was going to get ripped to shreds. He knelt on the edge and turned around unsteadily, feeling the lip of soft rock crumble slightly near his right knee as he positioned himself for the drop.

Flashing the light down to the narrow, rocky shelf below, suddenly the three metres looked more like thirty. The flashlight was going to prove a liability since he needed it not only to see what he was doing but also to see where the bears were located. Deciding to put the flashlight in his mouth, he clamped his lips and teeth around it to hold it tight. It glowed from his buccal cavity like a locomotive emerging from a darkened tunnel. He lay down on his belly along the lip of the ledge, slowly turning his legs out into the blackness to lower himself down.

Unfortunately, Bob Nichols upper body strength was not what it had been when he was younger. Like so many elderly people, his muscles had atrophied after decades of lack of exercise and neglect. What should have been a simple thing for a man of fifty or even sixty, for a man of seventy-five, like Bob, it was almost impossible.

He had enjoyed a privileged life, not having to break a sweat to make a living. Being the nephew of the owner of the Sinclair Development Corporation had certainly allowed him privileges while growing up, of that he was more than sure. And never having to do anything more strenuous than chasing a golf ball around the green or perhaps tip back his elbow to partake of another scotch and soda, he was about as physically unfit a specimen as had ever walked the planet.

His face pressed to the cold, dusty rock, Nichols splayed his arms across the edge of the ledge, his feet now dangling down into the darkness below. The intention had been to lower himself in something of a controlled manner. But the soft leather gloves he wore were not suited to gripping time-worn rock, and the smooth, supple hide slid over the eroded rock much too quickly as gravity pulled him over the edge.

The bears were almost upon him, less than a metre away now. The cub on the left, being closer to him, swept its paw out to try and snag him as he dropped down, its fresh, young claws looking wickedly long and sharp.

Bob continued his slide off the ledge and plummeted into the blackness below. His trip was a short one, but his brittle bones impacted the rock ledge with brutal force. The flashlight ejected from his mouth, and a shriek of pain burst from his lips. His left leg hit the narrow ledge first, shattering his ankle in a dozen places and the rest of his body landed on top moments later. Nichols now lay flat on his back along the ledge, right leg hanging into nothingness, his left ankle a white-hot brand of agony. "Oh Jesus Christ, God, it hurts!"

Nichols tried to move and was surprised to see he could still sit up, but his ankle screamed in pain at him once more, and he followed suit. Reaching toward the flashlight, he grabbed it away from the edge of the ledge where it rolled when he landed. He flicked the light's beam upward and looked into the ravenous faces of the cubs. Saliva dripped from their partially opened mouths onto his upturned face, and he wiped it away. The creatures knew their prey was now unobtainable and both roared again, this time in frustrated unison.

Bob cringed at the sound; his ankle pain temporarily forgotten. The cubs gave a final howl of frustration and turned away, perhaps going to look for a meal more easily accessible than the mewling, injured thing just out of their reach below.

Breathing a sigh of relief, the mayor said, "Thank God! Thank God!" He moved the light along the ledge, assessing his situation. The shelf of rock ran about four metres along the rockface to his left and then ended, dropping into oblivion below. Shining the light to his right, he saw he had only one metre or so before the rock did the same disappearing act into nothingness.

Nichols tried to stand. He scrabbled his hands along the rock wall to pull himself up. Once standing, he decided to put some weight on his ankle, and it rewarded him with more searing pain that made his vision go white.

Bob stretched up his hands to see if he could reach the ledge above to pull himself back up. His heart sank when he saw his grasping fingertips were still about a half-metre too far away.

He had no way up.

The flashlight in his hand had been a trusted companion up until now. Without warning, it began to dim, going from a brilliant white to a dull yellow in less than twenty seconds. "No, no, no!" He cursed at the light, "Work, you piece of shit, don't die on me now!" He smacked it with the palm of his hand, but nothing improved, and it continued to die.

Soon, the high-intensity flashlight was nothing more than a faint memory on the back of his retinas, fading slowly away until it was swallowed by the blackness that surrounded him. Now, the only sense he had left was sound. He listened to the white noise of the waterfall off to his left shooting into the chasm below. It was pitch black, and he couldn't see anything, anywhere. He was now effectively blind as well as injured. He slowly slid back down the rockface, wincing from his ankle pain once more as he sat. The rough, rocky ledge dug into his back and buttocks.

Mayor Bob Nichols peeled off his supple, kid-leather gloves one at a time and placed them neatly in his lap. With slow deliberation, he put his uncalloused hands to his face, covering it though no one was there to see, and he wept.

CHAPTER FIFTY-FOUR

Arctotherium Angustidens pawed at the single glass door remaining in the airlock, trying to make it open. Because the mechanism was off its base, it continually jammed and then reset itself, only allowing the door to move a couple of inches before slamming shut once more.

Trying a new tactic, the prehistoric bruin pressed its enormous head into the door, the steel frame around it squealing as it pushed harder and harder. The glass, already cracked after Edna's tragic demise, shattered inward in an explosive shower, coating the lobby floor with millions of glistening shards.

At the sight of the door shattering, the pack of swarming seniors shrieked, with several grey and blue heads fleeing toward the kitchen as directed by Alex. Others, however, refused to listen to the young whippersnapper and instead tried to jam inside the malfunctioning elevators, pushing and pressing into each other in an attempt to get to safety.

With the glass out of the frame now, the bear pressed forward, its gargantuan head thrusting into the lobby. It let loose a vocalisation that shook the bells on several of the slots. The seniors flew into a renewed frenzy of panicked screaming and shoving. Several were down on the ground now getting trampled by their fellow residents as they attempted to flee.

The beast pushed hard again. Another shriek of metal on metal came as it managed to wedge its shoulders into the airlock but was stopped halfway through by its massive girth and roared in frustration. The noise level inside the casino cranked to eleven on the dial as a new wave of screams rolled through the throng of petrified blue-hairs.

With a mighty heave, the animal pushed again and advanced into the lobby, straining to get through the secondary airlock. Now, the only thing keeping it from its upcoming meal of well-aged prey was its own gargantuan ass.

***

Austin ran through the now empty smoking room and slammed his hip into the emergency-release exit bar, not slowing down at all. His speed was so great that he slid several metres on the fresh coating of ice outside before coming to a stop.

Snow removal had been an issue around the casino, as usual, thanks to Ray Chance's continual budgetary cutbacks, and numerous sections still needed to be cleared and sanded. Several spots had piles of snow that had fallen off the roof and built up along the ground under the eaves of the building throughout the winter. It made navigating the terrain outside the smoke room exit extremely hazardous. It wasn't that the piles were large, but that they were hard-packed and icy, and not particularly conducive to running over the top of at high speeds unless one wanted to fall and break an arm or leg.

Austin wished he could solve the problem by running farther out from the building, but the fog was so thick that if he lost sight of the main structure, he'd be lost within seconds and then he, along with everyone else, would be royally screwed.

Rounding the building, he rapidly approached the lobby. The bear was almost through the secondary set of airlock doors, only its huge posterior sticking out of the entrance now, the rest of its muscular body disappearing into the lobby. The beast roared from inside the casino and tried to push farther inside; the seniors inside reached a new peak of panic.

"Shit and crackers!" Austin yelled out loud. Now running full tilt, he had thrown caution to the wind. Coming off the icy piles of snow, he hit the shallow, crimson pool that remained of Edna O'Toole, and went for a slide. Before he knew it, he found himself on his back, staring up at the canopy over the entrance. The T-Rex lay next to him on the ground in a puddle of gore. Pushing himself up on his elbows, he slipped in the sanguine slop once more and fell back on his buttocks.

An incredible shriek arose from the panicked seniors inside the casino. If he didn't get to them soon, they were going to be toast.

Reaching for the rifle, he jammed the stock into the ground and pulled himself upright using the gun as a crutch, his other hand steadying himself on the side of the building, and finally stood once more.

The bear had almost gotten its amazingly large butt through the door frame now. The half-dozen or so senior citizens still inside the lobby were crushed up against the elevator doors. They pushed and shoved, trying to get through them, if not to rise above the terror, perhaps to at least hide from the horror.

Near the front desk, some of the more agile oldsters began to climb the stairs, abandoning their walkers in the process. They pulled themselves slowly up the staircase, holding onto the railing for dear life. A couple of the more sprightly ones had actually made it halfway. Unfortunately, it looked like one or two of them had either had a coronary from fright and exertion or had been knocked down by their retirement home travel-mates as they attempted to flee.

Rivers of drool gushed from the beast's parted jaws as it tried to advance on its upcoming Senior Smorg Special at the Bonanza Buffet. Their screams grew louder and shriller, becoming a deafening discordance of despair. Almost through the entrance now, only one last bit of steel framing twisted around the creature's lower body held it back, ensnaring it in the doorway.

Austin moved cautiously across the blood-slicked ground, looking for a better angle. Things were going south very quickly. He stepped forward and knelt, assuming a firing stance. Propping the stock of the T-Rex firmly against his right shoulder, he lined the bear up in its sight.

Just as he was about to pull the trigger, inside the lobby, Alex jumped forward and started waving his arms and shouting near the beast.

Austin checked his trigger pull at the last instant. He shouted, "Jesus Christ! Alex! Get the hell out of the way!"

Alex looked to his father and saw what had almost happened, his face going white in the process. The boy complied and darted off to one side, heading for the smoke room exit and letting this dad do what he needed to do.

The Tyrannosaurus Rex boomed, the oversized rifle's muzzle flashing again and again as Austin pumped round after round at the beast. The sound was explosive in the closed confines of what remained of the casino entryway, and Austin's ears were ringing from the blasts.

Two of the rounds hit home, blowing chunks from the bear's ass-end. Two other shots went wild, executing a brightly coloured Royal Flush slot machine along one wall. Fortunately for the seniors, this assault on the beast's hindquarters had the desired effect on the bear. A shriek of anguish and anger came from the monster's throat as it turned toward him.

***

Alex bolted through the access into the smoking-room and burst outside into the fog.

He had an idea.

Running blindly forward, he almost ran face-first into the Gold Mountain maintenance truck that seemed to appear out of nowhere in front of him. He ripped the driver's door open and rummaged behind the driver's seat and found what he wanted, a storage locker. "Yes!" he shouted. Quickly rummaging through its contents, his heart suddenly beat faster at what he discovered inside.

With his new treasure tucked in his jacket, Alex jogged a bit farther into the fog and saw the faint outline of the Golden Castle Adventure bus. He suddenly felt a spark of inspiration and jogged toward it, hoping it contained what he was looking for.

Sliding to a halt near the driver's side of the minibus, the boy flinched, looking away from the mess inside, feeling like he was going to ralph. He ran around to the passenger entrance, prying the doors open with frozen fingers. A wave of nausea washed over him when he saw that the monster hadn't successfully removed the entire driver from the vehicle. Part of him still remained in his seat. A single leg, the right it appeared, had tangled in the seatbelt as the creature extracted him, ripping it off as it tore him from the window.

Alex turned away, feeling ill, then glanced behind the driver's seat to the small storage locker behind it with the red cross on top. He tore the lid open, rifling through the locker's contents, hoping he'd find what he was looking for somewhere inside.

***

Backing up and firing another shot, Austin now had the beast's undivided attention. In the excitement, he'd lost track of how many rounds he fired. Recalling Christine's sales pitch, he remembered it held eleven rounds but wasn't sure if he'd fired eight or nine already. Several of them had struck home hitting the bear's ass, while others had impacted the ground due to his firing too low. His shoulder was throbbing along with his ears from the repeated assault of the rifle's concussive blasts on his body, both physical and auditory. He needed to get the bear out of the casino and have it follow him, and he hoped to God that he had enough ammo to do so. He fired another shot at the monster as it pulled itself out of the casino entrance and turned toward him.

"Okay, so far, so good! Now I've got this thing extremely pissed at me and wanting to eat me instead of the seniors, just like I wanted. Peachy!"

The bruin roared, seemingly in agreement, and continued toward him. "That's right! C'mon, you big, ugly son of a bitch," he shouted, turning to flee. "Follow me!"

Austin moved as fast as he could along the slippery slope leading toward the back of the casino. If he went down now, he'd be next on the menu. He made sure to keep the snowbank on his left as he moved up the lane or else he'd be lost in the fog. Alex was MIA, and he wondered where he'd gone, concerned for the boy's safety.

Turning his attention back to the task at hand, it appeared the shells he'd pumped into the bear's hindquarters had been more than enough to keep its attention focused on him. It shrieked and roared once more, advancing toward him through the billowing ice fog, but it was moving slower, and obviously injured by the bites taken out of its ass by the T-Rex.

Austin moved toward the corner of the building and his face suddenly brightening into a broad grin when he saw what lay in front of him. "Holy crap! Awesome job!"

Disappearing into the fog, like a runway lit for take-off, were a series of bright orange flares, hissing and sputtering on the icy ground. Austin marvelled at what someone had thought to do. As the ice-fog smothered the remaining daylight, they blazed brightly, dazzling his eyes and acting as a marker trail, lighting a path for him through the mist toward the storage shed.

The beast steadily approached him, dragging the latticework of steel behind itself. The metal framing scraped huge chunks of ice and snow out of the ground as it moved. He waited a moment to make sure the animal didn't give up following him and double back on the Golden Castle seniors.

The beast suddenly whipped around, jaws snapping and teeth cracking, trying to tear away the steel struts entangled around its damaged posterior and legs. It snarled and bayed in frustration. This new sound was enough to get the seniors inside the casino screaming all over again, and the animal turned its head back toward them once more, suddenly recalling the plethora of prey waiting inside the building behind it.

Austin fired another round at the creature to jar its memory and remind it that he was still there as well and that he wasn't going anywhere. The shot missed and ricocheted off into the fog, but it was enough.

The beast snapped its head around and glared at the man standing defiantly before it, then began advancing toward him once more. It howled at this prey that had stung it repeatedly, and it raged anew, wanting to crush the cause of its pain between its salivating jaws, squashing the irritating little creature that was still annoying it.

Austin slung the rifle over his shoulder and turned, moving into the fog. The last of the daylight had disappeared, the sun finally setting behind mountains it had only hidden behind earlier. Illuminated by the sputtering flares, only a faint silhouette of the creature was visible as it surged through the fog. Austin called out Alex's name as he moved, searching for the boy. Where was he?

The beast's laboured breathing grew louder as it drew closer to him. He attempted to run, but his feet lost purchase on the sloping, icy ground. With the last of the daylight gone, the temperature continued to drop, and the buildup of ice was accelerating. In spite of the exceptional grip of his boots, he felt his feet began to slip repeatedly, and he went down painfully on one knee. Behind him, the scrape of claws on the frozen ground echoed in the fog as the beast continued moving up the lane toward him.

Austin pressed the butt of the T-Rex into the ground, trying to stand but began to slip once more. Suddenly, strong hands reached out and helped him to his feet. "You need to get up now!"

As Austin clamoured to his feet, he looked up into the face of his saviour. "Alex! Thank God!"

"You don't have time to rest, Dad!"

"I know! I wasn't resting. It's as icy as hell here!"

"That's why I have these." The boy held up his foot to show what he'd found in the resort maintenance truck. Ice-gripping elasticised cleats were stretched over the soles of his boots, allowing him to walk easily on the ice-slicked lane. "You said you were trying to head the bear toward the maintenance shed, so I laid those flares to guide you since I knew you'd have your hands full!"

"You're awesome, kiddo!"

"Thanks!" His son continued, "And I made this for you!" He held up something that looked a little larger than a two-litre bottle of pop and handed it to his father.

Turning it quickly over in his hands, Austin saw he was holding an M4 oxygen tank with an unlit flare attached to it. His son had used several metres of a true Canadian favourite to secure the flare to the bottom of the aluminum cylinder — it was swathed in duct tape. Alex concluded, "I saw someone do it in a movie once, and I thought you'd like to give the bear a warm welcome!"

"Great idea!" Austin beamed at his son. Tearing the cap off the fusee on the tank, he turned. The orange glare of the flares illuminated the predator's massive silhouette as it loomed in the fog. It was so close that Austin could smell the pungent stink of its matted pelt as it raged after them. He quickly slapped the flare's cap against the phosphorus inside to ignite it. The flare was positioned on the cylinder so that its molten, seven-hundred-degree Celsius tip would start burning near the bottom of the oxygen tank and hopefully turn the device into a makeshift bomb.

Backing up a bit more to give a couple of seconds for the bomb to cook a little, Austin threw the oxygen cylinder toward the creature. It clattered along the ice, coming to rest next to the beast's mammoth front paws.

The monster looked down at this sputtering, hissing thing at its feet and went to swipe it away. As it did, the oxygen container exploded with a flash and a bang that startled not only the bear but both Austin and Alex as well with its ferocity.

Pieces of shrapnel flew past father and son, missing them by only centimetres. The bear was not as lucky, and the bottle exploded near its right forepaw, blowing a huge chunk of flesh from it. The creature shrieked with pain and protectively held up its wounded limb as blood flowed profusely from the gaping hole.

Father and son turned and clambered up the lane's incline with Alex helping Austin gain purchase on the icy ground as they moved. They didn't need to look back to see what the bear was doing, its shrieks of rage and pain behind them was more than enough to let them know they were still foremost in the monster's mind and that they'd better haul ass or die.

The flares led them around another corner toward the maintenance shed. Austin saw the faint outline of the Lawless City Silverado parked next to the shed and hollered, "Trip! We're here, and we've got company! Get the party favour ready!"

Alex and Austin approached the large shed door, hearing the beast roaring behind them with renewed pain and anger. A low rumbling growl of building rage suddenly came from deep within the creature's throat. Its ruined forepaw no longer supported its weight, and it limped toward them, now only ten metres away, closing fast in the fog, despite its wounds.

They stood with their backs against the maintenance shed door. Looking with concern into the fog, fear strong in his voice, Alex said, "Uh, Dad, shouldn't we be getting out of here?"

"Hang on, hang on…" Austin said, holding his hand up to silence the boy.

"But Dad!"

"Just a second longer…"

The beast was so close now that they could smell the fetid stench of its numerous victims still lodged in its teeth. Alex's face wrinkled in disgust.

The tremendous bruin stood erect on its hind legs, rearing to its full height. It towered over the men; its head now level with the peak of the maintenance shed roof, five metres up. It shrieked in anger as its lifeblood poured from its wounds, ruined forepaw pumping a geyser that spattered onto the ice-covered ground, painting it with a rich swath of crimson.

"I hope you bleed to death, you big ugly bastard!" Austin said. He pounded heavily on the shed door with the back of his hand and hollered, "Now, Trip!"

The maintenance shed door at their backs rolled up on well-oiled hinges like an express elevator.

Austin dropped to the ground, pulling Alex down with him. Using his own body as a protective shield for his son, he shouted, "Cover your ears!" He put both of his heavy, leather-gloved hands over his own ears, feeling Alex do the same beneath him.

Inside the maintenance shed, Trip stood to the side of the howitzer cannon. Dayglo ear protectors on, one hand holding the lanyard, ready to pull the firing lever. His eyes widened when he saw the full height of the beast outside, now fully erect in front of him. Anger boiled up within him as he thought of all the people that died for no reason, other than to slake this creature's insatiable hunger.

"Baby says bye-bye!" He pulled the lanyard down, firing the howitzer.

The cannon didn't just 'go off', but instead seemed to explode in the confines of the small shed. Trip's eardrums would have surely ruptured had he not been wearing the ear protectors.

Blinding light erupted from the muzzle of the 105mm gun. It kicked backward, knocking into the rear wall of the shed as the explosive shell left the muzzle at a rate of over one and a half kilometres per second.

Trip's aim was low, but he struck the bear, knocking it backward to the ground as the shell vaporised its right leg. Shrieking, the beast lifted its monstrous head, looking toward Trip as if wondering how this small annoying creature could have injured it so, then it slumped back down, writhing and squealing in pain.

Liquified intestines and stomach contents sloshed out of the gaping hole where its leg had been. An entrail tidal wave spread across the maroon-coloured ice, stopping just before it washed over Alex and Austin's prone bodies.

Pulling himself off of his son, Austin Murphy allowed the boy to sit up. They looked toward the mewling bear, its life's blood pumping into the crystalline ice before them.

Alex said wonderingly, "Holy crap, Uncle Trip, I think you got it!"

"Yeah, but now I need to finish the job. Since I only had time to pack one shell for the howitzer, we'll have to do this the old-fashioned way." Trip moved toward the bear, avoiding the pile of intestines and gore spread across the ice. He unslung the .30-06 from his shoulder.

Angustidens Arctotherium swiped at Trip's legs as he approached, reaching out with its uninjured paw toward him, perhaps trying to snag him and eviscerate him, but it was a weak effort, its life force now coating the frozen ground.

Trip put the gun to the beast's temple, saying, "All it takes is one well-placed shot." He pulled the trigger. The shell penetrated the bear's brain, and its outstretched paw fell back to the ground, a final sigh of air escaping its bloody maw from now-stilled lungs.

Inside the maintenance shed next to the howitzer was a pair of snowmobiles. The shed usually housed four of them, but two had already been taken, presumably to the cavern along with Nichols, Chance and VanDusen, but no one knew for sure.

Seeing the keys already in the ignitions of the sleds, Austin climbed aboard the closest one, saying, "All right, let's get moving," Alex hopped on behind his father, with Trip straddling the second snowmobile.

"But Dad! What about Jerry, don't we need him?"

Austin said, "He's going to be our next stop. He got hit hard by one of the entrance doors, and I don't know how he is right now, but we're going to find out. Glad to see we're thinking along the same wavelength here, Sport. Let's hope he's okay since we don't have a GPS receiver with a location for that cavern now, not to mention the return of this fog complicates things as well, so we'll need his help finding Chris for sure."

"Well, I've got room for one more," Trip said. "Let's go see how our little geologist buddy is doing." He started his engine and revved it up.

The ice continued to build as they made their way down toward the casino. The aggressive treads of the Arctic Cats studded treads dug in with little problem, making the trip down the lane an uneventful one.

Approaching the entrance to the casino through the fog, Alex thought the place looked like one of those videos from the evening news where a terrorist's bomb had torn apart a busy marketplace. The blood from the woman who had been eaten was all over the place, sprayed amongst the twisted metal of the steel-framed entryway, and splashed along the splintered framework of the casino's walls that jutted out in spots. Several seniors wandered around near the entrance no doubt still shell-shocked from the trauma.

"Wow, what a mess," Alex said from behind his dad as they pulled up on the sleds.

The three men walked carefully on the ice-sheened ground, not wanting to slip and fall on any broken glass or metal shrapnel that lay scattered about from the bear's attack. Austin was first through the mangled entrance into the lobby and shook his head as he surveyed the damage.

Most of the seniors were huddled in the back corner of the casino near the video roulette table now. Some were poking their heads out of the galley door that lead to the kitchen. At the base of the Million Dollar Slots, a couple of elderly women were tending to Jerry, who was sprawled out, half-covered in casino tokens.

Austin was about to check on Jerry, when Stanley Scrill approached him, saying, "Say there, sonny!" The man's bushy white eyebrows were raised in consternation. Austin nodded toward him, watching the man get even more excited as he recognised him from earlier. "Say, aren't you the one who was shootin' up the casino?"

"That would be me," Austin admitted.

"Well, that was a hell of a racket, you just about gave me a coronary infartion!" the man exclaimed, mispronouncing the word, much to Austin's amusement. He continued, "And what in the hell happened out there? Did you kill that big bastardly thing?"

"Yes sir, it won't be causing any more problems."

"About time! It just about gave my Rosemarie a heart attack!" Austin nodded in sympathy.

Seeing Austin otherwise occupied, Trip made his way toward Jerry.

"I told you, Polly, don't move him!" one little blue-haired lady exclaimed to a second, equally blue-haired lady. The latter lady was attempting to pull Jerry upright into a sitting position using the crook of her cane on his neck.

"And I said I wasn't moving him, Holly!" the first woman snapped. "I was only trying to make him more comfortable and see if he was awake! Plus, I used to be a nurse, you know!"

"Yeah, I know, in a veterinary hospital!"

Trip walked up behind the two arguing seniors, his large circumference creating a shadow over the pair. Both jumped slightly and let out a small squeak of fright. He figured the silhouette of his doughnut-honed physique was enough to make them think the bear had returned, looking for some dessert, something containing some genuine granny goodness, perhaps. "Sorry, ladies, didn't mean to startle you."

"Well, ya did!" Holly said, her face wrinkling up in a mixture of surprise and relief.

"Damn straight!" Polly said, her own face trying to look stern, but the wideness of her eyes betrayed her fear.

"I'm just checking on my friend here," Trip said, nodding toward Jerry's supine form. "If you ladies don't mind, I'd like to check to see how he's doing?"

"He's doing just fine thanks to us!" Holly chimed in.

"Probably doesn't even know that damned bear helped him win the jackpot!" Holly concluded. "Anyway, suit yourself," Polly said. Stepping back, she released her support of Jerry's neck from the hook of her cane's handle.

Kneeling next to Jerry, Trip took his head gently in his hands and placed his fingers lightly onto Jerry's neck, checking his pulse. It was strong and steady, and he seemed to be breathing comfortably on his own, with no visible sign of trauma. Trip tried a little more stimulation and gently slapped Jerry's face with his open palm, saying, "C'mon Jerry, little buddy, wakey-wakey!"

After a couple of less gentle slaps, the man gradually came around, batting Trip's hands away, saying, "I told you I don't want to go to school today, Mom!"

"Sorry buddy, it's a school day," Trip said gently. He grabbed the man's face in his thick-fingered hands, saying, "Jerry, it's me, Trip, from the rescue. How're you doing?"

Jerry's jolted awake as if shocked by electricity, and he struggled upright, eyes wide open. "Did we get it? Where is it? Is it dead?"

Trip put a hand on the man's shoulder and said, "Calm down, little buddy. Yeah, we got him."

"Thank God!" Jerry felt his heart swell with relief. He looked at where he was sitting and suddenly recalled the front entrance door exploding into his face as he tried to help the prone woman and then remembered flying through the air.

"How's that woman doing?"

"Sorry, buddy, she didn't make it. But we can still help Chris and need to get up to the cavern. Since Austin received that text message, we haven't heard anything more from her. Plus, the quake hit right after she got there, so who knows what kind of trouble she might be in."

Austin finally extricated himself from Stanley Scrill's interrogation and approached the pair, interjecting, "Remember, we need your help to find her."

"Right... "Jerry trailed off for a moment, the joy of victory that puffed out his chest slowly deflated like a leaky balloon. It was quickly replaced, however, by a desire to help these men who had risked their own lives to save his and everyone else's at the resort. Jerry wanted to pay it forward and help the next person in need. He said, "Yes! Absolutely! I forgot in all the excitement! This unplanned nap I took here didn't help." Jerry tried to stand and then abruptly sat back down on his rump once more.

"Take it easy, buddy. Take it slow," Trip gently hooked one hand under Jerry's armpit on his uninjured, cast-free side, while Austin did the same on the other, grabbing him by the waist. Together, they slowly helped the man to his feet. Once standing for a few seconds, Jerry seemed to stabilise, and they released their grip on him. He swayed a moment but found his centre of gravity and seemed to be doing okay.

"How're you feeling now, my friend?" Austin asked.

"A little dizzy, and really sore, but I think I'll live."

Austin looked to Alex across the lobby who was now working crowd control near the main doors, fielding questions from a growing group of seniors that had come out of hiding to see what was happening.

A pretty, young, blonde girl wearing a red and orange casino uniform came from behind a closed door and walked rapidly up to Jerry. "Excuse me, sir!" She called out, proffering an envelope. "Here you are, sir." She said, smiling sweetly.

"What's this?" Jerry asked, looking at the girl's hand holding the envelope, noting how blood-like the red polish appeared on each of her exquisitely shaped fingernails.

"It's your voucher, sir, don't lose it. You'll need it!" Her voice was light and pert as she spoke as if nothing out of the ordinary had just happened around the place, though her wide eyes and the slight quaver in her voice said otherwise.

"My voucher? Voucher for what?"

"Why your cashier's cheque for your winnings, sir,"

"My What? Winnings? How? Where?"

"From them!"

An elderly man and woman stood nearby, smiling at him. They looked vaguely familiar.

The girl said, "I watched it happen from the security camera in my cashier's cage! I saw you warn that couple at the slot. Then, when you were trying to save that poor lady, and the door hit you, you spun into the machine!" Her voice rose in pitch as she excitedly described the event to Jerry.

"Which machine?" Jerry inquired slowly.

"That one!" The perky blonde said, pointing one crimson-coloured nail at the flashing Million Dollar Slots machine next to him, its large, colourful LCD screen still flashing, '$1,000,000 Winner!'. She finished, saying, "The couple who put the money into the slot wanted to share some of it with you since they figure you gave it a lucky whack when you smashed into it." The elderly duo stood next to the hostess and smiled, nodding in agreement.

Jerry gasped. He suddenly felt like he might need to sit down again. "Thanks, But…"

The girl offered the voucher once more. Jerry looked at it dumbfounded. Still speechless, he gently took it and gingerly tore it open. He pulled out a small, red cardboard folder that said, Golden Nugget Casino in large gilded letters. He opened it up and was stunned to find a cashier's cheque for five-hundred thousand dollars.

Trip swooped in quickly to grab Jerry's elbow as he wobbled on weak knees for a moment. Thanking the girl, Austin took the red folder containing the cheque from Jerry's clenched fingers and stuffed it into the front pocket of the man's bright neon-blue parka, zipping it up. Trip thanked the girl and the elderly couple once more for Jerry, who nodded toward them, absentmindedly. Together, Trip and Austin shuffled the befuddled Jerry away toward the front of the lobby.

Seeing Trip and his dad with Jerry, Alex was finally able to excuse himself from the crowd of concerned seniors, citing Christine's pending rescue as his reason to leave.

From the look of things, Austin thought, the boy had been doing quite well in allaying the senior's fears. As he departed the group, several of the men came up and shook the boy's hands, and a couple of the elderly ladies moved in to hug him. On butterscotch-scented breath, one petite woman whispered in his ear, "You come back and see me after you save your lady friend, young man, and I'll bake you a fresh batch of shortbread cookies." Alex thanked her, telling her it was one of his favourites and that his mom used to make them for him. The woman smiled back at him and patted his hand.

Austin smiled as his son approached. Once more, he was impressed with Alex's people skills, seeing another example of his natural charisma and civility.

On their way through the sticky, mangled lobby entrance to the parking lot and the sleds, Alex quickly recounted the fantastic tale of Jerry and the slot machine to Trip. The boy figured he should fill his uncle in on things he'd missed while he had been out at the maintenance shed having his own adventure.

Trip smiled at Alex's dramatic retelling of the story, impressed with Jerry's wherewithal and luck. He nodded toward the man, saying, "Well, little buddy, when we get back, I guess you're buying coffee and doughnuts at Timmies!" Tilting his head toward the back of his sled, Trip said, "Hop on board, my friend!"

Jerry sat down on the back of Trip's snowmobile with a pained sigh. Alex jumped behind Austin on the other sled. The pair of snowmobile's engines revved to life with a high-pitched drone that spiralled higher as the machines were shifted into gear. Their studded tracks dug in, kicking up chunks of ice and snow, throwing them into the fog-enshrouded night as the group made their way up the mountain toward Christine and whatever fate may have befallen her.

CHAPTER FIFTY-FIVE

Christine raced back toward the entrance of the cave system, feeling the moisture-laden air clot in her lungs. She figured it was partly from exertion but also from fear. Slowing to a jog, she concentrated on calming herself and regulating her breathing. Within a few seconds, she felt her constricted airways begin to relax, and she started to pick up the pace again.

Due to the house-sized boulders now blocking the way, she knew she couldn't escape through the front of the cavern. But the one thing that kept her running in that direction was something she remembered seeing earlier — a possible emergency exit, as long as the latest quake hadn't blocked that, too. She hadn't mentioned it to the cadre of crapheads earlier since she didn't want to give them any hope or assistance. Her plan was to get away from them somehow and then try to get out through the vent, so the last thing she wanted to tell them of was her possible escape route.

When Christine first arrived at the cavern, before this nightmare of shit had come down on her head, she'd remembered seeing a crevice running up the cavern wall, near the torn tent. At a casual glance, it looked just like a regular gap in the rock wall for the first five or six metres. But if you looked more closely, up into the stalactites near the cavern ceiling, you could see the fissure turned into a natural vent that stretched up into blackness.

Being a rock climber for a hobby, when Christine first noticed this natural volcanic chimney, she'd thought she just might have to come back to the cavern someday and see how far up it went. Well, she noted with a slight smile, apparently today was that day.

Christine knew without any conceit that she was the only person in this cavern physically capable of climbing the vent. As for anybody else inside it right now, well, she figured their odds of getting out of this were about as good as a snowball's chance in… She paused her thought for a moment, realising she was going to finish the thought with 'a snowball's chance in hell', but since they were already there, she figured it rendered the expression moot. So now, it was only a matter of getting to the vent to see if it actually was a viable route of escape from this steamy little slice of purgatory.

The tunnel widened out, and she found herself in the main cavern once more. She was moving as fast as she dared, still taking extra care to look where she ran. The thought of slipping and falling into one of the pools, or into one of the many assorted vertical lava tubes that randomly dotted the cavern's mist-covered floor was not an appealing thought.

Up ahead, off to her right, Christine saw the tent, and allowed herself a moment of hope. Before starting to climb, she decided it might be worthwhile to check inside it for anything that might aid her in her quest, such as her backpack and rifle. When she arrived, she was sad to discover that if there were anything of value in the rear of the tent, it no longer existed in three dimensions, and that included her rifle and pack, unfortunately. Thanks to the recent quake, the back of the tent now lay under a boulder the size of the new chest freezer at her shop, rendering everything beneath it not only inaccessible but obviously useless to boot.

Still hoping to find something to salvage, she opened the tent's flaps and entered, shielding her light as much as she could as she frantically searched for anything that could help her. Under a rumpled sleeping bag, to her surprise and delight, she found a large coil of dynamic climbing rope that looked to be at least sixty metres long. "Bonus!" she whispered excitedly to herself. Digging around further, she saw that she'd really hit the jackpot. Inside a small daypack, she found an EpiPen, gloves and a pair of adjustable climbing crampons (C2s, no less!).

She strapped the twelve-point metal-fanged footwear onto the soles of her boots and wondered why a gold miner would have this climbing gear unless they were excavating in some hard to reach areas? And an EpiPen? Were they around somebody who had anaphylaxis, yet still had an affinity for peanut butter? Or perhaps they'd found a prehistoric beehive nearby, and someone in the cavern was deathly allergic?

More sensibly, she thought, the gear was there because they were going to explore the very same vent she was going into, or perhaps maybe extract a vein of gold down the side of one of the pits? Who knew? Whatever the case, she silently thanked her unknown benefactor for their thoughtfulness and their generosity for leaving these things behind, and to the fates that be, for leaving them untouched by the latest quake.

Before exiting the tent, she turned the phone's dimmed flash off and peeked out to see what she might see. There was no sound outside the flaps, and darkness ruled. After listening silently for a moment, she eased herself out. There was no sign of VanDusen and his flashlit shotgun either, which was encouraging. "So far, so good," she whispered.

Christine turned the phone's flash back on, it's low-power battery saving mode not illuminating anything very far up the wall, but it was enough. It looked like she could quickly get started climbing the first three or so metres with minimal effort as she'd hoped, but the rest would be much harder, of that she was sure.

Tightening the wrist straps on her gloves, she started the climb and found she was correct, and it was very easy going for almost four metres. She paused after a few minutes of exertion, feeling her left leg threatening to cramp up once more and she tried to work it out while remaining wedged into the fissure and trying not to plummet to her doom.

Her back was jammed against one side of the fissure's walls with her feet thrust to the other side, supporting herself across the metre-wide crevasse. At least it was a metre-wide at this point, and she hoped it didn't become too narrow as she moved up, or too wide where she could no longer stretch all the way across. If she encountered either of those scenarios, she didn't think she'd have the strength to lower herself back down to the ground safely, and that would be the end of that -- hello gravity, goodbye Christine. When she started this climb, she knew it was going to be a one-way trip, and she smiled glumly. The rope, coiled over her shoulder, was unused at the moment as there was nothing to which she could tie it. Looking up into the narrow vent, she now knew what the Grinch felt like on his way up the chimney after stealing the very last crumb of food from Cindy-Lou Who's house.

Peering up into the dark recesses of the upper section of the fissure, she wasn't sure, but she thought she could see the faintest hint of dark blue, surrounded by the cavern's blackness. Oh my God, she thought, is that the sky outside?

Christine grabbed another breath, meaning to carry on with her climb and get up inside the chimney proper to see what her fate may be, newly inspired as she was. But just moments after she began moving again, a flashlight's beam bobbed up and down near the back of the cavern, coming her way fast.

She froze. Not wanting to make any noise that would give away her location, she paused where she was, five metres up the fissure, her legs tense. She waited and watched as the person with the light]headed toward the mass of boulders at the front entrance next to the tent. They were no doubt hoping to see if there was a way out through there. She couldn't see who it was but knew she wouldn't have to wait too long to find out and she already had her suspicions.

The light continued to bob up and down very rapidly as if the person were running from something, throwing caution to the wind as they fled through the pits and pools. The light stopped at the rockfall near the front, and she heard a voice. Somebody was muttering to themselves. "Shit! There's gotta be a way out of here." Barely audible, it was VanDusen's voice. She watched the chief playing his light over the jumble of immense rocks that blocked the entrance. "C'mon, C'mon…"

The light flitted back and forth over the boulders as he searched. He still mumbled under his breath as he went, looking for an escape route. The flashlight's beam started to move about the cavern in an increasingly erratic manner. Apparently, VanDusen's panic was beginning to bubble through to the surface, affecting his actions. She'd felt herself wanting to do the same earlier and had fought against it, not wanting to lose her own head to panic, as the chief was doing now.

Of more immediate concern to her than the chief's panic was her own rapidly cramping leg muscles, still sore from the snowshoeing she'd done several hours earlier. Not wanting to give her position away, Christine flexed her shoulders and legs slightly to try and provide them with some relief as she felt the rock of the fissure digging into her back. It ground into her spine from the pressure, directly into the sore spot where VanDusen had drilled her with the muzzle of his shotgun. She dared not move, as she didn't want the chief knowing her current location. It wasn't as if she thought he'd be able to climb up to where she was, far from it, but she didn't know if he had any shells left in that shotgun of his. Nor did she know if his service revolver was still with him, and she didn't want to find out if he was willing to waste any ammo on target practice, herself being the target.

Christine watched him move along the rockfall. Stopping halfway, he spotted something on the cavern floor, making a grunt of surprise as he did. He picked up whatever he'd found and put it in his pocket. Breathing heavily, VanDusen jogged back over near the tent, still unaware of Christine's presence, four metres up and wedged into the cavern wall. She watched from her perch as he shone his light amongst the large boulders piled there, looking for some sort of gap through which to escape, but could find nothing.

A whine of frustration like that of a petulant child escaped VanDusen's mouth, and he kicked a small rock at the boulders with one boot-covered foot. "Shit! Shit! Shi…"

The chief's final shit was interrupted by a faint, but unmistakable sound of rock being knocked over as something at the back of the cavern moved his way. VanDusen whipped around toward the direction of the noise.

Christine had front row seats to the show that was about to begin if her legs could take it. She remained wedged with her back against one side of the vent wall and her feet pressed into the other. She alternated stretching out one leg and then the next, trying to alleviate some of the cramping. Her vantage point afforded her a unique view, high above the mist generated by the boiling aquifers, and she settled in to watch the show below.

VanDusen shone his light toward the back of the cavern. He shouted, his voice a mixture of anger and fear, "Why can't you goddamned ugly sons of bitches just leave me alone?"

Whatever was coming his way, there was more than one of them. Judging by the tone of his voice, he'd already had a run-in with whatever they were once before. Apparently, that time had been more than enough for him.

Christine felt her legs start to tremble and she pressed harder into the vent wall with her feet. It helped a bit, and she felt the quiver steady somewhat. Holding her breath, she waited to see what was coming. She half-expected to see the sabre-toothed cat that had jumped Chance stroll into view, or a pack of them, perhaps.

When she saw what was revealed in the light, she was stunned. It appeared that the terror currently stalking Lawless had two mouths to feed at home. "Oh my God," she murmured to herself. The pair of cubs looked well-fed, but if they were anything like their mother, they were still very hungry.

Christine's left leg started to cramp again, and she felt herself begin to slip. She kicked in hard with both feet. Pressing her back into the unyielding rock with all her strength, she stopped her downward skid just in the nick of time. But her movement against the rock also yielded the unfortunate effect of several smaller stones being kicked loose from the side of the vent. They clattered down the crevasse, hitting the ground with a noise that did not go unnoticed by either the chief or the new nightmares that had just appeared. Both creatures lifted their heads and looked in her direction, sniffing the air, perhaps smelling her scent. VanDusen jerked his light toward the sound of the falling rocks, but then yanked it back toward the bears again almost immediately, not seeing Christine up above.

To VanDusen's relief and Christine's dismay, the twin bears were more intrigued by the falling rocks below her than by VanDusen's light, and they plodded toward where she had wedged herself into the wall. The chief kept the bears in his spotlight as they approached her position like they were star performers in an underground circus big-top ready to perform a fantastic feat of some sort or other.

At first, Christine thought the bears smelled her, but then she realised they were drawn to the air flow that they sensed moving through the cavern via the vent. The twins looked up toward where she was sequestered, and VanDusen's light followed their gaze, all the way up this time. The beam stopped when it hit Christine's tense form, still wedged three-quarters of the way up the wall fissure, but not quite to the vent. She squinted as VanDusen's torch pierced her eyes with its harsh white light.

"You!" VanDusen screeched. "I thought you were bear chow by now, you bitch!" He laughed crazily for a moment and said, "Looks like our new friends here find you more interesting than they do me!" He was separated by a distance of fewer than twenty metres from the bears, but thanks to a stream and boiling pool between them he was not as readily accessible as Christine seemed to be.

The chief continued to keep the cubs in his light, and Christine studied them as they looked up at her. They didn't look to be as large Angus, at least not judging by the size of the bear's tracks she'd been following off and on for the last couple of days. She was sure that bear out there had to be at least a third larger than these animals. But that being said, these twins were still monstrous, nonetheless.

His voice cracking with hysterical laughter, VanDusen said, "Looks like they want to have their dessert before the main course, and they want something sweet to eat!" He giggled to himself for a moment.

The bruins had reached Christine's location now, and one of them slowly stood on its hind legs sniffing at the air rushing through the vent and also taking in her scent finally, no doubt. It roared as it reached toward her with one razor-clawed paw, missing her thigh by only inches. Though not as large as their mother, these creatures still had a fantastic reach.

Christine felt a surge of adrenaline and managed to shimmy up another half metre, enough to finally be out of the reach of the creatures.

VanDusen watched this for a moment and then cackled quietly again to himself, turning away to look for a place to hide or an escape route.

Christine tried to push herself higher up into the vent but felt weakness overcoming her once more, the adrenaline's surge dissipating more rapidly than she'd expected. The standing bear roared and swung at her again. Though she found herself out of reach, she didn't feel confident about how long her height advantage would last — or how much longer she could keep herself wedged into this vent before her legs gave out entirely and she plummeted to the waiting jaws of the creatures below.

Luck was on her side, however, and the extra distance proved too much for the bear. It roared in frustration one final time, taking one more ineffectual swipe at Christine, then dropped down onto all fours once more.

In the real estate and business world, location is everything. If a client or customer didn't find your location particularly appealing or easy to get to for whatever reason, they would just go elsewhere. Predators, when faced with a similar situation for their next repast, will do the same. More often than not, it will choose the prey that's easier to take down, such as the old and infirm, or the very young, rather than the one that is healthy, swift and agile. But other times, a predator will choose prey that is just plain easier to reach.

Unfortunately for Chief Reggie VanDusen, this was one of those other times. And even more unfortunately for Reggie, the twin bears must have arrived at the same conclusion at the same time. As one, the beasts refocussed their culinary appetites on the prey that was much riper for the plucking and not located halfway up the cavern wall as their current target was. This new, tasty treat had the added bonus of being very easy to locate as well, thanks to the light that it kept flashing around, blinding both itself and them in a most annoying manner.

Suddenly this new prey seemed like a much more appealing target. Yes, location really was everything.

Christine watched the bears turn and silently make their way toward VanDusen's twinkling, guiding light. Ignoring the chief's predicament for a moment, as he ignored hers, Christine refocussed on her own dilemma.

She knew she had to keep going, and up was the only way out. She inhaled sharply in pain; unsure if she had the leg muscles left to do it. She hadn't had enough to eat today and was feeling weak from low blood sugar as well. Her legs trembled, ready to give out, and she knew there was no way she could go any further. She had no strength left to shimmy any more. Glancing higher, she could see there was nothing else to hold onto should she start to slip again. Christine figured she would fall back to the ground and be eaten by the bears as she writhed in pain from a broken spine or neck — if she weren't lucky enough to die on impact that was.

Wincing from the leg pain, this was not the way she'd ever seen herself going out. She jammed her hand into a jacket pocket and found the 9mm pistol. In all the excitement over the last few hours she'd completely forgotten about it. Her fingers caressed the nylon polymer body of the handgun, and she briefly toyed with using it as a way out of her predicament but rejected it almost immediately. It wasn't in her personality to just give up, and she thrust the pistol deep into her parka pocket.

Desperately cramming her hand into her other pocket, she came across the EpiPen. It was a risk to use it for a healthy person, but she knew the alternative was one that she wouldn't even waste her time thinking about. She figured that since her legs were weakening first, a boost of adrenaline there would undoubtedly help where she needed it most. It certainly couldn't hurt at this stage, she reasoned.

Uncapping the EpiPen, she jammed it into the meat of her left thigh, feeling the sting of the needle as it bit through the Gortex material covering her leg.

Electrified — she couldn't think of a better word; that's how she suddenly felt. She was soaring with energy, but she knew it wouldn't last. Her mind and senses were racing as well. Suddenly, VanDusen let out the most God-awful shriek from below. It felt like dozens of nails being dragged across her brain.

***

While thinking that the bears had been distracted with the blonde bitch, Reggie had been preoccupied trying to climb a chunk of rock next to one of the large boulders near the entrance. His plan was to try to clamour up onto a smaller rock, then up onto the larger boulder. He had actually done reasonably well, or so he thought. He'd managed to climb to the top of the chunk of rock and was trying to drag himself onto the boulder a little over two metres off the ground next to his current perch.

Things seemed to be improving for Reggie. He hadn't heard from that conservation cow in a little while now, and he was hoping that she was about to drop into the bear's drooling mouths from above. If that happened, maybe one of them would choke on her. Then he'd only have to try to cap the ass of one of these bastards as he stood atop his rocky bastion and fired his 9mm at them. He toyed with the idea of bringing the bitch down with a well-placed shot when he'd first seen her clinging up there like Spiderwoman, but he didn't want to waste his ammo. You can always dream, he thought. He smiled slightly as he studied the rocks in front of him with his light. It looked like he might be able to get a little higher if he grabbed...

VanDusen's back exploded in pain when the closest bear's claws raked through him. Still firmly zipped into his winter parka, he was flung through the air like the rag chew toy he threw around his backyard for his pit bull, Snotty. He skidded across the rocky cavern floor, slamming into some of the larger shards that covered it along the way. They sliced through his gloved hands and jacketed forearms as he tried to protect himself as he slid and rolled.

Groaning and retching with pain, VanDusen tried to stand, feeling sticky from the blood that now flowed from his torn hands and forearms. Reaching around to his ruined back, he felt around for a moment. Through the searing heat of pain, he probed carefully, finally pulling what he thought was a torn piece of his jacket out of his back wound. Instead, he pulled a large flap of lacerated skin the size of one of those goddamned graphic novels Roxanne was always pouring over at home. He began to feel like retching again but finally made it up onto wobbly legs, preparing to run.

Chief Reggie VanDusen quickly discovered he had nowhere to go. He was now on a peninsula of rock between two boiling pools that emptied into the icy cold blackness of the cavern's main lava tube at his back. It yawned wide like a hatchway to hell.

The bears rumbled deep in their throats as they lumbered toward him. "You mother-fucking bastards!" he hollered. His pain and fear were now forgotten, replaced by a heat of rage as these beasts from before time approached him.

Reggie was choked. Here were these two pieces of shit from the goddamned dark ages coming to take him out and it didn't look good. Yes, he was a greedy, arrogant, mean son-of-a-bitch, but he wasn't a stupid man. He could see the writing on the wall that this was only going to end in three possible ways. A) He gets ripped to shreds and eaten if he stands there and does nothing, B) He goes for a swim in one of the pools of boiling water and ends up like the catch of the day at Red Lobster, or C) He steps off the edge into the bottomless pit behind him and kisses his ass goodbye. Some choice, he thought bitterly.

With a flash of recall, he remembered his service revolver. He hoped it hadn't fallen out somewhere and his hands flew to his holster. Yes! The Glock was still there! He pulled it out and cocked it, alternating his aim between the two approaching beasts, saying, "C'mon you cocksuckers!"

With a deafening roar, the bears charged VanDusen. He screamed and started firing his 9mm. The shells did little to penetrate the thick hide of the approaching abominations, but he kept firing, pulling the trigger until the gun was clicking empty anyway. He fumbled for a second clip from his belt. The bear on his left took advantage of his distraction, and it crashed into him, pulling him into its arms in a deadly embrace and bringing him down to the ground. It enveloped his head with its mouth and began to stand on all fours, trying to drag VanDusen upright with it.

Reggie VanDusen was a big man, over one hundred and sixty kilograms of crooked cop, in fact. He was a ponderous weight, and when the bear tried to stand with him in its mouth, it proved too much for the creature especially while he kicked and thrashed.

Still alive with his face firmly clamped in the beast's mouth, his shrieks were muffled as he tried to pull free. The bear tried to yank him backward to get assistance from its twin, but the chief's weight proved too much, and they both toppled into the boiling pool at their side.

The cavern was suddenly filled with the combined shrieks of the bear and Chief VanDusen as their respective fur and skin boiled from their bodies in the searing, highly acidic water. As they stewed away, being cooked alive, the bear's twin stood near the pool roaring in anger and frustration, unable to help its sibling.

While the drama unfolded below, high above, Christine Moon heard none of it. She felt as if her entire body was being flooded with liquid fire as a tremendous surge of adrenaline coursed through her system.

She shimmied faster and faster up the vent and soon found herself quite far up inside of it but grew concerned when it narrowed most alarmingly. After several more tense metres, it widened back out, and she breathed a sigh of relief.

The speed burst provided by the EpiPen had only given her a temporary boost, and she felt the burn of power begin to diminish, her feelings of lethargy returning tenfold. She gave herself one more push but felt herself lagging further and further. With the stars just becoming visible, the small slice of dark-blue night sky above her head seemed to taunt Christine in her climb to freedom. So tantalisingly close, but just out of reach now as the last of her energy began to ebb away.

There was still nothing to which she could tie her rope inside of this smooth, volcanic vent. She suddenly knew she wasn't going to make it and wondered if this might be some of the last starlight she would ever see. Bracing one last time for as long as she could, Christine dug in, mentally psyching herself for her death plummet back into the cavern and its horrors below.

Never resigning herself to her fate, she couldn't stop trying to survive and was surprised she had gotten as far as she had. It was just part of her nature to keep trying, no matter what the odds — to be who she wanted to be, and to be who she needed to be and to survive no matter what life threw at her. She'd made her peace with the world many years before, and she was now ready to be done with everything. Closing her eyes, she said a silent prayer.

From above, a voice echoed down, "Need a hand?"

Christine blinked in amazement and looked up. There, outlined by the starlight, the shape of someone looking down at her from the top of the vent.

"Oh my God, Austin! Yes, please! Thank you! I can't make it any farther!" Her legs were trembling from the continued strain on them now. "Hurry, please, I think I'm going to slip!"

The outline of Austin disappeared from view, replaced by a larger silhouette. Her face broke into a smile when she heard Trip shout down, "Hey Chris! Tie this on, and we'll pull you up!" A rope dropped down in front of her face. She grabbed it and fastened it around her waist.

"Thanks, Trip! I'm already on it!" she hollered back.

After securing the rope around her waist, she gave it two good, hard tugs. With a jolt, she felt herself rising up the chimney, the circle of brightening starlight growing bigger and bigger by the moment.

And then she was outside.

Christine took in great gasping breaths of the cold night, tasting the frigid air flooding her exhausted lungs and loving every second of its cooling balm.

The sky was clear up here now, and Christine could see that the ice fog had come off the glacier and settled into the valley as predicted. The full moon shone high above, illuminating everything around her a luminous white. The small mountain town of Lawless, BC lay dark beneath a soft blanket of icy-white fog. Amid the nothingness, colourful high-intensity lights strobed atop emergency vehicles making their way about the valley bottom, appearing as if an alien mothership had just landed and was now picking up its ground crew, preparing for takeoff.

Her voice still trembling from her recent overload of emotions, Christine said, "How did you get up here?"

With a smile, his teeth glowing phosphorescently in the starlight, Alex pointed down the cliffside. "We used the stairs!" They were just above and to the side of the cavern's now blocked entrance, where the vent came out of the rock. The men had used an assortment of fallen boulders like a staircase, allowing them to climb partially up the mountainside to look for an alternate way inside.

Trip replied, "When we saw the main entrance blocked, we figured we'd better look for another one. Alex saw the vent here. He was climbing around like a regular mountain goat on these rocks then we followed him up. Don't know if I would've seen the hole. He's got great eyes!"

"That's right. My boy loves his carrots," Austin added, smiling at her warmly.

Christine looked around — her friends surrounded her. Austin, Trip, Alex and a man she had never met before all stood near her, smiling. Perhaps they were also pleased at their good fortune of being able to get to her in time to help her, and to have her now standing there in front of them, healthy, happy and whole. If that were the case, so was she. Overwhelmed once more, she couldn't speak for a moment. With tears in her eyes, she hugged each man in turn, thanking them individually for their help.

"Glad you're okay," Trip smiled. Christine tried to wrap her arms around him to hug him, but it proved too much of a challenge. She hugged the part of him that she could hug and did so fiercely. The tops of Trip's cheeks that peeked through his beard began turning a fierce shade of red.

Christine moved to Alex next and hugged this fantastic man-boy hard. She knew that if his father was anything to go by, this young man in her arms was going to grow up into an amazingly handsome, strong, healthy man. Alex smiled awkwardly and said nothing, his face going a brighter shade of red than Trip's currently rosy cheeks.

She turned to Austin finally and hugged him the hardest. Speaking quietly in his ear she whispered, "Thank you so much for being here for me. I don't know what to say."

Austin pulled her back and looked into her eyes kindly. "You don't need to say anything else, you're safe and amongst friends here." She hugged him once more and smiled.

Christine looked over at Jerry and said, "I don't know you, but what the heck." She reached over and hugged him hard anyway.

Jerry groaned slightly as Christine wrapped her arms around him. He introduced himself mid-hug, "Please to meet you, I'm Jerry Benson by the way." She stood back from the man and smiled up at him, saying, "Jerry! Right! I'm so glad to see you're doing better!"

With the greetings out of the way, Austin put his hand gently on her shoulder, saying, "Are you okay, Chris?" Concern was heavy in his voice.

"I think I need a vacation," She said tiredly. "Apart from that, I'm fine. A little bruised, but not bad. I wish I could say the same for Mayor Nichols, Ray Chance and Chief VanDusen."

"They're down there, too?" Austin asked incredulously.

"Yes," she responded. Then as an afterthought, she added, "Well, they were at least."

"What happened?" Trip inquired.

"I'll fill you in on all the gory details back at the bottom of the mountain. But for now, let me say it looks like Lawless might need to have a by-election for a new mayor and chief of police very shortly."

The group moved carefully down the jumbled, rocky staircase to the ridge below. The glistening starlight aided their descent, and soon Christine found herself next to the scree outside the cavern near the snowmobiles. She marvelled at the immense size of the boulders that had piled up outside of the entrance. Millions of tonnes of rock and ice blocked it, sealing it closed forever. "At least we don't have to worry about what to do with this cavern here."

"Yeah," Trip said, shaking his head, "I don't think we would have dug you out of there any time soon."

Christine shuddered as she spoke, thinking of all the people who had lost their lives over the golden fortune contained within the cavern, and almost all of them were now entombed along with it. "I don't think anybody is using the front door here ever again," she said.

Jerry interjected, "But we need to map this cavern somehow! I think we should be able to dig that rock away no problem with some heavy equipment! Or use that vent for access! The scientific discoveries inside that place must be amazing! Some of the systems at work in the cavern have possibly been going on for tens of thousands of years and could help the world's…" Jerry snapped out of teacher mode as the ground started to vibrate beneath his feet.

"Aftershock!" Austin shouted, grabbing Christine by the shoulders. He whisked her along to his snowmobile, saying, "Move, move, move!" He jumped aboard the sled first, grabbing the controls. Christine followed suit and climbed on behind Austin, wrapping her arms about his middle. Alex clamoured on last and latched his hands onto the chromed safety bar at his back. Christine looked across to the other snowmobile and was relieved to see the other two men already aboard with Jerry clinging to Trip's rounded back like a stuffed Garfield on a car's rear window.

Austin and Trip gunned their snowmobile's engines, and they shot away from the mountainside. The machines flew along the ice-slicked snow, jumping and skipping over its surface as the ground trembled beneath them, not slowing until they were almost a kilometre from the cavern. They pulled the sleds around to face the mountain, killing the engines.

In the distance, massive sections of the Kootenay Glacier sheared off and plummeted onto the house-sized boulders at its base, exploding into thousands of huge, blue-hued chunks. Parts of the mountainside caved inward like a monumental souffle deflating from the quake's jarring motions.

None of the group spoke as they watched the destruction, awed by the power of nature on display before them. The cavern, already inaccessible from the rockslide, now lay buried underneath millions of tonnes of time-worn ice.

As the ground beneath them gradually calmed its tectonic trembling, Jerry smiled sadly. Whatever other secrets the cavern contained were now lost to the world forever.

"Well, that's one thing you can scratch off your to-do list," Trip said, shaking his head.

The sled's engines revved up once more, their wasp-like drone slicing through the cold night air as the group continued their journey. The swirling fog hungrily gobbled the snowmobile's tail lights as they disappeared into the icy grey void, descending toward what remained of Lawless and whatever their future might bring.

At their backs, the Kootenay Glacier's newly exposed ice sparkled in the starlight. Its reign over the valley below continuing for the moment, a silent testament to the power, beauty and impermanence of nature.

Fin

CLAW

KATIE BERRY

Upcoming Releases:

CLAW: The Audiobook (July 31st, 2020)

ABANDONED: A Lively Deadmarsh Novel Book 1 (Oct.31, 2020)

ABANDONED: A Lively Deadmarsh Novel Book 2 (Dec.31, 2020)

CLAW: Emergence Novelettes 1-6 (Aug. 31, 2020 - April 2021)

CLAW: Emergence (Spring 2021)

CLAW: Resurgence (Spring 2021)

BESIEGED: A Lively Deadmarsh Novel (Spring 2022)

■■

If you enjoyed CLAW: A Canadian Thriller, please leave a review on Amazon at:
http://www.Amazon.com/gp/customer-reviews/write-a-review.html?asin=B081R1SND1

Goodreads is also a great place to leave one:
https://www.goodreads.com/review/new/48908398

Reviews help others to hear about CLAW. Doing so allows me to do more of what I love to do: write more stories for you to enjoy! So, by sharing your enjoyment and letting others know of CLAW, we all win! Thank you so much!

To stay up to date with my upcoming novels and series and find out about the other projects that I have planned, please visit my website. And while you're there, feel free to join my e-mail list to be sure not to miss a thing.

www.katieberry.ca

As a special thank you for those of you who join my e-mail list, you will receive an EXCLUSIVE short story set way back in the day when Lawless first earned its name, absolutely FREE!

This is my way of thanking you for purchasing this novel. Without people like you, I wouldn't be able to sit here and type this sentence for you to read right now. Feel good about your purchase, because you're allowing me to do what I love to do, write more stories that I love, which I hope you will, too.

••

Follow me on Facebook at:
www.facebook.com/katieberrybooks
or
Follow me on Twitter:
@KatieBerryBooks

or

Feel free to send me an email at:

katie@katieberry.ca

I'd love to hear from you!